Love
Remains

HOPE SPRINGS SERIES
Longing for Home
Hope Springs
Love Remains
My Dearest Love

REGENCY ROMANCES
The Kiss of a Stranger
Glimmer of Hope
An Unlikely Match
For Elise
All Regency Collection
British Isles Collection

THE JONQUIL BROTHERS SERIES
Friends and Foes
Drops of Gold
As You Are
A Fine Gentleman

THE LANCASTER FAMILY SERIES
Seeking Persephone
Courting Miss Lancaster
Romancing Daphne

TIMELESS ROMANCE ANTHOLOGIES
Winter Collection
Spring Vacation Collection
European Collection
Summer Wedding Collection
Love Letter Collection

HISTORICAL WESTERNS
The Sheriffs of Savage Wells
Old West Collection
Mail Order Bride Collection

A Hope Springs Novel

Sarah M. Eden

Interior design by Heather Justesen
Edited by Annette Lyon and Lisa Shepherd

Cover design by Mirror Press, LLC, and Rachael Anderson
Cover image © Victoria Davies / Trevillion Images

Published by Mirror Press, LLC

ISBN-10: 1-947152-02-5
ISBN-13: 978-1-947152-02-1

Dedicated to John and Mary,

I've stood where you once worshiped and walked where you once walked. Though your lives remain a mystery, I'll not give up searching until I know you better.

Chapter One

AUGUST 1871

HOPE SPRINGS, WYOMING TERRITORY

On the night of his thirtieth birthday, Tavish O'Connor resigned himself to a life of eternal bachelorhood. A man could only fall in love so many times. The best birthday gift he could give himself was to quit hoping that fate meant him to be anything other than unattached.

He certainly wouldn't be the first, nor the last, poor Irishman to live out life as a hermit. He had his land, his work, in addition to an ailing brother and broken family to occupy his time and thoughts. Those, he silently declared between bites of chocolate cake, were more than enough.

Convincing the women in his family of that truth, however, would be about as easy as convincing a cat to keep away from the cream pitcher.

Long after his siblings had returned to their respective homes, he sat at his parents' table, leaving only him and his da to listen while his ma continued her unrelenting mission of finding him a wife by whatever means necessary.

"The Macmillians have a daughter only two or three years younger than you are," she said as she dried a stack of plates.

There were no Macmillians in Hope Springs. Tavish could think of none back in New York, either.

"Have you reached all the way back to Ireland, then?" Tavish asked. Their tiny town hadn't many unwed women. Ma's efforts had turned international.

"The Macmillians were our dearest neighbors," Ma said. "What was their daughter's name, Thomas?" she asked Da. "Elizabeth or Mary or some such thing. You remember, the little one with red hair."

"She's likely married by now, dear," Da answered. "Provided she survived the Hunger. Few of our neighbors did, you'll remember."

Ma's eyes dropped to her clasped hands. For a moment, she didn't speak, didn't look at either of them. Tavish knew that expression of remembered sorrow. The dark years of the Famine had left many scars.

He reached out and patted her hand reassuringly. "I'd wager the Queen's jewels themselves that young Miss Macmillian is happy and healthy, and, I've no doubt, quite, quite married."

Da crossed to the sideboard and slid another slice of cake onto his plate. "No doubt."

Ma rallied quickly, though not entirely. Never entirely. "The Buchanans in New York," she said. "They had two or three daughters near Tavish's age. And though they aren't Irish, they are Scottish, which would have made my father tremendously happy."

"Two or three daughters, you say?" Tavish whistled long. "I'd have m' pick, wouldn't I? Perhaps you might root out a family with a full half-dozen daughters. That'd be a grand thing, wouldn't it?"

Ma swatted at him. "None of your cheek, lad. I'm helping you."

"Why don't you help me to another slice of that cake? I'd rather have that than all the redheaded Scotswomen you could dig up."

"She doesn't have to be a Scotswoman, nor a ginger," Ma insisted.

"Grand." Tavish grinned as broadly as he could manage. "I think I'll find m'self a golden-haired Englishwoman."

"Bite your tongue," Da said.

"You've objections to golden hair?"

Both of his parents leveled him looks of dry scolding. He assumed his most innocent expression, knowing perfectly well that the proposed hair color wasn't at all what his parents disliked.

Ma pointed at him with the last of her washed plates. "Despite your sass, we will find someone."

He didn't doubt she fully meant to try. He also knew perfectly well that no objections on his part would put her off the scent.

There was only one thing for him to do: set her on another scent altogether.

"I think it's time and past we decided what's to be done about Finbarr."

On the instant, his parents grew quiet. Finbarr, the youngest of Tavish's siblings at barely seventeen, weighed heavily on the minds of the entire family.

Seven months earlier, the lad had lost nearly all his sight in a horrific fire. Desperate to help him, Tavish had left his crop unharvested—his only source of income, knowing it would be ruined by the neglect—and had taken him to a specialist in St. Louis, who declared Finbarr's condition inarguably permanent. His sight would not return; neither would it improve. This was Finbarr's new life, and something had to be done to help him live it. The doctor provided the name of a school for the blind in St. Louis, as well as directions for contacting a tutor he highly recommended, should they choose that route instead.

Ma sat at the table across from Da. "I cannot countenance the idea of sending him away," Ma said. "He's far too young."

"He's seventeen years old," Tavish reminded her.

She shook her head. "It's too much to ask of him. And of us."

"Aye." Da's nod was more one of acknowledgment than agreement. "But he cannot go on as he is now. He spends too much time wallowing and fretting and pitying himself."

The lad was, in that moment, sitting out on the porch, alone, something he did far too often.

"If we're not to send him away," Tavish said, "we've no choice but to hire a tutor to come here as the doctor recommended." Tavish didn't care to push his parents, especially knowing how fragile they'd been of late, with worries pressing on them so heavily. But something had to be done.

Ma's shoulders drooped. "How are we to pay for a tutor?" Money was ever on their list of struggles.

"I'm taking Joseph Archer's crop to market for him, he being across the country." They'd made the arrangement before Joseph and his family left Hope Springs to see to his business concerns back east, as well as to visit the family of his new bride.

New bride. Still an odd phrase for him to digest in regards to Joseph.

He and Tavish had once been rivals for the affections of a particularly fiery Irishwoman. She was now Mrs. Archer, and Tavish was, once again, alone. Traveling with Finbarr meant he'd not been able to see to his own crop. Without Joseph's offer to leave his crop to Tavish's care in exchange for a percentage he sold it for at market, Tavish would've had almost nothing to live on until the next year's harvest.

"If I get enough for his grain, I'll have a bit left over we can use to pay a tutor," Tavish said. "If not, I'll send a telegram to Joseph, explaining the situation. I'm certain he'd lend us a bit." 'Twas a great risk, further mortgaging his land, but he refused to lose any more of his brother than he already had. "While I'm there, I'll send another telegram to Lincoln. That's where Dr. Jones said this Cecil Attwater is currently living."

Da rested his forearms on the table, his expression heavy. "If Mr. Attwater takes on the job, I'd wager he will prefer to live in the same house as Finbarr. Seeing as the lad lives with you, Tavish, housing the newcomer will fall to you."

"We'll be tight as Dick's hatband," Tavish said, "but we'll make do." He mentally compiled a list of things he needed to do in preparation for Mr. Attwater to live in his small home. Tavish's first duty, the one he least relished, would be making Finbarr aware of the decision that had been made.

"I am sorry so much of this burden has fallen on your shoulders." Ma clutched her hands more fiercely. "Perhaps we could make a try at having Finbarr back home again." She made the offer with a catch in her voice.

Da shook his head. "The lads will get on well enough."

A measure of tension left Ma's expression, a hint of guilt taking its place. Tavish ached at the sight of it. Convincing her to send Finbarr to his home months earlier had required every ounce of persuasion he could muster. She'd been falling to pieces trying to care for Finbarr. Her deterioration had only sped up his. And Da, watching the two of them slip farther away, had worried himself into a fitfulness that had quickly been eating away at his health, too. There'd been no other option.

Tavish made the journey every day or so to his parents' home to look in on them, as he did with the rest of his family. He'd two sisters in Hope Springs, both of whom had passed through difficulties of late. He'd an older brother in town as well. Ian had sustained a horrific injury the year before, from which he'd never fully recovered. Tavish's granny lived a pace down the street. Time was rendering her frailer with each passing year. Each passing *day*, it seemed. Tavish helped them all in any way he could, but they all needed so much. He was only one person.

He'd kept them all going, had kept them together, through some of the darkest moments of his life. He was tired. Exhausted. But they needed him. There was, indeed, no rest for the weary.

"We've room enough for a tutor," he assured his parents. "Mr. Attwater'll set the lad to rights. I'm certain of it."

He bid his parents farewell and stepped out onto the porch where Finbarr yet sat. "Come along, then, you lazy bum. Time to head home." He kept his tone light and teasing. Though doing so hadn't managed to bring a smile to Finbarr's face these past months, Tavish didn't know what else to do.

Finbarr rose and, as was their custom, grabbed hold of the arm Tavish offered. They moved off the porch slowly and carefully, Tavish warning Finbarr of each obstacle that might give him difficulty. They did this every day—Tavish walked him from bed to the parlor, from the parlor to the table, and anywhere else he needed to go. And though he was more than willing to do whatever his brother needed of him, Tavish could see that needing help at all grated on Finbarr.

Tavish waited to bring up the topic at hand until they'd reached home and Finbarr was settled in a chair near the fireplace.

"I'll not tiptoe around things," he said. "A decision's been made regarding your situation."

The expression on Finbarr's badly scarred face hardly changed. Only the slightest drop in his coloring told Tavish that his brother was even listening. "You're sending me away?" His voice hardly rose above a whisper.

"No." Tavish pulled a chair up. "No one is sending you away. No one wants to. Not anyone."

Finbarr didn't look relieved. He wore the same expression of vague worry and weariness he'd carried since the fire that had taken his sight.

"We're sending for the tutor Dr. Jones recommended. He'll come here, stay with us, and work with you. That'll be a fine thing, don't you think?"

"I don't need a tutor," Finbarr muttered. "I'll sort this out on my own."

"You've had a half a year to sort this out without managing it."

"You try living in the dark, Tavish." He spoke louder and with increasing frustration. "Then I wouldn't be the only failure in this family."

These were the moments that pierced Tavish the deepest. Finbarr had once been a cheerful sort of lad. He'd been quick with a smile, the first to reassure others that things would work out for the best. All of that had been left in the ashes.

"Maybe Mr. Attwater can teach you enough for you to get your old job back," Tavish said.

Finbarr shook his head. "What good would I be to Mr. Archer? I'd get lost out in his fields. He'd spend all day trying to find me."

"That's the sort of thing Mr. Attwater can teach you," Tavish reminded him.

"He can't teach me to see again," Finbarr snapped. "Nothing he does could change that."

"I know it. And I'm right sorry, I am." Tavish was, indeed. More than he could possibly say. "I'd much rather be arranging to take you somewhere to have your eyes made new again. But Dr. Jones said there's nothing to be done. This is all we can give you."

With a deep breath, Finbarr's shoulders rose and fell. Resignation filled his features, something Tavish saw happen on a daily basis. The lad had to reconcile himself to his condition over and over again, mourning anew with each unseen sunrise.

"How long before he comes?" Finbarr didn't sound at all pleased at the prospect.

"I don't know. He's in Lincoln, on another job." Much would depend on how much money Tavish received for Joseph's crop.

Finbarr only nodded.

They sat in silence as the minutes dragged on. Tavish watched his brother wrestling with demons. His brow furrowed deeply then smoothed out in a look of acceptance. His mouth alternately pulled in a tight line and tugged down in a frown. The hardest of all, however, was looking into the blue eyes that once sparkled with life and happiness, now empty. Was the change from the loss of sight, or from the loss of hope? Tavish couldn't rightly say. Whatever the cause, his heart broke to see it.

"I'd like to go to bed now," Finbarr said after a time.

Tavish guided him to the alcove behind the fireplace where he had slept before Finbarr had come to live with him. He pulled out Finbarr's nightclothes and set them on the straw tick then helped his brother change and dress for the night, something they accomplished every evening in silence.

"I'll see you in the morning, lad," he said once Finbarr was lying down and under his blankets.

"I'll be here." Finbarr always gave that response. It made sense. The lad wouldn't be seeing anyone the next day. Still, something in the phrase and downtrodden tone cracked Tavish's heart clean in two.

He stepped back into the parlor, sparing only a parting glance for the closed bedroom door he passed. He'd built that room the previous fall, fully expecting to share it with his new bride. But his Sweet Katie had chosen someone else. The room he'd had such plans for, such hopes, sat empty and unused. Finbarr slept in the alcove. Tavish slept in the loft.

He sat in a chair near the fireplace and slumped low, listening to the deafening silence. Nights were long and difficult, and had been more so these past months. Without the distractions daytime provided, he could not keep his worries tucked away.

Less than a year ago, Hope Springs had been a town at war. The

American townspeople had resented the presence of so many Irish immigrants, who, in turn, had resented the misery and injustice they'd endured at their neighbors' hands and had returned the treatment in kind.

Tavish didn't care to think on those times. Too much had been lost: livelihoods, property, even lives. His older brother Ian had nearly been one of those lost to violence. Try as he might, Tavish couldn't forget the sight of Ian, bloodied and beaten, fighting for his very life.

He leaned forward, elbows on his legs, and dropped his head into his upturned hands. Ian still wasn't truly well. His wife and children were struggling.

Their older sister, Mary, had worries of her own. Her husband had begun speaking of leaving Hope Springs, but all her family was here. A worrisome rift had grown between the couple.

His younger sister, Ciara, was now spending far less time with her siblings and parents than she once had, and no one knew why.

The town might have stopped tearing itself apart, but his family was still falling to pieces. He worked tirelessly to hold them all together, yet this was how he spent his nights: alone in his empty home.

It was always empty. Always had been. And that day he'd finally admitted to himself that it always would be. Fairy-tale endings were just that: fairy tales. The time had come to pull himself out of the clouds.

Falling in love never ended particularly well for him. How many women had he lost? He'd courted a couple of young lasses back in New York, though, none, he later admitted to himself, had been truly a serious attachment. Then he'd courted dear, kind, tenderhearted Bridget, who died of a fever six years back, mere weeks before they were to be married. A heart simply didn't recover from such loss.

Then Katie Macauley, who'd passed him over for Joseph

Archer. She was happy in her choice, and he was glad of that. But it still stung.

Sitting there in the dark as his birthday came to a close, Tavish congratulated himself on having made a logical decision about his future. He'd focus on Finbarr and his needs. He'd keep his family whole.

And he would leave the women to see to themselves.

Chapter Two

OCTOBER 1871

Cecily Attwater sat amidst the ceaseless noise of yet another train station, trying to separate voices from train whistles, footsteps from the thud of traveling trunks. Noisy places were always the most difficult. Silhouettes moved around, the outline of a train behind them. She clung to the paper with "Archer Family" written across it. They were supposed to collect her and take her back with them to the town of Hope Springs, where her newest student lived.

No matter how many times she traveled to an unfamiliar place and navigated her way through a new group of people, no matter how often she started over, it never grew easy. But she loved her work. She helped people and improved lives. And each job's salary aided her in the work dearest to her heart: creating a library for the blind.

She never knew how her pupils would receive her. Some, like the sweet little girl she'd worked with in Lincoln, were eager to learn new skills and adapt to their circumstances. Others, like the crotchety old man in Omaha, were too angry at the world to learn anything without a great deal of arguing.

Finbarr O'Connor. She repeated the name in her mind. This newest student was, from the sound of things, Irish. That worried her a bit. The Irish were, in her experience, often stubborn and difficult. She hoped, for his sake, he'd directed at least a portion of his Irish bullheadedness toward the task of learning to function in the world as a blind man. But the necessity of her presence indicated otherwise.

A silhouette approached her. The midday sun provided enough light for her to know that the stranger was a woman, though not a terribly tall one. She wore a broad-brimmed bonnet and a dress of either blue or purple, though how vibrant, Cecily couldn't say. Even in the brightest of lights, colors remained muted.

"Forgive me," the woman said. "I couldn't help but notice your sign."

An Irishwoman. This stranger was likely connected to Cecily's newest job.

"Is it the Archer family you'd be looking for?" the Irishwoman asked.

"Yes. Would you happen to be Mrs. Archer?"

"That's myself. I'm looking for Cecil Attwater. Are you holding this sign for him, then?"

Cecil Attwater? Good heavens. "My name is Cecily Attwater, but yes, I am quite certain I am the person for whom you are looking."

"You've been hired to tutor Finbarr O'Connor?" the woman pressed.

"I have."

The woman turned her head away, looking at the person standing behind her, a man, judging by the size and shape. He must have given Mrs. Archer some kind of reply, because she looked at Cecily once more. "It seems we confused our instructions a bit, Miss...?" She pulled the word out long like a question.

Cecily nodded.

". . . *Miss* Attwater," the woman said. "We'll be taking you on to Hope Springs, unless you've something you need to do here first."

"I have no further business here." Cecily had placed her traveling trunk directly to her right and her basket of foodstuffs beneath the bench. She set her hand on the trunk. "This one is mine."

The man stepped forward and lifted her trunk.

"Miss Attwater," the woman said, "this is my husband, Joseph Archer."

Cecily dipped her head a bit. "I'm pleased to make your acquaintance, Mr. Archer. I was instructed to obtain two days' worth of food for the journey to Hope Springs. I have that here."

She hunched down, reaching for her basket. She could just make out its shape in the dimness below the bench. By the time Cecily was standing fully upright two children in short dresses had joined the couple.

"Good morning," she greeted, looking down in their direction. She'd found people were less unnerved if she at least *appeared* to see everything they did. Her slightly darkened spectacles gave the illusion of focusing on people she couldn't entirely see, as well as hiding the odd milkiness of her eyes.

"This is Emma and Ivy," Mrs. Archer said.

"It is a pleasure to meet you both."

"You talk strange," a child's voice said. "Where are you from?"

"Ivy," Mrs. Archer reprimanded.

Cecily knew her manner of speaking sounded odd to American ears. "I am from England," she said. "Everyone there speaks as oddly as I do."

"Oh." Ivy seemed to take that as a very thorough explanation.

"We'd best be on our way," Mr. Archer said. "The day's getting away from us, and we have a great deal of ground to cover."

Mr. Archer spoke with the refined accent Cecily had often heard in the eastern cities of the United States, but not at all since coming

West. The Eastern accent was as close as anyone ever came to sounding like home. The farther west she traveled, the more she missed hearing those almost-familiar strains.

Cecily followed the family away from the depot, careful not to allow anyone to come between her and her escorts. Even in full sunlight, she would never be able to distinguish them from the crowd should any degree of distance separate them.

They wove through the crowds, past the smells of freshly baked bread and savory meats wafting from the depot restaurant, then out to the yard behind the station, where Cecily became instantly aware of the smell of horses. She could make out the wagons, some piled high with crates and barrels. Amongst the great many horses were nearly as many people moving about. Crowded places always created an overwhelming cacophony of sounds and smells. For a person dependent on those clues to make sense of the world, the experience was not a calming one.

"Would you be offended, Miss Attwater, if you are required to ride in the wagon bed?" Mr. Archer asked.

"Not in the least. I am weary enough, in fact, that I will likely simply lie down and fall asleep."

Mr. Archer lifted her trunk into the back of his wagon then helped his daughters into the wagon bed. Next, he stretched out his hand to help her into the wagon as well. Had he done so at dawn or dusk or, worse yet, in the dark of night, she wouldn't have seen his offer of assistance. She had a great deal of practice stepping up on the hub of wagon wheels and could manage the thing with very careful effort.

She was quickly situated in a snug spot in the wagon bed, her back pressed against a crate, her feet stretched in front of her. The two little girls sat nearby, whispering to one another. Her hearing had grown necessarily acute over the years, and she could make out their words, though she wasn't purposely listening. The girls weren't quite sure what to make of their strange traveling companion, most especially her green-hued spectacles. Cecily could appreciate that; she knew she made a rather odd picture.

The lurch of the wagon, and then the rumble of the wheels under her, signaled the beginning of their journey. The outline of buildings passed one at a time, and, slowly, the sounds of the bustling town faded away. Blessed, blessed silence. Tension eased from her shoulders. She could hear the clomp of hooves clearly enough to know that there were two horses. The little girls shifted around nearby.

As the day wore on, she listened to the family's conversations but kept more or less to herself. They were a loving family; that much was certain. They also clearly had a unique history. The little girls called Mrs. Archer "Katie," which likely meant she was not the girls' mother. Mr. Archer spoke to his wife with unmistakable kindness and caring, and the girls obviously adored her. Whatever the exact dynamics of the Archer family, they had precisely the affectionate closeness Cecily longed for. Her parents had both been gone for several years. She had no brothers or sisters. Though she always grew very fond of her students, in the end, her job required that she leave them.

She was very much alone in the world.

The world grew darker as they traveled. Fewer and fewer sights were discernible. Slowly, everything faded into blackness, though Cecily knew that the world itself had not yet been plunged into the full darkness of night. It was amazing how deeply one missed the light when one could see so little of it.

The wagon came to a stop, and everyone disembarked. Mr. Archer soon had a good fire going. Cecily kept near it, grateful for what little light it provided. In the dim and dancing shadows, she prepared her meal. Thank the heavens her father had seen fit to send her to school as her sight worsened. She wouldn't have known how to do much for herself otherwise. With her training, she functioned very nearly as well as any fully-sighted person.

Cecily sat on a blanket laid out within comfortable distance of the fire, her plate of food balancing precariously on her lap. The younger of the Archer girls, Ivy, quite unexpectedly came and sat beside her.

"Is England close to Ireland?" the little one asked.

"It is very close to Ireland. The two are neighbors, in fact."

Ivy inched closer. "We were in Ireland."

Though Mrs. Archer was clearly Irish, the little girls sounded as American as their father. "Were you there recently?"

Mr. Archer answered. They all sat near enough each other for their various conversations to be overheard by the rest of their small party. "We are just now returning home from our journey to Ireland and Baltimore."

"We were visiting our families." Mrs. Archer sat beside her husband, which made looking in her direction less of a guess.

"Did you enjoy returning home?"

A pause. "'Twas an important thing to have done." Mrs. Archer's response was not at all what Cecily had expected.

Father had longed to return to England, as had many of the English friends they'd had in America. And she'd often heard immigrants from other countries express the same longing. Did Mrs. Archer not feel the homeward pull?

"Everything was green," little Ivy said.

Cecily did not see colors very well anymore. She missed green most of all. Though England was not quite as green as the Emerald Isle, it was still the color she most closely associated with her childhood in England, the color of summer, of laughter, of happier times.

How well she remembered green. The *feeling* of it, at least.

"What did you enjoy most about Ireland?" she asked her tiny companion.

"Uncle Brennan," she said. "He is so funny." Ivy giggled, probably remembering a few moments with her uncle.

Cecily took a bite of her honey-drizzled drop scone. They traveled well; she'd eaten many over the years.

"What did you enjoy the most, Emma?" Mr. Archer asked.

"The music." Emma wasn't as loud nor as lively as her sister. "I loved the music."

Ivy hopped up and hurried away toward Mr. and Mrs. Archer. "Play for us, Katie," she said. "Please. Please, please, please."

"Would you, Katie?" Mr. Archer asked.

"Only if the girls agree to lie down while they listen. The night's growing late."

Emma and Ivy settled in for the night as Mrs. Archer retrieved and tuned her violin. By the time Cecily finished her meal, the music had begun. Something in the sound was hesitant, as though Mrs. Archer had not been playing for very long, or the songs she'd chosen weren't entirely familiar. Still, the music was soothing and heartfelt, with the plaintive sound so common to the music of Ireland, a sound that somehow spoke simultaneously of sorrow and hope.

In the silence between tunes, Cecily could hear the little ones' breathing grow slower. Cecily's eyelids were growing heavy. Though Mrs. Archer's playing lacked polish, it held such feeling. That emotion, that connection, wove a spell.

In time, there was no more rustling of blankets, no more whispered but eager song requests. All was still. Mrs. Archer stopped playing, leaving an incomplete sort of peace, as though the silence held life's worries at bay only momentarily.

No one spoke as Mrs. Archer put her instrument away. The click of the violin case melded with the pops and snaps of the fire, the only sounds in the darkness.

Then Mrs. Archer spoke again. "Miss Attwater, I'd not wanted to say anything while the girls were awake, but I'm wondering if the

O'Connors realize—That is, since they made no mention of your being—"

"A woman?" Cecily guessed. The Archers, after all, had been expecting a Mr. Cecil Attwater.

"Well, that, yes. Unless I misunderstood, they're under the impression you're a man."

"I imagine that will be straightened out quickly enough." But Cecily sensed there was more. "What else has you worried?"

"The O'Connors are Irish," Mrs. Archer said.

Cecily nodded. "I guessed as much."

"But do the O'Connors realize you're English? Your countrymen and ours haven't had the most pleasant history between us."

That was most certainly true. "But does that mean that here, in this new country, far from the site of our past difficulties, we who were not part of those struggles must continue in animosity toward one another?"

Mrs. Archer answered firmly. "Those you are about to meet were part of those struggles. They've very real, very personal complaints against the English."

"And they will hold that against me?"

"I cannot say with any certainty that they won't." To her credit, Mrs. Archer sounded genuinely sorry about the possibility of difficulties between Cecily and her pupil's family. "The past decades have not been good ones for the Irish. Add to that many centuries of hatred between our people, and we've quite a chasm separatin' us."

Hatred. The word hung heavy between them. These people she'd come to help may hate her from the first word out of her mouth.

Little else was said over the remainder of the night, and when someone did speak, the topics were light, skirting around what Mrs. Archer had spoken of. But her words were precisely where Cecily's mind remained. She'd more than once endured a less-than-enthusiastic reception from her pupils and their families. The very necessity of her services was often met with resentment. But never before had she arrived for a job already hated simply because of her birthplace.

She'd realized right off that her student was Irish but hadn't held that against him. Would the O'Connors be willing to do the same?

Centuries of hatred.

Centuries.

That did not bode well at all.

Chapter Three

Tavish stood on his front porch as Joseph Archer pulled his buggy to a stop in front of the house. Katie sat up alongside him—Katie, whom Tavish had once courted and cared for and dreamed of making a life with. Though he did his best to push her from his mind, he still thought about her now and then, and what might've been.

Watching her arrival, he couldn't deny that she looked happy. She always looked happy with Joseph. That was something of a consolation. Katie was happy, as she'd always deserved to be. He was glad of that; it eased his own regrets a bit.

In the very next moment, Biddy, his sister-in-law, rushed out of the house and straight for Katie, who'd only just been handed down by her husband.

Her husband. In time, he'd grow used to thinking of things in those terms. In the meantime, 'twas inarguably odd.

He pulled his thoughts away from his distraction. This gathering was not about him or Katie. It was about Mr. Attwater, whom they'd brought with them—and about Finbarr's future. Having a tutor would ease Da and Ma's burdens. The rest of the family worried for Finbarr as well. This step would help everyone.

Katie reached the porch. "Tavish O'Connor." She gave him one of her once-rare smiles. "How are you, then?"

"Well, Katie. I'm well." 'Twas the most he could say for himself. Life had been difficult these past months.

Apparently satisfied, she continued into the house. Joseph approached next. He shook Tavish's hand. A great deal of the tension that had existed between them before Joseph and Katie's marriage yet remained. Tavish had tried to make clear his intentions to not interfere or make trouble between them. Katie had made her decision, and he meant to be happy for her and Joseph both.

"How was your journey?" Tavish asked.

"Fine," Joseph answered.

"Did you find Mr. Attwater at the station?" 'Twas best to keep to safe topics.

"Not exactly."

They'd not found the tutor? Everything depended on Mr. Attwater.

For the first time, Tavish noticed the woman standing near Joseph. Golden curls, a natural touch of color in her cheeks, a rosebud mouth, a trim figure. She was breathtaking, even with the odd, green-tinted spectacles. How had he not spotted her immediately?

"Tavish, this is Finbarr's new tutor, Miss Cecily Attwater."

"*Cecily* Attwater? *Miss*?"

"Indeed." Ever the refined gentleman, Joseph completed the introductions. "Miss Attwater, this is Tavish O'Connor."

She turned and faced him. "Are you a relative of the young man I've come to tutor?"

At the sound of her voice, he grew instantly still. Miss Attwater was English. *English.* The situation was growing more complicated by the moment. Still, he knew how to be welcoming. A soft smile or two generally smoothed over even the most unpleasant of situations, and few things were as unpleasant as the English and Irish being forced to interact.

He tucked away his discomfort. "I'm Finbarr's older brother. He lives here with me."

"I would like to meet him," Miss Attwater said.

"Come inside," Tavish said. "The entire family's waiting to meet you." *And won't they be surprised?* "But I'll make no promises regarding Finbarr. He'll likely as not remain in his alcove at the back of the house."

"Will he refuse to make an appearance because he's embarrassed, or as a show of willfulness?"

She made terribly light of the situation. "He'll refuse because he's a seventeen-year-old boy whose entire world has gone dark."

"He's not the first to find himself in that situation, nor will he be the last."

If that wasn't the coldest response he'd heard since Finbarr'd lost his sight, Tavish didn't know what was. "For one who's made her life's work teaching the blind, you're not very quick with sympathy."

"Sympathy?" she asked. "Is that the approach you've taken thus far?"

"Of course." Finbarr needed their kindness.

Her chin inched up a notch. "And how has that been working, Mr. O'Connor?"

When he didn't manage to find an answer immediately, she pushed past him with a deliberate and determined stride, stepping into the house with the same triumphant tilt to her chin. Why was it he constantly found himself in company with stubborn women?

"This could be disastrous," Tavish muttered.

"That was Katie's feeling as well." He'd all but forgotten about Joseph on the porch.

"Was Miss Attwater this difficult all the way from the train station?"

Joseph seemed to think over it a moment. "She showed herself very independent and very determined. She'll either be the best thing for Finbarr, or an absolute nightmare for him."

"Care to place a bit of money on that wager?"

Joseph didn't take up the jest. "What I would really like is to see Finbarr. How is he? Truly?"

Tavish pushed out a heavy breath. "In all honesty, he's not well. He still hardly speaks, doesn't leave the house. He's not the same lad he was before the fire. Not at all."

"Would it help if I reminded him that his job is still waiting for him at my place?"

Tavish didn't have to ponder the question. "I can't say if he doesn't feel equal to the task, or if he simply doesn't care to try. Amounts to the same thing in the end."

"The boy's lost." Joseph finished the thought.

"That he is, but can Miss Attwater bring him back again?"

She'd not struck Tavish as the gentle, nurturing type that a frightened and wandering lad needed to guide him back to himself. She'd be more likely to push him farther away. If that happened, the tenuous thread holding the O'Connor family together—their fragile hopes for Finbarr—would snap.

"I don't intend to volunteer to drive her back to the train station, so I think you're stuck with her for the time being."

Tavish could appreciate the dry tone. "Shall we go see if the family has filleted Miss Attwater yet?"

"Or vice versa," Joseph said.

"You think she's managed to bring the entire O'Connor clan to its knees in only two minutes?"

When Joseph didn't appear the least bit amused, Tavish's humor faded. Either Miss Attwater had done something to convince Joseph of her fearsomeness, or Tavish hadn't hidden his family's fragile state as well as he'd thought.

Little Emma Archer stepped back out onto the front porch. Her eager expression had turned to disappointment.

"What has happened, Emma?" Joseph asked.

"He still won't talk to me," she said quietly.

No need asking who "he" was. Emma had visited Finbarr several days a week, every week, from the day of the fire until her family had left for their journey. While Finbarr had at first accepted her company, he'd started pushing her away more each visit.

"He's feeling nervous, sweetie," Tavish told her, hoping to ease the sting.

Her nod was too automatic to indicate she fully believed him.

"Let's go inside," Joseph told his daughter.

They stepped inside Tavish's house to find Miss Attwater seated, facing the O'Connor family with the regal bearing of a monarch. Her gaze didn't quite settle on any of them but hovered somewhere just above their heads. They looked noticeably puzzled. Joseph took position at Katie's side, leaving Tavish, alone, standing in front of them all.

"Perhaps you've a solution to this difficulty, Tavish," Da said.

"And which difficulty would that be?" There'd been any number of late.

"Miss Attwater," Da answered.

Tavish let his eyes dart to her. She didn't so much as flinch at being discussed; neither did she seem to mind the many pairs of eyes trained on her. Quite sure of herself, wasn't she?

"She objects to the housing arrangements." Ma spoke with great concern.

"You were hoping for finer accommodations?" he asked their royal visitor. "I'll warn you, you're not likely to find any. We've simple lives around here."

The English were forever looking down their noses at the poverty and simplicity of the Irish way of life, conveniently ignoring the role they themselves had played over the centuries in creating the disparity.

"Her objection, is to you in particular, son," Da corrected.

"Is it, now?" Tavish let his question sound like a challenge. "Am I not a fine enough fellow for you? Not possessing lofty manners and such?"

Miss Attwater shook her head in much the way one would when rolling one's eyes. The darkened spectacles made it impossible to see if she'd matched the impression. "You've done a remarkable job of twisting my words about," she said. "My objection is not personal but, rather, the very understandable unease an unmarried woman would feel at being housed under the same roof as two bachelors."

What a dunderhead he was to not think of that. "I suppose I can understand your worries. 'Twould be a hard thing resisting m' charms."

"I will do my utmost to be strong under their influence." Her tone was the driest he'd ever heard.

He thought he detected a bit of humor in her response. He never could resist a chance for a fine bit of banter. "And what of you?" He allowed a bit of flirtation to touch his words. "Thinking I might fall under *your* spell?"

"I simply asked if there were any other options, something that would be more proper and comfortable for all of us." Her reply didn't match his tone at all. "I am certain you will agree with the necessity of a different arrangement."

There, once again, was that very English talent of instant superiority. Though *they* were employing *her*, she was already issuing dictates and expecting obedience.

Still, he had to admit she was right. She couldn't live in his house as the man they'd been expecting could have. Tavish refused to pawn her off on his mother or sisters, who had trouble enough of their own.

A bolt of inspiration shot down from the very heavens. Granny. Few people in the world were a match for Tavish's granny in terms of headstrong tendencies, determination, and gumption. The woman was in her eighties and a touch frail, yet she could still match anyone wit for wit and emerge not even the slightest bit worse for wear. Under Granny's influence, their newly arrived queen would find herself without a throne.

"Across the road and back a pace lives a sweet, older woman with an empty room." He didn't look over at his family, knowing they'd likely all be holding back smirks. *Sweet* and *older* Granny certainly was, but she was also a force to be reckoned with.

"If I ask her," he said, "I imagine she'd be willing to take you in, though she's not able-bodied enough to cook for nor clean up after you."

That much actually was true. Tavish saw to the upkeep of her house. Half of the Irish in town saw that she was fed. Katie came 'round and cleaned regularly.

"I do not believe she will find me a burden."

The lass certainly didn't lack confidence.

"Does Finbarr intend to come out and meet me?" Miss Attwater asked.

"I warned you he might not."

"You did." She gave a decisive nod. "But I expect him to be here to greet me at eight o'clock in the morning. Not a moment later." Miss Attwater rose, not seeming to care at all that the many eyes in the room had pulled wide with surprise. "Mr. O'Connor, I would be grateful if you would show me to my new quarters."

"Very well, Miss Attwater." Tavish offered an exaggerated bow. "'Tis quite happy I am to escort you down the road."

She neither smiled nor shook her head nor gave any acknowledgement of his antics. He wasn't at all accustomed to a woman who didn't respond in any way to his teasing. Perhaps the

English didn't have a sense of humor. They certainly had odd taste in spectacles.

Tavish met his parents' worried gazes. "All will be well," he assured them quietly.

"What if it's not?" Ian, Tavish's older brother, voiced the very question Tavish saw in all their eyes.

"I'll make it right," he promised. "Don't you worry."

How many times had he said those very words to this very group of people in the past year? Too many to count.

What have I actually made right? Nothing.

"She's at the door already." Ian motioned across the room.

Miss Attwater's posture put him firmly in mind of a fence post. He didn't know whether her stiffness was more amusing or vexing. As always, he chose to lean more heavily toward being entertained. Life was unbearable otherwise.

Tavish crossed to her. "Shall we, Miss Attwater?"

"I will follow your lead," she said.

They stepped onto the porch.

"How long have you been in this country, Miss Attwater?" It seemed a good enough way to break the silence between them as they walked.

"I have resided in America nearly fourteen years." She spoke so formally, even for an Englishwoman. "How long ago did you leave Ireland?"

"Ireland?" He laid the accent on as thick as he could manage. "What is it that's making you suspect me of bein' Irish?"

"Certainly not your Christian name," she said. "'Tavish' is Scottish, I believe."

He stopped in his tracks. Never in his life had anyone outside his own family known the origins of his name without being told.

She stopped as he did. "Have I offended you?"

"How'd you know where my name hails from?"

"My childhood home was in the north of England," she said, "not far from the Scottish border. The butcher in town was named Tavish MacIntosh. He and his family were as Scottish as anyone I've ever known."

He continued walking, slower now. She matched his pace precisely. "This Tavish fellow sounds like a grand person, if you ask me."

"And your evaluation is based on nothing more than his name?"

He veered the tiniest bit as they crossed the road. She did as well. Exactly as much as he did, in exactly the same spot on the road. Exactly.

"Anyone named Tavish is bound to be a fine fellow," he said. "I believe there's a law."

Katie hadn't laughed at his teasing at first, either, but at least she'd looked as though she'd wanted to. Miss Attwater couldn't have appeared less amused if she'd been watching the grass grow. And she kept matching him movement for movement, down to the tiny wanderings that weren't the least bit important.

He stopped. So did she. "Just what is it you're doing?"

She watched him from behind her darkened spectacles. "I am following you to call upon an apparently frail, helpless, elderly woman, though I take leave to doubt she is either frail or helpless." She was quick; he'd allow that.

"You're doing more than merely following me. You're insisting on remaining a pace behind, taking every step I do, *exactly* as I do. You're full-on mimicking me, and, I suspect, mocking me as well, though I can't sort out why."

Miss Attwater stepped slowly and deliberately off the road then moved beside him and turned to face him once more. "How is following you across an unfamiliar road in an unfamiliar place whilst the setting sun renders the landscape dimmer by the moment 'mocking' you? I would rather not trip and fall on my face, though I will apologize if my desire to remain upright has offended you."

"Now who's the one twisting words?" He shot her another of his famous smiles. Again, it fell short of the mark; she didn't even seem to notice. "I'm of the impression, Miss Attwater, that you've already decided to hate me."

She shook her head in firm denial. "I hardly know you. If you wish for my opinion, good or otherwise, you'll have to earn it. At the moment, my feelings toward you are entirely neutral."

As was her expression. The woman didn't seem the least concerned about anything. Was she really so unshakingly confident, or was this all an act?

She motioned toward Granny Claire's house ahead. "Is this our destination?"

"It is that."

"Shall we?" With that, she continued up the path with the same measured step as always, her chin held high, shoulders back.

Rather a cold fish, this one. 'Twas a good thing for his sanity that he'd given up on women. Otherwise, he might've been tempted to find out if she had a heart underneath all that ice.

Chapter Four

Cecily had heard many a tale of Irish stubbornness, but witnessing it firsthand had convinced her of its enormity. Did Tavish—thinking of him as simply "Tavish" was too familiar, considering they'd only met, but she'd been introduced to two other Mr. O'Connors that night alone and needed to be able to distinguish them from one another—truly think she'd mimicked his movements to mock him rather than as her only safe means of crossing the dim, uneven road? What did the man expect from one who was nearly blind?

The windows, discernible by the light coming through them, sat high enough above the level where Cecily walked to tell her that the house she approached had a few steps leading to the front door. She slowed as she approached and raised her foot. The toe of her boot bumped the edge of something flat and wide—the front step, she guessed.

She raised her foot to the level of most stairs and found precisely what she was looking for. One step. Two. Three. Then no more. She committed that to memory. If she was to live in this house, she'd do well to know exactly how to navigate in and out.

Three more paces brought her to the edge of the house. Light spilled through a window not far to her right. Another window sat equally far to her left. The door likely sat centered between the two. She pressed her palm to the wall directly in front of her. The door. In the second before she knocked, Tavish's footsteps sounded behind her.

A silhouette appeared in the window to her right. "Well, then, Tavish, have you decided to finally offer a 'good day' to your old granny? You've neglected me something terrible these last days."

"I've not neglected you at all, y' old fibber." Tavish moved to the window as well, blocking most of the light Cecily could see. "I've brought you someone new to torture and question."

"Torture, is it?" the woman said. "I've not tortured anyone in years, though I've a mind to start up again."

Cecily heard something very tender in their teasing banter. Tavish clearly loved his grandmother, and she loved him in return. Cecily never could witness a caring family without being touched by it. And she never could entirely squelch her envy. She'd made the acquaintance of dozens upon dozens of people over the past years as she'd traveled about, tutoring, yet she was every bit as alone as she had been before taking up her profession.

"Might we wander on inside, then, Granny?" Tavish suggested.

"The door's not locked."

Cecily was adept at knowing instinctively where to find a doorknob. She grasped it, turned it, and pushed the door open, all without having to feel around. The house smelled of cabbage and tea. A taste of dust hung in the air; perhaps Granny lacked the fortitude for regular dusting. Tavish's house had smelled of something sweet—fruit or berries, or something of that nature. The scent had been so wholly unexpected that she'd noticed it even in its subtlety.

Granny's house was lighter inside than the dimly lit porch but not light enough for Cecily to make out much of her surroundings. It seemed her soon-to-be landlady was not one to light many candles or lanterns. Cecily would have to either offer to pay for the kerosene or candles she needed, or she'd need to memorize the house with enough precision to move about in the dark.

Tavish came in behind her; one couldn't help but sense his presence in a room, blind or not. Some people were simply that way. They filled a space without words, without movement, simply by being.

Cecily could see enough to make out a person—"Granny," no doubt—seated near the front door. Tavish moved toward the older woman and bent low.

"Granny." It was a greeting, one accompanied by either an embrace or a kiss on the cheek. Tavish straightened. "This here is Finbarr's tutor, newly arrived in town."

"Mr. Attwater is sporting an unusual figure, I must say. And he's in sore need of a haircut."

Cecily liked Granny already. "And I'm further afraid that my whiskers haven't come in yet." She shook her head as if it were a great shame. "What a disgrace I am to men everywhere."

"'Disgrace' is not quite the word I'd use," Tavish muttered.

"Quite frankly, Mr. Tavish, I am not overly concerned about which word you would use." She kept her gaze directed toward Granny's outline. "Your grandson has not furnished me with a name for you, other than 'Granny.' Neither has he taken a moment to explain to you why I am here, so I suppose that task has fallen to me."

Tavish objected immediately. "Are all Englishwomen as impatient as you are?"

"Are all Irishmen as slow to come to the point as you are?" Cecily addressed Granny once more. "You seem far less frail and helpless than Mr. Tavish told me you'd be."

"I said nothing of the sort." A smile hung behind the words—a promising sign. She far preferred pleasant to prickly.

"Come sit here with me, Mr. Attwater," Granny instructed. "Tell me what's brought you here with this troublesome lad."

With careful steps, Cecily moved in Granny's direction. She made out a chair and lowered herself into it. "I am, as Mr. Tavish said, come to be a tutor to Finbarr. Due to a miscommunication, the young man's family was expecting a man, one who could live at Mr. Tavish's home without whispers or scandal or discomfort. I, as you have noticed, am a rather odd version of a *Mr.* Attwater and haven't that luxury."

"Ah. The family sent you here, did they?" The runners of a rocking chair squeaked against the wood floor. "But am I to look after you, or do they mean for you to tend to me?"

"You know your family better than I do, ma'am. Which do you think they intended?"

The woman made a sound of pondering. "You're welcome to stay, though I'd rather not call you 'mister' for the rest of forever. What's your name, lass?"

"Cecily."

"How long ago did you leave England?"

The second time in less than an hour someone had asked her that. Mrs. Archer had warned her that the Irish in Hope Springs might hold her English origins against her. Thus far, she hadn't been badly treated, but the length of her residency in America was definitely a point of discussion.

"I left England when I was eleven years old. America has been my home for nearly fifteen years." She couldn't see their faces, and neither of them spoke, so she didn't know whether they approved. "Now it is my turn for questions. What am I to call you?"

"Mrs. Claire'll do nicely," was the answer. "And before you ask your next question, I'll answer it. I've lived in this country a long old while. Now, my turn again." She was sharp witted. "Do you think you can help our Finbarr?"

"Yes," Cecily said. "I know what it is to be in his place."

"Oh, do you, now?" Tavish jumped in again.

Cecily turned her head in his direction. "Are you still here? I'd completely forgotten about you."

Mrs. Claire laughed heartily. "You've wounded him, you have. No woman's ever forgotten about Tavish when he was about. Handsome as they come. Humor to keep a lass smiling for days on end. Personable."

"Judgmental," Cecily added. "And entirely too sure of himself."

"I believe we've something of a pot and kettle argument, Miss Attwater," Tavish said. "I might've said much the same about you."

"Ah, but you didn't." She turned her head in Mrs. Claire's direction once more. "We'd best add 'slow to enter his opinion in a conversation' to your list of his attributes."

Tavish's feet shuffled as his silhouette paced a bit away. Cecily had encountered people before who'd taken an immediate dislike to her. She understood; having someone come into their lives with the express purpose of changing it often brought out people's prickliness. She'd found that standing her ground from the beginning and showing them she was not to be intimidated generally set things on the appropriate footing. In time, her clients came to value her at the least, and generally decided to like her.

Mrs. Claire spoke into the somewhat awkward silence. "Off with you, Tavish. I'll see to it Mr. Attwater settles in."

Cecily suspected she'd be teased about being *Mr.* Attwater for the rest of her sojourn in Hope Springs. She looked forward to it; humor had seen her through many difficulties.

"Doesn't she have any traveling trunks or bags or any such thing?" Mrs. Claire asked.

"They're still over at my place," Tavish said. "I'll fetch them."

"Leave 'em on the porch, lad. Cecily and I need a chance to become better acquainted, and I'll not be needing you around jokin' with me nor snippin' at her."

"Snipping at her? Is that what you think this is?" Tavish didn't sound as though he agreed.

"Off with you." Mrs. Claire left no room for argument.

A moment later, he was gone. Cecily didn't know what to think of the Irishman. Not at all.

"Now, Cecily, answer me this: How is it you've found your way under Tavish's skin so quickly?" That was certainly direct.

"My work here will disrupt his life," she answered. "In my experience, that anticipated upheaval tends to put me on a difficult footing with people when we first meet."

"I suppose." The rocker continued to squeak. "Still, I can't say I've ever known him to not take to someone straight off, even to those who didn't care at all for him."

"It seems I am destined to be the exception to the rule. He even objected to how closely I followed him on the journey over." That worried her, truth be told. "If he is so impatient with the adaptations necessary for me to get about, how will he react when his brother is taught to utilize the same techniques?"

"I'd wager he'll be more understanding with his brother," Mrs. Claire said.

"Why, because he's his brother?"

"Because he's aware that *his brother* is blind."

Cecily sat a moment in stunned silence. Surely Mrs. Claire was wrong. "He doesn't know I am blind?" That seemed unlikely. "I undertook a long, drawn-out discussion with his family, then walked all the way here with him. I never mentioned it specifically, but he had to have realized."

"You've quite a knack for appearing as though you see things and people," Mrs. Claire said. "I m'self didn't realize it until you lowered yourself into the chair. M' dear husband couldn't hardly see toward the end of his days." *Squeak. Squeak.* "He'd reach out for the arms of a chair, then hold fast to them as he slowly turned about then lowered bit by bit, as if half-convinced his backside would miss the chair entirely. You did the same, only not as slowly."

"My backside has missed a few chairs in its time." She'd learned the importance of taking care.

"Are you entirely without sight?"

"Not entirely." *Not yet.* "I can see shapes and outlines when there's enough light. At a very close distance and with plenty of light, I can make out a few details." Not nearly as many as she would have liked. Flowers had become nothing more than generally colorful blobs. Faces were little but the basic parts and, in just the right lighting, perhaps an eye color, if the bearer permitted her a very close inspection. She could read words written in large enough letters. Generally.

"And why do you suppose my dear Tavish thinks you wear those green spectacles?" Mrs. Claire asked.

"I have absolutely no idea." He must think her mad. She rather liked the possibility.

"I've a grand idea, Cecily. A wonderfully, horribly grand idea." Mrs. Claire's voice held a note of mischief. "You move about as if you've a full view of the world. What a lark we'd have keepin' Tavish thinking you can see and makin' him wonder."

The family at Cecily's last job hadn't been very keen on humor and laughter. She'd missed those things. "How long do you believe we could fool him?"

"Long enough for a laugh or two," Mrs. Claire said. The rocking chair creaks came faster. "I'm looking forward to this."

"I find I am, as well," Cecily said. "Laughter is good for the soul."

Another ponderous sound followed. "That will take some getting used to."

"What will?" Cecily asked.

"An English voice in my house. The last time that happened, my family was being tossed off the land we'd worked for centuries." Though accusation touched Mrs. Claire's tone, it held plenty of wariness. "Our lives were ruined."

"I haven't come to ruin anyone's life," Cecily assured her.

"But you have come to change our lives. You said as much yourself."

"And help Finbarr," Cecily said. "My efforts will change his life for the better—all of the family's lives for the better."

The heaviest, tiniest moment passed. "We'll see."

Chapter Five

"Miss Attwater said you are to be out and awaiting her by eight o'clock," Tavish warned his brother. "That's in a mere five minutes."

He stood at the opening to the alcove. Finbarr sat on the low bed. They'd already enacted their morning routine—Tavish buttoning the lad up, tying his shoes, combing his hair, and Finbarr standing mute the whole time. Now he wore his usual expression of barely concealed sorrow.

"You need only step out and drop yourself into the chair. You've done that every day as it is. You're simply doing so on a schedule today."

Finbarr didn't move.

"At least come have some breakfast. It'll do you good."

"Maybe in a bit," Finbarr answered quietly.

Tavish didn't like the idea of Finbarr not eating. "I could bring it to you."

Finbarr only shrugged. The lad was ceaselessly somber, lost in his thoughts. Tavish didn't know what else to do, but Finbarr depended on him. He couldn't give up.

A knock sounded from the front door.

"That'll be the lady herself." Tavish watched his brother for any change of expression. None. "Could you not at least bid her a good morning? It's for your sake she's come."

"*I* didn't send for her." Finbarr turned away, his empty eyes facing the brick on the back of the fireplace. "I don't need her; I'm not helpless."

"Not a soul among us thinks that, lad."

He shook his head, and in whispered tones muttered, "Everyone thinks that."

A second knock prevented a response.

Finbarr would come out when he was ready. Miss Attwater would simply have to be patient.

Tavish left his brother in the alcove and crossed the house to the front door. He pulled it open. Miss Attwater stood on the threshold, a cane hooked over her wrist. She wasn't alone. "Granny? What brings you all this way?"

"All this way, says he. Why, I can see the man's house from mine. How is that 'all this way,' I'd like to know?"

"You know full well 'twasn't the distance but the state of your bones and the nip in the air I referred to." He leaned forward and kissed her cheek, then stepped back so the women could come inside.

Granny took small steps across the room. How long must it've taken to make the journey from her house? Whenever she wished to go visiting, Tavish always took her in the buggy he shared with Ian. She didn't walk well, nor fast, nor without pain.

"Were you fearful Miss Attwater couldn't find her way here on her own?" Tavish offered them both a smile, though he couldn't say for certain if Miss Attwater was truly looking at him. Her darkened spectacles kept her eyes well hidden. "As you said your own self, Granny, she can see my house from yours."

"Can she now?" Granny's answer sounded far too much like laughter. Even the stone-faced Miss Attwater bit back a smile. "You can see this house from ours, Cecily. Is that not a grand thing?"

"I can think of nothing grander."

Tavish's gaze moved from one of them to the other. A joke hovered between them as did a fair bit of tension. Beneath her humor, Granny, who never looked anything but entirely comfortable with everyone, dripped with wariness. She sat in the chair nearest the low-burning fire. Miss Attwater took up a position standing at the mantle.

"Now, where's Finbarr taken himself?" Granny asked. "I'd hoped to see him. He's not come by to visit me in weeks."

Finbarr hadn't "come by" anywhere in months, as Granny knew perfectly well. "The lad's not ready to join us this morning."

Miss Attwater turned her bespectacled gaze toward him, her expression no longer light and laughing. "You told him we were beginning at eight o'clock, did you not?"

"I did. He's just needing a moment to reconcile himself to this."

Surprise touched her expression. "He has had time and plenty for that."

"I don't expect you to comprehend the pain he's going through, Miss Attwater." He had, however, assumed she would have at least shown some sympathy; she made her living working with people in Finbarr's situation. But he'd rather not pick a fight with her when he'd already spent the morning arguing with his brother.

"Rather, *how* could I possibly comprehend, is what you mean." So very sure of herself, she was. "I'm merely a teacher for hire, a task master. What do I know of his struggles?"

"Seems you've summed things up nicely. Now that we understand one another—"

"Understand?" She stepped closer, moving in the same calculated, deliberate manner she'd employed the night before. So stiff. So haughty. "Believe me, Tavish O'Connor, I understand your brother's situation far better than you ever will."

"Do you, now? More than merely a teacher, you've the second sight, then?"

She laughed humorlessly. "I don't even have the *first* sight."

What did that mean?

Miss Attwater grasped her wooden cane firmly, the tip resting against the floor at least a foot in front of her. She turned her head back toward Granny. "In which direction is young Finbarr's hidey hole?"

Hidey hole?

"I will not allow you to make light of his troubles," Tavish warned.

She turned back to him. "And I will not allow you to coddle him into helplessness."

"I've done nothing of the sort."

She closed in. "I've witnessed the same situation dozens of times. A family sees a loved one struggling and cannot bear for him to be further injured, so they protect him, cushion him from any possible blow. And in doing so, they turn their loved one into a shell of a person. They destroy him, Mr. O'Connor. It is my job to undo that damage."

"You're accusing me of destroying my own brother?"

Granny whistled long and low. "I swear, the two of you are worse than a couple of Kilkenny cats. I don't know whether to laugh at you or separate you for your own safety."

Miss Attwater straightened her already ramrod posture. "Quite frankly, Mrs. Claire, I'm not overly concerned about Tavish. Where do I find Finbarr?"

Tavish swallowed back a retort. Though he'd have liked to set her straight on a thing or two, they needed to focus on Finbarr. Until he knew whether his best approach was to try to soften things a bit between himself and Miss Attwater or to meet her stubbornness with an equal measure of his own, he would do his best to keep the peace. "Finbarr's in the alcove tucked behind the fireplace."

She let out a puff of breath and turned to face Granny once more. "Would you mind giving me more detailed instructions? I don't believe he'll piece together this puzzle any time soon."

Puzzle? He was missing something, and both women knew what.

"Walk somewhere approaching six feet to your left," Granny said. "Then turn left and go near about as far again. On your left'll be the alcove where Finbarr lays his head."

Miss Attwater nodded. "Left. Left. Left. Thank you."

She followed Granny's instructions with precision. She kept the cane a bit in front of her, never placing any weight on it. The cane tip moved back and forth, brushing against a chair leg, then the edge of a rug, then the corner of the wall.

With a dawning as sudden as the firing of a gun, Tavish discovered the piece he'd been missing.

"There it is," Granny said with a laugh. "The look I've been watching for."

"She's blind," he said quietly.

"Very nearly. Though from what I've gathered, she hasn't always been."

A few paces shy of the alcove, Miss Attwater called back, "I'm blind, not deaf."

Under his breath, Tavish muttered, "And certainly not mute."

Miss Attwater didn't respond as she disappeared around the corner.

"Will you survive having her in your home, then, Granny?"

She looked quite suddenly done in. "'Twas a cruel trick, lad, dropping a stranger at my door."

"You adjusted quickly when Katie was left to your keeping."

He was proud of the steadiness of his voice when speaking of his one-time sweetheart.

"'Twasn't the same at all," Granny insisted. "Katie wasn't . . ." She searched about for the right word.

"Blind?" Tavish suggested.

Granny shook her head. "Miss Attwater's so capable I've my doubts I'll even notice her lack of sight."

"English, then?"

"That is proving a bit uncomfortable. But it's more than that. She's . . . she's very . . ."

"Top lofty?"

"Intimidating," Granny said. "I'm not accustomed to being intimidated."

He didn't like the worry in her tone. "Is she unkind to you? I'll not countenance anyone mistreating you."

"She's not been unkind."

Yet Granny didn't look pleased. "If having her there makes you truly unhappy, I'll make other arrangements."

She gave a halfhearted nod.

Tavish took her hands in his. "If anything goes wrong, anything at all, I'll make it right. I promise."

She gave him a fond look. "You always do. You never could bear for anyone to be unhappy. 'Tis the reason Finbarr weighs so much on your heart."

"Speaking of the poor, unhappy lad, I'd best go save m' brother from the hobgoblin." He made a show of squaring his shoulders. "If I don't return, tell Ma I was brave to the bitter end. And have someone sing 'Mo Ghille Mear' at my wake."

"Oh, Tavish." Granny sighed his name. "'Tis a grand thing to hear you teasing again. You've not done enough of that these past months."

"Let us hope my good humor lasts now that I've a banshee in

my house." There was a bit too much truth to that. Cecily wasn't at all the soft-spoken and patient guide he'd expected of his brother's tutor.

Tavish followed the same path Cecily had trod a moment earlier: left, left, left. Cecily had found the alcove and now stood facing it. Just how much could she see? Strange to think of someone as clearly independent as she was also being blind, or very nearly so.

"I am assuming, Finbarr," she said, "your parents taught you better manners than to ignore someone who bids you good day. Shall I try again? Or do you mean to sulk in silence?" She certainly didn't treat the lad with kid gloves, that was for sure and certain.

"Good day, Miss Attwater," Finbarr said quietly. His wasn't merely a sulking tone, but also a sad one. 'Twas always a sad one.

"Your brother told you that we were to begin at eight o'clock this morning. Why are you not in the sitting room, ready to begin?"

"I don't need you here," he said. "I'm getting on fine."

"Are you?" Cecily set both hands on her cane and leaned ever so slightly on it. "Did you dress yourself this morning? Eat your breakfast? When did you last bathe on your own? Leave this house on your own?"

She was hounding him, and Tavish didn't like it. He stepped closer to her so he could speak in a lowered voice. "Show the boy a bit of sympathy, will you?"

"He has been fed enough sympathy to choke on." She didn't turn toward Tavish. Indeed, she returned to haranguing Finbarr with her very next breath. "Have you eaten breakfast?"

"I'm not hungry," Finbarr muttered.

"You're a seventeen-year-old boy; of course you're hungry."

Finbarr offered no response. Miss Attwater didn't seem to require one.

"Now, do you mean to come out and begin your day properly, or do you intend to spend it here in this dark abyss?"

Finbarr's shoulders drooped. "My entire life is a dark abyss."

The words struck Tavish's heart like a hot fire poker. These were the moments he felt the most helpless. Finbarr had once been endlessly sunny. Now, nothing Tavish did ever brought the slightest glimpse of light back into his brother's expression.

"I will be here every Monday through Friday from eight in the morning until six in the evening," Cecily told Finbarr. "You are welcome to spend the remainder of your time feeling sorry for yourself if you wish. But while I am here, you will work, and you will learn. That is what I was sent for."

"*I* didn't send for you." 'Twas the retort Finbarr offered most often.

"Those who need me most never do. But your family did, and if you fail to learn what I am here to teach it will not be my fault." She shifted her cane a bit so she held it once more in her left hand. It jutted out a bit in front of her. "I will meet you at the fireplace in two minutes."

With no more ceremony than that, she turned and retraced the path she'd taken to the alcove. Tavish remained behind, watching her turn the corner and slip out of sight.

"I don't like her, Tavish," Finbarr muttered from the alcove.

Neither do I. But Tavish had to give this a chance. Cecily lived independently without full sight. She traveled the country, alone. She could show Finbarr how to live, how to function. She was their first hope of a future for the lad.

"What do you think I should do?" Finbarr asked.

"I'd suggest getting yourself to the front of the fireplace within two minutes. Elsewise, she's likely to crack your head with her cane."

Finbarr turned the tiniest bit in his direction. "She has a cane?"

"And she wears spectacles with green glass."

For the briefest, most wonderful of moments, a single corner of

Finbarr's mouth tugged upward. The lad hadn't smiled in ten months. Not once.

"Why do you suppose she wears green spectacles?" Finbarr asked.

"I've not the slightest idea." He had a thought and pushed ahead with it. "You ought to ask her about them, out of the blue. She'd have a terrible time trying to piece together just how you know she wears spectacles."

"I am still not deaf, Tavish O'Connor." Cecily called from out of sight.

"Shall we face her down, lad?"

"I will go sit by the fire." Finbarr rose as he spoke. "But I'll not promise anything beyond that."

"That is good enough for me."

But it likely wouldn't be enough for Cecily.

Chapter Six

The first weeks were always the hardest. Cecily had to convince not only her student but usually the student's well-meaning loved ones as well that they'd all do best to follow her instructions. Her brief moments with the O'Connor family the night before had told her in no uncertain terms that they were worried about Finbarr. She felt quite certain that Tavish was as well, but he was also frustrated with the boy, and that frustration could go a long way toward securing his cooperation. Eventually.

The one person she hadn't sorted out yet was Finbarr. She couldn't yet say if he was more angry or more afraid; she'd experienced significant amounts of both as her world had gone dark. Though she didn't generally admit it, even to herself, she still felt those same emotions as she faced further loss of sight.

The windows and low-burning embers provided just enough light for Cecily to make out moving shadows. She already knew Mrs. Claire sat in the chair across from her. She recognized Tavish when he stepped back into the room. And his brother entered on his arm. The young man's steps dragged. He hung back from the fireplace.

From distrust or stubbornness? Or both? Chipping away at his walls would take patience, a virtue she'd learned well during her years as a tutor. He would discover soon enough that her fortitude would outlast his obstinacy.

"Find a place to sit, Finbarr," she said. "Somewhere on my side of the room, if you would."

The slow scrape of his boots on the floor came a touch closer and then stopped. His shadow loomed too high for him to have sat.

"I mean to ask you a great many questions," she told him, "so, for your comfort, you would be well advised to sit."

Finbarr's arm jutted out, his hands searching for a chair. Had he not made the effort to memorize the room in which he spent his days? They had more ground to cover than she'd realized. Tavish helped his brother sit, then stood beside Finbarr's chair.

She dove straight to the heart of the matter. "How much can you see, Finbarr?"

"We included all of that in the papers we sent to you." Tavish's tone held almost a note of panic.

This happened every time. The family circled their wagons, not realizing their loved one was suffocating.

"Yes," she said. "But I want to hear it from him."

Tavish stepped closer to her and in a low and tense voice said, "He doesn't like to talk about it."

Which was why she always asked. Until the newly blind could acknowledge their condition, they could not come to terms with it.

She pressed on despite Tavish's objection. "Is one eye better than the other, Finbarr? Or are they both the same?"

"He doesn't like to—"

"Mr. O'Connor," Cecily broke in, "why don't you walk Mrs. Claire back home? I believe I can handle this."

"This, here, is how you handle it?" His silhouette moved away. "You've been here but a few minutes, and things are already a shambles."

"Which is why I am asking you to leave. If I am to address the shambles, I must remove the shambler."

His form shifted and, she would wager, turned back to look at her, but he didn't say a word. She had a feeling he wasn't accustomed to being left speechless—an opportunity she didn't mean to let pass.

"Your brother is not a child, nor does he seem like a simpleton, nor do I suspect his is a temper which flares so easily that he'll beat me senseless the moment you've stepped from the door. All things taken into consideration, I do believe he and I will be fine on our own for a few minutes." She punctuated the declaration with a nod of her head.

Mrs. Clair jumped in, thank heavens. "Let us go call on your mother, Tavish. I've not gabbed with her in a month of Sundays."

"And what of Finbarr?" Tavish sounded entirely unconvinced.

"I'm not a child," Finbarr muttered.

"Come along, then, Tavish." Mrs. Claire moved toward the door, Tavish moving with her. Cecily would wager he was being dragged.

At last, she was alone with her new student. Now they could accomplish something. "I haven't any brothers of my own, so I must ask. Has he always babied you this much, or is this new?"

"I am the youngest in the family. They've *all* always babied me. But it has been worse since . . . this." He didn't speak in specific terms about the fire in which his eyes were damaged. Had he ever?

"Speaking of 'this'"—she wouldn't push him to discuss the incident, not yet—"tell me, in your own words, the state of your vision, or lack thereof. Hearing from you what you are experiencing will help me understand."

"You don't understand." There was the anger she'd expected. "Everyone acts as though they know what this is like. 'It will all be fine,' they say. 'We know what you're going through,' they say. But they don't. No one does."

Anger. Isolation. How well she knew those emotions.

"Allow me to share my story. I believe hearing it will help you recognize just how well I do understand." She folded her hands on her lap. She'd told her history so often, it no longer hurt. "When I was eight years old, I experienced a sudden, unexplained pain in my eyes, accompanied by a subtle cloudiness in my vision. The pain subsided after a time, but my vision remained affected, not blurry like one in need of spectacles, but murky, as though I were viewing the world through a glass of dirty water.

"Over the next few years, I had more painful episodes, always resulting in ever-murkier vision. One doctor after another, from Edinburgh to London, evaluated my eyes, and every one of them agreed: my vision would continue to worsen, and nothing could be done to prevent or repair the damage. I would, they were all entirely certain, eventually be left with no vision at all."

Finbarr sat in silence. She hoped he was listening.

"My father, upon accepting the fate that awaited me, made inquiries, and, after a time, learned of a school here in America, the Missouri School for the Blind, which specializes in teaching the sightless and nearly sightless how to live their lives in the dark. Though I was, at the time, still in possession of most of my vision, he felt it best to prepare me for the unavoidable. He liked what he'd learned about this school more than he did the few such schools available in England.

"We sold our home, our lands, and nearly all our possessions and came to this country. I was eleven years old. In that school, I learned to be independent and productive, and how to live my life the way I wanted to live it."

There was a great deal more to the story, of course, but she only ever shared the parts that most helped her students accept their situations and her role in improving it.

"I know you do not want me here, and that you do not even think you need me. Perhaps you don't. Perhaps your life is playing out precisely as you'd like it to." That, she knew, was grossly untrue.

"I will sort it all out," he said. "Everyone is just babying me, like you said. Once they stop—"

"Believe me, Finbarr O'Connor, the babying stops today. I am the one with whom you will be interacting most, and I baby no one." She said no more. She would sit there, and he could take all the time he wanted to mull over her words. She couldn't force him to learn, but she could make refusing her help awfully difficult for him.

"Is your sight gone now?" He spoke almost too quietly to be heard.

"Not entirely. In enough light, I can make out shapes. I can even read very large lettering if I hold a candle nearly touching the paper. But eventually, even that will no longer be possible."

"I'm sorry."

"And I am sorry that there is a need for me to be here." She leaned forward, facing him directly. If his family's explanation was accurate, he could make out enough of the silhouettes around him to know she'd moved and was looking at him. "I will make you this promise: give me a chance, see if I can teach you anything useful, and in return, I vow to never treat you like someone who is broken."

"But—I am." His voice cracked on the words. "I used to be able to do anything. I was going to do so many things." Emotion rose as he spoke, and with it the fear Cecily had suspected hovered beneath his dour demeanor. "It's all broken now. My whole life. My future. Everything."

He needed hope back. He needed a future he could feel excited about. She could give those to him, if only he'd allow her to.

"That is why I'm here. You tell me which broken pieces of your life you want to reclaim, and I will help get them back."

"I just want my eyes back," he muttered.

"So do I." Heavens, it had been a long time since she'd admitted that to anyone. "But let us focus on something more practical. Did you dress yourself on your own this morning?"

"I can't see the buttons or laces."

"Neither can I, and I dress myself every day." She rose from her chair. "Tomorrow, you will do the same. And you will eat breakfast at eight o'clock, just as soon as I arrive."

"Do you expect me to cook it?" he asked dryly.

"Eventually."

"I can't cook. I can't see—"

"Finbarr." She stepped directly in front of him. "You will find some things to be beyond your ability, but until you've tried them, you are not to declare that you can't do them. That is a rule I will require you to live by. It is the only way you will ever know what you are capable of."

His outline slumped lower in his chair. "I didn't want you to come," he muttered.

"I know." She set her cane in front of her once more. "Now, you may sit here and sulk all you want today—*only* today—though I hope you'll spend some of your energy thinking about what I've said. We'll not worry about lessons until tomorrow. In the meantime, I need to memorize the specifics of this house."

She left him there to stew while she counted steps. Six from the sitting room to the alcove that served as Finbarr's bedroom. Four more brought her to a back wall. Four steps back up toward the alcove but along an opposite wall—almost like a very short corridor. There she found a door, something she hadn't expected to find. If she'd counted correctly—and she was always careful to count correctly—the front door sat directly across from the alcove.

"What's behind this door?" she asked, knowing Finbarr was close enough to hear.

"A bedroom."

Tavish's, no doubt. She continued counting steps. Around and around she went, retracing her same path. The sitting room, she discovered, functioned as both sitting area and kitchen. It constituted the entirety of the house, outside of the short, narrow "corridor" containing the alcove and the door to Tavish's bedroom. Near the fireplace, she found a ladder.

"Is there a loft?"

Finbarr made a noise of confirmation.

"Do you know if it has a window?"

"I don't remember."

She'd need to ask Tavish. A boy struggling to escape the darkness needed space of his own that was at least dimly lit. The dark confines of the alcove would never do.

Looking upward, she could not make out much difference between the light in the loft and that of the room below. There might very well be a window tucked around the corner, but she couldn't tell. It wasn't promising. Finbarr needed light.

She retraced her steps to the corridor and bedroom door. Tavish might be convinced to allow Finbarr to use his bedroom if it was light enough, though that would hardly be a permanent solution. Finbarr would likely feel himself an even greater burden if he displaced his brother in his own home.

She turned the knob, opened the door, and stepped inside—all she managed before amazement stopped her. The room was positively flooded with light. Windows graced three of the four walls, rendering the room as bright as if she were standing outside.

Cecily's hand moved of its own accord and pressed to her heart. She could hardly breathe. For seventeen years, she'd watched the world grow darker, especially indoors. But this room . . .

She could make out the furniture, including the bureau pressed against a wall. Usually walls were too shadowed for furniture to stand out. She could see the floor and even the far wall, not clearly as she would have once, but she could see them.

With a breath of apprehension, she lifted her hand from her heart and held it in front of her, arm outstretched. She moved her fingers about.

Good heavens. She could see each individual finger. Not merely the outline of her hand, but the hand itself. She could see this well out-of-doors still, but that hadn't been possible inside the dim confines of a room for more than two years.

She bent forward and lifted the hem of her dress a tiny bit. The tips of her boots were visible. Indoors. She could see these details indoors.

Cecily took another step inside. She pressed the tips of her fingers to her lips as she slowly turned in a full circle, taking in the bright expanse of this miraculous place. If she was ever fortunate enough to have a home of her own, with a room of her own, this is what she wanted. Windows. And light. Even when her sight went through its next inevitable worsening, this was a room in which she might retain some of what she would lose.

"What are you doing in here?" Tavish's voice boomed, shattering her reverent silence.

She sucked in a startled breath. "I'm sorry." There was no true reason to apologize, and yet she felt compelled to.

"No one is allowed in this room."

Her usual resolve had fled. This room had cast a spell, and she was struggling to free herself from it. For those brief moments, she'd forgotten her role as teacher, forgotten her struggling student and his stubborn brother. Nothing existed but this flood of light.

Without words, and hardly noting where she moved, she stumbled back into the dimness of the corridor. Tavish snapped the door shut. The spell broke.

The light was gone.

Chapter Seven

"How are you holding up, then?" Ian sat with Tavish in the barn, helping him mend rope. "Miss Attwater seems a handful."

"She is more than merely a handful. I've never met such a headstrong woman in all my born days." Tavish filled his tone with all the emphasis he could manage.

"'Tis a bold statement, that," his older brother said. "We're surrounded by headstrong women, you and I. We're drowning in them."

"This woman beats them all. She points out everything she sees amiss, whether it actually is or not, and lists all the things she thinks I'm likely to get wrong in the future. She dictates and bosses and declares herself the queen."

Ian pointed at him with the limp end of an unspliced rope. "Perhaps we ought to tell her that the Irish aren't terribly keen on monarchs."

"Were I to try that, you'd likely find m' lifeless body sprawled out on the floor." Tavish made a show of mourning his inevitable death. "Then Ma'd cry and make a big fuss, and Da would likely turn to drink. It'd be a full tragedy, it would. I think we'd best not risk it."

Ian's gaze narrowed on him even as a grin began tugging at one corner of his mouth. "You're afraid of her, aren't you?"

"Terrified."

Ian laughed, the sound genuine and light. Hearing it did Tavish's heart a world of good. His brother had been beaten nearly to death by a mob bent on revenge for any number of things, none of which Ian had been the least bit responsible for. He'd simply been Irish and nearby when their anger had reached its peak. For days, Ian had hovered between life and death. He hadn't been the same since.

Finbarr's injuries and suffering had rendered him withdrawn and distant, his spirits depressed. Ian's injuries had changed him in different ways. He was less patient, more easily frustrated; he was also unpredictable, shifting from his old, quick-with-a-jest self, to the new, irritable version with no real pattern.

Tavish was losing hope of ever getting his brother back again. Either brother.

Ian tossed aside a bit of rope that wasn't cooperating. He'd not yet fully regained coordination in his fingers. The blows he'd taken to the head had affected more than his personality. They'd left his body less agile as well. "How's Finbarr adjusting?"

"He sulks and mutters and generally refuses to do what she tells him to," Tavish said.

"What is it she asks him to do? Something terrible? Offer sacrifice to pagan gods? Take a dip in the cold river, naked as the day he was born?"

"I firmly suspect there's pagan sacrificing involved, I simply haven't any proof." Tavish finished with his rope and began winding it in a large loop. "She hasn't so much as a thimbleful of sympathy for the lad. He tells her he can't do something, and she won't listen. She pushes and pushes."

"Can he?"

"Can he *what*?" Tavish picked up the rope Ian hadn't been able to repair and set to work.

“Can Finbarr do the things she’s asking him to do?” Ian asked. “The lad’s a bit stubborn, you know.”

“I know it. The two of them are like a couple of terriers trying to growl each other down.” He’d watched exactly that over breakfast that morning, a standstill that had ended in Finbarr not eating, and Cecily not caring that he was hungry. “Have you ever watched two people—two people who can’t *see*, mind you—engaged in a staring match? ’Tis an odd and unsettling thing.”

“You’ve had that hard a time of it?” Ian asked.

“That I have. Misery, Ian. Pure misery.”

Ian looked as though he were silently laughing. “She’s only been working with the lad since yesterday morning.”

“Which shows you how impossible she is.” ’Twas a relieving thing to joke about their troubles. So much connected to Finbarr was heavy and worrisome. So much connected to Ian was, as well. To the entire family, in fact.

“I believe you said something similar about Katie when she first arrived.”

Tavish rose, instantly on edge. “She’s nothing like Katie.” He tossed aside the bit of unspliced rope.

“I’m sorry I couldn’t manage that one,” Ian said nodding toward the rope. “I’m not good for much these days.”

Tavish pulled himself out of his own doldrums so he could address his brother’s. “Don’t fret over the rope. I’ll fix it.”

A frustrated sigh escaped Ian’s lips. “I’m needing help with a few things over at my place. Things I can’t manage just now.”

That worried him. “Is your head aching you again?”

“When is it not?” Ian muttered. He puffed his cheeks and pushed out a full breath. “But, aye, it’s hurting me more again, and I’m forgettin’ things and struggling to do others.”

“I’ve time and plenty tomorrow. Give me the morning to see to a few chores, and then the afternoon is yours.” Tavish gave his brother his most reassuring look. “Together, we’ll have it all right as rain by day’s end. You’ll see.”

Ian rubbed at his temples. “We’re a burden on you, aren’t we, Finbarr and I?”

“A terrible burden,” he answered, making certain his teasing tone was obvious. “I cry buckets over it every night.”

“You jest about it,” Ian said, “but I know full well you’re neglecting your land and home seeing to the lot of us.”

He was, truth be told. But what other choice did he have? Ian and Finbarr were not the only O’Connors in crisis. His sisters needed him as well, as did his parents. He’d managed to sell Joseph Archer’s crop at a tidy profit, which had given him enough to live on—if he was careful—until next summer. He’d lost too much of his berry crop for making any deliveries this year. The situation weighed on Tavish’s mind. What if next year proved slim as well?

The barn door opened, and in stepped Cecily.

“What do you think Miss Attwater’s come for?” Ian asked.

“A pint of blood?”

Her cane brushed aside bits of hay scattered on the barn floor as it tapped against stall walls, guiding her directly to the open area where Tavish and Ian sat working.

“Welcome.” Despite his frustrations with the woman, Tavish spoke in his most friendly tone, hoping to avoid another confrontation. “What brings you to our humble corner of the barn?”

“Something must be done about Finbarr’s accommodations.”

Yes, Your Majesty. “And a fine good afternoon to you as well. ’Tis a pleasure, as always, to see you. How’s life been treating you?”

“Did I not spend enough time making this about *you*? Very well. Why, Tavish, what a pleasure. Do tell me what you’ve been up to and regale me with the details of your goals for the day. Finbarr? Finbarr who?” Her overly sweet tone gave way to one as dry as Wyoming in the dead of summer.

Ian, the great traitor, laughed right out loud. "You picked him up, tossed him about, and threw him back with all the fire and determination of an Irish warrior, Miss Attwater."

"You're the absolute worst brother, you know that?" But Tavish couldn't help the hint of a laugh in his words. Cecily *had* rather expertly put him in his place.

"If we have finished with the frivolities, I would like to discuss the true matter at hand." She addressed Ian, now all fine manners and patience. So did she only ruffle up at *him*? "I am concerned about your brother." She motioned vaguely in Tavish's direction. "Not this one, of course."

"Of course," Ian answered quite seriously. "I'll leave the two of you to slug this out." He gave Tavish a quick raise of an eyebrow. "Best of luck to you, then." And to Cecily, he said, "Give him what for, will you? He needs a challenge."

"What I need is an older brother who knows where his loyalties ought to lie."

Ian simply smiled. Tavish was glad to see it.

"Miss Attwater," Ian offered by way of goodbye.

She inclined her head ever so slightly in a regal goodbye of her own.

"Now, Cecily, what's your grievance with Finbarr's living quarters?" Tavish moved closer, leaning against the stall wall near her. "I realize they aren't fine or fancy, but he has a roof over his head, and that spot behind the fireplace is one of the warmest in the house. He has a bed to sleep on, a pillow for resting his head, and blankets aplenty."

"Why is it you continually assume I object to simplicity? What evidence do you have that I am so pretentiously supercilious?"

"For one thing, you use words like 'pretentiously supercilious.'" He only had a vague idea what that mouthful meant.

"For another . . . ?" She pressed.

He wasn't sure what she was aiming at. "For another *what*?"

"You indicated my vocabulary was one reason for your assumptions? What are the others?" She held her chin at that superior angle he was becoming well acquainted with.

"I've known a few English in my life, Cecee. I know what you're like."

"Cecee?" She managed to look surprised, ponderous, and vaguely offended all at the same time. She just as quickly shook it off. "We'll address the matter of my name later. In this moment, I take greater exception to the rest of what you said."

"I imagine you do." No one liked being told their faults.

She pointed a finger directly at his chest. Could she see enough to know that was where she was pointing, or had she meant her finger to be directed at his face? How short did she think he was?

"Mrs. Archer warned me that my reception might be a touch chilly amongst some of the Irish families in this town, owing to my country of birth."

It was still so uncomfortably odd hearing Katie referred to as Mrs. Archer. In that moment, he was grateful Cecily couldn't see the heat that must have stolen over his features. At least he hoped she couldn't.

"She warned me," Cecily continued, "but I felt confident that, at the very least, the family whom I had come to help wouldn't hold that against me."

"We've centuries of reasons to be wary," Tavish reminded her. "For us, approaching with caution has always been advisable in matters involving the English."

"You do not have to like my origins, or my mannerisms, or me, for that matter." She somehow managed to look down on him, despite being shorter, and most likely not knowing exactly where he stood. "But I am all that stands between your brother and a lifetime of sulking in the dark corners of your house. I suggest you find a means of accepting that and start working with me instead of against me."

She was correct, of course. No matter that she pricked at him, he needed to help her help Finbarr. "What is it about Finbarr's fireplace nook that concerns you?"

She shifted her cane to her other hand and leaned her shoulders against the wall. "I made a visit to your loft—"

"You climbed the ladder? In your condition?" Heavens, she could have tumbled off and broken a limb.

"I'm not crippled." Behind those green spectacles, she likely glared at him. How he wished he could see her eyes. One could learn a lot from seeing a person's eyes. "The loft is lit enough to tell me there is a window."

"There is. On the west wall."

She nodded. "Finbarr needs to be moved to the loft. He has very little vision, and what he does have requires light. By assigning him a corner of your house that is perpetually dark, you are plunging him further into blackness. The space he's been given isn't a comforting one. It is a reminder of what he's lost. He needs light."

Tavish hadn't thought of that. "I figured he'd be safer there, not having to climb up and all."

"He can manage the ladder. And the loft has a railing; I discovered it myself, so he shouldn't tumble over the edge."

"You truly think it would be best?"

"I know it would be." Cecily added in quieter tones, "No one needs the light so much as someone who receives very little of it."

He'd been mistaken, then, in placing Finbarr in the alcove. He'd made things worse. "I was only trying to protect him."

"I know." She smiled briefly, minutely, but it was enough to ease the tension between them. "Now it's time to *push* him."

"That's a hard thing to ask after all I've seen him pass through this year. The older brother in me can't help but try to save him from more of that."

She nodded. "I encounter that sentiment a lot. Sometimes my biggest challenge is my student's family."

He could appreciate that. "There's no challenge so enormous as the O'Connors when we've set our minds to something."

"So set your minds to giving Finbarr back his independence and his life." She stood fully upright once more, her cane at the ready. "When you're finished in here, please come help Finbarr move his things to the loft. But do so in a way that requires him to work as well. He needs to feel useful."

"Yes, Your Majesty."

Every muscle in her body seemed to tense. "I beg your pardon?" 'Twasn't a demand made from a place of disapproval, but a question heavily tinged with surprise.

"I said 'yes.' I'll set my mind to Finbarr and his independence."

Her lips pursed, and her brows pulled down in sharp lines. The woman was no simpleton. She likely knew perfectly well what he'd said, and likely understood why. But she didn't press the issue.

He watched her go, more intrigued than he was yet willing to admit. She could brangle with him, that was for certain. And her quick wit made their war of words a decided challenge. Life with Cecily Attwater around would certainly not be boring.

While part of him looked forward to contending with her, a growing part of him needed a bit of boring. He needed calm and quiet. Needed a moment to simply breathe.

He spent every waking moment, every thought, every ounce of energy holding his family together while, inside, he could feel himself beginning to fall apart.

Chapter Eight

In previous years Tavish'd had the luxury of pausing now and then during his work to take in the beauty of the distant mountains and the lush fields of his family's nearby farms. He often whistled as he worked, sometimes even sang a tune or two. This year he was too far behind for such quiet luxuries. His journey with Finbarr had come at a difficult time for one whose crop came in as early as Tavish's did. He'd lost a large portion of his berries. Only by scrambling had he saved the rest before they turned to mush on the bushes and vines. He spent his morning searching for any stragglers he'd missed. This year, every last berry counted.

He snatched his watch from his pocket, checking the time. Ian needed help over at his place, and Tavish had promised him the afternoon. Time was running short.

He put the watch away then lifted two baskets, one under each arm, both blessedly heavy. His stomach rumbled loudly, insisting he stop for a midday meal. No time for that. If fortune smiled upon him,

Biddy would give him a bite or two after he finished his work with Ian. He'd not ask for one, though. Money was terribly tight for his brother and sister-in-law just now, more so than for Tavish.

His gaze slipped to the window of the not-distant house as he passed by with his baskets of berries. Cecily stood visible through the glass, leaning against one side of the window frame with her back to the outdoors. He couldn't tell from his vantage point if she was talking, or more likely *scolding*, Finbarr. What else might she be doing, simply standing there as she was? Not watching the lad; Tavish didn't think her sight was keen enough for that.

At least Tavish knew she wasn't nosing around where she oughtn't anymore. She hadn't been in the house more than a few minutes before stepping inside the one room, the only space in the entire house, the entire town, sometimes it felt like the only place in the entire world, that was his and his alone. He'd built that room in preparation for a happy future that was never meant to be. He kept it quietly tucked away, a reminder of what he'd hoped for. That room was intensely personal and meant to be kept free of interruption and prying eyes, like a prayer chapel or a shrine, and she'd violated that sanctuary. He'd been harsher in his scolding than he'd intended, but she'd no business being in that room. He only hoped that, going forward, she'd leave it be.

He carried his baskets all the way to the trap door in the floor of the barn. With an ease borne of experience, he balanced his load in one arm and pulled open the door with his other hand. He quickly but carefully traversed the steps down into the cold storage. Most years his berry crop filled more than half the space. This year's 'twas but a few baskets' worth. He pushed that worry from his mind; he had enough others.

Once he had the berries safely tucked away, Tavish stepped inside the house, meaning to explain where he'd be for the next few hours, as well as to make certain neither combatant had throttled the other.

Finbarr sat where Tavish had left him that morning: slumped in a chair near the empty fireplace with his arms folded defiantly across his chest. Cecily still stood at the window, her gaze seemingly on her pupil. Could she see him?

"The two of you have clearly been busy," Tavish said.

Neither turned toward him or acknowledged his comment.

"I'm going over to Ian and Biddy's," he added. "I'll be back before you're done with . . . all you're doing today."

"We're not doing anything," Finbarr muttered.

"Speak for yourself," Cecily said. "I've spent the past few hours thinking about how to torture you next."

Tavish didn't know if the comment was meant in jest or spoken in earnest. Torture might very well have been one of her tactics. She hadn't let the lad eat, after all.

"He could come with me," Tavish said. "His niece and nephews would appreciate having him drop in, as would his brother and sister."

Cecily shook her head with a firmness that allowed no room for negotiation. "He has work to do here. That must come first."

"With us, family comes first," he told her.

"Then put *this* member of your family first," she countered. "He'll stay here until he does what has been asked of him."

If he hadn't been strapped for time, he might have stayed and argued with her. Should she begin regularly denying Finbarr the chance to spend time with his family, Tavish would need to say something. But for today, he'd leave things as they were.

"I'll be back before you need to leave for the day," he told her.

She simply nodded, not looking away from Finbarr. Could she see him? She was such a mystery, so well adapted to her situation, that a fellow, even an intelligent, observant one, could easily be mistaken in her abilities.

There seemed nothing else to be done but make good on his

word by leaving the two to their hours of stubborn silence. He only hoped Cecily had some plan in mind. If all she meant to do was sit about staring into the silence, the money they'd spent in bringing her to Hope Springs would be wasted.

His mind was no less at ease by the time he reached his brother's home. Ian's oldest, Michael, answered the knock. Tavish offered his nephew an easy and friendly smile. "A fine good afternoon to you, Michael."

The boy, as always, had a book tucked under his arm. He owned only two, and had read them cover to cover many times over. The lad was a dab hand with horses and would likely make a fine rancher someday, but he'd never have access to the book learning he craved. 'Twas one of the reasons Thomas, husband to Tavish's older sister, was contemplating leaving the tiny town of Hope Springs. He had children of his own who dreamed of something more than they could have in the vast emptiness of Wyoming.

"Now, Michael," Biddy's voice echoed forward from somewhere inside. "Don't leave Tavish standing about at the door like a vagabond."

"Yes, Ma." Michael stepped aside, and Tavish moved past him.

His sister-in-law greeted him with her usual warmth, though she looked a bit harried. The wee one, born not many months earlier, fussed in his mother's arms. Their daughter, who'd soon be six years old, sat on the floor, folding laundry from a large basket. Ian was nowhere to be seen.

"Has my bum of a brother taken to wandering about the fields, then?" Tavish asked, pretending to be gravely concerned.

Biddy didn't join in the jest. "He's having one of his difficult days. He may very well be 'wandering the fields.'"

The children were watching him with the same look of fearful pleading he'd seen so often. They worried for their father, and they looked to Tavish for reassurance. As Biddy did. And as Ma and Da did. And everyone else.

"Are his spirits low, or is it that he's feeling frustrated?" Tavish had seen Ian pass through long periods of both.

Biddy switched the baby to her other hip and eyed her two older children in turn before her gaze settled on Tavish once more. "Would you step outside with me a moment?"

That didn't bode well.

He followed her out the door and under the front overhang. He closed the door behind them, then turned to face her. "What's happened?"

"Ian's feeling himself a burden, taking you away from your own work because he can't manage his own. Wasting days laid up with terrible pains in his head, spending what little we have on powders instead of improvements to the home and land, or books and shoes and clothing for the children." Biddy brushed a hand over baby Patrick's peach-fuzz head. She met Tavish's eyes once more. "How do I convince the stubborn man that he's loved and wanted, even when he's struggling? He's begun saying that I couldn't possibly love him as I once did."

If not for Biddy's worried tone and expression, Tavish would've laughed out loud at the absurdity of such a thought. He knew what it was to lose the love of a woman he cared for. Ian was as cherished as he'd ever been.

"He's likely in pain," Tavish reassured his sister-in-law. "That'd scramble anyone's mind a bit, make it hard to hope for good and comforting things."

"If you can get him through today, perhaps tomorrow will be better," she said.

Tavish nodded. "I'll do what I can."

For the first time since his arrival, he received a smile from Biddy. Once, she'd been lighthearted, quick to laugh and grin at a fellow. The past year had changed her, as well. "I don't know what we'd do without you, Tavish."

"You'd fall clear to pieces, and you know it," he said, returning to his usual jesting tone.

The twinkle in Biddy's eyes muted a bit as she focused on something over his shoulder. "Ian's coming this way. Saints, I hope his spirits are up since last I saw him. It full breaks my heart to see him so cast down."

"You keep loving him the way you do," Tavish said. "It does a man a world of good to know he loves someone who loves him in return."

Biddy set a hand on his arm. "We'll find you someone, Tavish."

He did his best to laugh off the comment. "I wasn't ruing my lonely state, you meddlesome woman. I was speaking of your stubborn husband."

Biddy, true to character, was not deterred. Between his sisters, sister-in-law, and ma, he'd never fully escape these moments of pity and promise. "We will find someone."

"For my part," he tossed back, "the someone I've come to find is nearly at the door." He tipped his hat to her and turned to face his brother in the moment he reached them. "What have you for me to do, Ian? Your wife'll never stop speculating on the state of m' heart if I don't make a hasty retreat."

The exaggerated retelling earned him a look of amusement from both of them, precisely as he'd hoped.

"I'm meaning to mend the broken stall door in the barn today," Ian said. "If you run fast, my Biddy here will not be able to catch you."

Tavish clasped his hands together in front of him as if offering a prayer of gratitude. "Thank you, brother. It's my life you've saved." Then, in tones more serious but careful not to sound worried, he added, "Take a moment, though, before you follow, and give your wife a bit of sweetness, will you? She seems in need of it."

Ian turned immediately to his wife. "Are you unwell, love?"

She smiled gently and shook her head. “Only missing you, my dear. You’ve been far away today.”

“I was merely out in the fields,” Ian said.

She reached up her free hand and gently touched his cheek. “It felt farther.”

Ian set his arms around Biddy and pulled her and the baby into his embrace. Tavish left them in that loving arrangement. He couldn’t make all their problems disappear like chaff on the wind; he only hoped to ease them where he could.

Chapter Nine

Having arrived on a Wednesday, Cecily's first week working with Finbarr was a short one. Even so, by the time Saturday arrived, she was exhausted. The boy was fighting her far more than she'd expected. Theirs was not a physical struggle, but one of wills. He consistently refused to do anything she asked, choosing instead to sit stoically, repeating that he didn't want or need her there.

Students who started out this way always left an ache in her heart. A few never cooperated, ones on whom she had no choice but to give up. She couldn't teach if they weren't willing to learn. And those who did eventually allow her to help did so only after the weight they carried had crushed and broken them.

She didn't want Finbarr to go through that. Underneath his stubborn refusal to hear her was a frightened and scarred young man. When he knew she'd accomplished something he thought impossible for someone with limited vision, she had seen tiny, minuscule glimpses of hope in him. If only she could convince him to try his hand at a few of those things. She hadn't yet hit upon a means of convincing him. At least he'd accepted the move to the loft.

She herself had spent the last few days struggling with the challenge, both physical and emotional, of having a dimly lit bedchamber. She knew how to function in complete darkness, but she craved the light. Her small window couldn't illuminate much of anything. She'd intended to spend her Saturday working in her bedchamber, out of Mrs. Claire's way, but the light was insufficient. She would need to find a brighter spot out in the sitting room. As she felt about in her trunk, entirely dependent on touch to identify the contents, she thought longingly on Tavish's sunlit room.

Would he let her see it again? He'd been firm when he'd tossed her out of it a few days earlier. She didn't dare ask for permission; they'd butted heads enough the past few days without introducing a topic she knew would upset him.

She would simply make do with what light she had.

Her fingers knew well the feel of the items she needed. She quickly found the crisp plane and thin edges of a stack of stiff parchment. A wide wood frame, metal insert, and moveable, attached metal stencil sat at the bottom of her trunk, all easy enough to locate. Finding the specific book she needed proved more difficult.

Two of her five books were too thick to be the one she wished for; they were returned to the trunk. She tucked the remaining three under her arm, then rose, crossing to the window. She held the first book up to the light filtering in then leaned in close. The cover was red. She set it aside. The second two were close enough in color to be almost indistinguishable. She could see just enough of each cover to make out the golden swirls decorating the front of the book she wanted. The others went back into the trunk. Always returning things to their assigned spots was crucial to locating them again—often the hardest habit for her older students to develop.

She carried her wooden frame and stencil, parchment, and book, heading toward Mrs. Claire's table. The outer room smelled of soap.

Was Mrs. Claire cleaning? Cecily was met by the familiar sound of rocker runners squeaking against the floor.

"Good morning," Cecily greeted as she counted the steps to the table.

Movement on the other side of the room told her someone was present in addition to Mrs. Claire. The squeak of a floorboard in the other direction indicated yet a third person.

"You have visitors," Cecily said, setting her items on the table.

"How did you know?" The voice from the opposite side of the room was Mrs. Archer's; Cecily was nearly certain of it. "I didn't think we'd made any noise."

"You made very little," Cecily admitted. "I have simply learned to listen very closely."

"And are you able to teach Finbarr to do that?" Mrs. Archer's footsteps were sure and even as she came closer. "He's forever startling anytime someone speaks who he'd not realized was nearby."

Cecily gave a single inclination of her head. "I can teach him anything he's willing to learn."

"You've set yourself up against Irish stubbornness," Mrs. Claire said, entering the conversation. "No matter that the boy *sounds* American, it's Irish blood in those veins. It'll sooner boil than act sensibly."

"Stubbornness is not an exclusively Irish trait." Cecily spoke from experience.

A quick succession of footsteps preceded a quietly spoken, "Pardon me. I'll be going home now."

Cecily couldn't identify the voice, only that the speaker was female and Irish.

"Do stay, Biddy," Mrs. Archer pleaded. "We've not had a chance for much gabbing yet."

Biddy O'Connor, likely. Finbarr and Tavish's sister-in-law.

Cecily had spent time learning the connections within Finbarr's family. The more she knew of his life, the more likely she was to help him reclaim it.

"I'll come by for a gab later," Biddy said, just as rushed, just as quiet.

"I hadn't meant to disrupt," Cecily said. "You needn't mind me. I'll simply be doing some work here at the table."

"You see there, Biddy?" Mrs. Claire said. "You needn't run off."

The door opened, letting in enough light to illuminate the silhouette of the woman about to step outside.

"I—I'll come back later, when the house is . . ." She stepped out. "I'll come back later."

The door closed, dimming and silencing the room. Though Biddy hadn't said as much, Cecily firmly suspected she was the reason for Biddy's sudden departure. But why? They'd never met.

"Have I done something to upset her?" she asked. Except upset wasn't the right word for the tone Biddy had used. "Or to make her uncomfortable?" she amended.

"She is—" Mrs. Archer hesitated. "She's a bit shy of strangers."

A plausible enough explanation, yet something told Cecily that it wasn't entirely accurate. What, then, was the real reason?

"What else can you teach our Finbarr?" Mrs. Claire managed to turn the topic away from Biddy's swift departure. "Other than to listen, of course."

Mrs. Archer laughed. "Can anyone truly teach a seventeen-year-old boy to listen?"

"We'll work on making sense of what little he can see," Cecily said, "and on interpreting sounds, paying attention to the feel of things, making his memory as sharp as possible. Once he's mastered those things—"

"There'd be more than that?" Mrs. Archer sounded both

surprised and impressed. “Just how long do you expect to be here?” Mrs. Archer was sweeping the floor now. Cecily could hear it.

“The length of my stay depends entirely on young Finbarr.”

“Meaning, the longer he takes to cooperate, the longer you’ll need to be staying.” Mrs. Claire yet rocked. The prospect of Cecily staying didn’t seem to appeal to her.

“Not necessarily. If he doesn’t begin cooperating in the first few weeks, there will be no point in staying.” Cecily had been forced to resign her post when a student refused to learn. The regret of those failures never fully left her. “I understand that by December, travel out of this valley isn’t consistently possible. So I can only give him that long.”

“Six weeks?” Shock tinged Mrs. Archer’s voice. “Can he learn all he needs to in six weeks?”

Cecily shook her head. “He doesn’t have to be *finished* learning by then; he simply has to be *willing* by then.”

“Well, Granny,” Mrs. Archer said, “it seems we’ve a challenge laid before us.”

“Have we?”

“We’ve a lad in sore need of tutoring, and a tutor he won’t give the time of day,” Mrs. Archer said.

“Hmm.” Not enthusiastic volunteering from Mrs. Claire. “I don’t know that we can do much. The lad is, as you’ve said, stubborn.”

“You don’t believe we could convince him?” Mrs. Archer’s question might have been directed at either of them.

“We’ve not convinced him to let your Emma visit,” Mrs. Claire said. “They were thick as thieves before. He filled the role of protective older brother, and she his adoring little sister. If he’ll not accept her, I can’t imagine he’ll . . .” The sentence dangled unfinished.

“You can’t imagine he will accept *me*,” Cecily finished for her.

"That may very well be true. In the end, Finbarr will be the one who decides he is ready to learn and heal."

"And it's in the next few weeks that he's needing to decide this?" Mrs. Claire asked.

"Yes." Cecily herself felt the same uncertainty she heard in the older woman's voice. If only she had some strategy, more information to help her.

"Why is it the family chose to place Finbarr with Tavish? Not to speak ill of your grandson, Mrs. Claire, but Tavish O'Connor is . . . well, exasperating."

"Exasperating? Tavish?" She clearly disliked the description.

Mrs. Archer simply laughed.

Cecily wasn't sure what was so funny. Was it a commiserating laugh of agreement, or was the general opinion of Tavish far different from hers? The latter seemed unlikely. His cantankerousness was the first thing she'd noticed.

"Tavish is such a jovial and friendly sort of person." Mrs. Archer's voice grew louder as she came closer. "'Tis an odd thing to hear that he's regarded as peevish."

Jovial? Friendly? Cecily had seen moments of humor from him, but jovial and friendly would not have been at the top of her list when describing the man. "And everyone feels this way? Not merely his family?"

"He's charming, that one." Mrs. Claire spoke with such fondness. "He could convince Queen Victoria to give him her throne with a few honeyed words."

"Or simply toss her one of his heart-melting smiles," Mrs. Archer said. "No one can resist one of those."

"I can," Cecily said, taking the seat she'd stood next to since coming into the room.

"Are you so very sure of that?" Mrs. Claire spoke with more than a hint of a laugh. Clearly she doubted Cecily's endurance of her grandson's handsomeness.

"A breathtaking smile has little effect on one who cannot see it," she reminded them.

"I hadn't thought of that," Mrs. Archer said. "Tavish mustn't know quite what to do with you."

"I beg your pardon?"

"Heavens, but you speak with such a formal air." Mrs. Claire didn't sound overly put-out over the matter. "'Tis something we don't hear often in these parts."

"Why would Tavish be so turned about by me?" With Finbarr living at Tavish's home, Cecily needed to win over both of them.

"You can't see him," Mrs. Archer said simply. "Without making him sound vain—he's certainly not—Tavish has always won people over with his twinkling eyes and breath-snatching smile." Mrs. Archer sat in a chair across from Cecily. "Even I, who wasn't at all sure what to think of him when we first met, found m'self smiling when he did, and, soon enough, being charmed by him."

"He's frustrated with me because I don't realize he's handsome?" No matter that Mrs. Archer hadn't meant to make Tavish sound arrogant, she'd managed precisely that.

"I'm making a shambles of this," Mrs. Archer said. "Granny, help me explain."

The rocker stopped squeaking. Was that a good sign or a bad one? A moment later, shuffling footsteps approached the table. Mrs. Claire moved about on her own, but slowly. She sat next to Mrs. Archer.

"Will knowing Tavish better help you teach Finbarr?"

"Yes," Cecily said. "His support will allow Finbarr to feel safe proceeding."

That seemed to convince the older woman. "We can give you some ideas. I've known him forever and a day."

"And you, Mrs. Archer? Might you have some insights for me?"

"Call me Katie. Though I do still love to hear 'Mrs. Archer,' I've always ever been Katie, and it's what I prefer."

Katie. She would remember that.

"Tavish is most at ease when he can laugh and tease," Katie said. "Match him wit for wit, give him a reason to grin, and I'd wager he'll be not so likely to prickle up."

Laughter. Wit. She nodded as each item on the list was cataloged in her mind. "What else?"

"Nothing is so intriguing to him as a woman who's both stubborn and clever," Mrs. Claire said. "And though I'm not accustomed to speaking kindly of the English, I've my suspicions you're quite clever."

Her birth was being made an issue again. Would it always? "I haven't met many men who appreciate a woman for being intelligent."

"The ones worth knowing do." Mrs. Claire spoke with the firmness of conviction. "And there's not a man in the O'Connor family not worth knowing, young Finbarr included. Show him you're smart and know what you're about. And never, under any circumstances, let his stubbornness outlast your determination."

"Are we speaking of Finbarr now, or Tavish?"

"Both." Mrs. Claire and Katie spoke in near perfect unison.

Cecily needed to be firm, but she also needed to lighten a bit. Perhaps Tavish would then cease questioning everything, and Finbarr would begin attempting something.

"One last thing you could do," Katie said.

"I'll take any suggestions you have."

"Come to the *céilí*."

"The what?" That was not a word with which she was at all familiar.

"'Tis a party. We hold them every Saturday night at the elder O'Connors' home until the weather turns. We've music and food and stories and neighborliness. There's no one who isn't happiest at a *céilí*."

A party. That was a promising thing. "Does Finbarr attend?"

The sounds of hesitation answered her question in precisely the way she'd expected. Many of her students stopped doing the things they'd once loved, often because they knew the experience would be different from before. They were afraid to face the changes. Knowing what Finbarr was avoiding might help her understand better what he was feeling.

"I look forward to the *céilí*." She did her best to reproduce the word Katie had used.

Kay-lee. Something in her inflection wasn't quite correct, but she'd come close. "And I thank you both for the advice. I've been a little baffled. Now I will allow you to return to your cleaning, but with one request. Let me help. I've asked Mrs. Claire any number of times what I could do around here, but all she ever says is that 'Everything's—"

"—grand altogether.'" Katie said before Cecily could. Apparently, she wasn't the only one who'd received that answer. Katie's chair legs scraped along the floor. Her dress rustled. "Come along, then. I'll put you to work no matter what our headstrong granny says about it."

"Excellent." Cecily stood, feeling lighter than she had since arriving in Hope Springs, since before that, even. She felt hopeful about her student and his stubborn guardian. These women had offered her some much-needed advice and a greatly appreciated bit of friendliness.

And she was going to a party. She had never in all her life been invited to a party. How she had longed to be. Had her vision not begun deteriorating while she was yet a child, she might have attended any number of them. But fate had taken her away from home and the friends she might have known there. Now her work pulled her from place to place, never allowing her to be a full part of anyone's life.

Here, in this tiny hamlet in a quiet corner of the West, she had been offered an unexpected hand of friendship. She had a chance at being included in this town's socializing. At last she felt part of someone's life, however small and brief that part might be. She meant to seize the unexpected but blessed offering.

Chapter Ten

Tavish helped Ma set out her famous scones, the last on a long list of chores he'd been given as the weekly *céilí* began. All of Hope Springs attended the parties now, though they'd once belonged exclusively to the Irish. People who'd been sworn enemies had found friendships under the influence of food and music and laughter. The gatherings were considered miracles by the once war-torn town.

If only Finbarr would come. He'd loved the *céilís*.

Ian wove through the thick crowd directly to him. In a tone of sharing secrets, he said, "Thought I'd drop a warning in your ear, brother. We're to entertain royalty tonight."

Cecily. "Are we?" He looked about but didn't see her. "'Tis a fortunate thing I've been practicing bowing deep at the waist."

"She's lookin' us all over, I'll tell you that much." Ian looked back over his shoulder. "I've half a mind to go over there and beg her pardon for our peasant attire."

Tavish gave his brother a friendly shove. "You'll get us all beheaded, you will."

"So long as I'm faster on my feet than you are, I think m' head's safe." Did Ian realize the way his ever-present, though subtle, grimace added weight to those words? His head hadn't stopped aching since his beating. The doctor in St. Louis had warned that the pain might never entirely stop.

Ma found them in the next moment. "Miss Attwater is here." Worry, fear, something like panic, filled Ma's expression. "There are few things so Irish as a *céilí*, and the English never have approved of anything Irish."

Ma wiped her hands repeatedly on her apron, a nervous habit Tavish had seen her employ more often of late. Ian watched her with his own look of pained concern.

"Do not fret," he told them both. "Even if she dislikes the *céilí,* 'tisn't for her to be deciding if they're held or not. We'll not allow her to put an end to our gatherings."

"They've done too much good," Ian said by way of both agreement and reassurance.

"Precisely," Tavish said.

Ma didn't look as convinced. "You'll make certain of it?" she pressed.

"As always."

She nodded and took a deep breath. "You brought this on us, you know. Joking as you did about finding a golden-haired Englishwoman to court. Now one's here."

He set his hands on Ma's arms. "Rest assured, I've no intention of courting her or anyone else. I've learned my lesson, and I'm finding that bachelorhood suits me fine."

Ma pushed back, looking him in the eye. "Don't say that. You'll find your sweetheart. I know you will."

He already had, and she'd left him. Everyone always left him.

He forced a lighter expression. "I'll keep a weather eye out for any English storms. You set your mind to enjoying the evening, Ma. You, as well, Ian."

His brother moved away through the crowd.

Ma pressed a kiss to his cheek. "What would we do without you, my Tavish?"

"You'd have a lot fewer berry preserves in your cupboard, I'll tell you that."

She pinched his chin as she'd done when he was a lad. "None of that. You've more worth than you ever give yourself credit for."

Tavish wrapped his arms around her, pulling her into a close, adoring embrace. "You keep telling me that. Eventually I might believe it myself."

She squeezed him for one quick moment before hurrying off to see to more tasks.

He milled about, nodding and smiling to the people he passed. The *céilís* truly had become a town gathering since the people had begun putting their differences behind them.

He discovered Cecily sitting not far from the musicians, who'd already taken up a tune. Her back was straight as a ship's mast. She held her chin at a defiant angle. She'd fastened her hair in its usual golden knot at the back of her head. As always, her green-tinted spectacles hid her eyes.

"Are you enjoying yourself, then, Cecee?" He dropped into the seat next to hers.

"Even if I didn't recognize your voice, Tavish O'Connor, I would know you were the one speaking. No one else has ever called me something so ridiculous as 'Cecee.'"

Oh, yes, this conversation was taking a familiar path. Katie had objected to the nickname he'd fashioned for her as well, which, of course, had made using it regularly all the more essential. "But are you enjoying yourself?" he asked. "A person's not allowed at a *céilí* unless she's enjoying herself."

"The way Emma Archer explained it, a person can't help but be happy at a *céilí*."

Katie sat not far off, Joseph at her side and her girls gathered around her. "Did you come with the Archers?"

"I did. Emma, sweet girl, tried to convince Finbarr to join us. He wouldn't come down from the loft."

Not surprising. "Finbarr doesn't come to the *céilís* any longer."

"That is a shame." Cecily sounded sincere. "This is a lovely way to spend an evening."

For the first time since Cecily's arrival, Tavish didn't entirely want to throttle her. Perhaps teasing her a bit was a good strategy for keeping the peace. "We've a great deal of food. Are you hungry?"

"Not really."

What else? "There's a lot of room and some fine music. Are you wanting to dance?"

Did I just ask Her Majesty to dance?

"No, thank you." She wasn't being very helpful.

"Would you care to sit in with the musicians?" he suggested.

She shook her head. "I don't play any instruments."

"Do you care for storytelling?"

"I do." Her expression turned the tiniest bit eager. "When does that begin?"

"Another hour or more."

"What sort of stories will we hear?" Her interest surprised him. He would have expected her to turn her nose up at something so common as telling tales.

"We generally prefer stories that make us laugh or remind us of home. Those who aren't Irish have begun sharing tales as well, and we've found their preferences are much the same." He waited for her to dismiss the undertaking as a frivolous one. Instead she only grew more intrigued.

"And you do this every week?" she asked.

"Aye, while the weather holds."

Her brows pulled low, the tips tucking behind her green-hued spectacles. "Why is it you say, 'Aye'? Isn't it more Scottish than Irish?"

"For the same reason I've a Scottish given name. My ma's family are Scottish. We also hail from Ulster, an area of the Emerald Isle that's heavily influenced by Scotland."

"That does make sense." Always so formal.

"I'm pleased we meet with your approval," he said dryly.

She either didn't hear the comment or simply chose to ignore it. "So many aromas. I've spent nearly every moment sorting through them, and I still haven't identified them all."

"Are you saying we stink?"

"No, Tavish. Food aromas. *Food*."

"Ah." He chuckled lightly. "Well, that is fully relieving, that is."

She shook her head, but in an amused way. "I suspect you are a bit of a handful when you choose to be."

Tavish flashed her his most winning grin. "A *charming* handful," he clarified.

Her mouth pressed and twisted as if fighting a smile of its own. "That is the current rumor."

"Friends." Seamus Kelly stood in front of the musicians, addressing the partygoers as he often did. "We've a tradition at these *céilís* when someone new joins us." He turned and looked at Cecily. "We'll not ask you to dance, Miss Attwater, knowing your situation, but we do always offer a song in honor of a new arrival."

"I would like that, thank you." She spoke quietly, but confidently.

"'Tis also part of our tradition to choose a song particularly suited to the one for whom we're playing it." Seamus turned to the musicians. "Do you know any tunes about England, lads?"

Ah, begor. This could go wrong in a great many ways. Irish songs about the English were seldom polite.

Cecily showed no signs of concern.

The musicians struck up their selection without discussion or hesitation. This had been decided upon in advance, anticipating Cecily's attendance. Tavish recognized the tune after a moment, a relatively new song that didn't speak at all well of Ireland's least favorite neighbor.

It seemed Her Majesty was to be put in her place.

O Paddy dear, an' did ye hear the news that's goin' round?
The shamrock is by law forbid to grow on Irish ground;
St. Patrick's Day no more we'll keep, his color can't be seen,
For there's a cruel law against the wearin' o' the Green.

The crowd listened, adding sounds of agreement, after a time joining in as the lyrics grew even more critical. Cecily's concentration didn't waver.

Then since the color we must wear is England's cruel red,
Sure Ireland's sons will ne'er forget the blood that they have shed . . .

"This is clearly not a song celebrating England." Cecily spoke so quietly Tavish wasn't at all certain he was meant to overhear.

The song continued, growing ever more disparaging of the land that had ruled Ireland for so long. If Cecily noticed the biting criticism, she didn't let on. Her posture remained stiffly upright.

The tune came to its conclusion. The Irish in the crowd applauded enthusiastically. Few things united Tavish's countrymen like their feelings for the English. In general terms, he agreed with the sentiment, having experienced cruelty at their hands himself, but tossing those grievances at Cecily felt wrong.

She stood slowly and regally. The crowd took note and held their breath, waiting.

"I thank you for the song," she said.

Grins dotted the crowd. Tavish thought he heard a few snickers. There was no mistaking the look of satisfaction on the faces of the musicians, Seamus most especially. Tavish was rather glad Cecily couldn't see them, and he hoped they wouldn't speak. As she'd reminded him repeatedly on her first day at his house, she wasn't deaf.

The music began again, with many in the crowd stepping into the open space to dance.

Cecily turned her head in his direction. "Thank you for explaining the *céilí* to me. I assure you, you needn't explain the past few moments." She set the tip of her cane on the ground in front of her. "Clearly I misunderstood the invitation that was offered."

"Cecee—"

"Remind Finbarr that I will be expecting him to be ready at our usual time on Monday." Head held high, she turned and walked toward the edge of the gathering. The crowd parted as she approached, clearing a path for her. No one attempted to stop her. No one said anything.

Tavish watched her go. She passed through the crowd, who stood about watching the dancers, and made her way through those lingering around the edges. On she went, not stopping to chat or ask directions back to Granny's. Did she mean to attempt the walk back entirely on her own? Had she been in Hope Springs long enough to make that remotely possible?

He caught up to her just as Katie and Joseph did.

"Please allow us to take you home," Katie said.

"I would appreciate that. I'm not entirely certain I could find my way."

Joseph's eyes fell on Tavish. "The girls are with Biddy and Ian. Would you tell them Katie and I will be back in a few minutes?"

Tavish nodded his agreement.

"And if you feel so inclined," Katie jumped in, "tell Seamus and the rest of them that they're all a terrible bunch of hypocrites."

"Do not worry over it, Katie," Cecily said. "Tonight was not the first time I've found myself unwelcome, and it certainly won't be the last."

Her easy dismissal of the Irish townspeople's pointed disapproval somehow only added to the weight of guilt Tavish felt. He didn't care for her overly fine manners or her toplofty air, but he couldn't help but feel they'd all dealt her more of a blow than she was allowing them to see.

She'd been happy before the song—friendly, at least. Seeing that disappear so quickly, and so entirely, proved unexpectedly disheartening.

Cecily pushed open the door of Mrs. Claire's house, then turned back to face Katie and Mr. Archer. "Thank you for accompanying me. I likely would have become terribly lost if I'd attempted it alone. I do not know this town very well yet." Her heart thudded against her ribs at the memory of the song they had sung at her. In quieter tones, she added, "I clearly do not know this town at all."

"I am sorry for what happened," Katie said from the porch.

Cecily held up her hand to dismiss the necessity of an apology. "I know that, historically, my countrymen have not treated yours kindly. While I would, of course, rather not be made the whipping boy for seven centuries of animosity, you did warn me that I likely would be. I should have more closely heeded your warning."

"This is terribly unfair."

Cecily couldn't argue with that. "I will not keep you both any longer. Your daughters will be anxious for your return. And I will be fine here on my own."

"Are you certain?" Katie pressed. "I would be happy to stay with you, at least light a lantern or two."

Cecily shook her head. "I am not afraid of the dark. Besides, I can use this time to formulate next week's strategy for convincing Finbarr to not be afraid of it either."

That was, after all, the reason she was in Hope Springs. She'd been brought there to teach, not to attend parties or make friends. She would do well to remember that. Furthermore, while she enjoyed making friends wherever she taught, doing so wasn't a requirement. Friendships would only make her inevitable departure that much harder.

The Archers' footsteps faded as they made their way back to the gathering. Cecily carefully, quietly closed the door. She stood there a long while, fighting her disappointment. She'd always longed to attend a party, having witnessed a good many from the top of the stairs in her home growing up, her parents having been very social people. How she'd dreamed of one day attending a party herself instead of merely listening from afar. She had allowed herself to be excited about finally being invited to one.

There had been nothing excessively cruel about the song, but its message had been clear.

She was not welcome.

Chapter Eleven

"Either you build the fire as I asked, Finbarr, or you don't eat today." Cecily would've put the O'Connors' one-time factory foreman to shame with the unbending authority of her tone. Tavish hadn't expected a row first thing Monday morning, but perhaps he should have. "If you think I am not in earnest, then, please, continue with your stubborn refusal. Your stomach will eventually tell you how very resolute I am."

Cecily and Finbarr stood in front of the unlit stove, neither seeming the least willing to budge. Tavish sat at the table, near a basket Cecily had brought with her. He wasn't certain what was in it. Torture devices? A collection of poisons?

"I can't build a fire if I can't see the wood," Finbarr insisted.

"I've built any number of fires, and I can't see the wood."

Finbarr's frown grew ever fiercer. "I don't need you telling me what to do."

"Denying the lad food is cruel," Tavish said.

Cecily spun about on her cane and very nearly faced him. "He doesn't eat if he doesn't build the fire. This is not negotiable."

He should have known better than to argue with the Queen. "Your command is my . . . command."

Finbarr dragged himself away and sat in his usual chair near the empty fireplace, muttering something about traitorous brothers and overbearing women.

Tavish rose from the table and crossed to the stove where Cecily still stood. "How long is the lad meant to go hungry?"

"Until he complies."

Not exactly bubbling over with empathy, this lass. "And are you and I to suffer along with him? Without a fire in the stove, we'll not manage to eat much ourselves."

"Then you had best begin praying that your stubborn brother comes to his senses quickly."

'Twasn't the answer he'd been expecting. "I'm to suffer for Finbarr's mule-headedness, am I?"

"Well, you are your brother's keeper." There was a great deal of cheek in her remark.

Tavish leaned in a little closer and assumed a bantering tone. "You'll not make me starve, will you? You'd not be so cruel."

"I have my suspicions that you are casting me a flirtatious look." She leaned in close and whispered. "That works only when the recipient can see it."

"What if I describe it to you? I'll be certain to mention how ruggedly handsome I am and how m' eyes sparkle in the lantern light."

"No good, Tavish. I already picture you as an unkempt ogre living under a bridge."

"Do you, now?" He couldn't help some amusement at that. "And what did I do to earn that particular mental portrait?"

She turned toward the table, and, after only two attempts at finding the basket, caught hold of its handle. "You have it backwards. Everyone starts as an ogre. What a person earns is *not* being imagined as one."

He wasn't the most handsome man in all the world, but he'd

been told he was a pleasant sight. He'd not realized before how much he'd depended on that to make a good first impression.

"Am I likely to fall more toward the ogre side of things if I stroll on out to the barn and ask the animals to share a bite or two of hay with me?" He leaned against the sink, arms folded across his chest. "If they'll be generous, I'll not starve, and Finbarr'll still have an unlit stove to attend to."

His teasing didn't pull the tiniest bit of mirth from her. She was going to be a bigger challenge than most.

"I have something better than hay, if you're interested."

"Better than hay? You've caught my attention."

She pulled back the dishrag tucked into the basket, revealing several paper-wrapped bundles and three large glass jars. Tavish didn't know what was in any of them. He hazarded a guess.

"Witch's brew?"

"I generally save witch's brew for the third or fourth week of lessons. It is a special treat for my very best students."

Quick-witted. He liked that about her. All the O'Connors enjoyed lightning-fast banter.

"What we have here"—she set her hand just over the packages—"are sandwiches made fresh—" Her mouth pursed in thought. "Unless I have the basket backwards." She lightly touched the paper. "No. I was right. These are the sandwiches. In the jars are soups, which, of course, will be cold if our friend Finbarr doesn't get around to lighting the stove."

"Cold soup." Tavish summoned his most pitiful tone. "That is what comes of being one's brother's keeper."

She still didn't smile, but she did look the smallest bit amused. Her Majesty seemed very nearly human, as she had in the moments before the song at the *céilí*.

"Did Ma send the food over?" he asked.

"No. I made it," she said. "And I'd wager you are now giving me a look of profound doubt at the thought of a blind person cooking edible food."

How had she known that? "I'd say my expression is more one of surprise than doubt."

"And now you have adopted an, 'I'm lying to you about my previous expression' expression."

She kept a fellow on his toes, that was for certain. "For a woman who can't see very well, you see very well."

She pulled a sandwich from the basket and handed it to him. "When I first started working as a teacher for the blind, my vision was much better than it is now. I simply memorized the usual progression of expressions."

"You cooked these?"

"One does not cook a sandwich, Tavish." She laid the dishrag over the basket again.

"You are a great deal more fun to talk with than I expected when you first came."

"Likewise." Cecily stepped away.

Tavish caught her hand, stopping her departure. "If I ask a question, will you promise not to prickle up at me?"

"No."

The answer was so unexpected, he laughed out loud. "You'll not allow me to ask a question?"

"No, I will not promise not to prickle up."

What a challenge she was. He glanced toward the fireplace where Finbarr sat with his back to them. "Did you really cook these soups with your poor sight?"

"I have taught people with no sight whatsoever to cook and clean and dress themselves and work their jobs and live their lives." She set a jar of soup on the table. "My vision isn't entirely gone, so accomplishing this is a little easier for me than it is for many of my students." She looked directly into his eyes, or at least appeared to. "Now, if I ask you a question, will you promise not to prickle up?"

"No."

She gave a quick nod of acceptance. "Do you truly want your brother to regain his independence?" She had lowered her voice, no doubt wanting to keep the question from reaching Finbarr's ears.

How could she doubt that? "I have spent every moment of the last year attempting to give him back his life. Yet you question whether I want him to improve?"

His terse tone didn't ruffle her in the least. As calm as ever, she said, "I am only trying to understand."

"Then understand this: I love my brother. His welfare is this family's greatest concern just now. And that, Cecily Attwater, is saying something."

She made a sound of pondering, but said nothing as she moved confidently away from him toward the spot where Finbarr sat, her posture stiff and straight. He'd intended to tell her when she came today that he was sorry for her overly cold reception at the *céilí*. He'd not managed to do so before setting her back up. Again.

Why was it their interactions always seemed to end in one or both of them being put out with the other? 'Twas a very good thing he'd decided weeks ago to give up on women; he'd clearly lost his touch with them.

The door closed behind Tavish on his way to see to his daily work, no doubt. Just as well. Having Tavish question her methods at every turn would not help her make progress. What she couldn't decide was whether his objections came more from doubt in her as a teacher or from distaste for her as an Englishwoman.

Cecily knew the O'Connor family wanted Finbarr to succeed, so there had to be a reason they placed their dislike of the English ahead of their hopes for their brother and son. She hadn't expected

Finbarr to be fully convinced of her yet, but she'd never had a family go to such lengths to make certain she knew how displeased they were with her presence. Even if Finbarr suddenly became converted to her methods, she couldn't fight his family much longer without being forced to admit defeat. His recovery depended so much on them.

She would simply have to ponder whilst continuing her attempt at lessons. She set a pair of boots she'd borrowed from Tavish on the end table near Finbarr's chair.

Before she could give an explanation, Finbarr muttered into the silence between them. "Did you really make the soup?"

"I don't know why everyone finds that so surprising."

"Because you're broken." His words were under-enunciated to the point of being almost indiscernible. "Broken people can't do anything."

"Call me 'broken' one more time, Finbarr O'Connor, and I will belt you in the gob so hard your teeth will be falling out your ears."

Oh, how she wished she could see the shock that was, no doubt, registering on his face. His tone when he spoke next confirmed her suspicions. "'Belt me in the gob'? Do the English say that?"

"I borrowed the phrase from your brother Ian," she said. "But the threat stands. You continually speak of those with limited sight as worthless, and I have extremely limited sight. No one calls me useless. No one. You can think it of me all you want, but don't you ever say it. Am I understood?"

He made a sound deep in his throat, one she took as agreement. The rule was not at all about her feelings but rather his need to stop viewing himself so poorly.

"Now, here is your assignment for the day—other than building a fire in the stove. On the end table beside you is a pair of boots and a pair of laces." She crossed to the windows and snapped the curtains closed. "Your job is to lace the boots."

"It's too dark in here," he said. "There's no fire, and you just pulled the curtains."

"Very good."

"It's not very good. If there were more light, I could see some."

She knew that all too well. "If you can manage the task in blackness, you can manage it in the light."

A shifting of clothes and a creak of chair legs told her he'd sat up once more. "That's not fair."

"Life isn't fair. The sooner you stop expecting it to be, the easier that fact will be to accept." She would need a firm, determined approach with him, at least until he began trying. "Lace the boots and build the fire. That's all that is asked of you today."

"How can I lace them? I can't see the eyelets."

Good. He was addressing the problem. "That's true. But you do have four other fully functioning senses you can rely on."

He sighed in exactly the way one would expect a seventeen-year-old to. "I can't hear the eyelets."

"I wouldn't recommend tasting them either."

His clothes rustled against the seat again; he was slouching most likely. "You mean *feel* the eyelets."

"That seems to be the best course of action." As she walked past the end table, she nudged the boots closer to him. "Now get to work."

"I don't like you," he grumbled.

"I know." Her students, to whom she dedicated herself, for whom she worried and cheered and hoped, often hated her at first. Some never stopped hating her. But as she and Finbarr had established a moment ago, life was hardly fair. "I will be over here at the kitchen table when you've finished lacing the boots."

She pulled out the kitchen chair and sat. She'd laid out her items when she first arrived, knowing she would likely have a long wait. Her fingers ran along the edge of her neat pile of paper and the sealed letter resting on top. Just to the left was a box of matches. Above that was a lantern, ready and waiting.

She struck a match and lit the lantern wick. A dull light illuminated her small space.

"That sounded like a match," Finbarr said.

Cecily silently cheered. He was learning to distinguish sounds to which fully-sighted people paid little attention. "I am lighting a lantern so I can do my work."

"Why do you get a lantern, but I don't?" He sounded as though she'd done him a great injustice.

"Because I laced my own boots and built a fire this morning," she answered. "Do that, and you can have a light today as well."

She was answered with another very seventeen-year-old sigh. He was at a tough enough age without the added weight he carried.

Cecily pulled the lantern close. Warmth immediately suffused the air directly beside her. Burns were always a risk when one needed as much light as possible, but its welcome glow illuminated the table top. She could see her neat stack of paper, her unopened letter, her pen and capped bottle of ink. None of the items were as clear and detailed as they'd once been, but there was comfort in the dim sight of them.

She opened and unfolded her letter, then held the page as close to the light as she could without touching the paper to the hot glass. She leaned in closer.

The muddled mess turned into a very fuzzy collection of letters.

Dear M—

She couldn't make out the rest of the salutation, though she could guess at it. *Dear Miss Attwater.* The letter was from little Theodore Calhoun, whose parents had insisted on formal address. She hadn't minded. In the end, they'd become good friends.

I am leaving—

No, that wasn't right.

I am learning to cool—

The word wasn't cool. She studied the text more closely.

I am learning to cook on the stove. Mother says I am—

The next few words blurred. She tilted her head a bit to the side. Sometimes that helped.

But the letters still wouldn't come in to focus. She pulled the lantern so close that the heat was uncomfortable against her cheek. The rest of that second sentence remained unintelligible. She tried the next line with no better luck. The line after that contained a passage about *Father* and *a great deal of hair on the quilt*. That made no sense, but she couldn't decipher enough to fill in what she was missing.

She brushed away a trickle of sweat from her forehead. Her face had likely turned red from the lantern heat. Another try at reading the letter convinced her that she'd never manage it, at least not in this dim kitchen with nothing but a lantern.

Theodore had never been particularly good about writing in large lettering. She'd either need to convince his parents to work with him on his letters, or she'd need someone to read his letters to her. His vision had not been far enough gone to require him to learn Braille.

The Braille system of point writing had been the one preferred at her school. She'd learned several others, but preferred Braille as well and always offered to teach her students who would otherwise be left illiterate. Most eagerly agreed. A few didn't care to learn a new alphabet.

She closed her eyes and listened intently for the sound of Finbarr setting to his task. His clothes rustled. Perhaps he was at least making an attempt. Would he be willing to learn Braille? Did he even need raised lettering? He hadn't spoken in enough detail about his remaining sight for her to determine if he was able to see written text.

"I'm finished." Finbarr sounded utterly unimpressed with his task and himself.

She pushed away from the table and crossed to where he yet sat. Her fingers found the boots on the side table, both sitting askew. He would eventually learn the importance of being very particular about how and where he placed things.

She ran her fingers along the laces, matching eyelets as she went. Predictably, he'd done a haphazard job—probably hadn't really tried. A boy of his age must have laced dozens of boots over the years. Losing his sight made the task a bit trickier, but not so much he'd do *this* poorly.

She hooked her finger around the first of the crisscrossing laces and pulled them out.

"What are you doing?" Again, Finbarr was listening closely enough to make some sense of what he couldn't see.

"You have been afforded the opportunity to try again." She continued unlacing. "This time, pay more attention."

"I laced them like you told me to. I'm not doing it again."

"Build a fire. Lace your boots. Those are your assignments. Both must be done with care and attention to detail. *Especially* building the fire." She set the laces on top of the boots. "Lace them again. You may not get it completely right this time, either; it will take some practice. But I do expect your next attempt to be better. *Much* better."

His chair abruptly scraped against the floor. "I'll not do it again." His voice came from higher up than a moment ago.

"You will." The flare of temper was not unexpected. She had long ago become adept at maintaining her calm. "And when you get hungry enough, you'll also build a fire. Knowing the potential dangers of fires, and in light of your unwillingness to be careful with something as innocuous as shoelaces, I suggest you not attempt the fire until Tavish returns to keep an eye on you."

"Don't talk to me as if I'm a baby," he said tightly.

"Then do not act like one."

"You can lace the boots yourself." The boots thudded to the floor shoved off the end table.

As she always did when a student lashed out, she kept still and spoke evenly. "In my experience, tossing things about makes locating them significantly harder. Feeling about the floor on your hands and knees is probably your best approach."

"I am not going to crawl on the ground just because you want me to lace boots like an imbecile."

She crossed back to the kitchen table, trusting he'd hear her footsteps growing fainter. If he knew she wasn't overly concerned, his temper might cool off a little. "The sooner you find the boots, the sooner you can finish your first task for the day."

"Lace them yourself," he repeated, overly emphasizing the words.

"Finbarr—"

His footsteps drew closer. Furniture legs scraped along the floor as he collided with something in his path. "I don't need you here. I don't want you here."

Cecily swallowed hard and forced a breath. "Finbarr, rein in your temper."

"Don't tell me what to do." The lantern cast enough light to emphasize how tall Finbarr truly was.

"You must lace your boots," she said. "Lacing your boots for you is not part of my job."

"But 'belting me in the gob' is?" He towered over her. "Maybe I ought to belt you in—"

"Finbarr O'Connor." Tavish's rumbling voice shattered the air around them. When had he returned? People very seldom caught her by surprise. Either she'd been very distracted or he'd been exceptionally quiet. "You're not ever to talk to a woman that way. Not ever."

"Are you going to tell me what to do now, too?" Finbarr

snapped back. “I didn’t ask for this. I didn’t ask for any of this. Especially not *her*.”

“You’ll treat her the way you were taught to treat a lady, or—”

“I hate all of this. I hate you, and her, and I hate these boots.” They thudded across the floor again. Kicked, probably. “I hate it all.”

Finbarr’s stomps indicated a path toward the ladder leading up to the loft. Cecily let out the tense breath she hadn’t realized she’d been holding.

“Finbarr,” Tavish called after him.

“Let him go,” Cecily said. “He needs to let his temper rage a moment. He needs to get it out.”

“But he threatened you.”

Her pulse hadn’t entirely slowed. “I know.” She’d been expecting his anger to surface at some point, but his outburst had been more than she’d bargained for.

Tavish drew a touch closer. “Sometimes I fear I don’t know him any longer.”

Here was the concern for Finbarr she’d searched for beneath Tavish’s objections to her and her methods.

“He used to always be light and kind. He brightened rooms and lives.” More than concerned, Tavish sounded grieved. “*This* Finbarr is a stranger.”

“This Finbarr is angry and terrified.” She tried to look and sound reassuring. “Episodes of this nature will continue for a time, until he is ready to begin healing.”

“But to threaten you the way he did, looming and raging . . .” Tavish paced away, his footsteps echoing with exhaustion and worry.

“I do not believe he would have followed through with the threat.” She felt more certain as she spoke the words. The truth of the realization calmed her further. “I heard far more pain in his words than rage.”

"Still, I mean to keep an eye on the lad. And you'll tell me if you ever feel unsafe?"

She nodded even as she prayed the situation would never reach that point.

Chapter Twelve

"He threatened to hit her, Da." Tavish rubbed the back of his neck. "He was livid enough, I'd not've been surprised if he'd made good on the threat."

"Finbarr? Quiet, sweet-tempered, little Finbarr?" Da paced away, stopping at the nearest stall. Barns weren't the best place to have difficult conversations, but Tavish hadn't wanted Finbarr or Ma to overhear. "He'd not truly hit a woman, would he? I didn't raise any of m' boys to be the sort of men who'd hurt a woman."

"If you'd seen him in that moment, you'd be as unsure of that answer as I am." Tavish released a breath slowly, though the knot remained in his stomach, as did the weight on his mind. Had he been right to share this latest trouble? Da had aged a decade over the last year. It showed most in worry-filled moments like this, when the lines on his face deepened and exhaustion filled his eyes.

Da leaned his forearms on the upper slats of the stall, his eyes on the cow, though Tavish didn't think he was looking at anything in particular. "What did Her Majesty have to say about Finbarr's outburst?"

The title Tavish fashioned for Cecily had stuck and spread. He felt a little bad about that. "That outbursts are to be expected."

"Did she think he was going to strike her?"

"She said she didn't. But I saw a seed of fear in her face. I think she wasn't certain her own self." That flicker of worry had stayed with Tavish all the day long. It confirmed his own worries, ones he couldn't in good conscience ignore. "We'd be well advised to not leave her alone with him until we've a better idea about how much his temper may rage."

Da's shoulders slumped. Such weariness. Such defeat. Tavish ought not to have burdened him with this.

"The lad's in my care and living in my house," Tavish said. "I'll see to it someone's with him when I can't be."

That would be often. He had land and animals to see to, repairs to make before winter set in fully, his own meals and care to see to. But he'd not allow Finbarr to harm anyone.

"I can come by and sit with the lad. Ian will, too, I'd wager. And your sisters' husbands." Da's tone held very little hope, as if he couldn't be confident the plan would work. "Joseph Archer. Jeremiah Johnson. They'd all take it in turns."

Tavish knew a bad idea when he heard one. "And convince Finbarr we all think he's in need of a nursemaid? He'd likely only grow angrier."

"Katie, then?" Da pushed away from the stall wall and paced. "She has the beginnings of a friendship with Miss Attwater. Finbarr might believe the ladies were merely visiting."

That likely would work. Of course, that would mean having Katie in his house regularly. That possibility had once been his greatest hope. Now 'twas a painful necessity he'd have to endure. Perhaps if he added another person to the rotation of visitors, he wouldn't have to face her as often.

"We could ask Ma as well."

Da held up a hand to stop the suggestion before Tavish could finish making it. "We'll not tell your Ma any of this." He rubbed at his face and eyes. "We've got far too much pain in this family just now, with Ian's struggles, Mary and Thomas thinking of leaving us, and Ciara pulling away." Sorrow filled every syllable. "I can't bear to hear her cryin' anymore at night."

"She cries?"

Da nodded, slowly. "When she thinks I'm asleep."

Tavish set a hand on his da's shoulder. "I'll see to this latest difficulty with Finbarr. You and Ma don't worry over him. I'll sort it."

Exhausted relief filled the lines of Da's face. "Thank you, son. This family would never've survived the last months without you."

"We'll manage this latest bend in the road as well. I promise we will."

Tavish had expected one of his sisters or Biddy to come around the next day. All three did. To their credit, they'd managed a good excuse, citing their tradition of helping Tavish see to his crop, nothing that would raise Finbarr's suspicions.

The last of the berries ripened quite late in the season, and the crop wouldn't hold. Little time remained for preserving what he'd salvaged. The women helped him each year, along with Ma. She didn't come today, no doubt due to Da's wish to protect Ma from Finbarr's growing struggles.

The lad had resumed his usual sulking, slumped in the chair he always occupied near the fireplace. The boots he'd not even tried to lace today sat atop the small end table beside him. Cecily sat in a chair opposite him, waiting.

Mary and Ciara looked over at the pair of them repeatedly. Biddy didn't glance toward Cecily even once. It broke his heart to see how much Cecily's presence pained his tenderhearted sister-in-law, though no one knew entirely why.

Under the pretense of bringing her a new bowl of freshly washed berries, Tavish leaned a touch close to her and, voice lowered, said, "If you can't bear it, Biddy, you can head home. I'll not begrudge you that."

But she shook her head. "Finbarr needs us, and so do you, whether or not you'll admit it."

"When have I ever not admitted needing the lot of you?"

She shot him a look of dry disbelief. "You've never admitted to needing anyone."

"That seems a bit harsh." He was independent, certainly, and he'd needed to be strong for the sake of his crumbling family. But she'd taken that reality to a level of pride he didn't think he'd fairly earned.

Her gaze, however, turned tender. "I'd not meant to offend. I only wish we could do more for you than we do."

"You're doing plenty," he assured her. "So little of m' crop was salvageable by the time we returned to town, so your help in saving all the bits of it will make a difference come next year."

"And for that reason, I'll stay and help all I can, even considering your current company."

Tavish glanced at Cecily, still waiting patiently for Finbarr to begin lacing his boots. Biddy's family had a particularly difficult history with the English; some of her loved ones had been killed at the hands of Cecily's countrymen. He assumed those losses were at least part of the reason for her discomfort with Cecily.

"If it'll set your mind at ease," he said, "I truly think we've nothing to fear from her."

"Likely not," Biddy said quietly, "but I mean to keep my distance, just the same. 'Tis always safer that way."

'Twasn't a matter of safety so much as comfort. Either way, it left Tavish with something of a struggle on his hands. He cared too much for Biddy to see her grow as scarce in his life as Ciara had.

But what could be done? Finbarr couldn't be left to remain in his current state, and Cecily alone knew how to save him from it.

"I'll not lose your company," he told her, "or Ian's. Neither will I ask you to be miserable. That means, you realize, that Finbarr and I will likely be knocking on your door at all hours, expecting food and company and a great deal of entertainment."

A welcome hint of amusement crossed her features. Biddy had been too solemn of late. As had Mary. And Ciara. Heavens, his entire family was plagued with worries.

Mary met his eye from across the table.

"How's Thomas?" he asked.

"Same as always. Stubborn." She applied herself with extra force to the berry mashing. "And forgetful. The man doesn't seem to recall how miserable we all were in New York."

"He's thinking of taking your family as far as that?" Tavish didn't care for the thought of his sister and her brood being away from Hope Springs, but he'd assumed they were thinking of somewhere closer, like St. Louis.

"I'm not certain he knows what he wants," she said. "But he's convinced himself that if we stay here, the children'll wither and die of lost opportunities."

"And are they showing symptoms of withering?" He'd thought her young ones seemed content enough.

"They're in that difficult time between childhood and adulthood. Of course they're rebelling against any constraints they feel. 'Tis the way of things, but it's not a reason to uproot the lot of us."

Tavish had seldom heard such frustration from Mary, especially directed toward her Thomas. The two of them had been sweet on each other for ages, seeming as smitten more than a decade after marrying as they'd been when they were courting. The rift growing between the two was worrisome.

"Would it help if I spoke with him?" Tavish wouldn't relish the undertaking, but if it'd help at all, he'd do it willingly. Someone had to keep the family from falling apart.

"If he's still being difficult come spring, we need only convince him to plant his crop," Mary said. "He'll stay at least long enough to harvest it. That'll grant us a stay of execution."

Tavish didn't at all like the way she spoke, with such a loss of hope. He hadn't any idea how to fix it.

Biddy's little one, Patrick, began fussing. She, however, was at the stove, stirring the preserves. "I can't let this burn," she said. "Ciara, will you rock the baby a moment or two. He'll settle down straight away; I'm certain of it."

Ciara hesitated. "Mary could fetch him."

"I'm up to m' elbows in berries," Mary answered. "You're between batches. Be a help and see to the little lad."

"I've been a perfectly fine help today."

"I never said you hadn't been." Mary seemed intent on matching her sister's tone.

In the background, wee Patrick made his own objections to the delay in attention. His whimpers were fast turning to cries. Soon enough, he'd be wailing to bring down the rafters.

Ciara's eyes flickered in the baby's direction for only a moment. She squared her shoulders and raised her chin. "This would go faster if we had more than one stove working at a time." She took up a large basket of berries. "I have jars at my house. I'll make a batch there and bring it by in the morning."

Tavish hated to see her go. "Ciara—"

She didn't let him object. "You can trade me for the jars and the sugar."

Without a backward glance, she made for the door. Tavish rushed to catch up and stopped her on the porch. "Don't rush off," he said. "I've not seen you in weeks and weeks, it feels. I've missed you."

Her expression turned apologetic. "I like being at home, is all. I like the quiet and the peace."

He knew with certainty that quiet and peace weren't the entirety of her reasons for keeping away. "What is it that's weighing on you?"

"Nothing you need to worry over."

Not worry? She was his dear, sweet, baby sister. Of course her pain and sadness worried him. "Do you remember all those times in New York when we'd walk home from the factory in the dark of night, and you'd be tired or worn down or nervous around the shadowy corners? I'd sing to you as we walked down street after street, and you felt better, if only for the moment."

She shook her head, not in denial of the memory but in rejection of it. "Singing won't help now, Tavish. There are some things a song cannot heal."

With that, his heart fell further. "It needn't be a song. It was the being together that helped."

She took a step away. "You've people enough you're carrying just now. I'll not add my weight to theirs."

Oh, Ciara. He watched her walk away. *You weigh on my heart already.*

Chapter Thirteen

"Fire first. Then you can eat." Cecily had uttered the instruction so many times, she no longer had to think about what she was saying.

Finbarr never built the fire yesterday, or the day before, or the day before that. She hadn't expected him to, either. The boy's walls were thick and unlikely to come down easily. "My family won't let you starve me." His faith in his family's concern, though frustrating when used to undermine her, was encouraging. He must not feel entirely abandoned by them.

"Then they must find a way to make you build this fire. That is my requirement, and you will do it if you want to eat." She disliked making the threat, but if he was to eat as life went on, if he was to survive the harsh Wyoming winters, he needed to learn how to safely start, maintain, and extinguish a fire. No two ways about it.

Tavish had not yet left to see to his chores. Unlike the first time she'd told Finbarr that he would earn his meals by building the fire, Tavish didn't express any objections. She hoped that meant he saw some wisdom in the firmness of her approach.

A change as drastic as the one Finbarr had experienced often left a person feeling sorry for himself. That self-pity often prevented the person from learning to do for himself, which, in turn, prevented him from regaining any confidence, plunging him ever deeper into sorrow. The cycle was a difficult one to break.

He must've been eating something, probably sneaking food in the middle of the night. She didn't scold him for that, didn't mention it. He might very well recognize it as an accomplishment, and she didn't wish to take that away from him.

A knock sounded at the door. She guessed who it probably was.

She'd told Tavish several times that Finbarr's outburst was understandable, expected, even, and nothing she couldn't handle. He didn't believe her, and neither did any of the O'Connors. Ever since the day Finbarr had first lashed out at her, Tavish had kept a steady stream of people in the house. All of the grown women in his family except for his mother had come the day after Finbarr's flare of temper. They'd done so under the pretense of canning berry preserves, and had spoken a great deal under their breaths, wandering over regularly to check on Finbarr. The tone they'd struck, and their often stilted conversation, had spoken of discomfort. Though much of that, she'd guess, was due to tensions within the family, she firmly suspected that her presence played a not insignificant role.

Mary, the older sister, had come the second day. Biddy O'Connor the day after that.

Cecily wasn't sure who had been more miserable during that visit, her pupil or her assigned "protector." Both had remained all but silent. Finbarr had refused to leave his chair by the fire. Biddy had moved away from the windows only when absolutely necessary. It had been a terribly awkward day.

Mary had come again the day after that. A new week had begun, and Cecily didn't know who to expect today, as Ciara, the younger sister, had left on less-than-congenial terms three days earlier.

Tavish crossed the room and pulled open the door.

"Good morning to you, Tavish," Katie Archer said. "We've come for a visit."

The small silhouette beside Katie wore a dress. One of the Archer girls, no doubt. Ivy was the more active of the two, and this new arrival kept very still. Emma, then.

"Perfect. An audience again." Finbarr was in a rare mood this morning, even grumpier than usual.

"Mind your manners, Finbarr," Katie said without hesitation. "I know you were raised with them."

Finbarr answered by walking to the window, his back to the room.

"Isn't he happy to have us visit?" Emma asked quietly.

"He's had a difficult morning," Tavish said. "He'll be happy as a cat in a fish market soon enough."

No matter that Emma was only ten years old, she no doubt saw through Tavish's unwarranted optimism.

"Would you mind, terribly, if we borrowed your table for a bit?" Katie asked. "Emma is helping me with my reading, but Ivy's being disruptive. We need a quiet place."

As far as excuses went, it was the most creative Cecily had heard yet. Biddy had explained her arrival at her brother-in-law's house as a quiet place to get the baby to sleep. Mary had insisted she'd come to do some cleaning.

"A lantern is on the table," Tavish said. "You are welcome to practice there."

Whenever he spoke to Katie, an unmistakable discomfort mingled with fondness touched Tavish's tone. And he kept a noticeable distance. A history existed between the two of them; Cecily was sure of it.

She busied herself searching for the boots Finbarr was supposed to have laced. She found them still under the end table, where she placed them every day. She ran her fingers along them. The laces hung limply from the lowest eyelets.

“Finbarr, come here, please.”

He didn’t respond. His footsteps didn’t draw nearer.

“Do as you’re told, lad,” Tavish said firmly.

“Stop ordering me around.” Finbarr’s lack of independence bothered him. If only he understood that independence was exactly what she was offering him. “I’m not a child.”

“Only a child would throw a fit this way.” Tavish’s patience was growing uncharacteristically thin. Both of these O’Connor men were reaching their limits. Maybe that’s what it would take.

“I don’t throw fits.” Finbarr’s voice grew louder, more angry.

“You are throwing one now.” Tavish’s tone was quickly coming to match his brother’s.

“Tavish, enough,” Cecily insisted. Finbarr’s usual petulance had grown to something more, and she didn’t want to push him. “Finbarr, here are the boots you are supposed to be lacing. You must keep working on them. Once you can manage that skill without difficulty, we can move on to something else.”

He remained firmly on the other side of the room, half of his silhouette illuminated by light coming in the window behind him. He did that a lot, keeping near windows when the sun was up, or near the fireplace when the light outside was dim. He was clinging to what little sight he had, a tendency she understood all too well. But he needed to learn to be comfortable in the darkness also.

Long minutes passed without Finbarr coming any nearer the boots. He remained standing at the window, ignoring them all. Katie and Emma undertook their reading lesson. Up in the loft, Tavish pounded away at the railing he was reinforcing. Cecily kept near the hearth, debating.

What if she was taking the wrong approach this time? Her students almost always fought the need to relearn tasks. But this was different. The famous Irish stubbornness, perhaps? Or was it something bigger she was simply not aware of?

If she didn't see at least a small improvement soon, she'd have no choice but to plan her departure. Her heart broke at the idea of giving up on someone as lost and afraid as Finbarr. She knew that he would continue to entrench himself ever further in his isolation. He'd never find his way back again.

I can't lose Finbarr, not when he's so close. She could sense that his walls were on the verge of cracking; she simply needed to find the right brick to pull out.

The reading lesson was ongoing at the table.

"That's an odd way to spell the word *through*," Katie said. "Seems to me you've a few extra letters."

"English is strange," Emma said. "Papa told me that."

"I fear you'll be reading to me for the rest of forever." Katie laughed a little. "I don't know that I'll ever master this."

"You will," Emma said earnestly. "It takes time, is all. And patience."

Perhaps Emma could give Finbarr similar words of encouragement. She was telling Katie exactly what *he* needed to hear.

Cecily sat at the table, a bit apart from the visitors, and listened. Emma was quite good at explaining things in clear terms. She corrected without belittling, was patient, and clearly wanted to help. She would make a fine teacher one day if she chose to become one.

"Finbarr, lad," Tavish spoke from the loft far above all their heads, "you've not done the boots as Miss Attwater asked. It'll not take you but a moment if you put your mind to the task."

"I could help," Emma quickly offered. "I could tell you if you've missed a hole or done something crooked."

"I don't need help from you," Finbarr muttered.

"But you haven't finished the boots," Emma pointed out. "I could help."

"I don't want you to."

"I'm a good helper," she pled.

“You’ve helped enough.” His earlier mutter gave way to stinging tones. “If it weren’t for you, I wouldn’t be like this in the first place.”

The house went utterly silent. Not so much as the rustling of clothing or a single breath broke the moment. What had he meant “if it weren't for you”? What did Emma Archer have to do with Finbarr’s blindness?

Into the tense quiet, Emma whispered, “I am so sorry.” Her words broke with emotion. “It’s all my fault. It’s all my fault.”

Small footsteps fled the room. Katie’s chair scraped as she rushed from the table, following her little girl. Was there anyone in this town not drowning in hidden sorrows? Tavish’s heavy footfalls sounded on the latter rungs.

“Finbarr O’Connor, what the blazes are you thinking?”

Cecily jumped up. “Leave us for a minute, Tavish. Go see if you can soothe Emma.”

For once, the man didn’t question her.

Once alone with Finbarr, Cecily spoke. “I have tried these past days to determine who you are. It seems I have my answer now. You are a young man who makes little girls cry, who chooses the words you know will hurt the most. Emma tenderly reached out to you again and again, and you verbally slapped her without the smallest hint of remorse.”

Finbarr didn’t respond, didn’t defend himself. He simply stood silently.

“I can teach you to function in a world you cannot see. I can teach you to thrive, even without your sight. But I cannot teach you to have a heart. I cannot teach you to be a kind person if you are determined to be cruel.”

She allowed a moment for that to sink in. He was on a dangerous slope. If not corrected, this path would leave him bitter and alone. This moment, she knew, would either make or break him.

"I am going back to Mrs. Claire's home for the remainder of the day. Tomorrow, I will decide if there is any point in staying and trying to help you." She crossed with determined stride to the door. "Think about what you have become, Finbarr O'Connor. Think about whether that is who you want to be."

Chapter Fourteen

Tavish paced the length of his small porch, fighting the anger and worry building inside. Finbarr's words had been cruel. Vicious. That he'd been injured while helping Emma escape a tragic fire did not make his blindness her fault. But Tavish'd wager Emma already blamed herself. So to strike out at her with that guilt was inexcusable.

Tavish had tried to offer some comfort, but the poor child had been inconsolable. Katie had taken her home. Cecily had left as well, telling him only that she needed to decide if Finbarr was beyond her help.

What'll we do if he is?

The lad couldn't go on as he was. Perhaps they would have to take him to that school in Missouri. Leave him there, hoping someone could get through to him.

No. They couldn't do that. Ma'd never recover. Da had only just begun returning to himself. Ian was struggling, which meant Biddy bore a heavy burden. The entire O'Connor clan felt a breath away from falling to bits. Sending Finbarr to St. Louis would be disastrous. Unless, of course, he began lashing out at the family as well.

Tavish leaned his forehead against a porch post. What was he going to do?

The door opened.

"Tavish?" Finbarr asked hesitantly.

"Aye."

"Would you please drive me to the Archers' house?" His question lacked all the angry defiance that had punctuated his words of late.

"That'd depend on what you mean to do once you're there. I'll not subject Miss Emma to any more of your spite."

Finbarr paled. "I won't hurt her again. I swear to it."

Tavish wanted to believe him, and he hated that he couldn't entirely. "Joseph will've heard about your sharp words. He's likely to skin you alive when you knock at his door."

"I know."

"And I'd not put it past Katie to give you a lashing of her own," Tavish added.

"I know."

It might do the boy some good to get chewed up and spit out. Whether he ever learned to function well in his blindness, he could not go about hurting the people who cared for him.

"I'll hitch up the wagon," Tavish said.

Finbarr spoke not a word as they drove up the road and over the bridge that spanned Hope Springs' river. Joseph's home sat just on the other side.

"Can you climb down on your own, then?" Tavish asked upon bringing the wagon to a stop beside the Archer home. He'd taken to applying Cecily's advice of giving Finbarr every opportunity to do for himself.

Finbarr nodded silently and carefully made his way to the ground. Tavish wrapped the horse's reins around the hitching post, then joined his brother on the front walk.

"I'm not sure which way to go," Finbarr admitted. He sounded more like he had in the first months after the fire. Far less bitter and defiant. Far more afraid and alone.

Tavish set his hand on Finbarr's back and applied a small bit of pressure, guiding him toward the house.

"The first of the steps is just at your toes," he said. They slowly climbed to the porch. When they stood within arm's length of the door, he said, "Reach out and knock. A good, solid rap so they'll hear it."

Finbarr's hand shook as he held his arm out, his fingertips searching for the door. He took a breath, folded his fingers into a fist, and knocked. Tavish pushed down the surge of protectiveness he felt. The lad needed to suffer the consequences of what he'd said and the pain he'd inflicted.

Mrs. Smith, the Archers' housekeeper, answered. "What do you want?" The sternness of her expression was more unnerving than usual, and that was a feat.

When Finbarr didn't immediately answer, Tavish decided to make certain the lad knew Mrs. Smith's question had been directed at *him*. "Answer her, then, lad."

"May I speak to Mr. or Mrs. Archer?"

Tavish hadn't expected that request. 'Twas Emma to whom Finbarr owed an apology.

"I'll see if they'll oblige you," Mrs. Smith said. "You may wait there."

Finbarr had once worked for Joseph, had once been as near to family as a person could get without being blood, and he was being made to bide his time. 'Twas a sure sign his welcome was a shaky one.

Only a moment later, Joseph stepped out, silent and stern. He pulled the door closed behind him. "Perhaps, Finbarr, you'd be so good as to tell me why my daughter is weeping?"

Though Joseph's ire wasn't directed at Tavish, the intensity of it sent a shiver of apprehension through him.

"I said some things to her I shouldn't have," Finbarr said softly. "Things I didn't really mean. Things that aren't true."

"Do you realize that she believes they are? Do you realize, son, how much she blames herself for all the suffering of that night?" Joseph's calm declaration snapped like a flag in a gale. His words visibly sliced into Finbarr. Tavish had to take a step back to prevent himself from rescuing his brother from the much-deserved lashing. "She didn't set that fire. She didn't do anything to prevent you from escaping in time. Yet she carries a burden of guilt that is crushing her. In one thoughtless moment, you have undone what little progress Katie and I have made these past months."

"I know," Finbarr whispered.

"I was reluctant to send Emma with Katie today, afraid that seeing you struggling would cause her pain. I never entertained the possibility that you, yourself, would inflict that pain directly, callously, purposely."

"I'm sorry." Was Finbarr tearing up? Tavish hadn't seen him cry since the fire. Not once.

"Her fragile heart aches, worrying over whether you are well, if you have 'forgiven' her, fearing that you hate her for what happened to you. She loves you so deeply, and you have shattered her."

Finbarr hung his head.

"I will allow you to apologize to Emma," Joseph said. "Katie will be at her side, fiercely protecting her. If I've learned anything this past year, it's that one should never cross an Irishwoman where her family is concerned."

That was as true as the day was long.

Joseph waved someone over from inside. A moment later Emma, holding fast to Katie's hand, stepped onto the porch.

Tavish whispered, "Emma is here. She's standing a pace or two in front of you."

Finbarr must have been able to make out their silhouettes; his gaze was directed toward them. "I came to tell you how sorry I am," he said. "I was cruel to you, and I shouldn't have been."

Emma didn't speak, didn't move. She eyed Finbarr with equal parts fear and pain. Tavish didn't know how much of that his brother could see.

"I am sorry," Finbarr said.

"I come to see you all the time," Emma said. "And you are never happy that I'm there. You never listen to me or talk to me. You did today, but only so you could say something unkind." Her voice broke, but she pressed on. "All you do is hurt people. You hurt them and hurt them. I would rather not have any friends than to have a friend like that."

Finbarr had turned utterly ashen.

"You should go home." Emma held her head high in a show of firmness, but her quivering chin told another story. Beneath her resolve, the poor child's heart was breaking. "And I don't think you should come back."

With that, she rushed back into the house, Katie close on her heels. Joseph's gaze remained on the doorway, where his wife and daughter had been only a moment earlier. For his part, Tavish stood mute, caught entirely off guard by Emma's response.

Without warning, a sob shuddered through Finbarr; his whole frame shook with it. He reached out, his palm pressing flat against the side of the house. His breaths caught one after the other as he set his back against the wall and slid to the porch, his legs bent in front of him, his arms on his knees, and his head hanging.

"I hadn't expected her to reject you so wholly," Joseph said, "but I can't say I blame her. Nor will I ask her to place herself once more in a position of pain, not even for someone I care about as much as I do you, Finbarr. I'm sorry."

When Finbarr didn't answer, or even raise his head, Joseph turned his gaze to Tavish.

"Go on," Tavish recognized Joseph's dilemma and released him from it. "See to your family. I'll see to mine."

A quick nod, and then Joseph was gone, the door closed behind him. Tavish crossed to his brother and sat beside him.

"I hurt her." Finbarr's words were garbled with tears. "I was cruel, and I hurt her."

"That you did, and you did a terribly precise job of it. But this is not who you are. This pain and anger are not you. If you keep clinging to them, though, they'll change you, and not for the better. You have to let go of your bitterness."

"I don't know how," Finbarr said through his tears, his head still buried in his arms.

"I can't say that I do, either." He had been carrying his own pain and unhappiness these past six years, ever since his Bridget died. If he was being fully honest, that hurt had played a role in his failed courtship of Katie. And her choosing Joseph over him had only added to it.

"I feel myself getting angrier all the time," Finbarr said. "And I want to lash out at people, and throw things, and hit things. I—I don't recognize myself. I don't know who I am anymore."

Seeing the lad's armor crack sent a radiating ache through Tavish's heart. "Maybe knowing you're not the person you want to be is part of changing the path you're on."

Finbarr took a shaky breath.

"And maybe part of moving down that road is doing some of the things Cecily's been trying to teach you."

"She makes me angry," he admitted, though much of the sting had left his tone. "She doesn't care that things are hard or frustrating."

That didn't ring quite true. "I think she does care," Tavish said. "She simply worries that you'll give up if she doesn't keep pushing."

Another moment passed in silence. Tavish would sit there beside him for as long as he needed him to.

Finbarr slowly regained his composure. Tavish let him sit and think. He didn't know what exactly had happened that day, nor if it would help Finbarr heal. But he hoped and prayed that it would.

He wanted his brother back.

Chapter Fifteen

Cecily struggled to focus on counting her steps as she made her way to Tavish's house the next day. The sky was dimmer in the mornings than it had been. She needed to concentrate but found she couldn't.

If she arrived and found Finbarr every bit as defiant as before, she would call an end to her efforts as his teacher. She refused to waste his family's hard-earned money. She'd had to make that choice only a few times before, but those students still weighed on her conscience. Giving up on people did not come naturally to her.

Finbarr needed what she could give him. He *needed* it. If only he would try.

Tavish opened the door. She knew it was him by the height of his silhouette and the breadth of his shoulders. Finbarr was understandably smaller in those respects.

"Good morning to you," he greeted.

"Why is it that none of you say, 'Top of the morning to you'?" she asked as she stepped inside. As always, his home smelled vaguely of berries and a scent she suspected was his shaving soap. "I thought that was the quintessential Irish greeting."

"'Tis not nearly so common as some think. 'Good morrow to you,' is a frequently heard one. 'You're lookin' fine as rain,' would be another. But if you'd prefer I toss out something you feel is more Irish, I'm happy to oblige."

"Do you know your accent grows thicker when you're teasing?" She crossed further into the room.

"I don't have an accent, lass. But you do, sure enough."

"Perhaps we could ask the Americans in town which of us they feel has the accent," Cecily said. "Then again, we may not be able to understand their answer, seeing as they have—"

"—the thickest accents of all," Tavish finished, with the very train of thought she'd been chasing.

How she hoped his light banter meant Finbarr was doing better. She looked about, but didn't spy her pupil's outline. He might very well simply be out of range of her limited vision.

"Is Finbarr up and about yet?"

If he hadn't dragged himself down, that didn't bode well.

"He is awake, in fact. Up in the loft at the moment, but I'd wager he'll be down shortly."

She clutched her cane more tightly. "How is he today?"

"I'll let you decide that for your own self," Tavish said. "He's climbing down just now."

Turning in the direction of the loft ladder, she made out the blurry colors of Finbarr making his descent. If she wasn't mistaken, he held something in one of his hands.

"Miss Attwater's come," Tavish said. "She's but a few paces behind you."

"I heard her voice," Finbarr said. He crossed to her. "Miss Attwater, I owe you an apology."

He might have knocked her over with a feather. Angry, defiant Finbarr intended to apologize?

"I've been hurting people, you included." Though she could tell this was a rehearsed speech, she didn't for a moment doubt his sincerity. "I never gave you a chance, but I'm hoping you'll give me another one. I can't promise to be a perfect pupil, or even a good one, but I want to try."

"We have not yet reached any difficult skills," she warned him.

His shape moved and changed, and whatever he had in his hand, he now held out to her.

She reached for the dark blob. A pair of boots. She cradled them against her enough to free her hand, then ran her fingers along the front. *Laced and tied.*

"You finished your first task."

"I did it wrong over and over, but I finally figured it out last night. I just needed to pay more attention and be patient with myself."

Relief washed over her in waves. Patience was the first lesson she'd been trying to teach him. "That is the same way you should approach everything you are relearning. Be patient. Take your time. Use your other senses."

"I dressed myself this morning, as well," he said. "Tavish said I did a fine job of it, but I realized afterward that I'd misbuttoned."

"And did you redo it?"

"I did."

Mercy, but this was a change. "What about the fire in the stove?"

"I haven't tried that yet. Tavish suggested I wait for you since he's never tried lighting one with his eyes closed."

Even Tavish was being cooperative. "I think I might have stumbled into the wrong house by accident. I don't recognize either of you."

"I told you myself we were fine fellows," Tavish said. "We've just been hiding it well."

"Ridiculously well." She tried to summon her next thought despite her shock. "Is there wood inside ready to be used?"

"Not yet," Tavish answered. "I thought maybe you'd want him to haul it in as well."

She was nearly speechless. She'd seen students make abrupt turnarounds, but this was astounding. "Take him outside and talk him through selecting logs that won't topple your wood pile. He'll have to learn to recognize that by touch, so think it through and give advice."

"I can do that," Tavish said.

"But under no circumstances is he to fetch it on his own until he is completely confident doing so, and until you are convinced he won't bring the pile down on himself," she quickly added.

"I'll not let the lad kill himself," Tavish promised. "Come on, then, Finbarr. Let's fetch some wood, and see if we can't get this lass swoonin' with how very manly we are."

The two brothers moved toward the door. Cecily stood, rooted to the spot, her emotions bubbling up unexpectedly. She wasn't one who cried often or easily, and there weren't actual tears surfacing now, but her emotions were real and potent.

She pressed her fingers to her lips and took deliberate breaths, willing her mind to slow and calm. Finbarr was ready to learn. He was ready.

Pacing seemed her best option as she thought through what needed to come next. The remainder of the week likely ought to be spent refining the skills he had begun working on. He would grow more confident as he mastered them.

Though most seventeen-year-old boys were not keen on tidiness, Finbarr needed to gain that skill. Keeping his belongings in specific places, and being careful to always return them there, would make his life far easier.

She crossed to the ladder and climbed up. Enough light spilled in through the single window to dimly illuminate the space. The place was a shambles. The air smelled of dust and unwashed clothes.

This would definitely be her next task: teaching him to organize and clean his space.

She carefully made her way to the window, stepping over and around the things Finbarr had left strewn about. The dimness of the light spilling in spoke of glass in need of cleaning. Cecily ran a finger down the window pane and rubbed her thumb and finger together. The unmistakable feel of grime. Finbarr would quickly gain an appreciation for the extra light provided by a clean window.

Cecily raised her hand to eye level and rubbed a small bit of the window clean, letting a few extra rays of sunlight inside. She couldn't see any details beyond the glass except for those things nearest the window and a vague outline of mountains on the horizon.

Though she was in Wyoming, where she'd heard the land was oft' times sparse and unyielding, with dots of precious green overwhelmed by the browns of the desert, her mind simply refused to fill in the empty spaces of her vision with anything other than the lush fields and tall trees of home.

When she was growing up, a stream had run through the fields not far from her bedchamber window. She'd often sat on the window seat, watching the water trip over stones and around bends, pleased at the picture it painted but never fully treasuring it as she ought. What a shame she'd never taken the time to learn the sound of her stream and the wind rustling the branches of the trees that lined its bank.

She'd been caught so unaware by the disease that was stealing the world around her. And she'd been so young.

"You will find a way to build a life," Father had assured her when he'd come to visit during her last year at the Missouri School for the Blind. She'd told him how worried she was about her schooling ending and not having the slightest idea what would come afterward. "You could stay here and teach."

"I couldn't bear that, not going anywhere, not experiencing the world while I still can." Seven years later, she could still feel the panic that had bubbled. "I want to see the ocean again and see the Rocky Mountains—I'm told they are large enough and tall enough that, provided I don't wait until my vision has deteriorated terribly, even I would be able to see at least their outline. And I cannot countenance the thought of spending the remaining decades of my life as a spinster teacher in a school, where my only companions are my students, and my only true company is that of the other teachers."

Her instructors hadn't been unhappy necessarily, but she had always imagined herself after her schooling living with Father again, finding some means of supporting herself. That had been her dream: being part of a family again and seeing the country with him. But her father had died mere weeks before she graduated.

She'd begun traveling, reaching out to those souls too far distant to attend a school. She'd seen the country, as she'd told her father she'd wanted to. Wyoming brought her closer to the Rocky Mountains. Perhaps after Finbarr had learned all she could teach him, she would search out a position in California or Oregon, somewhere near the coast. She would pass through the Rockies on her way. She still had vision enough to see waves crashing against sand on a bright, sunny day. She could stand on the beach and memorize the sight and sounds of the sea.

The door opened below, and Tavish's lyrical voice floated up to her. The Irish were known for the musical quality of their speech, but somehow Tavish's voice had it in extra measure. She'd heard any number of whispers during her brief moments at the *céilí* amongst the younger women, those too young for anything to come of their observations, that Tavish was breathtakingly handsome. And though she and he had undertaken their share of disagreements, she couldn't deny that he was witty and personable and likely could charm the socks off a snake when he wished to.

Why, then, was he still unattached? A handsome, charming man with a quick wit, who loved his family and worked hard ought to have been snatched up long ago.

That was a far more personal bit of pondering than she'd ever intended to entertain about Tavish O'Connor. She shook off the distraction and, with her hand on the railing, made her way back to the ladder. She quickly but carefully descended and followed the voices to the kitchen side of the room.

"Were you explorin', then?" Tavish asked.

He'd obviously seen her climb down from the loft. "I was deciding on Finbarr's tasks for the week." She stopped near the table, concentrating on placing Tavish and Finbarr within the dim room. "He'll focus on dressing himself, becoming more adept and swift at the task. He'll practice safely lighting a fire, though mastering that will take longer than a week. And the rest of his time will be spent organizing and cleaning the loft."

"You're planning to convince a lad his age to tidy his space?"

She cocked an eyebrow at him. "Are you impressed?"

Tavish's low rumbling laugh brought her smile out a bit. "Manage that, Cecee, and my ma might stop dislikin' you."

That declaration hit her like a slap of cold wind. She knew that the Irish families, including the O'Connors, disliked her, but hearing the truth of the matter spoken so directly pinched her already raw emotions.

Cecily turned her attention to the stove. She didn't care to think too closely on everyone's poor opinion of her. Nor did she wish to examine why their dislike hurt so much. "Shall we light a fire?"

The men accepted the abrupt change of topic. Cecily, on the other hand, knew her continued rejection by the town would prick at the back of her mind for days on end.

Cecily sat at the small desk she'd placed under one of Mrs. Claire's front windows, with her lantern lit, and attempted to focus on the book laid open in front of her. She didn't usually struggle to concentrate, but the sounds of the O'Connor women, Katie, and Mrs. Claire, in conversation behind her, repeatedly pulled her attention.

"You must bring your berry tart again, Katie," Mrs. O'Connor said. "No one bakes a tart as well as you do."

"Having access to the best berries in the West certainly doesn't hurt," Katie said.

"Don't tell Tavish that. His head'll swell big, and we'll never hear the end of it." Precisely the type of comment one would expect from a man's older sister.

Cecily shook off this most recent moment of distraction. She focused once more on her book. With both the lantern and the sunlight from the window, she could make out the words, but only just: *The king tried to have patience, but he succeeded very badly.*

She read the passage silently twice over, making certain she was not misreading any of the words.

Her familiar wood frame with attached metal stencil sat at the ready. She took up the metal stylus and began pressing dot after dot, forming in Braille the letters and words she'd just read. She read and transcribed another sentence. Then another.

The Light Princess was the seventeenth book she would transcribe into Braille in the last seven years, and the fifth for children. So few Braille books existed in English, and few of those available in the United States. Those that were could be obtained only at significant cost or borrowed locally from those who owned them. Her books were being sent throughout the West. She'd made the arrangements years earlier, running a lending library with the help of her former school.

Her heart soared at the thought of her students—who would otherwise have been unable to—reading. Even miles and years apart, she was still helping them. And these books would continue bringing joy to new generations of the blind and severely poor-sighted. They would feel a little less lost and a little less alone.

"Thomas must've been pleased with the crop this year," Mrs. O'Connor said. "We've not brought in such a yield in some time. And the men received top price for it. We've a bit more breathing room than usual."

Mary's husband was Thomas, whom Cecily had not formally met. "'Tisn't the money turning his thoughts eastward, but the opportunities."

"And what 'opportunities' did we have in New York?" Biddy asked. "Perhaps Thomas doesn't remember the misery we endured there. The Irish are as unwelcome in the Eastern cities as ever we have been here. More so, in many ways."

"The children don't sound as Irish as we do," Mary said. "They'd not have so difficult a time of it as we did."

"But they'd be away from their family," Mrs. O'Connor said. "You all would be. Surely Thomas doesn't wish for that."

Cecily hadn't intended to eavesdrop, but the conversation was loud, and her hearing was acute. Besides, they were discussing a topic far too relatable for her to not take notice of it. Her father had uprooted their family for the sake of giving *her* opportunities. She knew the worry associated with such an endeavor as well as the sacrifices.

Perhaps she could share her thoughts and experiences on the matter. She might be of some use to them, and they might appreciate her insights. They might even find between them all the beginnings of a friendship.

"Will we be seeing Ian at church tomorrow?" Mrs. Claire asked.

"I can't say," was Biddy's quiet response. "His head's been aching terribly, and he's having more of his spells."

"Has he?" Mrs. O'Connor whispered. "I hadn't heard he'd grown worse."

"Tavish finished his own work this morning and is with him now," Biddy said. "The children are spending the day with the McCanns. I needed a little time away."

"But who is with Finbarr?" Mrs. O'Connor's tone of worry only grew. "Ought he to be left alone?"

"He's been alone before." Mrs. Claire voiced Cecily's exact thought. Here was the "babying" Finbarr had complained of on her first day.

"I've heard," one of the sisters said, her voice low and filled with warning, "he's been building fires. He certainly shouldn't be doing that all by his lonesome."

Mrs. O'Connor adamantly agreed.

"He is not building fires by himself," Cecily said.

The women grew instantly quiet. She'd interrupted, inserting herself into the conversation.

"How is it you know what the lad's doing when he's alone?" Challenge. Distrust. Contempt. Mrs. O'Connor managed to fit all three into a single sentence. "Do you know him so well, then?"

"Him, personally? No. But I have been where he is, in the darkness, afraid and uncertain. He is inching his way out, not running."

A moment's silence followed, broken only by the pop of needles through the tightly pulled fabric of the quilt they were tying. Did their lack of response mean they were satisfied with her explanation, or more doubtful?

"I specifically told him not to build fires unless Tavish or I am there to instruct him. I believe he accepts my authority," Cecily assured them. "He knows that I know best."

Rustling fabric and scraping chair legs. Someone had stood. "I need to be on my way." Biddy.

"But we've not yet had our tea," Mrs. Claire said.

"I've tea at home," Biddy said. "I'll not go wanting."

"You'll be wanting for company," Katie said. "Stay a spell. Tavish'll look after Ian."

The others erupted with words of agreement and pleas for her to remain. But Biddy was undeterred. She crossed to the door, bid them a quiet farewell, and left.

"I've never known her not to stay for a bee," Mrs. O'Connor said. "Do you suppose Ian is in poorer health than she let on?"

Mary offered her own explanation. "I'll wager it isn't concern at home that's sent her fleeing but"—she lowered her voice to a whisper—"discomfort *here*."

They all responded with aahs and mm-hmms and general sounds of agreement. Biddy left to avoid being in company with one particular person: Cecily.

She set her foggy gaze on her book once more but couldn't concentrate. She was unwelcome. Unwanted. And so very, very lonely.

Chapter Sixteen

A month had passed since Cecily had arrived in Hope Springs. Though she was grateful Finbarr had finally begun making progress, she couldn't deny that he was often disheartened by how slowly he learned new skills. He regularly returned to his sulking and muttering, which made their days together long and wearying.

Worn down, tired, and a full hour past her usual departure time, Cecily pulled her coat off its hook near the door and hung it over her arm, taking her cane in the other hand. Tavish was near the stove with Finbarr, working on their dinner. Finbarr had been more frustrated than usual this afternoon but was finally focusing again. She didn't want to disrupt simply to offer a farewell.

She stepped outside, and her breath caught in her lungs. The temperature had plummeted over the course of the day. She could hardly bear to take the air in. What had brought on this sudden turn in the weather? Before stepping out and away from the protection of the house, she set her cane against the side of the house. Her hands free, she pulled her coat on and buttoned it high, hoping to offer a little respite from the iciness. She took up her cane once more and stepped out from under the protective covering of the porch.

The driving wind was unrelenting and loud. She took a step. Then another. But the third was unsure, and she wobbled. The storm robbed the landscape of what little light there might have been. Keeping to a straight path was crucial to reaching Mrs. Claire's home. If Cecily was thrown off even the smallest bit, she'd find herself wandering in the vastness, completely lost.

She took careful, deliberate steps, searching with her cane for any rocks or dips in her path. After only a moment or two, a sudden gust toppled her entirely, sending her sprawling to the ground.

Splinters. Howling wind. Sharp pain surging through her side. Her heart pounded hard in her neck. She couldn't catch her breath.

Snow pelted her face in the darkness. There was no light. Not a single ray or point. Cloud cover had rendered everything dark. Which way had she been facing when she fell? She couldn't see her landmarks, not one.

Oh, heavens. Which way was Mrs. Claire's? Tavish's? Was she even on the road anymore?

She shifted to her hands and knees. The punishing wind didn't relent. She felt about and found her cane. Found two pieces. That was the splintering she'd heard. She'd have to stumble her way back without its help.

If she stood up facing the same way she'd been when she fell, Tavish's house would be on her left. Or would it? A dangerous thing to be wrong about. She could find herself wandering farther and farther afield.

Slowly, carefully, she moved to her feet, clutching the pieces of her useless cane. She turned her head to the left. No lights. No clues. Snow fell harder. The bite of frigid air punishing. A core-deep shiver shook her hard as the arctic temperatures clutched at her.

She was lost. Completely turned around.

She forced slow breaths. What should she do? She couldn't simply wander around aimlessly, but neither could she stand there and freeze to death as the night wore on. Tavish and Finbarr would never guess she hadn't successfully returned to Mrs. Claire's house, and the old woman would likely think she'd chosen to remain at Tavish's house rather than brave the weather.

She wrapped her arms around herself, trying to fight off the invading cold. Pain clawed at her hands and face.

"Cecee?" The wind carried Tavish voice.

"Tavish!" She called back, praying he was near enough to hear. "Tavish!"

Suddenly he was there. His hands were warm against her face "I was afraid you'd be farther down the road. The storm's growing bad. You'd best come back inside."

"I don't know where the house is." Her teeth chattered as she spoke. "I can't see it. I tripped and found myself turned around. I didn't—"

He pressed his fingers to her lips, cutting off her words. "I know these storms, and we've but a moment before even I won't be able to see the house. We have to get back inside as quickly as possible."

He put his arm around her, pulling her in close as he led her swiftly away. The snow must have been thick. The toe of her boot hit the first step of the porch before she could see the tiniest hint of light from the house.

"I never would have found my way back," she said quietly. "If you hadn't come looking for me . . ."

"The weather's been threatening to turn this way." He led her past the porch and inside the blessedly warm house and the welcome light within. "I should've thought to check before you set out." He kept his arm across her back as they stepped farther into the warmth of his house. "Sit near the fire. I'll fetch—You've broken your cane."

She nodded against her increasing shivers. "I fell on it."

"Are you hurt?" He ran his hands down her arms. "I don't see any blood."

"I think my side'll be bruised, but nothing—nothing worse than—" Her emotions rose without warning, clogging her throat, preventing the very words she was attempting to speak. She pressed her eyes closed, trying to hold back tears. Her body shook, giving away the turmoil she couldn't hide.

"Cecee?" Tavish's voice was soft, concerned.

She held up a hand, hoping to cut off the inquiry she sensed was coming. An onslaught of questions would push her past the point of recovery. Her composure was too fragile.

"Your hand's trembling," Tavish said.

Her entire body was trembling. She was falling to pieces.

Outside had been so dark. She'd been utterly lost.

"I didn't know which way to go." Her near whisper twisted with delayed panic. Although the crisis had passed, her emotions seemed to be only just recognizing the danger she'd been in. "If you hadn't found me—" She couldn't finish the sentence.

She struggled for breath. She'd been lost in the grip of an intense storm. So dark. So cold. The trembling spread, leaving her shaking from head to toe. A hot tear escaped her eyes.

"It was so dark." Her whisper broke as her strength ebbed.

His hands slipped from her arms to her back, and he pulled her into an embrace. "You are safe now. And you needn't leave again until the weather has calmed."

Cecily couldn't remember the last time she'd been held like this. She'd received goodbye embraces from grateful students and their families. On occasion, one of her younger students had given her an enthusiastic hug after mastering a skill. But this was different.

Tavish was offering comfort and support. This embrace was not about what she could or had done to help him; he was meeting a need in her. Noticing her. Caring. Such a tender embrace was not truly appropriate between them, but she needed it too desperately to end it on account of propriety.

"Thank you for finding me," she whispered, not moving the slightest bit from the reassurance he offered. "I haven't been so frightened in a very long time."

"If I'd known I'd be rewarded with an embrace from a beautiful woman, I'd've gone about rescuing them from snowstorms long ago."

Oh, how she needed his humor in that difficult moment. The fear that yet gripped her heart eased the smallest bit. She could breathe more easily. And with the easing of tension in her lungs, she could think more clearly as well.

She'd allowed herself to panic, something she didn't often experience. For years, she'd taught her students the value of logic and calm. Maintaining her composure, especially in front of them, had always been crucial. Her current student was, she feared, seeing a different side of her.

"Is Finbarr witnessing all of this, as well?"

"Aye. He's but a pace away, listening to every word."

She, then, had undermined her own teachings by letting herself be overwhelmed. "He will not give my word the tiniest bit of authority now, having seen me turn so watery."

Tavish adjusted so he stood beside her and then guided her to a nearby chair, calling to his brother, "You'll not toss away all her good advice, will you, lad?"

She heard Finbarr take a tense breath. "You couldn't find your way back?" Real fear touched his words. "I hadn't—I hadn't thought of that danger."

Cecily sat in the chair Tavish offered her. He took her broken cane and stepped aside, allowing her a view of his brother's outline, pacing.

"What happened this evening was my own fault." She rubbed her still-chilled hands together, hoping to warm them. "I did not take the time to evaluate the weather or visibility before I set out. If I had, I would have known not to venture forth. I was careless."

"But if *you* can forget something like that so easily, *I* probably will every time." He leaned against the brick fireplace. "I'll never be able to go anywhere alone. I'll be trapped."

Her heart sank at his defeated tone. He was far too much the despondent Finbarr she'd met upon first arriving in Hope Springs, and all on account of her foolishness.

"I have travelled all over this country," she reminded him. "Losing your vision does not have to stop you from doing what you want."

He walked off as he muttered, "It stops everything."

Cecily was sorely tempted to follow his lead and do a bit of muttering and foot dragging herself. Though Finbarr likely wouldn't have guessed, and she'd never tell him, she was every bit as discouraged and overwhelmed as he was. Often, a world without sight was indeed a frightening place, and she hated feeling helpless. But she had decided long ago that she, not her vision, would determine the course of her life. Almost daily she fought against the worry and disappointment of encroaching darkness, but she never surrendered. She might not be able to stop the deterioration of her sight, but she refused to simply lie down and accept it.

Tavish moved to follow Finbarr.

"Allow him a moment," Cecily said. "Discouragement will be his frequent companion. He must discover for himself how to navigate those feelings."

"Is that something you've learned to do?" he asked.

"I am an expert at it."

Tavish abandoned the pursuit of his brother and moved, instead, to the window. "Saints, what a storm. 'Tis a regular Grand Pounding."

"What's a Grand Pounding?" She stretched her legs out, moving her toes closer to the warmth of the fire.

"We Irish coined that phrase early in our years here. A Grand

Pounding is a fierce storm that rages for days on end, leaving high drifts and icy bits everywhere. We had one like this two winters ago. The snow piled higher than the door and windows."

"Good heavens." She could hardly imagine. "How long will I have to stay here?"

"That'd be difficult to guess," Tavish answered. "Once the snow lets up, we can test it, see if it's solid enough for walking on. Could be days, though."

"What about Mrs. Claire?" Her heart pounded once more. "If she's snowed in all alone—"

"I'd wager she'll not have left my parents' house yet," Tavish said. "They'll take one look at all of this and keep her there."

"*You* didn't notice it," Cecily pointed out.

"Only because you didn't tell me you were leaving," Tavish said. "Slipped out without a word, you did."

"I didn't want to disrupt you and Finbarr."

"Should the matter arise again, I'll tell you with no uncertainty that I'd very much prefer you to 'disrupt' me before departing. Our weather's full mad this time of year."

She nodded her head in agreement. "I will."

"Easy as that?" He sounded truly surprised. "You'll not argue about bein' independent and not needing help?"

An interesting response, that. "Do people often reject your offers of assistance?"

"One person in particular." He spoke a bit under his breath.

Very interesting, indeed. She didn't have an opportunity to press further, nor did she know if doing so was advisable.

"I'll climb up to the loft and clear m'self a spot," Tavish said, using his full voice once more. "You'll be using the alcove tonight. 'Tis a fair bit warmer there, and I'd say, of the three of us, you're most in need of a warm corner."

"Why would my using the alcove place you in the loft?" He had a bedroom, one with magical windows and an awe-inspiring amount of light. Why would anyone give that up to sleep in a dark and cramped loft? "I don't walk about in my sleep nor will I knock on your door at all hours, if that is what is concerning you. Neither do I feel uneasy at the thought of you being across the way. You needn't abandon your bedchamber on my account."

"It isn't mine."

"It isn't Finbarr's." Who else was there?

"It isn't anyone's," Tavish said. "And that isn't likely to change, so there's little point beating the topic to death. I'll clear a place for me in the loft, and you can use the alcove." Apparently, he'd been sleeping in the alcove.

"I won't take your bed away from you, Tavish. I can make do out here."

He spoke through a tight jaw. "I may not have a fine English upbringing in manners and civility and such, but I do know how to treat a guest."

Was he upset that she'd asked him about the mysterious room of light, or had he truly taken offense at her offer not to toss him out of his own bed? Both, perhaps?

"I hadn't meant to imply that you were uncouth," she insisted.

"When have the Irish ever *not* been viewed that way by—" He cut himself off, but Cecily knew what he'd intended to say: by the English.

Only moments before, he'd been so kind, so comforting. Then, quick as anything, she was his enemy again. Surely he couldn't deny that she had never held his origins against him. Perhaps it was too much to ask for the same consideration in return.

"I will leave it to the two of you to decide what the arrangements will be tonight," Cecily said, "and I will follow your lead. In the meantime, I would appreciate a bit of peace and quiet."

"Her Majesty has spoken." The comment was made with a hint of jest but not enough to take out the sting.

How was it that this man could feel like a safe haven one moment yet turn on her the next?

As she settled into the alcove that night, she pushed thoughts of Tavish and his changeable personality out of her mind. But that left ample room for ruminating on what had nearly happened in the snow. She hadn't been able to save her own life.

What would she do when her vision was gone entirely? That was an utterly unavoidable eventuality. The unfamiliar and bustling train stations that her job required her to pass through would no longer be navigable. She knew how to listen for clues but still needed a bit of vision to orient herself at times. The day would come when she wouldn't have any.

Would she have to stop traveling? Would she be forced to give up the remaining items on her wish list? To never see the ocean again, or the Rocky Mountains? Stop taking on new students? How would she earn a living? Her Braille transcriptions brought her tremendous satisfaction, but no income.

From her bed in the alcove, she stared up into the darkness, pangs of uncertainty gnawing at her. *This will not defeat me. If I only work hard enough, find strength enough, this will not defeat me. Somehow.*

Chapter Seventeen

Tavish had held a number of women over the years. While he wouldn't consider himself immune to the feeling of a woman in his arms, he'd not expected the effect of Cecily filling his embrace.

Not once since her arrival at his doorstep weeks earlier had he let himself wonder what it'd be like to hold her. She'd been too prickly. Too stiff and off-putting. She'd not've welcomed familiarity with the peasantry.

There you go again, Tavish, thinking of her like Her Majesty. Indeed, he'd blundered and called her that to her very face. Though she'd made a show of being above such insults, he'd noted undeniable hurt in her expression. Perhaps the English and the Irish were simply never meant to get along.

None of that had mattered, though, during those moments with her in his arms. She'd been hurting and afraid, and offering her comfort had been the most natural thing in the world. Their embrace hadn't been filled with the hilarity and joyousness of his time with Bridget, nor the unmistakable challenge posed almost constantly by Katie. This moment had been . . . peaceful. For the length of that embrace, one meant to reassure *her*, he'd set aside his own worries and concerns. He'd known an unexpected—and unnerving—sense of having found a haven from the far too frequent storms of life.

He lay on his back in the dark loft, trying to make sense of it all. He liked Cecily well enough, the way anyone might like a neighbor who lends a hand in a crisis. But there'd been nothing comforting or peaceful about their interactions before. His response to their embrace was, in a word, ridiculous.

Perhaps she was becoming a friend. That change would certainly be a bit jarring. Yes, that was it. He was simply struggling to grasp the idea of her, of all people, beginning to feel like a friend.

Friends. Despite his rather sharp words to her earlier, he knew how to be someone's friend. He could manage friendship moving forward.

In the dark stillness of the house, he thought he heard the front door open. 'Twasn't Finbarr, for he slept on the far side of the loft. Cecily, then. But why would she be stepping into the storm after such a harrowing experience?

Perhaps she walked about in her sleep. Tavish snatched up his trousers and pulled them on hastily. While his long nightshirt would have been sufficient, he had no wish to prance about with no trousers with a woman staying in the house.

He climbed down then lit the lantern hanging on a peg near the ladder. If she'd gone wandering, he'd need the light to find her. In the dimness, however, he spotted her standing in the doorway, looking out into the night.

After a moment, she stepped back inside and silently closed the door. She pressed an open palm against it, then rested her forehead there. A posture of such sadness and defeat.

"Were you hoping to go for a bit of a jaunt?"

"I wasn't going to go out in the storm." She spoke calmly, not the smallest bit startled. Apparently, he'd not been as quiet as he'd thought.

He crossed to her, still leaning against the closed door. "You wanted a bit of a cold breeze, then? Or the bite of wind-driven snow against your face?"

"Do not mock me, Tavish." She made to push past him, but he stopped her with a gentle hand on her arm.

"I wasn't mocking, I swear to you. I tease a great deal. 'Tis simply my way."

She turned her head the tiniest bit in his direction. Where were her spectacles? He'd never seen her without them. He'd wondered at their purpose, but seeing how she kept her eyes closed now, he guessed they protected her eyes in some way.

"I suppose I'm a little sensitive," she said. "My reception here has not been entirely warm."

He slipped his hand around hers, intending to apologize for the treatment she'd endured. But the frigidity of her fingers forced a change of subject. "Come over to the hearth. I'll build the fire up again."

She was either tired or in complete agreement; she made not the slightest resistance. He fetched her blanket from the alcove, then brought it back, laying it over her lap.

"Thank you." She pulled it up all the way to her neck. "I hadn't expected to be hit with snow while under the porch overhang."

"That's a Wyoming storm for you." He took the fire poker to the embers, stirring air into them so they'd burn a bit hotter. "The wind here never stops; it simply shifts between somewhat gentle and trying to knock your house over." He carefully laid some kindling, then blew on it a bit to help the fire catch and grow.

"How long will the storm last?"

"Could taper off by morning. Or it might be a day or two. 'Tis a hard thing to know." He shifted back on his feet and watched the fire. "This is our eleventh winter here, so we've learned to prepare for the worst. We've a great deal of firewood at every house, a stock of food as well. Once this storm blows past, we'll hitch up a sleigh or two and head out to chop more wood to replenish our supplies."

"Is that how long ago you left Ireland? Eleven years?"

"Heavens, no. We left when I was but a lad. Finbarr was born in this country." He set a log on the fire, watching to make certain it caught.

"But you all still sound so Irish."

He chuckled to himself. "You left England a good while ago, and you still sound very English."

A reluctant smile tugged at her lips. "Point taken."

Her eyes were still closed. His curiosity was full eating at him, but he felt instinctively that asking about her eyes would not be a welcome intrusion.

"Do you miss Ireland?" she asked.

"Ireland is my mother, the place of my birth. 'Tis where my grandparents are now buried, and all my family before them. Who I am, who my family is, was shaped by Ireland. She's in our blood."

"I feel the same about England." Her expression turned more contemplative. "And yet, America has begun to feel like home."

"Aye. She has a way of doing that to a person." He pulled a chair up beside hers. "Those who've lived here all their lives struggle to understand how we can feel a loyalty to both places at once, how we can feel the pull of our homeland while still thinking of this land as home."

She tucked her legs up beside her, turning a bit so she faced him a little more. "What do you remember most about Ireland?"

"Green," he answered fondly. "A rather generic answer, considering she's known far and wide as The Emerald Isle, but that is truly what I think of. So many shades of green everywhere. For a land so devastated by battles and wars and famines and death, Ireland is somehow still the very picture of life and vibrancy. I've never seen her equal. M' grandfather used to say, 'There are as many shades of green as there are types of people in this world, and though they look different, they're all beautiful and worth takin' note of.'"

"I miss green, too."

He nodded slowly. "I've heard England is near about as green as Ireland."

She shook her head. "I don't mean that green is what I miss *about England.* I miss green in general. I can hardly see it now. I only see very muddied and murky versions of the color." Her mouth turned downward. "I miss it."

He hadn't thought of that. Could Finbarr still see colors? The lad had never said. And what else did Finbarr miss with the same sadness now in Cecily's voice?

What would it take to transform that heavy tone to a jesting one once more? Or a happier one at the very least?

"What was one of your favorite things about England?" He'd hoped speaking of her homeland would bring her some measure of enjoyment.

Her solemn countenance remained. "You'll only laugh."

"I do laugh a great deal," he acknowledged, "but never *at* people."

She took what appeared to be a fortifying breath. Something about sharing her memories with him was, apparently, nerve-racking. "I grew up in the north of England, where it snowed in the wintertime. I used to love sitting at the window of my bedchamber and watching the snow fall. Sometimes it fluttered and danced to the earth. Other times, it came down driven and harsh. I used to imagine that the snow matched Mother Nature's mood. When she was happy, the snow fell soft and gentle. When she was angry, the snow was punishing. But no matter her feelings as it fell, the result was always beautiful: a world blanketed in white. I loved that. Snow is amongst my clearest, most comforting memories of home."

And yet, the memory seemed clouded in sadness.

"Is that why you went out just now? To watch the snow?"

Her shoulders drooped. "I know full well my vision is too far gone for that; there is simply not enough light. But my heart seems unable to accept that. I convinced myself once again that I'd be able to see what I no longer can, so I pulled myself out of a warm bed on a fool's errand." Such heartache hung in her words.

"And could you see it?"

"Of course not." She turned away from him again. "That is what comes of letting emotions and memories get the best of one's judgement."

If ever a woman needed cheering, this one did. "I will strike a deal with you, Cecee. Come morning, when the animals need tending, no matter Mother Nature's mood, I'll allow you to make the trek to the barn in my place. That way, even though you cannot see the snow, you'll be able to experience it. I'd make that great sacrifice for you."

"Oh, would you? How very generous of you."

Thank heavens she'd recognized his teasing. Katie had often misunderstood his attempts to cheer her with jests. "I am a very generous fellow, really."

"It is rather silly of me, I know, wanting so badly to see the snow."

"There's not a thing silly about missing something that means so much to you." He mourned many things and people who had been taken from him.

"But I tell my students not to dwell on what they've lost. It tears a person to pieces." Her shoulders rose and fell with a deep, pained breath. "I'm a hypocrite."

Tavish slipped his hand around hers once more. "No. You don't dwell on what you've lost, Cecee. You have moments when missing it is a hard thing, and no one would fault you for that. During the in-between times, though, you live your life just as you've told Finbarr to do. You need not be so harsh with yourself."

“Will you remind me of that now and then?”

He squeezed her fingers. “If you promise to laugh with me now and then. That’s how I manage to not dwell on the things life has taken from me.”

“Gladly.” She spoke with palpable relief. “I dearly love to laugh. The family I worked for last was quite somber and disinclined to tease or jest. I had a very difficult time with them.”

“It seems we see eye to eye on something,” he said.

“I promise not to tell anyone if you won’t.” She offered him a conspiratorial look, but with her eyes still closed.

“Agreed.”

And, quick as that, he’d formed an alliance with a woman he hadn’t even liked in the beginning. If that wasn’t the very recipe for disaster, he wasn’t sure what was.

Chapter Eighteen

Cecily wasn't usually one for making personal confessions. Yet the night before, she'd told Tavish O'Connor her deepest worries and secrets. The man knew how much she missed watching the snow, something she'd never confessed to anyone. She hadn't been wearing her spectacles, a risk she didn't generally take. In her sleepiness, she might very well have opened her eyes and laid bare just how hideous a sight they were now that the milkiness had grown nearly opaque and all-consuming.

"How do I know if the eggs are ready to flip over?" Finbarr asked, pulling Cecily's thoughts back to the moment.

She'd been up and about for more than an hour, but her mind continually returned to those uncharacteristic moments the night before.

"Memorize how long, approximately, each preparation method requires and time it," she told him. "In cases where you've lost track of the time, listen to the sizzle and pay attention to the smell." She was beyond pleased that Finbarr was finally so willing to learn. "Of course, if you smell charring, you've waited too long."

He laughed softly. "I figured that much on my own. What do you think? Is it time to flip them?"

She listened and took in the scent. "Yes, I think so. You won't have to cook as long on the other side."

"I'll probably break the yokes," Finbarr warned.

"For the most part, you'll be cooking for yourself, so appearance will be of absolutely no concern. Anyone else you cook for will simply need to learn to be grateful for the food and not worry over the presentation."

"I need to develop a thick skin, is what you're saying?"

She could hear his wooden spoon scraping the inside of the pan. Once he set his mind to something, he stuck to it. That trait would serve him well. "A thick skin, yes, but also a sense of accomplishment that doesn't depend on others' approval."

"Will people be harder on me, or easier, do you think?" An intelligent question. He seemed to understand his unique situation better than she might have expected of one who'd only recently been forced into it.

"Both," she answered. "Some people will dismiss what you do because they don't think it's good enough. Others will see your blindness as a reason to think of you in the same terms as a child. When you find someone who treats you like a whole person, keep them in your life. They're gold."

"I wondered why you were so tough when you first came. You didn't accept any excuses, and you pushed and pushed me. But you were just showing me that I could do more than I was doing."

She felt like shouting for joy. He understood. He recognized what she had been working toward.

"The eggs smell done," he said. "I think." In time, he would grow more confident.

"I think so, too. Move the pan to the other side of the stove, then pull down some plates. Bear in mind, when you return, you'll need to take a moment to remind yourself which side of the stove is hot so you don't get burned."

She left him to his task, which he'd taken to quickly. Against the din of clanking plates and pans, her thoughts drifted back to Tavish. He'd gone out earlier to tend to his animals, insisting he'd be back in an hour. She knew more time had passed than that. Logic told her he had likely come across more work than he'd anticipated: frozen water troughs, perhaps a leak in the roof somewhere.

"How long does Tavish usually spend in the barn in the mornings?" she asked Finbarr.

"An hour before breakfast," he said. "Then he goes back out afterward to finish up."

Tavish ought to have been back by now. The snow hadn't let up, so he'd tied a rope between the house and the barn. She could hold and follow that if need be. But if he was simply working, what good would her checking do? She'd end up turning around and coming directly back to the house after making a fool of herself.

What if he hadn't merely fallen behind his time? What if he was hurt or in need of help?

Finbarr knows far more about tending animals than I do. But he didn't yet know how to be truly useful in his sightless state.

She told herself to wait another quarter-hour. If Tavish wasn't back by then, she'd be fully justified in checking on him.

Finbarr's careful footsteps took him from the stove to the table. The clank of the serving plate on the wooden tabletop signaled the setting out of breakfast. "I don't know if I can pour milk into everyone's glasses without making a mess," he confessed uneasily. "Maybe if I had a little more time to practice . . ."

"Everyone can pour their own. I'm certain your brother would be willing to fill your glass for you, if you'd like. You've done quite a lot already today. There's no need to push yourself harder than you can go."

"I feel ridiculous, though. These are all things I used to do without thinking about them."

She set a reassuring hand on his arm. "Few things will be as easy as they once were. But they will get easier."

Still no sign of Tavish.

"Do you think we ought to eat without your brother? I don't want your breakfast to get cold—mine, either, for that matter. But I'd hate to start without him."

"He'll be back soon; I'm sure of it." Finbarr pulled a chair out. Rustling fabric told her he sat down in it. A hungry, growing boy wasn't likely to wait on a latecomer.

"Maybe I'll go check to see how much longer he'll be." She moved to the door and the hook on which her coat hung. "You eat. We'll neither of us begrudge you a meal that you worked so hard to make."

But the door opened before she reached it, a blast of frigid air immediately filling the space, snow coming in with it and reaching her still a good few feet inside.

"'Tis coming down something fierce out there." His broad silhouette crossed directly to the kitchen stove. "I had to give the animals extra bedding to help keep them warm."

"Sit down and have your breakfast," Cecily instructed. "That'll warm you."

"I never turn down a hot meal," he said.

From the far side of the table, Finbarr offered a caveat. "Even if that hot meal was prepared by a blind man?"

The young man was forever fluctuating between determined, doubtful, and despondent. Cecily didn't yet understand him well enough to know how to help him find and keep his confidence.

"*Begor*, Finbarr." Tavish whistled low. "You made the meal this morning? You truly did?"

"It's only eggs," Finbarr said.

"But eggs you made your own self, lad. You know what this means, don't you?"

Please, Tavish. Don't make him feel condescended to.

"That I'm no longer a baby," Finbarr muttered.

"You've not been a baby for years and years. What this means is I can start on my sinister plan to make you my oppressed and under-appreciated manservant. At last!"

Finbarr laughed deep from the belly. The sound was devoid of the worry and defeat so often present in him. Thank the heavens for Tavish and his teasing.

"You do realize, Tavish," Finbarr said, "the Irish don't respond peaceably to oppression."

"They also don't respond well to early mornings. I'll simply agree to meet you on the field of rebellion at an unholy hour and win by default."

"But you're Irish as well," Finbarr reminded him. "No one can win if neither of us is awake."

"Then we'll set our skirmish for noon, and I'll still be the victor."

"You wouldn't stand a chance, old man."

Tavish stepped closer. "'Old man,' is it?"

Their silhouettes immediately undertook a jovial tussle, despite Finbarr being seated and Tavish yet standing. They tossed back and forth increasingly ridiculous insults and challenges, punctuated by laughter. Cecily leaned against the wall not far from the stove. She pressed a hand to her heart as an unexpected surge of emotion stole over her. Both men seemed happier in that moment than she could remember them being. They were interacting without the frustration of earlier weeks and without the cloud of worry that hung over the entire O'Connor family.

"Call me old again, lad. I'm daring you to."

She could just see enough of them to know that Tavish held his brother bent low, one arm pinning his head against Tavish's side. Finbarr didn't appear to be fighting the position. Indeed, he hadn't stopped laughing.

"For someone so ancient, you're surprisingly strong," Finbarr said.

Tavish didn't release his brother. "Are you hearing this, Cecee? Are you hearing the abuse this lad is heapin' on his innocent brother?"

"It seems you have a truly Irish uprising on your hands," she said.

"I'm staging an *Irish* uprising?" Finbarr sounded rather theatrically horrified. "I'm going to die!"

Tavish's laughter returned, deeper and louder than before. He pushed his brother away. "'I'm going to die,' he says." He sat at the table. "Saints, the blasphemy pouring out of this boy's mouth. His Irish ancestors are likely to come haunt him for what he's said about them."

"That they're all dead?" Finbarr tossed back from the far end of the table. "I doubt my observation took them by surprise."

Tavish chuckled once more. Finbarr joined in.

They were laughing, enjoying each other's company in a way that fit them far better than their usual tense discomfort. Her throat turned thick as her eyes began to burn. She tried to blink the tears away, but her heart was overflowing.

She'd been so certain a mere week earlier that Finbarr was a lost cause. She'd braced herself to lose another student. But there was hope now.

The brothers' tussle ended rather abruptly, silence settling over the room.

"Cecee?" Tavish's joviality had been quickly replaced with concern.

Her emotions must have been showing on her face. She tried to wave his comment off, but found she couldn't. She always did this—she let herself care so deeply that her students' suffering and fears, joys and triumphs, affected her on a very personal level.

"Excuse me a moment." She spoke quickly and moved away.

She bumped hard into something. Her hand shot out and struck a kitchen chair. She'd misjudged her distance from the table. The sooner she replaced her cane, the better. With measured steps, she moved toward the fireplace. The slow progress was embarrassing, but continuing to wear her emotions on her sleeve would be more embarrassing. She needed a moment to get herself firmly under control.

She fumbled her way to the alcove. The spot was far enough removed from the kitchen corner to grant her a little privacy. However, Tavish followed her there.

"Are you upset, Cecily?" he asked. "We were only jesting. Finbarr's not upset."

"I know." She didn't turn back. A few more deep breaths were all she'd need, and she'd be composed enough to face him. "And I'm not upset."

"But you looked it just now when you walked away."

She thought quickly. "I was only mourning the loss of my cane. I'm bumping into things left and right without it."

The smell of hay wafted about as he stepped up next to her. "You were upset before you took a single step. 'Twasn't anything to do with knocking into that chair."

"I'm not upset," she insisted.

His hand rested warm on her arm. "Cecily?"

She turned the tiniest bit toward him. "I really am not. I was actually happy."

"Do you often cry when you're happy?" His incredulous tone nearly brought a laugh to the surface. Did men not understand the reality of happy tears?

She had regained much of her composure. Finbarr had remained at the table, distant enough that, if she lowered her voice, he wasn't likely to overhear.

"I've been so worried about him," she said quietly. "He's been learning a great deal, but he still seems incredibly unhappy. So hearing him laugh—"

"I know it," Tavish matched her volume. "I feel like I'm getting my brother back by bits. He's been so far away for too long."

She felt in control enough to turn to him more fully. "Finbarr will still have difficult days. A great many of them. But I finally feel hopeful that he'll pull through his troubles."

"This family's been through a great many troubles." He sighed. "It'd be nice for one of us to emerge happier on the other side."

That was an unexpected thing to say. "Have you not emerged from your troubles happier, Tavish?"

He didn't answer for a drawn-out moment. "I've ended wiser. That's good enough."

Good enough, perhaps, but not at all the same. Here, then, was another piece of the O'Connor family puzzle: Tavish, who teased and jested and laughed his way through most everything, was not happy.

Chapter Nineteen

Tavish came in from shoveling snow in the afternoon to find Cecily sitting at the kitchen table, leaning dangerously close to the lantern. "You'll burn your face, lass."

She straightened and tossed a folded piece of paper onto the table. "I can't read it."

"What is it?" He crossed to her.

"A letter from a former student." She rubbed her forehead. "Usually, if I hold a paper close enough to a lantern and lean in, I can make out the words, but I've been trying for a couple of weeks now, and I can't see the letters well enough."

"I'm sorry to hear it," he said.

"I'm sorry to say it."

Though her expression wasn't pained or angry, it held a sadness that called out for comfort. Tavish leaned against the table. "Are you needing to talk to someone, Cecee?"

She shook her head firmly and without hesitation. "I'll not burden you with my troubles."

"'Tisn't a burden to lend an ear," he said. "I'm a fine listener."

"When I finish pouring out all of my miseries, will you promise to make me laugh?"

He pressed his hand to his heart. "My word of honor."

She stood and paced away, clutching her hands tightly in front of her. "My poor sight is the result of a disease, rather than an injury. This disease causes repeated episodes of vision loss. Usually when my vision begins deteriorating again, I experience pain—heavens, so much pain—but there hasn't been any lately."

"Pain in your eyes?" That sounded horrible.

She nodded, pacing back toward him. "Without pain, I've assumed my sight wasn't slipping again. But I can't read the letter, though I've tried over and over in different amounts of light. So it must be my vision after all." Her next breath was slow and heavy. When she spoke again, her voice was quiet. "I'm not ready for more darkness yet, Tavish. There are so many things I haven't seen yet."

Oh, she needed cheering. She needed it badly. And he *had* promised to make her laugh. "For example, you've not seen my handsome face yet."

A smile pulled at her lips. "Yes, that is what I am most hoping to see with my last bits of vision."

"As well it should be." He took the chair next to the one she'd been using. "Grown women have been known to swoon at the merest glimpse. Grown men have been consumed with envy."

"What a burden to carry all these years." Laughter touched her tone, so near the surface. What would it take to pull that laugh from her fully?

"I think I've borne it well. I've done the family name proud, which is the important thing." He spoke as solemnly as he could manage. "Though I suppose food on the table and a roof over one's head would come a very close second."

"It is good to know you have your priorities straight." She sat once more. Her smile was firmly in place. "Thank you."

"For what, Cecee?"

She bumped his shoulder with hers. "For giving me a reason to smile when I felt like crying. That is a fine thing."

"I've always felt that way, myself, though not everyone does."

Katie, in fact, had found his jesting during difficult moments more frustrating than helpful. He'd been so helpless to see her through her troubles. Nothing he did had ever seemed to be what she'd wanted or needed.

He glanced at Cecily's discarded letter. "The lettering on this note of yours is a bit faint. That may account for you not being able to make out the words."

"Do you think so? And, please, say you do even if you don't. I need a reason other than my inevitable blindness to explain this."

"I *do* think so."

She turned her head in his direction, those green spectacles of hers hiding her eyes as always. "Are you able to read it to me, by chance?"

Good grief. "Try to endure your shock, lass, but there *are* a few among the Irish who aren't illiterate."

She growled low in her throat, a sound he would never have expected to hear. "No one in this town is ever going to give me the benefit of the doubt, not even you."

"You asked if I was able to read," he reminded her. "A rather belittling question, you have to admit."

She shook her head in clear frustration. "I meant, 'Given all the work you have to accomplish around here, have you the time to read my letter to me, or are you too busy?' Of course, why should you assume I meant something fair and reasonable when there is any possibility of interpreting my words in the most negative light possible? Where would be the triumph in that?" Her tone was as dry as a desert.

He wanted to insist that she was being unfair, that her people's treatment of his more than warranted some wariness and assumptions on his part. When it came to being friends with an Irishman, the English . . . need not apply.

Need not apply. A phrase he knew all too well.

Saints, he was doing to her what so many had done to him and his countrymen. How often had he railed against the treatment the Irish endured in this new country? Yet he was treating her no better. He'd heard her manner of speech, learned of her English origins, and had promptly begun treating her as someone less than deserving of consideration.

"I'm sorry, Cecily." He crossed to where she stood. "I'm letting old hurts color my view of you. 'Tis unfair of me."

"It most certainly is."

"I, honestly, am surprised you don't seem to hold our Irishness against us," he said. "This age-old animosity goes both ways."

She shrugged a single shoulder. "I will admit I was not raised to have a favorable view of the Irish. But then I found myself part of a group of people who had little power over our own destinies and who were too often at the mercy of those who cared not at all what fate awaited us."

The blind, she meant.

"It opened my eyes, if you'll pardon the expression. I found I could no longer cling to assumptions about others, many of whom were powerless and oppressed in their own ways." She held her hands out in a show of acceptance. "I found myself hurting for them rather than blaming them for hurting. Compassion, I discovered, is a great equalizer."

"And a great humbler," Tavish added, feeling more than a little meek himself. "Will you forgive me, Cecee? For my comments just now, for the many unkind things I've said since you came, for fashionin' you such an unfeeling nickname?"

"You don't think 'Your Majesty' is fitting?"

"Not in the way I intended it to be."

Her lips tightened. "I'm not certain that's a better answer."

He reached out and grabbed her discarded note. "I'll read your letter to you if you'd still like me to."

She kept her head turned in his direction, not so much as glancing at the letter. "You don't mean to tell me in what way 'Your Majesty' is still fitting?"

"I'm determined to maintain my aura of mystery. 'Tis the most interesting thing about me."

"I thought that was your handsome face," she said.

He leaned closer and whispered, "It's both."

She laid her jaw on her upturned palm, her elbow on the table, almost smiling despite their disagreement. She had her share of worries and troubles, too many of which had been brought on by his family and the other Irish townspeople, yet she maintained a happy outlook. He liked that. He liked it a terrible lot.

"Now"—he turned his attention to the letter—"shall we see what this former student of yours has to say?"

"Yes, please." Quick as that, she seemed to have forgiven him, at least a little.

"'Dear Miss Attwater.'" He lowered the letter. "*This* student knows you're a 'miss.' 'Tis more than we knew, you'll recall."

She shook her head, and, he'd wager, behind those spectacles, she rolled her eyes.

He returned to his reading. "'I am learning to cook on the stove. Mother says I am doing very well. I am not supposed to light the fire, though, as Father says I'm not careful enough yet.'" He lowered the paper once more. He assumed a teasing tone. "Can't light a fire? Can he tie his own shoes, I'd like to know. Our Finbarr managed that."

"This student is only eight years old."

"Excuses, Cecee. Eight years is old enough to be useful. I built the Crystal Palace in New York when I was eight years old."

She yet rested her head against her hand. "You were a very industrious child."

"Indeed. I'm no lay about sort of fellow, not like the lazy bones in this letter."

She laughed. Only a moment earlier, he'd wondered if he could pull a laugh from her. The task had proven easier than he'd imagined. "Thomas is a dear boy. You speak kindly of him, you grumpy old man."

"Be nice. I'm doing you a favor, you prickly old woman."

She tucked a strand of golden hair behind her ear. "I wish you'd been around the past few years, Tavish. I've needed someone to laugh with."

"So've I." Heavens, he had. Bridget had smiled and jested along with him. Even Katie had on occasion. But they were both gone, and he'd spent a far sight too many hours alone, searching for a reason to be happy again.

"What else does Thomas have to say?" Cecily asked.

He read her the rest of her letter, one filled with recounting lessons the boy had been diligently completing and a troublesome puppy that left hair all over the house. All in all, it was a sweet letter, one that spoke both of fondness and respect for Cecily as well as for the role she'd played in his life.

When Cecily told him that the boy had likely written the letter himself, a new surge of hope sprung up in Tavish. Finbarr could learn to write again as well. Perhaps he'd never read—Cecily herself struggled with that—but there seemed a great many things he could relearn to do if he was willing. And he had a capable teacher. A capable, kind, caring, beautiful . . . teacher.

Finbarr had said very little all afternoon. Cecily was certain he sat slouched in his chair, sulking. Despite his lighthearted moment with Tavish that morning, an afternoon of despondency was not unexpected. Her students fluctuated between hopeful and hopeless while they adjusted to their new lives. She had, herself. Still did on occasion.

"If the snow holds off and we manage to clear out the field beside Ma and Da's place, we'll be holding one last *céilí*." Tavish said. "You should come, Finbarr."

No response.

Cecily crossed to the fire. She held out her hands to warm them.

"What about you, Cecee? Would you come to the *céilí*?"

The laugh she attempted to hold back emerged as a snort. "I may be blind, but I'm not stupid. No one at the party wished me to be there. Returning would only make everyone miserable."

"I'm certain—"

"Tavish, they sang a song about how terrible I am." Surely he remembered that.

"Not you in particular."

Did he truly think it was not intended to be personal? "They sang of the country of which I am considered a symbol. I half expected to discover I was to be burned in effigy."

"We did have a large bonfire conveniently located nearby," Tavish said.

As if agreeing, the fire currently located nearby popped.

Cecily turned enough to direct her next words to Finbarr. "I've been told you always enjoyed the *céilís*."

He made an indecipherable noise.

She tried a different tactic. "What was your favorite part of the gatherings?"

"I don't know." He was back to muttering. Not a good sign.

"The storytelling?"

Another wordless noise.

"The music? Do you play an instrument?"

"No," Finbarr said.

"You do so," Tavish interjected. "The lad plays the penny whistle."

"Not anymore," Finbarr muttered.

Here was another insight in to his struggles. "Do you no longer play because of your eyes? You can still play without clear sight, you know."

"How?" It was as much a demand as a sincere question.

"The same way you tie your shoes: by feel and sound." That had not emerged quite right. "The whistle by sound I mean, not the shoes."

He didn't respond, and she couldn't see him well enough to know if he'd shrugged or nodded or brushed her words aside.

"Did you ever dance at the *céilís*?" she asked Finbarr. "A young man your age must have enjoyed taking a young lady in his arms for the length of a tune."

Finbarr remained firmly entrenched in his silence.

"In case you're curious," Tavish said, "the lad's blushing like a schoolgirl."

She'd hit the nail on the head, then. It wasn't the penny whistle that kept him away. He'd attended the *céilís* to socialize and woo young ladies. But how did a blind man dance if he couldn't see the other couples or the boundaries of the dancing floor?

"I'm not sure how to help with that," she admitted. "As a woman, I don't have the same trouble. I can rely on my partner's lead to keep me from wandering too far afield."

"Do you dance, Cecee?"

"You've asked me that before," she reminded him.

"But you didn't really answer," he shot back. "Do you dance?"

"I do, and I'm told I am not terrible at it."

"Shall we see if she's as 'not terrible' as she claims, Finbarr?" The chair squeaked as Tavish stood. "We've a decent amount of open room here. Finbarr'd whistle a tune for us, I'm sure. And I happen to be a very fine dancer."

"Is he exaggerating, Finbarr?"

"All I will say is the lasses have been lining up for years, and they keep coming back. Dancing with him can't be too miserable an experience for them."

She was feeling uncharacteristically cheeky. "I've heard about the Catholic adherence to the need for paying penance. Perhaps dancing with him is an act of purifying punishment."

"Oh, now you've set m' pride on the line, you have." Tavish was up next to her in an instant. He took her hand. "You'll be begging my pardon after a single turn about the room."

"Or begging you to stop," she suggested.

"Whistle something sweet and slow, Finbarr. Cecee here's going to be danced with." He slid his right arm around her waist and took her right hand in his left.

"You haven't told me yet which dance we're dancing."

"The waltz, you loon," he said in tones of mock scolding. "What other dance lets a fellow hold a woman like this?"

"And that's why you like it?"

His face filled the space beside hers with warmth and the musky scent of his shaving lotion. "In this moment, I'm liking it very much."

"You are a tease."

"And you enjoy it, dear," he whispered. Then he called out to his brother. "*The Beardless Boy.* Nice and steady."

Finbarr obliged. Tavish swept Cecily into the dance without the slightest catch in his step or hesitation in his movements. Sometimes she'd found that trusting her partners to be mindful of her inability to see her surroundings was a difficult thing. In those cases, she spent the length of the song tense and worried, anticipating a painful collision or stumble at any moment.

She waited for that feeling to come with Tavish. It didn't. After a moment, she simply relaxed and let him lead her about the room. For the first time in a very long while she didn't constantly evaluate every sound, every smell. She didn't have to worry about the clues she'd missed or if she was navigating the world safely. She trusted him enough to simply enjoy the dance.

He spun her around as the whistled tune continued. Around and around. It felt almost like flying. And though she didn't want to end the magical moment, she couldn't help her impulse to tease him a bit.

As they made another turn, she flinched. "Ooh." She hopped backward. "My toe. Ooh."

"Heavens, did I stub your toe?"

She meant to keep the ruse going a bit longer, but couldn't hold back her laugh.

"You vexing colleen. Your toe's not stubbed at all, is it?" Far from sounding offended, Tavish began laughing along with her.

"I couldn't resist," she said.

"You most certainly could have," he countered.

"I had no one to laugh with in Lincoln," she said. "I've missed it terribly."

He pulled her a touch closer as he spun her about in the dance, still chuckling lightly and, she imagined, grinning broadly. "You laugh and tease all you want here, Cecee. 'Tis one of my favorite things."

Cecily leaned her head on his shoulder. She didn't know where the impulse had come from, but the gesture was so natural, she couldn't fight it. She was near enough to see, however vaguely, his chin and neck. Odd how not being able to see a person made such innocuous details feel very personal. She closed her eyes and concentrated on those bits of him that were familiar. His scent. The sound of his boots on the floor. The rich baritone of his voice. The infectiousness of his laugh.

The past few days he'd been quite charming, truth be told. But this moment was different. Dancing with him, Tavish felt like home.

"Despite the damage you've done to my toes, you are proving yourself a fine dancer."

"Vexing. Vexing." He held her so close that she felt the words as he spoke them. "I've been falsely accused, I have."

"Will you forgive me enough to help me think of a way for Finbarr to dance at the *céilís* if he wants to? I haven't the slightest idea how, at least, not yet, but between the three of us, we'll think of something."

"A fine goal," Tavish said. "It'd be good to see you there again, lad." That brought Finbarr's whistling to a halt, and not, she guessed, to one of eager anticipation. "For you to dance would be a fine thing for the lasses."

"I doubt they've missed me much," Finbarr said.

And there was another issue Cecily hadn't thought of: being admired by girls his age would be an important thing for him. Of course it would. He was likely convinced he was looked on with nothing more than pity. That would be a blow to his pride, his hopes, and his fragile confidence all at once.

The tune had stopped, but Tavish still held her close. "We must find a way to help him feel confident enough to spend time with his friends again, to view himself as worthy of wooing a young lady."

"I know." Tavish spoke just as quietly, leaning low so their conversation would be private. "How do we do that?"

"I don't know." She leaned more fully against him once more. "I don't know."

Footsteps sounded on the porch. A quick wrap on the door was followed by its opening. "Tavish?" The voice was Mrs. O'Connor's. "We've come to—" Her words stopped abruptly. "Good heavens, what in the name of Mary Mack is going on here?"

"Cecee was showing Finbarr how someone who can't see can still dance," Tavish said.

"And do all people who can't see end their dances with a . . . hug?"

Tavish laughed, quite as if he couldn't hear the tone of heavy censure in his mother's voice. "If so, I think I'd best find myself a blind woman, as I very much enjoy ending a dance with an embrace."

He was making this worse. Cecily swore she could hear Mrs. O'Connor growing alarmed. And if Cecily was correctly interpreting the second set of heavier footsteps, Mr. O'Connor was there as well, no doubt, just as horrified.

Cecily slipped from Tavish's arms, doing her best to place the others in the room. "Is the road clear enough to leave the house now?"

"It is." Heavens, Mrs. O'Connor's words were cold and clipped.

"I had best make my way back to Mrs. Claire's now," Cecily said. "I'll have no hope of successfully arriving in the dark."

"I'll walk you over," Tavish offered.

"No." She held her hands up in a frantic attempt to stop him. "You stay here with your family."

"Are you certain you can make the return safely? You haven't your cane anymore."

"I'll be careful." She crossed to the coat hooks by the doorway. "Until tomorrow, then."

"Perhaps you could take the next day or two off," Mr. O'Connor said. "You've been trapped here for a couple of days. I'd wager you could all use some time apart." He spoke softly and not truly unkindly, but his words were more demand than suggestion.

"Yes, sir," she answered with a quick dip of her head. "I'll wait until Monday to return."

"That'd be best," Mrs. O'Connor said.

Cecily slipped out, keeping her chin up and her emotions clamped down.

She understood Mr. and Mrs. O'Connor's objection to the very personal circumstances in which they'd found her and Tavish, though truly, nothing untoward had happened. But they'd dismissed

Tavish's explanation out of hand and hadn't seemed to hear in his jesting tone any reassurance that the situation wasn't serious.

Perhaps it didn't matter. Even friendship between her and their elder son was more than they were willing to accept.

The local Irish were unlikely to ever welcome her among them; their song of "greeting" made that clear. She had, however, held out hope that the O'Connors, at least, would allow her a portion of their good opinion.

They seemed grateful enough for her work with Finbarr, but it seemed they'd never allow her to be anything but an enemy.

Chapter Twenty

"She was showing Finbarr how to dance, was she?" Ma was fair glaring Tavish into an early grave. "Why, then, was she in *your* arms?"

"Because the lad would likely have danced her into the fire." He tossed his da a smile that, surprisingly, wasn't returned. "She's still working out a way for Finbarr to dance safely."

"And this demonstration was meant for the benefit of a boy who likely couldn't see it?" Ma said.

"He's not entirely blind," Tavish reminded them.

"It's a dangerous game you're playing, son." Da spoke as he passed on his way to the table, a burlap bag over his shoulder.

"What game is that, then?" Tavish was clearly being accused of something, and he'd very much like to know what.

"They mean flirting with Cecily," Finbarr said.

"Miss Attwater, lad," Ma said. "You're to call her Miss Attwater. She's your teacher, not your friend."

Finbarr slouched in his chair once more. "She said to call her Cecily."

Ma sat near the fireplace. "I don't like how familiar she's

becoming. With either of you." She had a way of biting her lips closed when she was trying hard to be tactful. At the moment, her teeth were near about to pop through her lips.

Tavish crossed to the door. "I need to make certain she finds her way to Granny's."

"She said she could manage on her own," Ma reminded him.

"I imagine she can, but it'll set my mind at ease knowing she's not wandering all over Wyoming." He stepped onto the porch. The cold air stung his face. No matter that he'd been in Hope Springs eleven years, the bitterness of winter here still surprised him.

Cecily was crossing the street at a snail's pace, taking painstakingly careful steps along the path he'd shoveled in the snow that morning. She held one hand out in front of her. The woman needed a cane. Perhaps Mr. Johnson had one at the mercantile. She reached the far side of the road.

A few weeks earlier, she'd tied a rope from Granny's front porch to a bush at the north end of Granny's property. The bush, she'd explained, was easier to spot than the unmarked head of the narrow walking path. Tavish had also shoveled a path following the rope, knowing she'd be returning to Granny's. He was glad to have helped, but part of him wished he'd left it alone. Maybe she wouldn't have run off so quickly.

Da joined him on the porch. "'Tis a reassuring thing to see how independent she is. Gives me hope that our Finbarr'll find his way."

"I think he will," Tavish said.

"We've passed a long year watching him struggle."

Tavish was painfully familiar with the heaviness of Da's tone. The year had been more than long; it'd been terrible. Heartbreaking. "Next year's bound to be better."

"We begin a new year soon," Da said.

"In a few weeks," Tavish said with a nod. They'd not yet reached Christmas.

"No, I mean Wednesday. One year since the fire."

A year. Only a year. Tavish felt in many ways as if a lifetime had passed, a heartbreaking, exhausting lifetime. One look at Da told him 'twas time again to set aside his own burdens and offer reassurance.

"Finbarr has had more moments of being himself again. Just this morning he was laughing and giving me grief."

"Aye, but he's sulking right now," Da pointed out.

"Cecee says that's to be expected. She says he'll go through times when he's discouraged and mournful, but that he'll do better overall. She says to be patient." He could feel Da's gaze on him, so he turned his head slowly that direction. Sure enough, Da watched him with narrowed eyes. "Have I a bit of lunch on m' face or something?"

"Why do you call her 'Cecee'?"

Tavish shrugged. "'Cecily' seemed too formal a name, too prim and stodgy and—"

"And English?" Da tossed in dryly.

Tavish chuckled. "I suppose."

Da wasn't as amused. "You're attempting to make her something she isn't. I'd wager you're also spending a good amount of time teasing her and pestering her so she'll smile and laugh."

"She smiles and laughs plenty on her own." He couldn't help a grin at the memory of her making him think he'd stepped on her toes. He hadn't laughed that easily in some time.

"You did the same with Katie," Da said.

Tavish turned back to the house. "I don't talk about—"

"I know you don't, son. But it's time you did before you get yourself hurt again. You teased Katie into laughing with you the way you'd prefer, and you fashioned her a pet name that didn't fit the person you met but the person you were looking for. In the end, it didn't work between you because she wasn't the woman you were trying to make her into."

"You're not telling me anything I don't know."

"And what if you fall for this Englishwoman?" Da pressed. "You've nothing in common. You were born to hunger and poverty. She was born to privilege. Your early years were spent in a factory. Hers were the idyllic days of a daughter of a manor. You've scraped together all you have. She was given an education and an occupation."

"I think you're getting far ahead of yourself, there."

Da was not put off the topic. "Even if the two of you found a way to overlook all of that, she'd be at odds with half this town for the rest of her life."

"Do you not think the Irish are capable of letting old grudges go? We've done a fine job of it this past year, making amends with our neighbors."

Da shook his head. "Our troubles with Americans go back only a few years. The English've been slaughtering and enslaving us for centuries. Hundreds of years' worth of history is not so easily overcome. There'd always be a chasm, a level of distrust between them. What kind of future would that be?"

In Da's *them* was a terrible strong amount of *us*. Tavish wasn't considering courtship with Cecily. But the arguments his da was making brought to mind her own complaints earlier that day—her very real conviction that no one in Hope Springs would ever allow her to be secure in their good opinion. Tavish hated how true that was beginning to feel.

"I know you're lonely, son, but you can't make people into something they're not and expect to find happiness. Bridget was light and joyful even when the two of you were apart," Da said. "She teased you as much as you teased her. You didn't need to change her. She fit you, Tavish. The two of you were each other's match."

"Yes, but she's dead." He set his hand on the doorknob. "I found my match, and the heavens snatched her away."

"I don't want to see you hurt again."

"Set your mind at ease, Da, and tell Ma to do the same." Tavish shook his head. "I've joked about finding myself a golden-haired Englishwoman to fall in love with, but I've no intention of doing so. None." He'd given up on women. "She's Finbarr's teacher and a friend. Nothing beyond."

"Are you certain of that, son?"

He met his da's eyes. "Quite." He'd learned his lesson; the vengeful heavens had made absolutely certain of that.

A man could find a great many things to do when he wished to distract himself. Tavish kept very busy the day Cecily returned.

He'd missed her more than he'd expected to. It seemed Da was at least partly correct; Tavish had let himself grow attached to her, something not at all advisable. Not only was the entire town rather unfond of her—of her roots, at least—his own family didn't care for Cecily either. Beyond that, she'd leave as soon as she'd taught Finbarr all he needed to know.

Every person Tavish let himself care about left him. Every single one. He couldn't let himself care like that again.

So when she returned to teach Finbarr on Monday, Tavish took on extra chores in the barn, and on Tuesday he mended a section of fence in the bone-chilling wind and nearly knee-deep snow, anything to keep him away from the house. He'd agreed to be her friend—he *wanted* to be—but friendship seemed less and less wise. His family worried about his interactions with Cecily, and they had worries enough already.

He trudged through the snow, his bag of tools slung over his back, his coat buttoned up to his neck to keep out the weather. He'd head home long enough to have a bite to eat and thaw his frozen body, but he'd keep his distance from Cecily. His family would fret less if he did. When his loved ones were hurting, he made it right. No matter what it took.

He shook the snow from his feet and hat before stepping inside the house. Cecily stood near the fireplace. Finbarr sat in his usual chair. After hanging his hat on its peg, Tavish crossed to the stove, intending to eat quickly and be on his way.

"Are you feeling unwell, Finbarr?" Cecily asked.

"No."

"Did you sleep well last night?" she pressed.

"I slept fine." His tone was clipped. Something was definitely bothering the lad. He had taken to brooding silence ever since their parents' visit, and Tavish wasn't entirely sure why.

"Are you concerned about helping at the wood pile tomorrow?"

Tavish, himself, was a bit nervous about that. Even sighted, a person needed to be particularly careful not to topple a wood pile.

"I am certain you feel I am being unforgivably nosey," Cecily said. "But, Finbarr, I am a little concerned that your reticence today is the result of frustration with our lessons. I can't change what I am doing if I don't know what is bothering you."

Finbarr shook his head. Sometimes even he forgot that Cecily couldn't see him.

"Are the tasks I'm giving you too difficult?"

"No."

"Too easy?"

"No."

She was getting nowhere. Tavish stepped in. "Would you tell us, lad, whether 'tis Cecily or myself you're put-out with?"

"Neither." He rose abruptly.

"Then Da or Ma?"

"No." Finbarr dragged his feet all the way to the ladder. "Not Mary or Ciara or Biddy or anyone else, either. I told you I was fine, and I am." He went up the first rung.

"Fin—"

"I'm fine." He climbed. "I'm not upset. I'm not frustrated. And I'm not going tomorrow." He disappeared into the darkness above.

Tomorrow. Wednesday. Saints preserve us.

"What's tomorrow?" Cecily lowered her voice.

"It's the anniversary of the fire." Saying the words struck him with stomach-turning force. "There's to be a ceremony."

"The fire in which Finbarr lost his sight?" Cecily asked.

"Aye."

Cecily pressed her hands together and rested her fingertips against her lips. "It's no wonder, then, that he's in turmoil. His grief is still so very raw. What a horrifying prospect—passing through that pain with all the town watching."

'Twould be a difficult thing for the lad, that was for certain. "I don't know whether to tell him he can stay here, or if it'd be best for him to attend." He hoped she would have a better idea than he did. She'd worked with students whose sight had been taken in traumatic ways.

After a long moment, she squared her shoulders. "He won't thank either of us for insisting on it, but he needs to go. Marking the anniversary of that tragedy understandably terrifies him. The day will be terribly difficult. But, Tavish, your brother has been hiding too long."

Chapter Twenty-one

The next day, Finbarr sat in stony silence at the back of the schoolhouse as the rest of the town filed in for the ceremony. The glare on his fire-scarred face acted as a warning. No one spoke to him. No one approached. He was left utterly alone, which Tavish didn't doubt had been his goal.

Reverend Ford rose and stood at the front of the somber gathering. "Friends," he began. "I wish we were assembled to mark a less-solemn occasion."

Though much had changed over the past year, changes that deserved celebrating, the tragedy that had triggered those changes was a horrific one.

Near the front, Katie sat in Joseph's embrace. The two Archer girls leaned against the both of them. This would be a difficult day for their family, as well.

Finbarr's glower didn't subside in the least. The fleeting smiles and moments of laughter the lad had indulged in of late were nowhere to be seen. "Why did I have to come?" he muttered not yet two minutes into the ceremony.

"Because you were part of that day," Tavish whispered back.

Finbarr folded his arms across his chest. “I’m nothing but a monument, something the town stares at so they won’t forget something terrible.”

“No one thinks of you that way, lad.”

“They all do.” Finbarr had been so much his old self the past couple of weeks that seeing the return of his moping and muttering side was proving difficult to endure.

“This is a difficult anniversary to mark,” Reverend Ford continued. “So much was lost that night.”

Finbarr grew paler. He rocked forward and backward, clutching and unclutching his fingers. His jaw worked furiously, though he made not a sound.

“For that reason,” the reverend continued, “we will mark this day each year, to make certain this town never forgets the price of hatred, prejudice, and divisiveness.”

Finbarr stood and, hands following the back wall, made his way quickly and gracelessly out of the small chapel. Fortunately, they were seated near the back; his exit wouldn’t be noticed by very many.

Yet, somehow, Cecily noticed from the row in front of them. She followed closer on Finbarr’s heels than Tavish did.

“How did you—?”

“I know the sound of someone stumbling toward a door he cannot see,” she whispered.

The winter was cold, and the room unheated. Everyone had kept hold of their coats, which had only made Finbarr’s exit that much faster, as he’d not needed to stop to bundle himself against the weather. He was outside and on his way with only the shortest of hesitations.

Tavish and Cecily were a few paces behind. The sun was out and shining brightly, but it did little to warm the air. Tavish shoved his hands into the warmth of his pockets, watching Finbarr walk away from the school house.

"Is he at least headed in the right direction?" Cecily asked.

"He's headed toward home," Tavish said. "I wonder if that is where he thinks he is heading."

"May I hold your arm?" she asked. "I don't know this area of the road at all, and I still haven't replaced my cane."

He took her hand and slipped it through his arm. "Is this a formal turn about the town? Shall I ask your chaperone for permission?"

She tugged his arm, urging him on. "Finbarr has never made this trip on his own. We need to keep within eyesight in case he gets turned around."

We. How long has it been since a woman tucked the two of us so casually into that word? 'Twasn't a difficult question to answer once he thought on it. Katie used to say *we* with tremendous ease. Before her, Bridget had fully and lovingly thought of the two of them in that way. As had he. Heavens, he missed her.

Thinking of Cecily in a way that at all resembled Katie or Bridget hardly aligned with his vow to keep his distance. But he wasn't courting or flirting, he assured himself. Yet he was certainly enjoying her company.

Friendly acquaintances, Tavish. Aim for "friendly acquaintances."

"The lad's slowed down," Tavish told her. "Now he's tipping his head a bit to the side."

"He's listening for the river, most likely. Sound is one of the most important senses out of doors." Her step faltered a moment. "Remind me, though, that we need to get him a cane now that he's wanting to be more independent."

"I talked to Jeremiah Johnson, who runs the mercantile," Tavish said. "He doesn't have a single cane."

"Why were you talking to him about canes?"

"Yours splintered out of all recognition. I was trying to find you a replacement." He wasn't sure if the cold air was making her cheeks redden, or if she was blushing yet again.

"That was very thoughtful of you." Her quiet, thick tone told him the answer: a blush.

Tavish liked that far more than he ought to have. With a firmness of purpose, he returned to the topic at hand. "Seems a good thing that Finbarr's attempting to make his way back on his own."

"It is. Once I've taught him to use a cane, he'll be even more independent. I'll warn you, though, he'll probably hate it at first." She laughed a very little. "I abhorred my cane when my teachers first insisted I learn to use it. But I could never do all that I do without it, especially when navigating unfamiliar places."

He knew a great many people who would never attempt to navigate unfamiliar places even with full use of all their senses.

"What is Finbarr doing now?" she asked.

"He appears to be searching for the bridge. At what point do I figure I ought to just pull m' shirt off and dive into the river to catch him?"

"I am sad I won't be able to see that."

How easily she gave him reason to be lighthearted, even for a moment. "Were you wanting to see me without my shirt on, lass? Seems a touch scandalous, that."

"I'm merely attempting to shed my 'prim and proper' persona. Do you think expressing a growing interest in your bare chest would be sufficient?"

He laughed out loud, but she immediately shushed him.

"We don't want Finbarr to know we're following," she said.

Tavish slowed their pace, keeping a distance. At last Finbarr found the bridge and made his way across.

"Good for him," Cecily said.

"How did you—?"

"I heard his boots on the wood. I told you sound is an important sense."

Tavish hadn't even noticed the sound.

"In fact," she continued, "we should probably wait until he is a little farther down the road before crossing the bridge ourselves. He'll be paying very close attention to every sound around him. He'll hear our footsteps and realize he's being followed."

"Do you think he already knows we're following?"

She shook her head no. "He's not that good yet."

"But you are?" He'd begun the remark as a tease, but realized before the first word was out of his mouth that he already knew the answer.

"I am a nearly sightless woman who travels the country alone. I learned long ago the value of knowing whether someone is following me."

Tavish stopped mid-step. In horror, he pivoted his head to stare at her. "Has that happened? Have you been followed?"

She looked at him in much the way one does with an adorably thick child. "I have also learned the value of carrying a cudgel."

"You have a shillelagh?"

"I do, given to me by a family from Donegal, in fact." She raised her head his direction. "If I told your Irish neighbors that, perhaps they'd stop hating me quite so much. Although, being the evil Englishwoman that I am, even that might not be enough."

He wished he could tell her she was exaggerating. She wasn't. "I like you, Cecee. Englishness and all."

"That is very good of you," she said in a theatrically solemn voice.

He matched her tone. "Yes. Yes, it is."

"I am going to ask a question you will likely find terribly nosey," she said, "but I suspect there are a few things that I will wish I had known sooner."

There were a great many topics he'd rather not discuss. Yet, she'd never been one to pry without good reason. Hesitantly, he told her to ask her question.

"What exactly happened in that barn a year ago? I know there was a fire, and that Finbarr lost his sight, but outside of that, I know nothing." She'd picked quite a topic.

"'Tis a long and ugly story," he warned her.

"I suspected as much," she insisted.

Tavish took a moment to convince his mind to dive back into that terrible day and everything that led to it. No one in town cared to talk about it; the pain was still too fresh. Yet he couldn't imagine Cecily asking out of mere curiosity. She needed to know what happened to help Finbarr. He'd wade through that abyss again for his brother.

"A year ago, Hope Springs was a town at war with itself. Down our road lived house after house of Irish families. And down the Red Road, as it was known then, lived house after house of families who were not Irish in the least. The Reds hated the Irish. The Irish hated the Reds. Both sides were dedicated to fighting each other to the last."

She listened in complete silence. Her expression didn't change. Without the tiniest peek at her eyes behind the green spectacles, Tavish hadn't the slightest idea how she was reacting to the story.

"At that time, we had a man here in town, a man whose name is no longer spoken among us." Indeed, Tavish shuddered even thinking of him. "His hatred was boundless, and white hot. Joseph Archer played peacemaker between sides, a lost cause if ever there was one. In vengeance for Joseph's unwillingness to side against the Irish, this man set fire to Joseph's barn. The man never would admit whether he knew as much at the time, and none of us is sure to this day, but Joseph's two girls and the daughter of the local merchant were in the loft when he set the barn ablaze."

"Oh, good heavens," Cecily whispered.

"Katie Mac—" He cut himself short. "Katie *Archer* saw the fire and knew someone was in the loft. Finbarr spotted the fire as well and went inside to release the animals, only to learn from Katie that more lives were at stake than the horses and cow."

Only with effort had they pieced together what had occurred that night. Finbarr's memories weren't whole, owing to the severity of his injuries. Katie's recollections were every bit as broken and incomplete. Everyone suspected that the Archer girls remembered every terrifying moment, but Ivy's explanations, given as they were by a five-year-old child, had been difficult to sort through. Emma wouldn't speak of the events except in the broadest, barest of terms.

"As near as we could discover," he continued on, "Katie and Finbarr coaxed the wee ones down into the leaping flames, their only option for escape. The two Archer girls, who've long thought of Finbarr as a brother and Katie as a mother, were more easily convinced than their friend, Marianne. Katie ran for the doors with her girls. Finbarr carried Marianne.

"The fire brought the roof down just before Katie escaped. Finbarr and Marianne were still inside as well. The weight threw them to the ground. 'Twas clear by how the two were found that my brave, tenderhearted"—the word choked him a bit—"little brother shielded his precious bundle, but the impact was still too brutal."

Tavish swallowed back the thick lump of emotion that always accompanied these memories. "Little Marianne landed with tremendous force and in precisely the wrong position. Her neck was broken. When they were found, she was dead in his arms."

"Oh, mercy."

Tavish took a breath and continued. "Finbarr didn't wake for more than a day. He had a great many broken bones. I know you likely can't see the scars, but his face was badly burned in places."

"Including his eyes," Cecily said.

They walked on in heavy silence. Her mouth pulled down at the corners, though not in a frown. She was pondering. Deeply.

"We've only just reached the point where any of us can talk about it with each other." It had been a very difficult year.

"I've been going about this all wrong." Her sigh was one of exhaustion as much as frustration. "He is a very young man who experienced a horrific ordeal but survived, while someone, a tiny someone in his care, did not. Much more than frustration and sadness are attached to Finbarr's vision loss. There is a crushing guilt. Guilt for failing to save her. Guilt for having survived instead of her."

Guilt. Tavish could see the truth of that. Buried under the sadness and anger and shutting out of the world, the lad blamed himself for what had happened every bit as much as little Emma did.

"We've told him he's not to blame," Tavish said. "He's been hailed a hero. Without him, they'd all've died."

"Pain distorts logic," she said. "Guilt can seldom be reasoned away."

"How is it you've become such an expert in guilt?" He guided her around a patch of ice on the road.

Finbarr was still a great many paces ahead, though he'd noticeably slowed down.

"Guilt is often part of grieving," Cecily said. "My students all grieve for the lives they once had and for the futures they'd expected."

She might've been describing Tavish himself. He still mourned for Bridget's loss, though much of the pain had dulled. And if he were being entirely honest, he still carried around a vast deal of guilt over her passing.

Why had she grown ill, but he hadn't? What if he'd done something different in nursing her? What if . . . What if her death was all his fault?

Cecily stumbled the slightest bit on a rock, but quickly righted herself. Tavish vowed to pay a little closer attention; she was trusting him to help her navigate.

"For Finbarr," she said, "the guilt associated with this tragedy is likely holding him back every bit as much as the adjustment to darkness. Likely even more."

"What can we do?" Tavish hated the idea of his brother hurting so deeply.

She thought a moment. "What did he enjoy doing before the fire?"

"Laughing with the other lads his age. Flirting with the lasses." That last was a particular favorite of all the O'Connor men during their single years. "He worked every day for Joseph Archer, and he loved being there. Those little girls held his heart in their hands. And Joseph was something of a hero to him."

"Has he associated much with the Archers since the fire?" Cecily asked.

"Hardly at all. He's kept away from most people, including his family."

"I think spending time with them would help him. It would offer a sense of reclaiming some of what was lost, as well as allowing him to associate with someone he admires."

"The Archers are a little put-out with him just now," Tavish reminded her. "He twisted Emma's own guilt rather painfully."

Cecily turned her face up toward him again. How much of his face could she see? Or did she look at people as she spoke merely out of habit?

"The Archers have seen Emma through her guilt and mourning. They can help us help Finbarr."

Tavish had been so alone in his desperate struggle to help his brother. Whenever he'd pulled in one of his family members, they'd crumbled a bit themselves.

"I could use the help." Somehow the admission didn't humiliate him as much as he expected. "I can't keep doing this alone."

"You are less alone than you realize," she said quietly. Before he could inquire into the statement, she spoke again. "Does Finbarr seem likely to find the house on his own, or is it time we intervened?"

"He has just walked past the house. Shall we stage a rescue?"

"Only if you promise to be very daring and adventurous. No rescue is worth enacting if it's boring."

A jest during difficulties. A smile in the midst of worry. He needed those things. Saints above, he needed them.

Chapter Twenty-two

Tavish drove his buggy over the bridge and pulled up beside the Archers' barn. In the months since Katie and Joseph's wedding, he'd done his best to avoid the Archer place. Even when working to bring in Joseph's crop while the family were all far away, he'd steered clear of the house itself. He didn't begrudge them their happiness. 'Twas simply awkward yet.

Cecily moved to climb down.

"You'd best wait," he warned her. "The snow left a great many drifts, and I can't say with certainty you'd not simply drop into one."

"So I am to pay for your poor driving? That seems unfair."

"Be patient, lass. I'm walking through the snow for you, after all."

She gave him a perplexed look. "I thought the reason you were driving was so that we could avoid walking in the snow. I am quickly losing faith in you as a buggy driver."

Despite his efforts to keep a distance between them, Tavish had grown quite fond of her teasing. She was his friend, which wouldn't sit well with his neighbors or his family. When she left, they would likely cheer. He, however, would miss her.

He hopped down then tied the horse's rein to the hitching post. "Stay put, Cecee." He'd spied her shifting toward the end of the bench. He stepped over to her side of the buggy. Not simply snowy, the ground was icy. "Don't chop my head off, but I think I'd best lead you to safer ground."

"Am I surrounded by rabid dogs or something?"

"Stop your sassing. I'm trying to be a gentleman." He reached up and took her hands in his.

"If you start doing that now, how will I recognize you?"

He held her fast as she stepped onto the icy ground. "Put your arm about my middle, and I'll do the same," he instructed. She obliged, and with a little maneuvering, they began their walk up the snowy path. "Now, what exactly do you mean to say to the high and mighty Mr. Archer?"

"'High and Mighty'? Is that anything like 'Your Majesty'?"

"They're in the same vein," he admitted.

"You don't like him either?"

"First of all, you troublesome colleen, I don't dislike you no matter that you've apparently decided otherwise." He guided her around a particularly treacherous-looking patch of ice. "And secondly, I don't dislike Joseph, either."

He could hear that his last words weren't entirely sincere. It seemed he had not yet let bygones be bygones.

Cecily didn't press the issue, but neither did she seem to believe him. "Have we passed the blood-thirsty hounds, or the life-threatening ice patches, or whatever danger it is you set me in the midst of?"

"One can never be too careful." Truth be told, he was enjoying having her up close to him once more.

Da would've scolded him to the ends of the earth for it. But Da had no idea what it was like to be alone. Cecily laughed with him and genuinely enjoyed his jesting and lighthearted approach to difficulties. Beyond that, she trusted him with her thoughts and questions. She asked for his input and offered hers to him in response. It was . . . refreshing.

"At times, I wish life had allowed me to remain quiet and bookish." She smiled a touch ruefully. "I used to be terribly shy, you know."

He could almost picture Cecily as a shy, keep-to-herself type. "Well if you're ever wanting to be quiet and bookish again for a spell, you say the word. I'll keep an eye on everything while you hide away."

"You would do that for me?"

'Twas hardly a question worth asking. "I do that for everyone."

Her brow pulled low and worried, her mouth following suit.

"What's brought on this sudden look of sadness?" He didn't like seeing it.

She quickly pulled herself together, waving off his question. "Point me in the direction of the door."

"If you'll make a quarter turn to your right, you'll be facing the door just a few steps ahead of you."

She turned, then lifted her hand, holding it out in front of her as a barrier as she stepped cautiously forward. "This is far less embarrassing with my cane," she said. "It taps the side of buildings before my face does."

Her fingers brushed the door. She knocked firmly. Mrs. Smith answered, then ushered them inside. Tavish held his breath. This was Katie's domain. He wasn't certain he could enter it without jumping clean out of his skin.

They stepped into the parlor, and there Katie was with little Ivy asleep in her arms and Emma napping on the sofa beside her. She rocked the small girl gently, a contentment in her face that Tavish had seldom seen before she'd become a permanent part of the Archer family. She belonged here. He knew it. But it still hurt.

"Come in, both of you," she quietly invited. "What brings you around?"

"I need to speak with you and your husband about Finbarr," Cecily said. She had a way of moving from jesting to sober so quickly and efficiently that Tavish wondered how anyone kept pace with her.

"Joseph's just out in the barn. Please have a seat; he'll return shortly."

Cecily turned her head a bit toward him and whispered, "Is that a chair directly in front of me?"

"Perhaps you could tap it with your face and find out."

She pointed a finger at him. "Don't make me tap *your* face, Tavish O'Connor."

"I'm quaking in m' boots." He set his hand on her back and guided her to the chair.

"How is Finbarr?" Katie asked. "I saw him leave the ceremony yesterday. I've been terrible worried ever since."

"He's made progress learning how to function in his new state," Cecily said, carefully lowering herself into the chair. "But he hasn't yet learned how to live. That is why I'm here."

"You think we can help with that?" Katie kept her voice low, still rocking her little girl, but her tone and expression had turned earnest.

"I believe so," Cecily answered. "I hope so."

"We will do whatever we can." Joseph's voice reached them from the doorway to the dining room. He'd come in so quietly no one had realized he was there. He sat on the sofa and set his arm around Katie.

Seeing the two of them together still wasn't at all comfortable. Tavish felt it best to wander a little toward the door once more.

"Before we begin in earnest," Cecily said, "I do want to make certain your little Emma is not in the room. I know Finbarr is a difficult topic for her, and I don't want to make her unhappy."

"She is here, but she is sleeping. She and Ivy both. Yesterday was a difficult one."

"Until yesterday, I did not know the exact circumstances under which Finbarr lost his sight," Cecily said. "Now I recognize that beneath Finbarr's anger and stubbornness is a tremendous amount of guilt. I am hopeful that in your efforts to see your daughters through their own struggles with all that's happened, you might have some idea about what could help Finbarr."

Joseph and Katie exchanged looks, whispering between themselves. Tavish paced farther away. He still found their connection and contentment uncomfortable, which made him feel guilty. If there was one thing the Irish were good at, it was guilt.

"I think what has helped her most," Joseph said, "was making life as normal again as we could."

"Normal." Tavish shook his head. "Nothing about Finbarr's life is normal any longer."

"I am well aware of that." Joseph clearly didn't appreciate the correction. "Despite appearances, life isn't normal for our girls, either. Ivy is plagued with nightmares. Emma is sent into a panic at the slightest thing. She cries often. Some days she won't leave her room. Believe me, Tavish O'Connor, I am fully aware that life will never be the same for anyone who passed through the events of that night."

Katie jumped in. "We're all worried, but picking at one another will help no one."

"Tavish did toss me from the wagon into a pack of rabid dogs," Cecily said. "I think that has earned him a little picking."

"Traitor," Tavish chuckled.

She turned a bit to face him. "Before the fire, what was Finbarr's daily routine?"

Tavish pulled the chair from the writing desk and placed it next to hers. "He lived with our parents." He sat as he answered her question. "He came here every day to work for the Archers. In the evenings, he helped Da or sometimes Ian or me with our chores, or he spent time with our nieces and nephews. Now and then, he'd have a lark with other young men in town."

"Could he return to living at your parents' house?" Katie asked.

"Ma struggles too much with all of this." 'Twas the reason Finbarr had come to live with Tavish in the first place.

"So that aspect of his previous life cannot be restored." Cecily sat quietly a moment, thinking. "Could he have his job back?"

"I have offered it to him many times," Joseph said. "He has refused."

"Has his refusal been due to disinterest, do you think?" she asked.

Joseph shook his head no.

"You'll have to answer out loud," Tavish said. "She can't see you movin' your head."

"My apologies, Miss Attwater. It is easy to forget that your sight is diminished when you move about with such ease and look unfailingly in the direction of the people you speak to."

Cecily leaned a touch closer to Tavish. "He would be singing a different tune if he'd seen me turned about in that snow storm, now, wouldn't he?"

"That he would," Tavish answered. "Why, he'd've stood there amidst the tugging and tossing of the wind, pondering nothing but how very unseeing you seemed to be. It would've been a grand bit of pondering, it would."

"You'll have to interpret for me, Katie," Cecily said. "With that accent of his, I didn't understand a word he just said."

Katie didn't join in the jest. Her gaze narrowed as she looked from Tavish to Cecily and back several times in succession. Hers was very much the look Da had given him while warning that the Irish would never be comfortable with an Englishwoman in their midst. Katie was one of the local Irish.

Cecily faced the sofa once more. Joseph was right on one score; she made it easy to forget she was nearly blind.

"What chores did Finbarr do when he worked here?" she asked.

"A little of everything," Joseph said. "He tended to the animals, mended equipment, helped plant and harvest."

Cecily folded her arms. "He won't be able to do most of those things, at least not yet." Her brow drew with thought. "But he needs to feel he has a purpose, that he is working toward something. This would be the right first step, I think. I can help you identify chores he could be taught to do blind."

Joseph nodded, but then seemed to catch himself. "I will do whatever I can for the boy. I've worried about him this past year, and we've all missed him."

"Tavish?" Cecily turned her head in his direction once more. "I would value your input on this as well."

He set his hand on Cecily's, hoping to convey through the gesture his support of her efforts, since he couldn't do so with a look. "Finbarr hasn't undertaken any chores at my place, so I can't say what he's able to do. We've talked a little about the woodpile, and he listened intently, but I'd not trust him to manage it on his own."

Cecily nodded. "We would do well to begin with chores that aren't inherently dangerous."

They spent the next hour discussing chores Finbarr had done before his accident, what he'd done since. Cecily asked a lot of questions, delving into the smallest details. Katie offered some insights as well. They decided, in the end, that Joseph had enough tasks Finbarr could quickly relearn to keep him busy at least one day per week. Through it all, Cecily kept her hand in his. The gesture wasn't flirtatious or lovey-dovey, but more friendly and comfortable.

"Finbarr has turned down any number of Joseph's requests to return to work," Katie said. Ivy began to stir, and Katie again soothed the girl. "How do we convince him to come?"

"Suppose," Tavish said, "rather than offer him his job back, Joseph were to come by asking Finbarr to help him with something small that wouldn't likely take more than a few hours or a single day?"

"He'd feel less overwhelmed." Cecily nodded. "It would work, provided the request is sincere, something that does, in fact, need to be done, and something Joseph truly does need help accomplishing."

"A great many things need attention around here," Joseph said.

Cecily looked noticeably relieved. "I believe this will be a good start."

"I do hope so," Joseph said.

Cecily turned to Tavish. "Shall we be on our way?"

He helped her to her feet. They'd only reached the front entryway when Katie's voice stopped them.

"Tavish, might I bend your ear a minute?"

He tossed her a grin. "That'd be a mighty short conversation."

She still held Ivy. Katie's arms must have been terribly tired.

Cecily slipped her hand from his. "I'll wait on the front porch."

"It may be a bit icy," Tavish warned.

"I'll be careful." With that she stepped out and closed the door behind her.

"What have you on your mind, Katie?" He'd finally broken himself of the habit of calling her "Sweet Katie." The nickname belonged to another time when things had been different between them.

"Why do you call her 'Cecee'?"

"Because she objects to 'Your Majesty.'"

Far from laughing at the teasing tone Tavish had employed, Katie only eyed him more closely. "I objected to 'Sweet Katie,' but you never stopped using it."

"You objected because you didn't think it fit you. She objected because she thought it was unkind."

"Was it?"

Tavish felt as if he were on trial. "In all honesty, yes. I meant it to mock her."

She lightly rubbed Ivy's back. "You changed your name for her out of consideration for her feelings?"

Tavish buttoned up his coat. "Turns out I'm a decent human being."

"You've always been far better than 'decent.'" She eyed him too closely for comfort. "You're quite fond of her, I'd wager."

"I am that. You, yourself, seem to have been getting along with her well enough."

Katie shook her head. "You know perfectly well 'tisn't what I meant at all. She's touched your heart."

He held his hand up in a show of surrender. "She's Finbarr's teacher."

"She's more than that."

He stepped over to the door. "No woman'll ever be more than that."

"Please, Tavish, don't let old hurts—"

"Good day to you, Katie." 'Twasn't the most gracious of exits, but he'd not stand about talking with Katie about "old hurts."

As promised, Cecily was waiting on the porch. She didn't turn as he approached, though he was certain she heard him. She looked ponderous, no doubt worrying over Finbarr.

"Do you think this'll work?" he asked her.

"No," she said.

"No?"

"Hiding from pain and regrets never truly works."

He set his hand on her arm to help guide her back to the wagon. "Finbarr'll be coming here soon enough. He'll not be hiding."

"Finbarr isn't the only one at your house hiding from his past."

Now that was a pointed remark. "Why is it you think I am?"

She tipped her head. Her mouth twisted in disbelief. "Can you honestly tell me you aren't?"

Tension in his jaw clenched his teeth. He forced himself to relax. "I can 'honestly tell you' that I'm ready to go home."

Cecily clasped her hands in front of her, but not in a posture of defeat. "Hiding from pain does not heal it."

He slipped his hat on his head. "Leave it be, Cecee. Leave it be."

She nodded. Tavish, however, firmly suspected she didn't intend to let anything be.

Chapter Twenty-three

"Tavish O'Connor is, quite possibly, the most frustrating man I have ever known, and I include in that evaluation an eighty-year-old former pugilist who refused to speak directly to me for the first two months I worked with him."

Cecily hadn't intended to air her frustrations, but they had all spilled out as she and Katie had stepped inside the mercantile. Katie had come to gather supplies for Mrs. Claire, and Joseph had graciously offered to bring Cecily along so she could obtain a few things herself.

"One moment Tavish is sharing his concerns and thoughts," Cecily continued, "and the very next, he is telling me to keep myself out of his affairs. He'll speak kindly to me for hours and then, without so much as a moment's warning, he'll call me 'Your Majesty' in that mocking tone of his."

"Has you a bit ruffled, does he?" Katie asked.

"I'm not a bit ruffled. I'm downright miffed."

"Isn't that turn of phrase a bit unrefined for an Englishwoman?" Katie managed to ask the question without adding any censure to her words. Few of her countrymen accomplished that when referencing Cecily's roots.

"Believe me," she said, "there are a number of even less-refined turns of phrase I've been biting back of late."

Katie laughed. "I like you, Cecily."

"Because I'm frustrated with your friend?"

"Because he is frustrated with you."

Cecily stopped near to what she was relatively certain was the mercantile counter. "He is decidedly frustrated with me."

Katie didn't follow her to the counter, but stopped to speak with someone. Cecily could hardly make out her outline and couldn't say with any certainty to whom she spoke. The store was dim, yes, but it was more than that. Cecily saw less and less detail of late. The customer waiting at the counter had the build of a man, tall with broad shoulders, but she couldn't see well enough to identify him.

"You've grown rather friendly with her, Katie." The woman who made the hushed observation was Irish, but Cecily couldn't identify her beyond that. Had the speaker been one of the O'Connors, she would have recognized the voice. "Does she not make you nervous?"

"Why would Miss Attwater make me nervous?" Katie replied, her voice equally soft. People often forgot that Cecily had very acute hearing developed out of necessity in a world she could not see.

"Have you not forgotten 'twas an English landlord who threw you out of your home when you were only a child?"

A chill crept over Cecily. She knew full well her countrymen had done some terrible things to the people of Ireland. She didn't imagine anything could bridge the chasm that their shared history put between her and the Irish in Hope Springs.

"I've also not forgotten that the man who burned our home to the ground all those years ago was, in fact, Irish," Katie said. "But don't fret, Anne. I'll not hold that against you."

Cecily held back the smile she felt forming. If she was caught out listening in on their conversation, that would simply be one more thing this town held against her.

"Does she not make you nervous, then?" Anne pressed, her voice almost a whisper now.

"A small part of me—I'd imagine the part that is still the terrified little girl who lost her home—feels a bit chilled when I hear her very English style of speaking." Katie's admission pained Cecily. "But the rest of me, the part that is thinking and feeling and strong and fair reminds the rest of me that Miss Attwater was not the author of my suffering, nor is she responsible for all that her countrymen have done, and she deserves to be judged for who she is and not merely where she came from."

"That is easier said than done," Anne said.

"I know it."

Cecily knew it as well.

A man arrived on the other side of the counter—Mr. Johnson, the mercantile owner, no doubt. "Here you are, Mr. Scott." Something was set on the counter with a clank. "Can I get you anything else?" He, judging from the sound of his voice, hailed from America's South. Cecily had worked with more than one student who sounded very much like he did.

Mr. Scott, who had checked in on Mrs. Claire earlier that week, answered that he didn't need anything more. He spoke little as his purchase was calculated. When Mr. Scott visited, Cecily had been in her room. In his brief conversation with Mrs. Claire, he'd shown himself a kindhearted person, but he, too, had asked after "the Englishwoman" in tones of distrust and uncertainty.

Cecily smiled in his direction as he stepped away from the counter. She didn't know if he saw the gesture, but she hoped so, and that it did some good.

"May I help you?" Mr. Johnson asked her.

"I need Dover Powder, a small jar, please." She hadn't used the pain-relieving remedy in some time, but her eyes had begun aching something awful. She knew how this would play out: soon the pain would be nearly unbearable without something to ease it. Then everything would grow darker.

He turned around and stepped far enough away to grow quite blurry. She really was having more trouble indoors. She pushed down the recurring worry that had accompanied the realization over the past few days. There were so many things she wanted to see before her vision deteriorated entirely, and she was running out of time.

"Are you injured, Cecily?" Katie asked, having joined her at the counter.

"Why would you ask that?"

"You're purchasing Dover Powder."

"It is for my eyes." She didn't care to discuss the situation more than that. Generally, if people heard her explanation, they treated her with either pity or dismissal. Far easier and more comfortable to keep her conversation simple.

"Do you think Finbarr's eyes hurt as well?" Katie sounded immediately concerned. "Oh, heavens, I hope not."

Did Finbarr have the least idea how much he was loved by this town?

"Now that his face and eyes are healed, I don't believe so." But she meant to ask him, to be certain.

Mr. Johnson returned to the counter. The sound of glass clinking against wood said he'd found the bottle. "Can I get you anything else, Miss Attwater?"

Only three people in town called her Cecily rather than the more formal Miss Attwater: Katie, Joseph, and Tavish. Finbarr had returned to "Miss Attwater." Only a moment ago, Anne Scott had called Katie by her given name. Biddy O'Connor was always called "Biddy." Tavish's sisters were addressed more personally by the other women in town. But not Cecily. The contrast stood as a recurrent reminder that she was an outsider.

"I am in sore need of a cane, as mine was broken beyond repair," she answered, "but Tavish tells me you do not carry any."

Silence followed. Instinct filled in the blank.

"I imagine you are either shaking or nodding your head," Cecily said. "I am afraid my vision is not sharp enough for me to know."

"My apologies. I can order a cane, but I won't receive any new goods until spring," Mr. Johnson said. "Will Finbarr need a cane as well?"

"He will." Though how she was to teach him to use a cane when she didn't have one was beyond her.

"I'll order one for him come spring." Mr. Johnson said. "Tell me precisely what he needs, and I will find it."

Such support. Such kindness. Not everyone was so blessed. "How much for the powder?"

He quoted her the price, and she carefully counted out the correct coins. Something else she needed to teach Finbarr: recognizing, by touch, which coin was which.

She carefully reached for the bottle, not entirely trusting herself to have correctly judged its location. Her fingers brushed against it. She wrapped her hand around the familiar square glass bottle. It fit almost perfectly in her fist.

Ivy Archer's skipping steps gave away her arrival. The girls had followed them.

"What is in your bottle?" Ivy asked.

"Medicine for my eyes," Cecily answered, stepping back from the counter, bottle in hand.

"Pompah said I could have a butterscotch," she said. "It is my most, most favorite. Mr. Tavish always gives me a butterscotch when I see him."

Though he was often grumpy and grumbly with her, Cecily had seen enough evidence of Tavish's kind and gentle nature to fully believe he treated the children of Hope Springs with tenderness.

"Skip up to Katie, Ivy. You as well, Emma." Joseph spoke from just behind Cecily. "She'll pay for your sweets."

Two sets of small footsteps moved in the direction of the counter, followed by Joseph's lowered voice in Cecily's ear. "I believe I've thought of something I might ask Finbarr to help me with."

"I'm glad to hear it. He has only grown more distant and despondent. Something must pull him from it before he is mired beyond rescue." She'd seen that happen to others, and it was always a tragedy.

"Katie and I were hoping to drop in at Tavish's place to speak with Finbarr before taking you on to Granny Claire's."

Cecily nodded approval. It was a good plan. "I *would*, however, suggest extending the invitation for next week sometime, so he has the weekend to think on it, and, if he wishes, he'll have time to consult with me about the best way to prepare."

"I will do that."

In very little time, the lot of them arrived at Tavish's home. Katie was careful to guide Cecily around snowdrifts. Emma, sweet girl that she was, took Cecily's hand and led her with utmost care to the door.

It opened, and Tavish's voice greeted them all. Though he jested and laughed as he ushered them inside, Cecily heard a strain under his cheerful tone.

"What's happened?" she asked quietly.

"He broke a plate this morning, and it's sent him into the worst state of blue-devilment I've seen in ages."

Setbacks were to be expected, but the timing could not have been worse. "This visit, then, will either be very helpful or an utter disaster."

"Care to place a wager?" Tavish's dry whisper lifted a weight from her heart. He'd keep an eye on things and do his best to prevent a catastrophe. "What's brought everyone around?"

"Joseph has come to make his request of Finbarr."

Tavish pushed out an audible breath. “Are you a praying woman, Cecee?”

“I’ve been known to petition the heavens.”

He rested a hand on her back and gently guided her farther inside. “Then do your best petitioning, lass. This could get messy.”

Tavish was exhausted and quickly losing patience. Finbarr had been difficult all day. All week. Honestly, all year.

“Finbarr!” Ivy cried with absolute glee and ran across the room, throwing herself against Finbarr, holding fast to his legs. “I haven’t seen you since I was little.”

For a moment, Finbarr stood frozen, his brows pulled in worry and uncertainty. He slowly, painstakingly, moved one hand and laid it gently on the top of her head. His lips pressed together. His chest rose and fell with a deep breath.

“You’ve grown taller,” he said quietly.

“Katie says it was the Irish air. It made me get bigger and bigger.”

Cecily leaned in close to Tavish and whispered, “Is he pushing her away?”

“No,” he answered as quietly. “But he’s not comfortable, either.”

The lad had avoided the Archer girls for nearly a year. Would he accept their desperately offered adoration, or push them away again?

“Has—has Emma grown as well?” Heavy hesitation hung in Finbarr’s question.

“Not as much as me. Katie’s mother said Emma was a ‘pretty pea.’ Katie said that meant she’s little. Pompah said it meant she’s pretty. Which do you think it is?”

Emma had chosen a seat near the window and was decidedly not looking at Finbarr. But Tavish wagered she was listening. Did Finbarr know she was there?

"Well, sweet Ivy." Finbarr's hand slid from the top of her head, down her long braid, and settled on her shoulder—as near to an embrace as Finbarr'd given anyone in the past year. He was reaching out, with however small a gesture. "Compared to an adult, Emma would be little. But she's also always been pretty. So I would wager Katie's mother meant both."

Well done, brother.

"Uncle Brennan said I was a regular handful." Ivy took pride in the description. "And he said Emma is the sweetest girl he'd ever met in all his life. That made her ears turn red."

"How is Emma?" Finbarr asked.

Though Tavish couldn't see her face, he was certain Ivy rolled her eyes. "She's sitting by the window." Ivy pulled away from Finbarr and crossed to Joseph sitting near the fire. She climbed onto her father's lap.

Every eye in the room moved from Finbarr to Emma and back. Tavish didn't think Finbarr could see her from where he stood. Emma didn't turn to look at him. Both were as stiff as boards, and the room had gone utterly still.

Finbarr, say something to the lass.

Silence hung over the room a moment longer before Finbarr muttered, "I'm supposed to be making lunch." He turned about, and, hands outstretched to warn him of anything in his path, returned to the stove at the far side of the room.

"That wound is still raw," Cecily whispered.

The impulse to jump in and save his brother from further pain was almost too strong for Tavish to ignore. "Remind me that I must let him fix this."

"You must let him fix this." She spoke with just enough teasing to bring a little smile to his face.

He set his arm around her shoulders and tugged her into a friendly side embrace. "I don't know what we'd do without you, Cecee."

"Come spring, you'll get to find out."

'Twas a splash of icy water. How easy it was to forget that her stay in Hope Springs was a temporary one. He was growing attached, and that, history had taught him, was a dangerous thing. Tavish let his arm drop away. Distance was best.

Joseph set Ivy on her feet and rose from his chair. "Could I talk with you a minute, Finbarr?"

Tavish followed to the kitchen side of the room, where Finbarr stood, not doing much of anything. He wore such a look of hurt it pulled painfully at Tavish's heart.

Joseph wasted not a moment. "If you think your brother could spare you, I have an unexpected bit of extra work this week, and I could use another set of hands."

"This set of hands doesn't come with a working pair of eyes," Finbarr muttered.

"The two tasks I need you for are ones I think can be managed without sight," Joseph said. "First, milking the cow—just sitting in one place. I'm so busy of late that I don't always get to the milking before the poor beast is miserable. This week is going to be even busier than usual. You taking on that chore for me would be a great help."

Finbarr's brow drew low in thought. His scars pulled unevenly, adding a foreboding quality to the expression. Tavish hadn't yet learned to recognize when the added flavor was intentional, and when it was simply an accident of healing.

"I haven't tried milking a cow yet." Finbarr sounded curious, a far cry from his common angry retorts when a new task was suggested.

"I'd wager you could sort it out with a bit of strategizing,"

Tavish said, trying to keep his tone light. If Finbarr sensed the slightest hint of pity, he'd likely retreat.

"I'd probably knock over the milk pail." Finbarr phrased it almost as a question, as if he was hoping to be reassured.

Joseph took the cue. "I've done that myself on occasion. I wouldn't hold it against you. Much."

A single corner of Finbarr's mouth twitched. "I suppose I would just have to learn to be careful."

Was he considering it, then? Tavish hoped so.

"What's the other task?" Finbarr asked.

Joseph lowered his voice to a whisper. "I've been making a rocking chair for Katie, and it needs to be sanded. It's meant to be a Christmas gift, but I won't have time to sand it smooth and still see to all of my other chores."

"I'd probably be slow, and likely miss spots." The hint of hope mingled with pain in Finbarr's warning pierced Tavish straight through.

The lad needed this victory. And, Tavish realized, *he* needed it as well. After a year of watching his brother wander about, lost in darkness, he needed to see Finbarr take a step back into the light.

"No matter how slow, you would still be helpful," Joseph said.

Tavish joined his voice to Joseph's. "And using touch to search for spots you've missed, as you'd be doing, would likely mean you'd find rough patches that might be missed if one were relying on sight."

Finbarr hesitated only a moment longer. "I suppose I could try."

Tavish held back the surge of triumph that immediately surfaced. Finbarr would hear it and likely interpret it as pity. If only he could share a silent expression of victory with Cecily.

Joseph, ever calm and focused, moved ahead without hesitation. "When can you come?"

"Monday morning." An unmistakable eagerness hid in

Finbarr's hesitant tone. "That is, if Tavish doesn't mind, and if Miss Attwater says I can miss my lessons."

"Why don't you ask her?" Tavish suggested. "She's sitting over by the fire."

Finbarr nodded. With a determination too often missing in him, the lad carefully moved that direction. "Miss Attwater?"

"Yes?"

Nervousness filled Finbarr's next breath. "Mr. Archer says he needs some help next week. May I be excused from our lessons for a day or two to go work with him?"

"Of course. I'll come by in the evenings so you can tell me what you've been doing, and we can discuss any adjustments that might be made in your approach to the chores you've taken on."

Finbarr nodded. "I can do that."

Ivy, seated on the floor near Katie's feet, looked up at Finbarr. "You are coming to our house again?"

Finbarr shrugged a little. "I suppose I am."

She squealed, hopped up, and rushed to Finbarr, throwing herself against him with such force she nearly knocked him over. "You're coming back!"

Emma didn't speak a word, but she had turned a little toward them all, a whisper of interest pulling at her features. Joseph and Katie looked as relieved as Tavish felt. And Cecily, who had seemed so unfeeling and indifferent when she'd first arrived in Hope Springs, looked happier than all of them.

A weight had lifted from Tavish's shoulders. For the first time in a year, he truly felt his brother was coming back to him.

Chapter Twenty-four

Sundays were generally quiet at Mrs. Claire's house. Cecily chose not to attend church with her hostess, knowing her presence would likely not be appreciated. Mrs. Claire usually spent the rest of the day at Mr. and Mrs. O'Connor's home. That left Cecily with hours on her own, hours she put to good use working on her Braille transcription of *The Light Princess*.

This Sunday, however, hadn't gone according to plan.

Even at the desk she had placed under one of Granny's front windows, the room was too dim. The day must have been very overcast for so little light to be coming in the large window.

She still hadn't chosen an alternate activity when Mrs. Claire returned home, Tavish at her side.

"Don't mind us," Mrs. Claire said. "Tavish has come to see to the rocking chair, is all."

Cecily assured them she was not the least put out by their return, yet she found herself focusing closely on their figures. They stood near Granny's chair, which was only on the other side of the door, a mere fifteen feet away at most. She could hardly make out their blurred shapes.

"I couldn't be certain I wouldn't simply fall out m' seat with the state this is in," Mrs. Claire said. "A shame. A right shame."

Was this why Mrs. Claire hadn't sat in her usual place the past few days—something had happened to her rocker?

The runners squeaked. "'Tis but one cracked slat," Tavish said. "You'd not tumble out on account of that."

"Are you certain? I'd hate for you to come visit next week, only to find me lying in a heap on the floor."

"I'd hate that as well," Tavish said.

Cecily could hear movement, but couldn't make out any change in their vague shapes.

"You'd miss me, would you?" Mrs. Claire asked.

"More than I've words to say."

Such a fondness between them. Cecily had noticed it from the first and had grown ever more sure with each interaction she'd witnessed. For all his lack of cooperation with her personally when she'd first arrived, he had certainly shown himself to be goodhearted and kind.

"Now, have a sit down before you have a fall," Tavish instructed. "The rocker is sound enough to hold you safely, though I'll whittle you a replacement for the split slat."

"I've a fine grandson, do I not, Mr. Attwater?" She still called Cecily that when she was in good spirits.

"I believe he is," she answered. "Though is he as adept at stopping drafts coming in a window as he is at whittling rocking chair slats? That would be a truly fine thing."

"Have you a drafty window?" Immediate concern filled his words, without a hint of annoyance.

"The one there by the rocker," Cecily said. "Anytime the wind picks up, Mrs. Claire's hit with an icy blast."

"Granny." A hint of scold entered Tavish's tone. "Why didn't you tell me sooner? I'd've come and seen to this first thing."

"You're already supporting your ma, lifting your da's worries, tending Ian's animals during his latest setback. You spent most of yesterday helping Ciara and Keefe mend a length of fallen fence, though what your sister has done to earn your devotion of late, I'll never know. And last evening, you looked after Mary's older children while she and Thomas nursed the youngest through his cough. Not to mention the year you've spent shouldering the responsibility of taking care of Finbarr. You've troubles enough without me adding to them."

"My dear Granny." He'd moved. Cecily could hear it; she simply couldn't see it. "You are my family. There is nothin' in all this world I wouldn't do for my family. And 'tisn't a burden in the least, but a privilege."

An ache of envy surged through Cecily. She had to turn away, back to her book and her stencil and the lanterns attempting to fight back the darkness. She'd not been a part of anyone's family for so very long. She spent months amongst families, interacting with them, coming to care for them, but in the end, she always moved on, leaving those connections behind. In the end, she was always alone.

How she wanted what the O'Connors had. She longed to have someone love her the way Tavish loved them. The way her father had loved her. More than that, she wanted to belong, to be loved, and wanted, and needed.

She forced her thoughts to empty of such things. Her eyes hurt enough without adding the sting of tears. The powders she'd taken that morning were wearing thin, but she could not take more until her midday meal. The familiarity of these bouts of pain and encroaching darkness did not make them any less difficult to endure.

She pressed the palms of her hands against her burning eyes. The pressure never entirely relieved the pain, but it helped a little. She likely had very few episodes left before her vision was gone entirely. Time was running out. The Braille lending library she hoped to create seemed less and less likely to be anything but a small handful of volumes.

"The window's not closing properly," Tavish said. "It seems to be catching along the track. I'll fetch some tools and see if I can't smooth it out a bit. I'll return shortly."

With that, he was gone. One thing that could be said for Tavish O'Connor: he certainly didn't want for energy.

"He has grown into a fine man," Mrs. Claire said. "I worried for him after Bridget died. He was lost for so long."

Cecily didn't have the slightest idea who Bridget was but chose not to press the matter. Mrs. Claire was never overtly unwelcoming or unkind, but there'd always been something of a distance between them, one, Cecily guessed, was almost exactly the size of England.

"He is a very good person," Cecily said. "I have had to admit to myself that I misjudged him in my first weeks here. He seemed so . . ." She struggled for the right word.

Mrs. Claire found it for her. "Exasperating."

Cecily bit her lips closed in guilty amusement. "I did call him that, didn't I?"

Mrs. Claire laughed lightly, a sound Cecily seldom heard from her unless Katie was visiting. Biddy had managed to lighten Mrs. Claire's mood as well, but she'd stopped visiting. The laughter was welcome. Cecily needed a distraction from the pain.

"Though I wasn't willing to admit it then," Mrs. Claire said, "you'd reason for feeling that way. He was fightin' you and making things hard for you. Life has asked far too much of that man. When you arrived, he'd all but reached the end of his endurance. He was frustrated and angry and so very tired. None of us wished to see or acknowledge the truth of it, as you attempted to do, because we knew we were the cause of his trouble, placing our burdens on him as we've done these months and more."

The sadness and guilt in Mrs. Claire's words tugged at Cecily.

"You are his family, and he loves you. Every one of you." She left her desk and carefully moved to the spindle-back chair that always sat beside the rocker. She scooted it a touch closer and sat. "The moment he sees a need in any of you, he immediately jumps to help whenever and wherever he can. There is never hesitation. Never any question. His burdens have been great, but I do not for a moment believe they have been forced upon him."

Mrs. Claire took a shaky breath. "I still feel the old guilt, though. I'm not even truly his family."

"You're not?" How was a grandmother not family?

"He was to marry my granddaughter, Bridget. But she died of a fever many years ago. She and all of my family."

All of my family. The tears she forced back fought ever harder for release. "I, too, have lost every member of my family. I would not wish that pain on anyone."

Mrs. Claire patted her hand, gently and kindly. "'Tis a misery almost past bearing."

"It is that."

"I thought when they were buried that I would be all alone. But Tavish never stopped seeing me as his Granny, as I was meant to have been. He loved me the same as he always had. He looked after me. He cared about me. Soon the entire O'Connor family made me one of their own."

"Perhaps that is the reason I chose to be a traveling tutor." Cecily spoke the thought as it formed. "Perhaps I am looking for a family that will make me one of their own, one that will fill the ache my family left behind."

"And have any of them?"

"No." Cecily took a fortifying breath. She didn't like dwelling on the empty spaces in her heart. "I have been treated with kindness for the most part, and I have made some cherished friendships."

"Ah, but 'tisn't the same thing, now is it?"

Her voice dropped even as her heart did. "No, it isn't."

A gust of wind rattled the windows. Cold air sliced through every layer Cecily wore. "Thank heavens Tavish is going to see to that draft," she said. "We'd freeze to death in here otherwise."

"I've a mind to move my rocking chair, but I like being able to look out the window and see the world. What I can see of it, at least. My vision's not what it used to be."

Cecily nodded solemnly. "Neither is mine."

Another of Mrs. Claire's small laughs filled the space between them. "I do like you, Mr. Attwater, no matter that you're English and therefore a terrible person."

Too much jesting lay in the words for any degree of offense to be taken. "That is very generous of you, Mrs. Claire," Cecily answered, unable to keep her grin back.

"Granny," she said. "Call me Granny."

"Are you certain?" That seemed more personal and familiar than the Irish had allowed her to be.

"Quite certain."

Warmth swelled inside Cecily. *Granny.* She could almost imagine that they were family. "Will you call me Cecily? Unless, of course, you are still overly attached to Mr. Attwater."

Granny made a sound of pondering. "Perhaps I'll settle on Mr. Cecily Attwater. What say you to that?"

"I like it." Cecily rose, her heart noticeably lighter. For a few brief moments, she'd been able to forget her worries and burdens and even push back, to the farthest reaches of her mind, the ever-increasing pain in her eyes.

"Why don't I make us some tea?" she offered. "It will warm us up, and, if I don't miss my mark, will make a fine thank you for your grandson's efforts with the window."

Making the tea, however, was easier said than done. The area around the stove was far from any windows, so it was nearly black as night. She stumbled around a bit, trying to locate things, before settling in to the familiar routine of touch. She'd allowed herself to grow accustomed to light.

The kettle was warming by the time Tavish returned. The wind was also still blowing.

"Saints above," Tavish said. "That's a mighty draft. How can you bear to sit so close?"

"I want to see out the window," Granny answered.

"But you'll catch your death. And don't think I didn't notice you coughing in church today. You need a warmer spot."

Cecily moved a step closer. "I could move my writing desk away from the other window, and she could sit there."

"You need the light," Granny insisted.

She didn't truly *need* it, but, heaven knew, she longed for it. Still Granny needed a respite from the cold.

"Only until Tavish stops the draft. I am happy to relinquish my spot until then." She moved with careful steps to her desk.

Tavish met her there. "'Twill go faster with both of us working. Only tell me where you want it put."

"Anywhere out of the way," she said.

Tavish moved the desk. She couldn't see where he put it, but she listened closely, placing it in the room by sound alone. She set the chair in place, knocking its legs against the desk only twice. As she made to return to the kitchen, Tavish stopped her with a gentle hand on her arm. The touch sent an unexpected shiver over her in waves of warmth that even the ongoing draft couldn't dispel.

He leaned in close and whispered, "Thank you, Cecee. Giving up your light is a sacrifice, I know. And I thank you for doing that for my granny."

"I am happy to," she answered, matching his volume.

"Where shall I place my rocker?"

Cecily turned in the direction of Granny's voice. "Does she mean to move it herself?"

Tavish groaned. “I am forever surrounded by stubborn women.”

“Aren’t you fortunate?” Cecily tossed out along with a grin.

“Traitor.”

While Tavish worked on the window and Granny regaled him with stories and gossip, Cecily returned to the task of making tea and then putting together a meal. Though she only occasionally participated in the conversation going on across the way, she thoroughly enjoyed listening to it. Granny and Tavish were different in each other’s company—lighter and happier. She seemed younger. He did, as well.

She’d sensed in him a hidden heartache, a pain he kept tucked away, but she hadn’t been able to identify the source. Granny had offered invaluable insight.

Tavish had lost his fiancée. That was an ache unlikely to ever fully heal.

But had it healed at all?

Chapter Twenty-five

A week had passed with Finbarr working at the Archer home on and off. With the lad gone and Cecily not due to come by until dinnertime, the house was quiet. Uncomfortably so. Tavish had too much space and too much silence in which to think. Again and again, he pulled his thoughts away from the fire, away from Finbarr's uncertain future. Away from his growing and confusing attachment to Cecily. He managed to, for a time. For small periods, those things would leave him in peace.

But not Bridget. Not ever Bridget.

Her death had fractured him. The passage of six years had dulled the ache, but the pain never entirely left. She had been sweet and tenderhearted. She had laughed and smiled with him. Every moment they'd been together was filled with sunshine. He'd been endlessly searching for even a piece of that ever since.

He'd had moments of it with Katie—fewer and fewer toward the end—enough to have fleeting glimpses of what he'd lost. Having that happiness almost in his grasp once more, only to lose it again had dealt a sharper blow than he'd yet been willing to admit.

Even in his distraction, he managed to finish repairing the fence around the pigpen with an hour to spare before dinner. He had work enough to do, but his hands ached with the cold. Gloves only kept them warm for so long. He turned up his collar against the wind and made his way inside to thaw out.

Winters were hard in Wyoming, hard and isolating. But Tavish had come to enjoy them. He liked the bite of cold when he was working. He looked forward to sitting by the fire each evening. He spent the winter months planning his crop and land improvements for the next year. Winters were calm and slow, and over the years, he'd learned to appreciate the pace.

Would Bridget have learned to enjoy winters as well? They'd both felt rather cooped up during the cold, dark months. He hadn't valued the peace of a snow-covered earth or the joy of a crackling fire on frigid nights back then.

The last six years had changed him in a great many ways. Those years would have changed her as well. But the two of them would have grown and changed together.

Put her out of your mind, Tavish. Does you no good to dwell on her.

He stomped the snow off his boots before pushing open the front door and stepping inside. A bonnet sat on the end table beside the armchair, and a coat hung on a hook by the door. Cecily had come early. But where was she?

Tavish hung up his own coat, then his hat, looking about.

She wouldn't have gone outside without her coat and bonnet. The house wasn't large by any stretch of the imagination, so finding her oughtn't've been difficult.

The door to the bedroom was open. The bedroom no one used. The bedroom no one was supposed to go in. He'd told her that. He'd been very specific.

He stepped up to the threshold, intending to firmly remind Cecily of the boundary. But every word, every thought fled at the sight that met him.

Only a few feet inside the room, Cecily was kneeling on the floor, quietly sobbing.

"Cecee?"

She didn't look up. Her shoulders shook as she continued to cry.

"Saints, *a chara.* What's happened?"

She shook her head but didn't speak. He'd never seen her upset like this. Her emotions were always kept firmly in check.

Tavish knelt beside her, panic surging. She was honestly sobbing. This was no small thing. "Are you hurt? Are you in pain?"

She nodded. His stomach dropped; he hadn't expected pain to be the reason for her tears. He set his hands on her arms and gently rubbed them.

"Did you fall or bump into something?"

"My eyes," she said between shaky breaths. She'd told him that her eyes pained her every time her sight deteriorated further. It was the sign she'd been dreading.

"Oh, Cecily." He brushed a tear that dripped along her jaw line. Based on the depths of her sobs, she must have been in agony.

She leaned the smallest bit toward him, her head resting lightly against his chest. "I'm not ready for this."

"I can't imagine you would be." Losing one's sight must be harrowing, no matter how familiar.

She still hadn't lifted her head. If anything, her posture slumped further.

Tavish set his arms around her and, sitting back, pulled her fully into his embrace. He'd seen this same anguish in Finbarr in the days and weeks after he'd realized his vision would not return. Finbarr had never cried, but the sorrow had been unmistakable. Tavish had wanted to comfort and reassure his brother but had never been permitted to do so. Cecily, however, had turned to him. She was allowing him to see her hurting and struggling; she let him comfort her.

"I know I'm not supposed to be in here," she said, "but I love this room."

He wasn't upset about that anymore. "It is a nice room."

"It is so bright." She shifted a little, fitting herself into his embrace. Odd that something as strange as sitting on the floor in the middle of the day felt so natural. "I've never been in a room filled with as much light as this one."

"The view is breathtaking. I chose to put in a lot of windows to see the mountains."

"I love mountains. I wanted to see the Rocky Mountains before—" She took a shaky breath. "—before I was no longer able."

He leaned back against the foot of the bed, resting the side of his face on the top of her head, his arms still around her. "What else do you want to see while you still can?"

"The Pacific Ocean." She answered without having to think. "And New York City. I know it's not possible, but I'd hoped to go home one more time to see the house I grew up in, and to sit on the banks of the stream that ran near my bedroom window. I wanted to see the stone church in our village."

He knew the longing in her voice all too well. "Home never ceases to tug at the heart, does it?"

She brushed a tear from her cheek. "My mother is buried there. I wanted to see her grave once more. I know that's ridiculous; it's not as though seeing her headstone would make me miss her any less. It would just feel . . . I would worry less that she is going to be forgotten. And my father is buried in Missouri. They're both so far away."

"I am sorry, Cecee."

Her breath quivered, but she seemed a touch calmer. "You probably think I'm pathetic."

"No one is required to be strong all the time, dear," he said. "And wishing to visit the resting places of your loved ones is hardly pathetic. My Bridget is buried here in Hope Springs, but I've not made that pilgrimage even once since the day she was buried. *That* is pathetic."

"You're hurting," she said.

"For six years?" He felt ridiculous to still be struggling with that loss after so long.

"Losing someone you love never fully stops hurting, Tavish." How was it that she was offering him comfort in her time of sorrow? "It does get better."

"I suppose." He hadn't been crushed by the pain of Bridget's death in recent years but mostly because he refused to think about it.

They sat a moment, neither speaking. She didn't pull away. She seemed less burdened. He, for once, wasn't fighting the emotions that came up after speaking of Bridget's death. Holding Cecily in his arms was peaceful. *Peaceful.* He used that word a lot when describing Cecily's company.

"Thank you for not being angry with me," she said. "I know I'm not supposed to come in here."

"Why did you? Besides liking the room, that is."

She breathed deeply, not quivering with the effort as she had earlier. Perhaps he'd offered her a measure of peace as well. "For the past few days, I haven't been able to see things indoors that I could see before. Everything seemed dim and murky."

"You did knock into a few things yesterday." He hoped his teasing didn't offend her. Katie hadn't cared to be teased when she was upset.

"I was simply trying to entertain you and Granny," she said. "Your own personal Punch and Judy show."

"Well, now, isn't that a fine thing to have a show just for us?"

She laughed a little, but it quickly died off. "I realized last night that the sun setting didn't change how well I could see indoors. Sunlight hadn't been lacking; my sight was." She leaned more heavily against him. “I came in here to see if I could still see in this room, since it’s so much brighter than most.”

“Can you?” He hoped so. She’d spoken once of how much those who depended on light longed for it.

She held her arm up, fingers outstretched. “I can see my hand, not in tremendous detail, but I can see it.” She lowered her hand once more. “That’s what made me cry. I was glad to be able to see in here, however, minimally, but disappointed that I need so much light to make out even an outline. I can’t deny it any longer: I’m losing more of my sight again.”

“Sounds to me as though we ought to move the things you’re wanting to see into this room.”

She tipped her head his direction. “I think you would have a difficult time fitting the Rocky Mountains in this room.”

“I’d be willing to try.”

Her elusive smile reappeared. Relief washed over him. Seeing her suffering, hearing the ache in her words, had pierced him.

“Barring that, the MacAllisters have a very ugly dog I’d be happy to fetch. You’d have a fine view of it in here.”

“A dream come true.” A hint of laughter edged out some of the pain in her voice.

“And you could finally get a good look at my handsome mug. I’m certain you’ve heard plenty of talk about how fine-looking a man I really am.”

“I have, but mostly from you.”

He couldn’t hold back a chuckle at that. She’d a fine sense of humor, this woman who’d been so prickly upon their first meeting.

She sat up more fully, facing him more directly. “The two things I have heard about you most since my arrival are that you are jovial and handsome. Considering how grumpy you were with me in the beginning, I find myself inclined not to fully believe either description.”

"Come now, I've not been grumpy in weeks."

She tossed him a look of doubt. "Is this your humble way of telling me that you really are a fine-looking man?"

Heavens, it was nice to see her lighthearted again, even for a moment. Her pain had been so terribly acute. "This room'd be a fine place to test your theory."

She shifted to a kneeling position. "Will you close your eyes?"

"Why?"

"My spectacles dim the light. I will be able to see you better without them."

She didn't want him to see her without her spectacles? "What is it that worries you, Cecee?"

She clasped her hands on her lap. "My eyes are diseased. It has altered their appearance, and not in a pleasant way. I first began wearing darkened spectacles after witnessing the expressions of horror people wore when looking at me. I kept wearing them because the gasps of revulsion and overly loud whispers were equally dreadful."

"It can't be as bad as all that."

"I have quite literally frightened small children, Tavish. It can absolutely be 'as bad as all that.'"

"Well, now, *a chara,* let me tell you this." He slipped his hand around hers, squeezing her fingers reassuringly. "I've thought from the first time I saw you the day you arrived that you were near about the most beautiful woman I'd ever seen in all m' days. I'm not likely to change my mind on account of your eyes having an oddness to them."

Color touched her cheeks. "I'd like to think I'm not a vain person, but I know perfectly well that I'm fragile on this matter."

"I'll not argue with you then." He obediently closed his eyes. An odd scraping noise sounded in the next moment. "What's that?"

"I'm scooting closer. Honestly, do sighted people pay no attention to the world around them?"

"We're the worst."

She gave a quick laugh. No lectures about not being somber enough. No scolding him for jesting during a difficult time. She simply laughed, as he'd hoped she would.

"I *will* need to get very close to your face," she warned. "Uncomfortably close."

He nodded. "'Tis a good thing, then, that my eyes'll be closed."

"You will be able to hear me breathe."

He shrugged. "Fortunately, we sighted people never pay attention to sounds."

"How attentive are you to smells?" She did sound much closer.

"Is that your way of telling me you haven't bathed in a while?"

Another laugh. "I thought subtlety was the best approach."

"I'll brace m'self." But the scent that filled the air around him wasn't unpleasant in the least. 'Twas a light, flowery scent, one he'd vaguely smelled before. It was Cecily. And the increased warmth was her as well.

He could feel her soft breath against his face. She must have been mere inches away, if that. He'd promised to keep his eyes closed, but heavens, he was tempted to look at her.

"What color are your eyes?" she asked.

"'Tis hard to tell with them closed, isn't it?"

The briefest of pauses followed. "You promised not to press me on this."

She was right, of course. 'Twas unfair of him.

"My eyes are blue. A very light blue, like m' grandfather's were." Ma had told him time and again that he had her father's eyes. "What color are yours?"

"They were brown."

Were. Had her disease changed their color, then? He didn't ask; he didn't press. Instead he said, quietly, "I've always liked brown eyes."

"I've always liked blue." Her tone and volume matched his.

'Twas an unexpectedly intimate moment, though they weren't touching or gazing into each other's eyes. They exchanged no flirting or banter. Yet his heart tugged even as he fought a grin.

"How do you feel about dark hair?" he asked.

"Hmm." The feel of her lightly brushing his hair back from his temple very nearly paralyzed his lungs. "I am finding I rather like dark hair."

A fine answer, that.

"I prefer light hair, personally," he said.

"Do you?"

Oh how he wished she'd let him open his eyes. He could so easily picture her saucy, challenging look. "I do, in fact. Not long before you came, I told m' parents I meant to find myself a golden-haired Englishwoman."

"And were they properly horrified?"

"Indeed."

The same light scraping he'd heard before sounded again. "You're scooting," he said.

"And you're listening."

He was, but he couldn't sort the rest of the noises. Rustling and something else.

"May I open my eyes yet?"

"I suppose," she said.

When he opened his eyes, she had her spectacles on already. His curiosity was nearly killing him, but he could respect her wish for privacy.

"What's your verdict? Am I as handsome as everyone says?" He put as much feigned arrogance in his words as he could manage and was rewarded with her smile.

"Even in this light, I couldn't see much." Some of her sadness had returned, though she didn't look as miserable as she had earlier. "But thank you for letting me try."

He moved closer to her.

"You're scooting," she said.

"And you're listening." He knelt directly in front of her. He set his hands gently on either side of her face and pressed a kiss to her forehead. "Anytime you need to sit in the light, *a chara,* simply come. No need to ask."

She laid her hands against his chest and whispered a thank you. His heart threatened to leap through his ribs. He swallowed against the sudden thickness in his throat.

"Tavish." A whisper.

His lungs strained with every breath. He slid his hands from her face and down her neck, along her shoulders, pulling her so close that warmth and the fragrance of flowers filled the air once more.

"Cecee." Her name emerged a bit strangled and broken. "I—I—"

"Merciful heavens!" An alarmingly familiar voice interrupted. "What in the name of Saints Bridget and Michael is happening in here?"

Though neither he nor Cecily had heard the new arrival come in, Tavish knew exactly who it was, and further knew he'd just landed himself in a world of trouble. Few people could guilt a soul as quickly and thoroughly as an Irish mother.

Chapter Twenty-six

Cecily sat on the porch, bundled against the cold, waiting for Finbarr to return, whilst Tavish was inside, silently enduring a tongue lashing the likes of which she'd not heard before. All of Hope Springs was likely privy to the lecture. Mr. and Mrs. O'Connor were certainly not holding back.

"We'd never have approved of Finbarr's returning to Joseph's home if we'd had the least suspicion of you and that woman being up to mischief in his absence."

That woman. Mrs. O'Connor had yet to refer to Cecily by her name.

"'Twasn't any mischief, Ma. She was upset. I was attempting to console her."

"In your *bedchamber*?" Mr. O'Connor sounded as unconvinced as his wife.

"She'd stepped inside to take advantage of the light from the windows. Like Finbarr, she needs a great deal to see. I happened to find her there, upset and sorrowful. Would you have had me turn my back on a crying woman?"

Had his gesture been nothing, then, but kindness and civility? She'd thought there'd been something more personal in it.

"Do not twist this into a scold for being kind." His father's usually calm and casual tone had taken on an edge that set Cecily on alert. "You are playing with fire, and you know it. She is sharp and pretty, with a quick wit—a combination for which you've always had a particular weakness. And you, son, are lonely."

Mr. O'Connor's declaration contained a painful degree of truth. She'd sensed Tavish's loneliness and heavy heart early on, had recognized it by its familiarity. She herself felt very much alone in this world.

"I don't want to see you entrapped," Mr. O'Connor continued, "forced into a situation that'd only make both of you miserable."

His family not only thought her a woman bent on leading their son down a honeyed path, but one so mismatched that he would rue the very day he met her. She wasn't looking to marry or fall top over tail in love, but she didn't think herself such a bad choice as all that. And, heaven help her, she'd grown terribly fond of Tavish. Her heart rather liked the idea of him returning her regard in some degree.

"I think it'd be best if she doesn't return here again." Mrs. O'Connor likely couldn't have sounded more resolved.

"I am not a child, Ma. You can't order me about, nor say who I'm to spend m' days with."

"No, but Finbarr is not yet a grown man. She was brought here to tutor him, and we've the right to determine when her services are no longer necessary."

They would deny one son his lessons to prevent the other from growing attached to her? Could they possibly object to her that much? She rubbed at her temples and tried desperately to ignore the growing pain in her eyes.

"What of Finbarr?" Tavish asked. "He has not yet learned all he needs to."

"He can find Miss Attwater at Granny's," Mr. O'Connor said. "She can answer any questions he may have until spring when the roads are open."

"You're making mountains out of mole—"

"I agree with your mother on this, lad. 'Twould be best for everyone if she doesn't spend her days at your home any longer."

If not for the thick layer of snow blanketing the valley, the O'Connors would be sending her away now. But she still had so much to teach Finbarr. If fate proved kind, the spring thaw would arrive late, granting her more time to teach the young man what he needed to learn.

"After all she's done for the lad, you'd toss her aside because you'd rather your son not grow overly friendly with an Englishwoman?" Tavish, bless him, defended her presence even in the face of his parents' unyielding disapproval.

"Whether or not 'tis the least bit fair, she represents centuries of suffering and loss. That's something none of your neighbors can entirely overlook." Mr. O'Connor sounded a little worried. "'Twould be best for everyone if she finished her time here quietly rather than summoning up old hurts and losses. Ian, in particular, would appreciate it."

"Ian? What has he to do with Cecily?"

Cecily lowered her head, for once letting herself focus on the pain. That might be enough to distract her from their words.

"Have you not noticed, son," Tavish's mother said, "that Biddy, though she is generally friendly and welcoming, has never warmed to Miss Attwater?"

Cecily had most certainly noticed, but she'd tried not to dwell on it. Katie had become her friend, and she'd hoped that Biddy, Katie's dearest friend, would come to like her as well. Instead, Biddy went to great lengths to avoid her.

"During the Hunger, Biddy's grandfather was beaten to death by their English landlord for the crime of making off with a bit of wheat to feed his family," his mother said.

Oh, dear heavens.

She wasn't finished. "Biddy's uncles were imprisoned for the same crime and sentenced to transportation," Mrs. O'Connor continued. "Only two survived the squalid conditions of the prison long enough to board the prison ship for Botany Bay. Though we're not completely certain of it—her mother was never able to speak of the matter, and Biddy herself has seldom spoken of it—there's every evidence her father suffered the same fate. She and her mother were left alone in the world; they never saw her father again."

I will never win Biddy over, not with that history between our people.

"None of that is Cecily's fault," Tavish said. "She wasn't the one who—"

"It isn't fair," Mr. O'Connor said, interrupting. "But it is what it is."

"I'll confess I ought not to have been in such a . . . private situation with her," Tavish said after a moment. "But you're taking things all out of proportion. I'm not in love with her, and I've no plans to be. She's a friend, nothing more."

No matter that she'd not sought his affection nor expected it, Tavish's declaration registered as pain in her heart. Just a friend. Nothing more.

"Are you certain of that?" Mrs. O'Connor asked.

Cecily held her breath, waiting for his answer. For though he seemed certain, she was far from it. Her mind insisted that he had offered an accurate assessment of his feelings, but her heart was not at all convinced.

"I'm certain," Tavish said. "And don't fret. From now on, I'll send Finbarr to Granny's if he has questions or needs instruction. The house'll be free of English."

Free of English. That's all she was to him now, an Englishwoman and a problem. This man, who'd held her as no one else had, who'd comforted her in her time of anguish, who had, she was certain, very nearly kissed her, dismissed her with hardly a thought.

This was what came of letting herself care too deeply—being sent away and forgotten, but leaving a bit of herself behind.

With a deep breath of frigid air, she rose from her seat. Dusk was fast approaching, and she could barely see as it was.

She folded the quilt and set it on the chair. Carefully, slowly, she made her way off the porch. She set her sights, dim as they were, on the shrub that marked her destination across and down the street. Soon enough, she wouldn't be able to see that either. Perhaps it was for the best for her to be confined to Granny's house now that the days were darker and shorter.

Granny Claire spent most of her days at the O'Connors' home. Finbarr had begun spending at least a couple of days a week at the Archers'. Cecily would be alone most of the time, without even transcription to bring her some joy. She'd be spending her days alone in the dark.

Cecily opened the front door and stepped inside Granny's dark house. Her hostess was not home, which was not unusual. Cecily didn't bother lighting the lantern. She needed to adjust to the deterioration of her vision, and spending time in the dark seemed the best way to do that.

She found the way to her bedroom and lay down on her bed. Somehow she needed to find a way to make her remaining time in Hope Springs productive and helpful for Finbarr. Sitting alone in this room, waiting out the end of winter, would be a waste of her time and would ruin Finbarr's chance at a future.

"But how can I help him if the O'Connors won't let me?" They'd made their feelings clear. They'd rather send her away than allow her to help their son or belong to the town.

She wouldn't try to force them to accept her. But that didn't mean she didn't have work left to do.

"Is that you, Cecily?"

Why was Granny home?

Cecily sat up on her bed. “I’m in here.”

Shuffling footsteps grew louder. Soon she could hear the rustling of a dress. “I didn’t expect you so soon,” Granny said.

“I could say the same to you.”

The bed shifted with Granny’s weight as she sat. The very faint aroma of smoke and wax told Cecily that Granny had brought a candle with her. She could not make out its flame. The realization swelled as tears in her throat, which she forced back angrily. Why did this have to happen so soon?

“I’m feeling quite done in this evening,” Granny said. “I had to cut my visit short.” Which explained why Mr. and Mrs. O’Connor had arrived at Tavish’s when they had. “What brings you back so soon, lass?”

“My eyes hurt.” It was true, just not the entire truth.

“I know the look of one whose heart is hurting, dear. You’re wearing it now.”

Was she so transparent? Cecily released a tense and overwhelmed breath. “The O’Connors have decided they no longer want an Englishwoman in their midst. I am to stay here at all times.”

“You’ve been banished?”

Cecily nodded. “Finbarr will come here when he needs instruction. I would not be surprised if they soon disallow that, as well.”

“Is Finbarr ready to end his lessons?”

Cecily pulled her legs up beside her. “No. But their distaste for my countrymen is, it seems, too great an obstacle. I don’t know how to convince them otherwise.”

“This town made its peace at the *céilís*,” Granny said.

“They aren’t held in the winter.” Tavish had told her as much. “And I wasn’t welcome at the one I attended.”

“We can be a terribly stubborn people, I’m afraid.” Granny spoke dramatically. “But we are very fond of parties.”

Cecily could almost smile at Granny's exaggerated tone. "Then I suppose I simply need to hold a party of my own if I am to win them over."

"Only if there is a great deal of food."

A party of my own.

The idea felt suddenly less of a jest. "Would it help, though?" she asked.

"Would *what* help?"

"If I invited the O'Connors over for a little party, a bit of food and socializing. Would that help soften them at all?" The more she talked about it, the more the idea appealed. "They may find that they enjoy my company, or at least that they don't have reason to hate me."

Granny didn't immediately answer.

"Does their fondness for parties not extend that far?" What hope did she have of making peace with the O'Connors if even the promise of a winter-time *céilí* wouldn't convince them to endure her presence?

"I believe they would come," Granny said carefully. "They're wary and unsure, but they're not unkind. Not truly."

"And it's nearly Christmas." Cecily liked the idea more and more. "The season is excuse enough for a party. Perhaps I could convince Ciara to attend; if I remember correctly, she's the sister who has distanced herself from them of late."

"'Twould be something of a miracle if you managed all that," Granny said.

"I can at least try." This might very well be the miraculous approach she'd been looking for. "And if Ciara doesn't agree to join us, the rest of the family would still enjoy themselves."

Granny patted Cecily's hand, a gesture she'd employed often of late. "That'll do the trick, Mr. Attwater, you'll see. You'll win them over."

"I intend to," Cecily said. "I fully intend to."

"Miss Attwater." Mary Dempsey, the O'Connors' elder daughter, could not have sounded more displeased to have found herself in her company.

For her part, Cecily was relieved at the unforeseen encounter. She had invitations for both O'Connor sisters and did not wish to overly burden Katie with the necessity of driving her up and down the road to make her deliveries. Her friend was waiting in the buggy as it was, willingly spending her day helping Cecily. To have reached the door of Ciara Fulton, nee O'Connor, at nearly the same instance as Mary was a bit of unforeseen good fortune.

"Have you come to call on Ciara?" Mary asked incredulously.

"Only to deliver an invitation." Cecily turned to face Mary, who stood very nearly behind her. "I have one for you as well." She reached into her drawstring wrist bag and pulled out an invitation, which she held out. She could make out Mary's outline and a few very minor details, yet she depended upon her other senses to fill in far too many empty spaces. The folded paper did not shift at all in her hand; Mary had not taken it from her, nor, as near as she could tell, had she reached for it.

The door beside them opened on protesting hinges. Enough light illuminated the space thanks to what Cecily suspected was a cloudless day for her to make out the silhouette of a woman in a long dress. Ciara, no doubt.

"Miss Attwater?" Did the sisters realize how very similar their voices were? If not for the fact that they stood on opposite sides of her, Cecily would have struggled to know which of them was speaking.

"Good morning," she said. "I've come to deliver an invitation."

"To me?" Ciara sounded surprised.

"And your husband." Cecily did her best to sound confident. While the family wasn't overly fond of her, this sibling offered a unique challenge. Being a bit distanced from her own family, Ciara wasn't likely to be warm with someone almost universally disliked. Still, Cecily meant to try.

"Did my family send you?"

Mary answered from behind Cecily before she could. "Do you think an Englishwoman would do the bidding of the Irish?"

Cecily forced her expression to remain neutral despite the derisive declaration. If all went well, the party to which she was attempting to deliver invitations would be the first step toward overcoming the distrust she'd inherited.

"But she has come with you," Ciara said to her sister.

"We arrived at the same time is all," Mary said. "I came to see if you'd care to join Ma and me for a bit of quilting this afternoon."

"I've a great deal to do here." Her tone sounded odd, but in a subtle way. Cecily would've expected determination or stubbornness in the rejection, or at the very least, conviction. Instead, she heard sadness and something bordering on desperation.

"You've not spent an afternoon with us in ages," Mary insisted. "Surely your chores can wait until evening."

"I've a great deal to do," Ciara repeated.

Silence descended on the two women. Neither spoke, and neither left. Cecily couldn't see enough to know if they were looking at each other. But one did not need a clear view to know that a world of hurt lay between them.

Cecily did not know Ciara's reasons for shutting her family out, but she was entirely certain it was a matter of deep-seated pain. The O'Connors were a family in agony.

"I must return to my work," Ciara said, her voice taking on a determined edge that rang a little too strong. She was making a show of being unbendable. An invitation might be exactly the excuse she needed to venture from the exile in which she had, for reasons yet unknown, placed herself.

"I won't keep you," Cecily said, turning her head toward each of them in turn. "Either of you. I only wished to deliver these." She handed them both an invitation. This time, they both accepted the offering. "I hope to see you there."

They made vague responses, owing to not having read the invitations yet, most likely. Cecily smiled and stepped carefully back in the direction of Katie's waiting buggy.

"Any difficulties?" Katie asked when Cecily drew near.

"Such a tension between them," Cecily said as she settled into her seat once more.

"That, there is. Ciara's pulled into herself these past months, but not a soul has any idea why."

The buggy lurched forward before settling into a relatively smooth clip.

"Has Ciara always been uncomfortable around children?" Cecily asked.

"What makes you think she is?" Katie's doubtful tone made Cecily question the conclusion she'd come to.

"Several weeks ago, Ciara was at Tavish's home with the other O'Connor women. She seemed to be getting on with them well enough, if perhaps distantly, until she was asked to tend to Biddy's little one. Then Ciara sounded quite suddenly on edge, and she made a swift departure."

"Odd, that," Katie said.

Either the discomfort was, indeed, connected to the baby, or something else in the interaction Cecily hadn't noticed or been aware of. It truly was not for her to insert herself into the affairs of someone she hardly knew, someone who had not invited her evaluation, but the pain she'd heard in Ciara's voice a moment ago wouldn't let her mind rest on the issue. Cecily never could be easy in the face of another person's suffering.

"Is her husband equally distant?"

"A bit, yes." Katie seemed to think on it a moment. "He isn't as distant as she is, though."

"Do they ever seem at odds with each other?" She was being unforgivably nosey.

Still, Katie didn't seem to object. "No. What little I've seen of them tells me they're as close as ever. Closer, even."

Circling the wagons. Cecily had seen it often enough. Something difficult had happened, she'd wager, so Ciara and her husband had turned to each other for strength. In the process, they'd turned others away, however unintentional or counterproductive.

Ciara's isolation was more pronounced than her husband's, Katie had said.

"I wonder what is breaking her heart," Cecily wondered quietly.

"You think it's a matter of pain?" Katie asked.

"I am certain of it. Her voice held a heavy note of sorrow just now."

"I doubt the O'Connors realize as much," Katie said. "They speak of her absence at family functions in terms of rejection and defiance."

Her absence likely felt that way to them, especially added to their other struggles.

"Perhaps you might suggest a different perspective," Cecily said. "They are more likely to listen to you."

"I'll consider it." Katie brought her to her next stop: Ian and Biddy O'Connor's home. Cecily made her way to the door, invitation in hand. Based on the dress and height of the woman who answered the door, she assumed it was Biddy. But from somewhere inside, Biddy's voice asked after the newcomer.

"'Tis Miss Attwater." Mrs. O'Connor, then, stood before her.

Mary had said something about the women gathering for some quilting. This must be where they'd gathered.

"I've come with an invitation," Cecily said. She grabbed a second invitation and held both out to Mrs. O'Connor. "I am holding a small Christmastime party, and I hope you and your husband can come. I also have an invitation for Ian and Biddy and their family. I would dearly love for all of you to attend."

"A Christmas party?" Mrs. O'Connor sounded more surprised than confused.

"A small gathering." Nervousness clutched at Cecily's mind. Her lungs shrank with uncertainty. She wanted to ease the difficulties between herself and her student's family, but the invitation was more than that. She wanted a friend. A connection. She was reaching out and begging for someone to reach back. She was asking for someone to see her loneliness and care enough to alleviate the isolation if only for the length of one evening.

"You are inviting us?" Mrs. O'Connor asked.

Cecily nodded. Though the gesture was not useful when others utilized it with her, it worked perfectly well when she directed it at others. "Your family as well as the Archers."

"Mrs. Claire does not mind the influx of people in her home?"

Cecily had made quite sure of that. "She does not mind."

"I will give Biddy your invitation," Mrs. O'Connor said. It was not an acceptance, but neither was it a rejection out-of-hand.

"Thank you."

No one had refused her invitations. No one had mocked her for extending them.

A glimmer of hope, however small, hovered on the horizon.

Chapter Twenty-seven

The evening of Cecily's party arrived full of promise. She'd delivered the invitations and had chosen a day near enough to Christmas for the O'Connors to feel festive without the party interfering with their holiday plans. The weather cooperated. The roads stood clear.

She felt hopeful. More than that, she was excited. Cecily remembered fondly the parties her mother held at their home so many years ago. The entire house had overflowed with happiness and friendship and welcome.

Before her eyes had begun their descent into blindness, Cecily often imagined being the hostess of such an evening. It wasn't the fine gowns or elegant decorations or fancy guest list that had appealed to her, but the joy that accompanied such gatherings. To know she had friends who cherished her company, and to bring happiness to people she cared about. The very possibility had warmed her heart.

She set her fingers on the lip of the table and slowly made her way around it, squinting at the plates of goodies on the surface. She couldn't make them out with any degree of clarity. She double-checked the stack of plates and napkins, quite a few of which she'd borrowed from Katie, not having access to enough.

She could show the O'Connors that she was a person worth knowing. She could convince them to allow Finbarr to return to his previous lessons and schedule. And she would get to spend time with Tavish. All in all, the night's prospects were good.

Tavish hadn't been by since her banishment, though Finbarr had. The young man had returned to Joseph Archer's home a few times to work, and he'd sought her out, needing advice on being more efficient in the tasks he'd taken on. The lessons proved a challenge, as she had to sort out chores she'd never done herself and think of ways to help him tackle them. She enjoyed the undertaking immensely. But in all of that, Tavish never came by, never dropped in to offer a good day, never sent a greeting with Finbarr.

She told herself he was simply being careful to maintain family harmony. He was being cautious and considerate of his parents' concerns. That would improve after tonight, when his family realized she wasn't a threat. After tonight, she would be at least marginally accepted. Then Tavish could resume their . . . friendship.

That word didn't sit well on her mind or in her heart. She felt more than that for him. Pointless though it was, she'd begun to fall the tiniest bit in love with the charming Irishman.

"One thing I will say for you, Mr. Attwater, you set a tasty table."

"Does everything appear correct?" Cecily asked. "None of it smells burnt, and I think I managed to arrange it pleasantly, but I see so poorly in the dim light that I cannot be sure."

"Mrs. O'Connor frets in precisely the same manner before every *céilí*, convinced the world'll stop spinning if a single tart or biscuit is out of place." Granny's rocker squeaked against the floor. "But I've never heard a lick of complaint."

Yes, but the people of Hope Springs already liked Mrs.

O'Connor. She wasn't attempting to prove herself to the neighbors. If her offering succeeded or failed, it made little difference; the town would love her just the same. Cecily had no such reassurance.

"What is the time?" she asked Granny. The clock was no longer visible to her.

"A touch after six o'clock."

"*After* six o'clock?" The party was scheduled to have begun at six.

"Only a touch, dear."

The gathering was intended to be a casual one, she reminded herself. The guests would, no doubt, come and go as the evening wore on. Everything would be fine.

She made her way to the front window. Granny's rocker sat directly beneath it, as Tavish had fixed the draft. Cecily carefully lowered herself into the vacant seat beside Granny. She was near enough to the window that she would hear any approaching wagons or voices. She took a deep breath and forced her shoulders to relax.

Why was the evening's gathering making her so nervous? One of the things she remembered most vividly about her mother was her graciousness as a hostess. Cecily would simply imitate her beloved mother, call on those long-ago memories, and all would be well.

Hope Springs was the only place she'd accepted a job where she'd felt utterly unwelcome. Her students had often been difficult. Her efforts had sometimes been dismissed. But overall, she'd been treated well. She'd found friends and acceptance.

But this town, this family, were breaking her heart.

"They will come." Her whispered declaration was a desperate one.

"Of course they will," Granny said.

Cecily waited. For fifteen minutes.

An hour.

Two hours.

No one came. Not one single person. Not Katie. Not Finbarr. Not Tavish.

Granny's rocker made only the occasional squeak. She hadn't spoken in some time.

"Granny?" Cecily had to repeat her name twice more before getting a mumbled response. "It's time for bed. You won't sleep well sitting in your rocker."

"But what—what about your party?"

"All finished," Cecily said. "I'm going to clean up. You go get some sleep."

Granny must have realized there had been no party. Even so, she rose and shuffled toward her room. "I will see you in the morning."

"Good night." Cecily maintained her light and easy expression until she heard Granny's door close.

Alone, she let her shoulders droop and her heart drop clear to her boots. No one had come. Not any of them. That was a message impossible to misunderstand. It was a fist to the gut and a slap to the face. Little point pretending otherwise.

Her mother's legacy of graciousness offered little solace and even fewer answers. What kind of hostess never had a single guest to welcome?

A pathetic and unwanted one.

She wrapped the uneaten sweets and pastries in paper, tying the packages with twine, then setting them in the cupboard. She wiped down the table, swept the floor, and blew out the lanterns. In the darkness, she stood alone, swallowing down tears that threatened.

The O'Connors had made their point.

She wouldn't try again.

"I used to like Christmas." Tavish stood at his front window, watching the gray sky. The entire O'Connor clan, including Ciara, though she hadn't stayed long nor said much, had gathered at Tavish's home on Christmas morning. "We've passed a rather gloomy couple of years."

Ian's gaze was on Tavish rather than the threatening clouds. "Last year we'd a brother no one was certain would live to see the new year. That put something of a damper on the festivities."

"Aye. 'Twas a difficult time, that."

Ian's gaze only grew more focused on him. "What has you in the doldrums this year? Finbarr's improving. The town is at peace. Yet here you stand frowning and glowering."

"Maybe I've simply become a grump in my old age." Tavish turned from the window, though he didn't move to join the rest of the family. "Or maybe you just have overly loud children."

"You are turning into a grump."

Tavish sat on a stool near the window. "Katie told me often enough that I needed to be more somber. Seems I'm finally managing to." His gaze wandered to Finbarr, who sat a bit removed from the family, though he didn't look as miserable as he had in months past. "He's doing a little better."

"Do you think he'll ever be the Finbarr we used to know?"

Tavish shook his head. "Cecee says he won't, that passing through the sorrows he has will've changed him. But she seems to think he can be happy again."

"I'd be more likely to believe that if *she* seemed happy," Ian said. "But I've seldom seen her anything but sour."

That sounded nothing like the Cecily he knew, yet he'd thought much the same about her when they first met. He understood her better now.

"She had to be forceful when she first arrived," he said. "Finbarr would never've listened to a word she'd said otherwise. Most've the rest of us still don't."

"You seem to pay her enough heed," Ian said.

Tavish held his hands up in a show of surrender. "Da already ran me down with that particular train of thought. You needn't travel those tracks as well."

"We none of us wish to see you hurt again." Ian was wearing the *poor Tavish* look of his once more. Pity was a hard pill to swallow, and Tavish had been doing just that for years.

"I've no plans to be hurt again. I've no time for it. Between our baby brother, my land, this family, and my dear ol' granny, I've enough to keep me plenty busy."

Ian's gaze turned to the window. "Speaking of dear old women, where is Granny? She was supposed to be here this morning."

'Twas odd for Granny to be so late. Tavish crossed to his front door and pulled it open. The rush of cold wind set the entire family loudly requesting he close it once more.

"Just wanted to make certain you were all awake," Tavish tossed back with a grin.

He stepped outside. If he didn't spot Granny straight off, he'd go trekking after her. But there she was, at the edge of the road, walking arm in arm with Cecily.

His worries eased at the sight of his beloved adopted grandmother. But seeing Cecily again after two weeks brought a sense of relief so strong it nearly set him off balance. 'Twas almost as if he'd been holding his breath for the entire fortnight, only to finally have air again.

Closer she came, Granny at her side. Up the walk. Up the steps.

Stay away from the women, he'd told himself all those months ago as he'd eaten his birthday cake. *Stay away. Keep your distance. Guard your heart.*

He was doing a mighty poor job of following his own counsel.

"My apologies," Granny said, reaching the door. "We dropped in at Archers and found Katie in need of cheering. Cecily, here, is as much a dab hand at bringing laughter to tearful eyes as you are, lad."

"Is she?" He kept his tone and expression light. His heart may have betrayed him a bit, but that didn't mean his head wouldn't win out in the end. "Perhaps Cecee would favor us all with a tale at the next *céilí.*"

Cecily gave a firm shake of her head. "I think I'd do best to avoid parties. They do not tend to turn out well for me."

The one *céilí* she had attended hadn't gone well, so she likely didn't care to attend another. That was probably for the best anyway. The town would never welcome her no matter how diverting her stories might've proven.

"Go on inside," Cecily said, slipping her hand free of Granny's arm. "And please assure the O'Connors that I don't mean to foist myself upon them tonight."

Foist herself? Cecily was welcome if she wished to stay. This was his home, and it was Christmas. Granny stepped past him, moving with slow steps. Tavish kept an eye on her until she'd set herself safely near the fire, then he returned his attention to Cecily.

She held up a small, paper-wrapped package. "I've only come along to offer these, a few goodies from two nights ago."

Two nights ago? What was two nights ago? "You've confused me, I'll tell you that much."

"No need for confusion." She all but forced the package into his hands. "I made a gesture and heard the response quite clearly. I will not impose again, but I do not wish the food to go to waste."

"You're not making the tiniest bit of sense." He placed her package inside the house and pulled the door closed behind him, leaving only the two of them on the porch.

"Your parents will be out here in a heartbeat, demanding to know why you're interacting with me," Cecily warned.

"I'm only seeing to it that you reach home safely."

"I don't have a home. Not really."

He'd not heard such a tone of defeat from her before. He shoved his hands in his pockets, resisting the urge to reach out to her. This was precisely the path he needed to avoid. The path of friendship was fine. Being a decent human being, certainly. But giving her a place in his heart? Out of the question.

"Granny said Katie needed cheering," Tavish said, "but I suspect you do as well. Do I need to summon my most entertaining tales of folly?"

Katie's voice immediately echoed in his mind, words she said often in the last weeks of their courtship. "I'm in no mood to laugh just now," and, "Teasing won't fix this."

But Cecily was not Katie.

"Only if you promise the tale is particularly embarrassing to you and will make me feel better about my own recent humiliation," she said.

"Oh, I can full promise you that, *a chara*." He chuckled lightly at the wide range of stories that had jumped to his thoughts. "You need only pick an age or a continent."

Though she didn't truly look unburdened, she did seem a bit less crushed by whatever weight she was carrying.

"I have a likely ridiculous question for you," she said.

"Ask while I walk you home, and I'll agree to answer it."

She nodded and allowed him to pull her arm through his. As they walked down his front walkway, she made good on her request. "What does *a chara* mean? You call me that now and then. It doesn't sound like an insult, but, given all that has happened, I wonder a little if it might be."

An insult? Here he was worrying that he was allowing himself to care for her too much, while she stood convinced he was calling her derogatory names.

"Is it, perhaps, the Irish phrase for 'Your Majesty'?" She did have reason to wonder.

"'Tis a term for a friend," he said. "Not a vague or casual friend, but a particular one. A friend that a person is fond of. One he holds dear."

Two spots of color appeared and slowly spread over her face. Though the cold might've accounted for it, Tavish rather suspected the cause was something else entirely. This path they were treading had more pitfalls than he'd feared.

"In the end, though," he added, "'tis only a friend."

That was not entirely true; the phrase could be used for someone more than that, but he couldn't allow that kind of relationship again.

"I know," she said. "I understand what I was told the other night. I won't overstep my role again."

He guided her carefully across the road. Pockets of ice dotted the landscape, and she was still without a cane. He took utmost care to make certain she made the short journey safely. "This 'other night' . . . is this the same night the package of goodies are from?"

She nodded.

"You speak of it as if I ought to know what you're referring to, but I'll admit, Cecee, I've not the slightest idea."

She stopped their forward journey. "The Christmas party I hosted," she said, brows pulled low in confusion.

"You hosted a Christmas party two nights ago?"

"I meant to." Her brow pulled low. "I sent Finbarr home with an invitation for you."

"He never gave me anything," Tavish said. "Did you tell him what was written on it?"

Uncertainty touched her expression. "I asked him to try reading it in the lamp light—it would be a good exercise for him—but to give it to you if he wasn't able."

Well, there was the answer to that mystery. "He's seventeen and stubborn," Tavish reminded her. "He likely couldn't read it, and wasn't willing to admit defeat and hand it over."

He nudged her along, and she resumed walking. The day was

growing colder; he'd get her home and make certain she had a fire to keep her warm. "Perhaps you'd best tell me what I was meant to have received."

"I thought if I invited your family to a Christmas party, they might decide I'm not quite as horrible as they'd like to believe."

From the sound of it, her plan hadn't played out well. "You invited my entire family?"

"I am nothing if not determined." She made a valiant attempt at a lighter tone.

They reached Granny's front path. Tavish tucked her closer to him. The path, dotted with patches of ice and mounds of frozen snow, was even more uneven than the road. "And how many O'Connors accepted your invitation?"

"They all took the written invitation I gave them." She said nothing more than that

"You've given me the milk without the cream, dear."

Her mouth and eyes scrunched in confusion.

"You've not answered the question," he explained. "How many in my family came to your party?"

She paused a moment. Voice lowered, she said, "No one came."

"What, no one?" That couldn't be.

"Not a soul." She made a gesture of dismissal, but her tone spoke too clearly of disappointment for him to accept it. "Their message hit its mark, I assure you."

No one had come. Her offer of friendship and kindness had been utterly rejected. "I mean to give them a piece of my mind."

"Tavish, no." She stepped up on to the porch. "I cannot tell you how relieving it is to know that you, at least, did not thumb your nose at the invitation. We are . . . *friends*, after all."

"Of course we are." Why did those words stick on the way out?

"And as such," she continued, "I will not cause discord between you and your family. Please reassure them that I will continue to work with Finbarr, and that his education will be completed to the best of my ability, but that I will not attempt to insert myself into their lives any more than is absolutely necessary."

"Cecee—"

"They can consider it my Christmas gift to all of them." She turned the knob and pushed the door open. "And a gift to you. You've fought this past year to keep your family whole—I've heard enough of what's happened, and have witnessed enough of your efforts, to know that their happiness is essential to your own. I will not undo that happiness."

'Twas exactly what he'd been telling himself for weeks. And, yet . . .

"But you will be all alone."

"I've been alone for a long time, Tavish," she answered. "Do not worry for me, *a chara*."

A chara. Friend. Why did such an uplifting phrase suddenly strike him as heartbreaking?

Chapter Twenty-eight

Cecily spent the week after Christmas formulating a plan for the remainder of Finbarr's education. He could more or less function around the house now. With Joseph and Tavish's help, he was learning to tackle various jobs around the farm. She'd taught Finbarr how to evaluate a new task and determine how to best approach it. He could use those principles to face unexpected challenges; he wouldn't need her for those things. But two things remained she could teach him. Two things she *needed* to teach him.

The first required a cane, which she didn't yet have. The other, though, she was prepared to begin on immediately. Finbarr arrived at Granny's early in the morning a few days after the new year. Cecily motioned him inside and indicated he should sit at the table.

She joined him there. "I think it is time I taught you to read."

"I know how to read," he insisted. "If this is about the invitation, I'm sorry I didn't tell Tavish. I didn't know what it was. I couldn't see it, and I was afraid if I got too close to the lantern, it would catch fire."

"I wasn't implying that you are illiterate." Tavish had jumped to the same conclusion a few weeks earlier. "I meant that it was time I teach you to read in the dark."

"Is—is that possible?" Finbarr was still uncertain, but he was no longer defeated.

"Yes," she said confidently. "First we will test whether your eyes function well enough to read given the right circumstances, whether that means bright light on the paper or having the paper very near your eyes, or perhaps both. You can also learn to write using a ruler as a guide. I have taught fully blind individuals to do so."

"And if my vision's too far gone for reading?" There was the all-too-familiar discouragement.

"Those who cannot read with their eyes can be taught to read with their fingers." She opened her copy of The Gospels, one of the few raised-type books she traveled with, and one she believed he would be familiar with. His family were church-goers. "Run your fingertips over these pages."

A moment's silence followed. She couldn't see Finbarr with any degree of clarity, but she hoped he was following her instructions.

"It's lumpy," he said.

"This is called Braille. The letters, rather than being written with ink, are instead written with a series of dots pressed upward from under the paper. They are raised so they can be felt."

The book scraped against the tabletop. He was pulling it closer to himself; that was encouraging. "And this really works?"

"It does. A few different raised-type systems are used, none of which is perfect, but they open up entirely new possibilities."

"But no one around here knows about it," he said. "No one could send me letters this way. And I couldn't write to other people, either, because they wouldn't be able to read it."

"True," she admitted, "but as I said, your vision may allow you to read in the right circumstances, and you can still write with ink. Using raised type, you could write to others with diminished sight, keep lists for yourself, balance a ledger of your expenses. And you could read books printed in Braille."

"Books?" The enthusiasm in his voice warmed her heart.

Learning to read raised type nearly a decade earlier had changed her entire outlook about her own future. It could change Finbarr's as well.

"I could send letters and the recipients could read them?"

"Yes. You'll use ink for those who do not read Braille. Braille for those who do and for yourself."

"My family cannot afford to buy books," he said quietly.

A great many of her students were in that situation. "I have established a lending library using a collection of books in Missouri that I created. The students at the school where I was educated take turns running the library. You need only send a letter or a telegram requesting a book, and it will be sent to you. Once you return it, you can request another. I've been adding to the collection for years."

"Does it have a lot of books?" More of the hesitant hopefulness.

"Quite a few, yes. Once my vision is gone entirely, and I can no longer travel as a teacher, I will return to a school setting, likely the school I attended." She would far rather have a home of her own, perhaps continue to travel, spend time with her transcriptions. But she had to have an income, and working at the school would provide that. "I hope to spend my free time translating more books into Braille."

"And you'd let me borrow some?"

"Happily." She'd send him all of the books he could possibly hope for. In return, she'd hear from him now and then, perhaps learn how his family was getting along—his brother, in particular.

"Is this Braille difficult to learn?"

She scooted her chair closer to his. "Not at all, especially since you can already read. You would only be learning to recognize the pattern of dots that represents each letter, and then learn how to use a stylus and stencil to create your own raised type. It will take some effort; I won't lie to you on that score. And at times it will be frustrating, but I haven't the slightest doubt that you will pick it up quickly."

"Don't the English generally view the Irish as . . . simple?"

Was there no end to their assumptions about her? "Unfortunately, many English do think that. I, however, prefer to wait and decide what a person is like until after I get to know that person myself. A novel idea, I realize, but one that has served me well."

"I'm sorry about my family," he said quietly.

"So am I." She took a quick breath and squared her shoulders. "But we have something far more pleasant to focus on just now."

"Reading in the dark." A hint of wonder touched his tone. "It sounds almost like magic."

"Don't tell your family that," Cecily said. "They'll deem me a witch."

Granny chose that moment to enter the conversation. "The way you've captured Tavish's attention, who swore he'd have nothing more to do with women, I've no explanation but dark magic."

Cecily didn't know where to begin responding to that declaration. "I've not bewitched anyone, and certainly not him. He calls me 'Your Majesty,' you realize, and not as anything resembling a compliment."

"He hasn't called you that in ages," Finbarr said.

"And he hasn't called *on* me in ages either," Cecily returned. "That doesn't sound like the behavior of a man who is under a woman's spell."

"He may not come by, but he asks about you every time I've been here," Finbarr said. "Every single time. He didn't even do that with Katie."

"With Katie?" What did she have to do with this?

"He courted her for a time," Granny said, answering Cecily's unspoken question. "But she was a better fit for Joseph, and he for her."

That was two lost loves. Little wonder he seemed so burdened. Between his family and his own heartache, he'd endured a great deal.

Granny's rocker squeaked once more. Back and forth. Back and forth. "He's not truly opened himself up to anyone since Bridget died."

She'd seen that for herself. "He hasn't allowed himself to mourn her," Cecily said. "He can't heal if he doesn't do that."

"Don't we know it," Granny answered. "But we've none of us managed to convince *him* of it. He'll not speak of her."

"He's spoken to me about her," Cecily said.

"He has?" Granny and Finbarr answered nearly in unison, their shocked tones matching each other's.

"Yes. On more than one occasion."

"Now isn't that something . . ." Granny's contemplative voice trailed off.

Finbarr hadn't mourned his losses, nor faced his feelings of guilt either. If only the two could open up to each other, they would both benefit.

She reviewed her unspoken list: Teach Finbarr to read and stencil Braille, especially if he hasn't the vision to read words in ink, feel at home working for Joseph again, use a cane. She added an item: convince Finbarr and Tavish to face their regrets. A lot to accomplish in only a handful of months. She had best set herself to the first task.

"Would you like to learn Braille only if you cannot read, even when close to bright light? Or would you like to learn it either way?"

Finbarr didn't answer immediately. When he did, his words were heavy with uncertainty. "I might not always have a lantern."

"That is true." But it wasn't a complete answer.

Again he hesitated. "The Braille might be good to know."

"Well, then. Let's begin." Cecily slid the book away and set a sheet of heavy parchment in its place. "I have written out the alphabet on this sheet of parchment using Braille. I'm going to place your fingers where they should be."

She felt about for his arm, then pulled his hand to the upper left corner of the paper and gently laid his fingertips there.

"Run your fingers over this small corner," she instructed. "Tell me what you feel."

"Lumps."

How well she remembered her earliest encounters with raised type. "That is precisely what it will feel like for a time. Once your fingers are more familiar with the sensation of reading, you will be able to feel each small dot. Each set of dots makes a unique pattern that represents a letter. Once you learn to recognize those letters—"

"—I'll be able to read again."

"Precisely."

"And keep accounts and lists and records and . . . and all of those things."

"Yes." She set her hands atop his. "This is why your family sent for me. The past year has been too full of darkness for you, but I know how you can get some of that back. Tell me what it is you wish to do with your life, and I will help you find a way to do it."

He pulled back. "What I want to do isn't possible any longer."

"I have done the impossible," she said. "I've given people things they never dreamed they could reclaim."

"I—" He pushed out a breath that sounded something like a growl. "For the past few years, I've been working for Joseph to buy a parcel of land he is holding for me."

Ah. "You wish to have a home and land of your own."

"I was going to raise crops and build a house for myself, have a family, live a quiet life a little removed from my enormous family. Granny, don't tell them I said that."

"Said *what*, lad?" Granny tossed back.

"Why do you think you can't still do those things?" Cecily

asked. "Working with Joseph will allow you to face the challenges of undertaking common chores around a farm. Between him and Tavish, you will have ample opportunity to discover the best means of caring for animals. You're already learning to cook for yourself and to keep your spaces tidy."

"I suppose." He did not sound at all convinced.

"What still worries you?" she asked.

His chair pushed away from the table. Footfalls paced behind her. "The fields would cover acres and acres. Even before the fire, I sometimes got turned about in Joseph's fields. If I tried to move about them on my own, blind, I'd likely end up off in the mountains, completely lost."

That was a legitimate concern, and one she had never tackled before.

"How can I make *that* work?" Finbarr asked, still pacing. He was moving around the room with ease. Did he realize how much of a triumph something as simple as that already was? Mere months earlier, he'd been too afraid to leave his chair all day.

"I don't have an answer to that yet. *Yet*," she emphasized. "But if you will promise to work diligently on learning to read raised type, to continue working with Joseph, and to not give up, then I promise to ponder the challenge of a farm until I have a solution. I am certain there is one, and I will work tirelessly until I discover it."

His footsteps stopped. "My parents say you're leaving in the spring. That's not much time to fix something you've never fixed before."

"And that is the beauty of learning raised type, Finbarr. I needn't be here in person for us to converse. I can write to you, and you can write to me." If he wrote to her in Braille, she could read his letters after her vision was entirely gone. "If by the time I leave Hope Springs, we don't have an answer, that does not mean the opportunity is lost. I have made connections throughout the country with people from all walks of life and all occupations. Someone among them has likely faced the same difficulty, or one similar to it. I can write to any number of people in search of answers, then write to tell you what I've learned. If an approach you are trying isn't working, you need only write back, and we'll continue to adjust."

"You mean to continue being my teacher even after you leave?"

How could she make him understand? "Teaching you has never been merely a job. I asked about your dreams, what you wished to do with your life, because *that* is my life's work: bringing hope to those in darkness. There are no limits of time or location on hope."

His chair scraped and creaked. He sat near her, but didn't speak for a drawn-out moment.

"I don't know why my family is so unkind to you," he whispered. "Or why you keep helping me when they treat you badly."

"They're afraid," she answered. "When people are afraid, they do things they wouldn't otherwise."

"But you've never given them any reason to be afraid."

If only fear were that rational.

"I sound different from them. Based on what little I know of your family's beliefs, I'm relatively certain that I hail from a different religious tradition. I come from a different area of the world. My homeland has a difficult history with theirs. Those things shouldn't be enough to make one person view another as somehow less acceptable, but too often fear has resulted in exactly that."

"I don't think of you that way," Finbarr said. "Granny doesn't. Neither does Katie. Or Joseph. Tavish certainly doesn't."

"Then perhaps they will write to me as well." Truth be told, she almost hoped Tavish wouldn't. She ached at the thought of receiving letters from him, of Tavish continuing to be a part of her life, occupying the place in her heart he'd somehow managed to claim.

She'd sought so long for love and companionship, of belonging somewhere and with someone. But having him in the most vulnerable places of her soul, yet forever out of reach, would only make her hurt that much more.

Chapter Twenty-nine

One did not ignore a summons from Granny Claire. Stepping over her threshold, Tavish discovered his parents were there, as were Ian and Biddy, and his sisters, even Ciara. 'Twas a regular family gathering, only without the laughing voices and smiling eyes. Everyone, to a person, looked as wholly confused as he felt.

He passed by them, crossing to the far wall where Da stood near the kitchen cupboard.

"Any notion what this gathering's meant for?" Da asked.

"Not the slightest," Tavish quietly replied. He leaned one shoulder against the wall.

Granny, in her rocker as ever, spoke. "Now that we're all here, and the two who I'm meaning to discuss are not, I'm calling a beginning to this meeting."

"A meeting, is it?" Tavish eyed her, trying to gauge her intentions. "You mean to give us assignments?"

"I mean to give you a sermon." Granny skewered every last one of them with a look so pointed it left no doubt of her earnestness. "Though we're not kin, you've claimed me as your own. You've treated me with a kindness and compassion that does our Irish ancestry proud."

For a sermon, 'twas beginning on a friendly tone.

"When we came to this country, we were viewed as a scourge. We sounded odd, saw the world differently, worshipped differently, hailed from another area of the world. So many in this place saw all of that as proof that we'd come to unravel the very moral fabric of their society. They believed that we, in our poverty and want, served no purpose other than to ruin their lives and destroy their country."

Granny leaned forward, her rocking coming to a halt, as she eyed them all. The condemnation in her eyes set most of his siblings fidgeting. Tavish had been on the receiving end of her glare in the past, but even he squirmed a bit. Biddy, standing near the door, a bit apart from the rest of the family, wrapped her arms around her middle, not looking at any of them.

"And now," Granny continued, "here is this same family looking at a woman among us who sounds odd, sees the world differently, likely worships differently, and hails from another area of the world than we do. And are we showing her the compassion we insisted America ought to've given us? No. We're proving ourselves no better than those we condemned."

"Granny—" Ma began, but she was cut off.

"This here's a sermon, not a discussion." Granny made to speak again but was seized with a coughing fit.

Tavish quickly stepped to the sink and pumped enough water to fill a glass. He rushed the glass over to her. She sipped while he lightly rubbed her back. His family yet sat, mute, confused, and more than a touch guilty. Biddy stepped away from them all and stood with her arms crossed, looking out the window near Cecily's desk.

Granny returned her half-full cup to Tavish and continued with her lecture. "Finbarr told Cecily of the dreams he's given up, the things he wishes for in his life but doesn't believe'll ever be his."

Finbarr didn't tell anyone of his fears and worries. Not Ma or Da. Not Tavish. Yet he'd told Cecily. Tears sprang to Ma's eyes. Pa stood with his mouth a bit agape. Ian met Tavish's shocked gaze with one of his own.

"Cecily promised not to rest until she'd done all she could to help him live those dreams," Granny said. "In the most solemn of tones, she promised to never give up on him. And he, in turn, felt compelled to tell her how very sorry he was that his family was so terrible to her."

If ever a family looked ashamed, the O'Connors did in that moment.

Granny coughed again. She waved away Tavish's offer of her water glass. "Cecily spoke kindly of us," she said. "She eased Finbarr's distress. She, who's received every unkindness at our hands, saved his opinion of us all."

"That isn't a surprise to me at all," Tavish said. "She's a fine person. Far better than any of us've been willing to admit."

"We've reason to be wary." Biddy still hadn't rejoined them all, remaining not far from the door, as if ready to flee at any moment. "Whenever English and Irish live together, we are the ones who suffer. Always and always."

"I'm not suggesting we make her a member of the family," Granny said. "Nor that she be your dearest friend."

"What are you suggesting, Granny?" Da asked.

"That we give Finbarr reason to look on his family with pride rather than shame."

The hesitant silence that followed did not set Tavish's mind fully at ease. Yet, they were listening, which was a decided step in the right direction.

"We can be peaceable," Granny added. "And we can help her help him." She began rocking once more and peered through the window nearest her chair. "This'll be her, returning with Katie Archer. They've been to town." Her gaze returned to the family. "Tell me what you've decided."

"We'll behave." Tavish eyed his family. "Won't we?"

He received nods, even a look of encouragement from Ian. Biddy moved to a position behind the group, far from the door and very nearly out of sight. The others remained where they were, but no one said a word. When the door opened, the room, in fact, was unnaturally quiet. Katie stepped inside first, stopping in her tracks at the sight that met her. Cecily came in behind her and stopped very quickly as well.

She tipped her head to one side, and after a moment, said, "More than five, but fewer than twelve."

What did that mean?

Cecily's nostrils flared with a deep sniff. "And one of them is Tavish."

Ian laughed.

"And Ian," Cecily added.

"There are ten of us, you troublesome woman," Tavish said. "And I'd very much like to know what smell it was that told you I was present."

"Berries," she answered.

"Truly?" He'd not worked his berries in months, the harvest being over long before winter set in.

"Yes, Tavish. You exude the essence of berries year round," she said dryly.

"Troublesome, troublesome." Heavens, he'd missed her humor.

"Who else is here?" she asked, her unseeing gaze falling over the room.

"M' sisters and parents."

Her amusement disappeared on the instant, replaced with undeniable worry. "Are they angry with me?" she asked quietly.

Tavish threw a look of censure at them all before answering Cecily. "No. We've come to see if we can help with Finbarr." He suspected Granny wouldn't care to be made responsible for this.

"I am pleased to hear that." She took a single step forward, holding her hand out tentatively. "I haven't replaced my cane. Am I on the verge of walking into anything or anyone?"

"You've plenty of open space." Da, of all people, offered the assistance.

Cecily took a couple of steps, stopping in front of them. "Finbarr shared with me one of his worries for the future, and I'm not certain I can sort out the best way to address it. Having your help and your minds spinning over the issue would be a godsend."

She'd just referred to a family who'd been unkind to her from the first as heaven sent. How could they not see how remarkable she was?

"He still dreams of taking possession of the land Joseph is holding for him," Cecily continued. "While he's more hopeful about his ability to tend to animals and work in the barn and around a house, he cannot fathom how he could possibly work his fields, not being able to see where he is or where he's going."

Since the fire, Finbarr hadn't spoken of the future in any specifics. How had she managed to pull that confession from him? Could she teach Tavish to do the same? He wanted to reach out to his brother but didn't know how.

"I have never worked in a field," Cecily said. "While I can conceptualize it to a degree, I would only be guessing at the exact details and therefore I'd be guessing at what and how to teach him. I need your help with that. *He* needs your help."

Only the briefest pause followed before the room erupted into a myriad of conversations. Words like "field" and "rows" and "plow" bounced off the walls. Even Ciara joined in the conversation. Ciara, who'd not spoken at length to any of them in months. Tavish didn't see anyone else looking at Cecily, so none of them saw the utter relief that crossed her features.

He stepped up next to her.

"I knew I wasn't equal to solving this on my own," she said. "But I didn't dare approach your family. This is almost miraculous."

How did she always know when he was the one who approached? Did he have such a unique scent? Or was it something else?

"Katie promised to set the question to Joseph," Cecily continued, "but having this many minds working on the problem sets mine at ease."

"Do you think Finbarr could someday live on his own, then?" Tavish hoped so.

Cecily nodded. "When his house is built, some adjustments can be made so he has an easier time getting about in it."

"What kinds of things?"

"Large windows, for one thing," she said. "His vision is not entirely gone, and having light would help tremendously. Cupboards and cabinets with a great many drawers and shelves for organizing those things that most people would leave lying about but which he'd have a more difficult time locating without very specific places to store them. A bedchamber on the ground floor so he need not climb a ladder; he is capable of climbing but would appreciate not having to do so. Things of that nature can be taken into consideration when building his home."

Perhaps Tavish could implement a few of those things in his house so the lad would function better while living there. "What else?"

"The paths between outbuildings can be lined with fences so he won't get lost moving from place to place." She didn't even pause to think, a clear indication she'd already pondered the matter. "The family of one of my youngest students trained a dog to go about with him and steer him back in the direction of their house if ever he began to wander. While that wouldn't entirely solve the difficulties Finbarr would face in his fields, I do think a dog would be very helpful. I would also suggest a wind chime or hanging bells on the porch. During times of bad weather, the sound would help give him a sense of direction."

He could live in his own house, on his own land. Independent. His own man. Amazement filled Tavish at the idea. "You will have given him his life back."

"That is why I do what I do," she said.

"Even when your student's family is mule-headed."

She smiled broadly. "*Especially* then."

"You're a gem, you know."

"Am I? Because Seamus Kelly was at the mercantile just now, and I did not get the impression that he feels the same way."

Tavish wasn't overly surprised. "Well, the O'Connors aren't the only mule-headed ones in Hope Springs."

She shrugged, but the dismissive gesture did not quite ring true. Cecily quickly changed the topic. "Mr. Johnson asked me to tell you that he and his oldest boy have been pondering ways to get Finbarr a cane sooner rather than waiting until the spring thaw."

In the few months she'd been in Hope Springs, Cecily had managed to efficiently focus the efforts of those who cared about Finbarr in ways no one else had in the year before she'd come.

"And have they thought of a way?" Tavish asked.

"They are whittling down a broomstick," she said. "It should be ready in another week or so."

How perfect. "And are they whittling one for you, as well?" She'd been without hers for over a month already.

"They are not so fond of me as they are of Finbarr."

"I'll do it," he offered.

"Do what?"

"Whittle you a cane." Indeed, he felt the fool for not having thought of it sooner.

"Your family would have a collective stroke."

There was some truth to that. "They'd not begrudge you a cane."

"They would if *you* made it."

He set a hand on her arm. "But you need a cane."

She smiled a little. He liked her smile. He liked it a lot.

"This is one problem you don't have to fix, Tavish. I'll get another cane when I can."

He slipped his hand in hers, unsure where the impulse came from. "Well, dear, don't be surprised should you find a hand-whittled broomstick waiting for you one morning."

"Don't be surprised if I tell your family about your mischief."

"Traitor," he muttered in unison with her, and then she joined in as he laughed.

Granny's rattling cough pulled his attention. He watched her frail shoulders shake with effort.

"I don't like the sound of that," he whispered.

Cecily, her hand still in his, whispered, "She has begun coughing at night. I bring her water, but it doesn't seem to help."

Not for the first time, Tavish wished Hope Springs had a doctor. "I don't know how to help her either. I've not the slightest bit of medical training."

Cecily wrapped her arm around his. "I've been bemoaning the same gap in my education."

"At times, Cecee, I can't understand a word you say."

She bumped him with her shoulder. "Says the man who doesn't always speak entirely in English."

"Tavish," Ma's voice snapped.

On instinct, Tavish dropped Cecily's hand. She must have felt the same moment of panic; she hastily unwrapped her arm from his.

"What can I do for you, Ma?"

She stopped directly in front of them both. "I'm needing to speak with Miss Attwater."

Then why was he being scolded? The answer, of course, was

that he was being friendly with the enemy. The O'Connors might be helping with Finbarr's dilemma, but that didn't mean they felt any different about her as a person. He'd generally seen the family's stubbornness as a strength, but seeing them hold fast to their notions about Cecily made him wonder if perhaps stubbornness wasn't their greatest weakness after all.

Cecily remained as unruffled as ever. "What can I do for you, Mrs. O'Connor?"

"Granny says you're teaching Finbarr to read and write."

Cecily clutched and unclutched her fingers. She took what sounded like a fortifying breath and pushed onward. "In a manner of speaking, yes. He already knows how to read and write; I am simply teaching him how to 'see' words with his fingers."

"This book"—Ma held up a thick volume—"is made with the special printing that you are teaching him?"

"It likely is. I left one of my books on the table this afternoon."

"Would you show me how it works?"

Cecily's brows shot upward. For a moment, she neither spoke nor moved. Then, slowly, she turned her head in Tavish's direction. "I'll need you to hold the book for me, as I require both hands to read. Open to any page you'd like."

Tavish took the book, opened it up, and held it out flat for her. The pages were covered in dots, but not dots made of ink. They were made *of* paper, paper pressed upward. She found the book, and then her fingers slid lightly over the pages to the left-hand side. Then, ever so carefully, she ran the pads of her fingers over the paper.

She read aloud.

"What though on homely fare we dine,
Wear hoddin grey and all that,
Give fools their silks and knaves their wine,
A man's a man for all that."

"Robert Burns." Amazement touched Ma's words.

Cecily nodded. "My childhood home sat very near the Scottish border. I was raised with a love of Burns."

If her kind words for a Scotsman softened Ma's opinion of her, it didn't show. "And those dots are words? You can read them?"

"Yes. I can read four different systems of raised type. This one, I think, is the most useful and efficient."

Ma's gaze became intent on Cecily's face. "And Finbarr could learn to read it?"

"He is learning it—both how to read and write it," she answered. "He isn't proficient yet, but that will come."

"Do you think—?" Ma took a breath, apparently uncertain of what she meant to ask. "Do you think . . . I could learn it?"

Ma? Asking Cecily to teach her? Volunteering to spend time with her enemy? Tavish could've been knocked down with a feather, so great was his shock.

Cecily simply answered, "Yes."

"Learning to write it would mean I could write a letter or a note to him, and he could read it." Ma hadn't looked away from Cecily.

"I am teaching him to write in ink as well, so he could write to you that way. But if you learn to decode the dots, he could write to you in this method, which I have found is easier for those with poor vision."

"Life has been hard enough for the lad," Ma said. "I want to be part of making it better."

Cecily showed not a hint of begrudging Ma the suspicions and unkindnesses she'd been shown. How she'd endured his family without turning bitter, Tavish couldn't say.

"This will help," Cecily said. "The blind so often feel a barrier between themselves and the sighted world. He ought not feel that with his own family."

Was that part of the chasm Tavish had felt over the last year? Finbarr sat in a world apart from them, one they didn't fully understand. Perhaps they weren't the only ones unsure how to bridge that gap. Perhaps Finbarr felt as helpless as they did.

"I want to learn," Ma said earnestly. "We are not wealthy people; we haven't the means of paying for additional lessons. But I could knit you a scarf—I notice the one you use is not very thick. I can't imagine it's warm enough. Or I could bake your favorite sweet or cook a meal. Or do all of those things. Whatever you deem fair."

"Mrs. O'Connor." Cecily reached out and somehow managed to set her hand on Ma's arm with her first attempt. More miraculous still, Ma didn't pull away. "I consider myself more than a teacher of skills. My goal is always to give back what blindness has taken from the people I teach. Their freedom, their futures, their families. Giving you this connection to him, and him this connection to you, is part of why I am here."

Ma's eyes turned a telling shade of red. Her lips, pressed tightly together, quivered noticeably. She nodded her silent understanding and acceptance of Cecily's words of reassurance and compassion.

"She's nodding," Tavish whispered, knowing Cecily wouldn't see it.

Cecily gave a quick nod of her own. "Would you like to learn along with Finbarr—attend his lessons—or separately, on your own?"

A hint of excitement touched Ma's features, something Tavish hadn't seen in over a year. "I'd like to surprise him. Simply write him a letter one day."

"I think that is a lovely idea." Cecily's enthusiasm dampened, however. "To write in Braille—that is the name of this system—one must have a special stylus and stencil. I have mine and the set I gave to Finbarr, but I don't have another."

"Perhaps if I were to show m' husband the contraption, he could manage to think of something to take its place."

"Certainly." Cecily turned to Tavish. "I'll need help navigating the room with so many people here."

"I'm fairly reliable," he said. "Leave it to me, dear. I'll see you safely over the passage."

"You stay here, Tavish." Ma left no room for disagreement. Recognizing Cecily was a good teacher didn't make her any less English. "I'll go with Miss Attwater."

The two women left and had only been gone a fraction of a moment when Katie, who had apparently been nearby the entire time, spoke up. "Do you suppose Cecily would teach Joseph this writing method? 'Twould likely help the two of them in their work."

"I'm certain she would."

Ian stepped closer as well. "Would she teach me?"

"Aye." The eyes of many in the family were on him, all asking the same question. "I've no doubt she'll teach anyone who cares to learn. We need only help her fashion the needed equipment."

Excitement, curiosity, and determination all flitted across the faces around him. They were eager and unified and facing a problem directly.

Tavish met Granny's eye. She gave him a nod of approval. He felt, as she so clearly did, that though far from whole, his stubborn, worried, fearful family was finally beginning to heal.

Chapter Thirty

Tavish felt like quite the rebel slipping over to Granny's while Finbarr was at Joseph Archer's. He'd done so the past two days with Finbarr's Braille stencil and stylus in hand, having nipped them after Finbarr had left for the day. He and Cecee had work to do.

She opened the door and motioned him inside. "Has he noticed yet?" Cecily didn't need to say who.

"I've been careful to leave the contraption just as I found it. I must be doing a fine job, because Finbarr's not said a word."

She pushed out a relieved breath, turning back to the table where she'd laid out all the needed supplies. With her back turned, he pulled from behind his back the item he'd hidden there. He meant it to be a surprise.

"I can appreciate your family's desire to make this a pleasant surprise for Finbarr," she said, moving to the table. "But attempting to teach—how many are we up to now, an even dozen?—to read and write Braille without him being the wiser, and when my stencil and stylus are not available, is proving a bit tricky."

"Ah, but 'tis a fine excuse for me to come over and banter a bit with you. Surely that's worth a bit of bother."

"And a fair bit of bother it is, to be sure." Heavens, but she could manage an Irish manner of speaking when she decided to. She pulled her chair away from the table. "Shall we set to work?"

"But first, I've brought something for you."

"You have?"

Tavish set Finbarr's Braille slate on the table near her stack of thick parchment. He held out a long, rough-hewn walking stick. "'Tis nothing fancy. I hadn't a spare broomstick, so I made it from a tree limb. It's a bit crooked, but I'm hoping it'll prove a usable substitute until Jeremiah Johnson can order you a proper one."

Her gaze was fully on the stick, though he felt certain she couldn't truly see it. Nothing in her expression told him whether she was pleased or put out.

"You've said your stick is important to your independence, and I've noticed you don't leave the house as often as you once did."

She reached out and touched the stick. Perhaps she could see it after all. She ran her fingers down the length of the branch he'd meticulously sanded. How he hoped he hadn't missed any spots. His offering would be far less welcome if it left splinters in her hands.

"It's not perfectly straight," he said again when her silence pulled long. "I hope it'll still work."

Cecily looked up at him once more. "You've given me back my freedom." Her voice broke a little on the words.

"I'm a rather wonderful fellow, aren't I?"

She set her hand tenderly to the side of his face then raised up on her toes and pressed a light kiss to his cheek. "You are a very 'wonderful fellow,' Tavish O'Connor."

He cleared his throat of a sudden thickness. He could do nothing to stop the pounding that had taken hold of his pulse. Cecily had stood close before. He'd held her as they'd danced. But this moment held more affection than any previous one had.

Either she particularly liked her cane, or she particularly liked him. For his part, he hoped both were true.

Cecily stepped away and set her cane ahead of her as he'd seen her do with her old one. "Once the Johnsons have finished Finbarr's cane, I can begin teaching him to use it. That will open up possibilities for him."

How quickly she returned to the tasks before her. What would it take to convince her to set aside her responsibilities, even for a few minutes, and simply talk, as they'd once done? He'd missed their conversations, her endearing way of jumping from earnest to jesting, from topics of importance to amusing anecdotes.

Cecily felt along the tabletop until she found the slate and stylus he'd placed there. She took her seat and leaned her stick against the table. She ran her finger along the edges of the wooden slate, finding the screws holding the long metal stencil in place and, with a precision a sighted person would be hard-pressed to possess, slid the stencil to the top of the slate and screwed it in place once more. She pulled a sheet of paper from the stack and slid it between the metal stencil and the slate beneath.

She took up the stylus and made quick work of her first line of pressed printing. Her efforts moved from right to left, something Tavish imagined would take some getting used to. She unscrewed and moved the stencil down a bit, then quickly pressed out the second line. He watched the graceful movement of her hands, the confidence of her speed, the determination in her posture. She was something of a marvel, truth be told.

As she worked, Tavish sat next to her and prepared his pen, ready for the task she'd given him the day before as well. She freed the paper from the slate and flipped it over, the dots raised on that side. She laid the sheet between them on the tabletop. Her fingers found the uppermost set on the left.

"A," she confirmed.

He leaned over and carefully wrote the letter in the space just above the dots that represented it.

"B."

This was their method. She made the alphabet in Braille. He wrote it out in longhand after she confirmed it was in the right place and that she hadn't made an error. They'd completed several sets the day before and meant to finish today. These were keys to be used by the sighted members of the family while they learned the coded language. She insisted they make extras should anything happen to the originals, or should others decide they wanted to learn.

"You enjoy this," he said as they finished up the first sheet. "You've seldom been so close to giddy as you have been the past days while we've worked on these."

"This writing system, and others like it, give the blind back a bit of their lives. Bringing these miracles to them is my passion. Too many are lost in darkness with no one to show them the light."

He set aside the completed paper and took her hand in his, raising it to his lips and pressing a kiss to her fingers. She blushed so red 'twould've put his raspberries to shame, were they yet on the vine.

"What was that for?" she asked.

He couldn't help a jesting reply, not only because that's what came most natural to him, but also because he knew she'd appreciate it. "I thought that was the proper way to finish making one of these keys. Dots. Ink. Kiss."

She laughed unabashedly. "If that's the case, I may be able to convince more sighted people to learn Braille."

"Perhaps schools for the blind could use that to advertise and increase their enrollment. 'Come get an education—and a kiss now and then.'"

"Oh, good heavens." She shook her head as she often did when he was teasing her, with her lovely smile firmly in place. "That would cause quite the scandal, seeing as most students are very young. I was only eleven."

"You were away from your family at eleven?" He couldn't imagine having been separated from his at so young an age.

"I'd already lost my mother, and the family never felt whole after that. I suppose my time at school didn't feel much lonelier than I had been surrounded by the silence of my father's breaking heart."

A heaviness settled over him. "Losing a loved one leaves a vast void in a person's soul."

She held more tightly to his hand. "You, *a chara,* have lost more than your share of loved ones."

"But you are giving me back Finbarr," he said. "And for that, I cannot thank you enough."

She rotated on her chair and faced him more fully, though he knew her eyes, hidden behind her colored spectacles, could not actually see him. "Has Finbarr spoken of the fire or the little girl who died? He is progressing in many respects, but I worry a great deal about that. He hasn't mourned what happened that day, and that burden takes a terrible toll."

"I don't know that he has. The O'Connors are good at many things, but grieving isn't one of them."

"Granny doesn't often speak of Bridget," Cecily said. Hearing that name again didn't pierce him the way it usually did. "I think she is afraid to; she doesn't want to hurt you."

"Thinking about Bridget is painful," he admitted, rising from his chair and slipping his hand from hers. "I don't often allow myself the memories, let alone speak of her."

"I'm a very good listener," Cecily said. "If you'd like to try."

Try speaking of Bridget? Could he manage such a thing? To his surprise, he found himself wanting to make the attempt.

"She was two years younger than I. So very sweet and happy. She was . . . it was as if someone had captured pure sunshine in a jar, and she carried it about with her. A person simply couldn't be unhappy in her company."

"That is a rare and beautiful quality," Cecily said.

"'Twas, indeed." He forced himself to breathe, to push ahead. Talking about Bridget didn't break him the way he'd expected it to, but neither was it proving easy. "I don't know that we ever disagreed about anything. Looking back, I can't say if that was because we shared the same opinions or because we were both young and relatively unacquainted with the world. Perhaps neither of us had the heart to risk undoing the almost magical quality of our connection."

Cecily offered no insights or guesses. She simply remained in her chair, facing him, listening.

"Six years ago, at the last *céilí* of the season, she agreed to marry me." He paced a bit away. "Not a month later, she was gone, dead of a fever, buried alongside all her family except Granny." He swallowed the emotion that quickly rose at the spoken memory of one of the worst times in his life. "My homeland had been taken from me, as had my grandparents and two older brothers. Half this town died of that fever, and the woman I loved had as well. I was more than sad, more than brokenhearted. I was . . . lost."

"You *were* lost or you *are*?" Cecee asked.

He rubbed at the back of his neck, where tension was building. "I'm not so broken as I was those first months and years. But I don't know that I've ever truly found myself again. There was no time for mourning; the first victims were buried within a week of the fever's arrival." Those had been dark days. "All through it, Bridget kept sewing the dress she meant to wear on our wedding day. She'd chosen the fabric herself: pink flowers—she liked pink—on a cream background. A bit of Irish lace at each wrist." He could still picture that dress. She'd shown him her progress every day, so proud of it, so pleased.

He breathed through the pain stabbing at his heart. "She was buried in it."

Cecily rose from her seat. She slowly crossed to him. Dredging up these memories ought to have left him wishing her to Hades, wishing himself alone. Instead, his arms reached for her. He pulled her into his embrace. She, in turn, wrapped her arms around him.

Neither spoke. Neither pulled away. He closed his eyes and let himself breathe for what felt like the first time in six years. He'd not been strong enough to examine his pain alone, but he'd found in Cecily Attwater an ally to stand with him as he felt the anguish and offer strength to him as he faced that chapter of his life again.

Speaking of Bridget hadn't brought sudden healing or forgetfulness. He didn't for a moment believe that all his grief and pain were behind him. He simply felt, finally, as if he might at last be able to face it, if only he knew how.

"I've spent the past year trying to help my family face their losses, but I haven't the first idea how to do that myself." He managed a tense and difficult breath. "I've never been to her grave. I attend church every Sunday, painfully aware that the churchyard where she's buried lies mere steps away. I've tried to make that journey any number of times, but I can't do it."

"Because if you do, it becomes real." How she understood that so instinctively, he didn't know.

He nodded. "I think I need to go, though." His stomach twisted at the thought. "And Finbarr needs to go, to let himself weep for little Marianne Johnson."

"Perhaps knowing that you've managed that difficult journey will help him feel safe enough to make his own," she said. "He may not be ready for some time yet, but he'll need to go, eventually. And when that time comes, he'll have you, who understands that struggle better than anyone. You can help him conquer it."

But only if he, himself, managed to conquer it first.

That Sunday, Cecily's heart felt heavy all through services, the first she'd attended since arriving in Hope Springs. Reverend Ford's sermon wasn't lacking in any way. She simply knew that Tavish had to be hurting fiercely; after the service, he would finally be making the pilgrimage to Bridget Claire's grave. Cecily had witnessed enough mourning over the years to know that the journey, and even the anticipation of it, would likely be excruciating.

After the service, she waited for him at the far corner of the churchyard, the cane he'd fashioned for her held firmly in her hand. When he'd promised her a cane, she'd thought it had been in jest. She ought not to have doubted his thoughtfulness.

The bright light of day illuminated the church steps and a mass of colors and shapes she knew to be people. Her vision was not entirely gone, but had diminished to the point she couldn't make out individuals. She recognized the rhythm of Tavish's steps approaching the spot where she stood.

The breeze brought her the familiar scent of him—his soap mingled with something that was his and his alone.

"Do you still want to do this, Tavish?" she asked gently.

"It's a little unnerving the way you do that. I'd not said a word yet." His next breath shook a little. "I don't know why I'm so nervous."

"I do. You are about to face a ghost of your past, face pain and heartache. That would make the stoutest of hearts nervous."

"Are you saying I'm 'the stoutest of heart'? A regular knight on a charger? A conquering hero?"

"What you are is stalling." She tempered the words with a smile. "You don't have to do this if you're not ready."

"I'll never be ready," he said. "But I'm willing, and that'll be enough."

"Well, then, Sir Tavish, Knight of the Realm, go slay your dragon."

"Would—will you go with me?" He made a sound of distaste. "Some hero I'm proving to be, needing someone to hold m' hand."

She held her arm up, fingers outstretched, not entirely sure where his was, and felt his warm hand wrap around hers.

"Needing people is not a weakness," she said. "In fact, letting yourself acknowledge that need takes a great deal of strength. You keep people at a distance, my friend. It is time to let them in."

He tugged her next to him and threaded her arm through his. Though she'd not told him specifically, he'd come to realize that holding his arm in that way helped her navigate. She held the cane in her other hand, high enough to not bump the ground. With him beside her, she didn't need it to guide her.

"Here we go then." He spoke with tremendous uncertainty.

"Tell me more about her," Cecily requested. A little distraction might help him take those arduous steps.

"What would you like to know?"

She thought on it a moment. Something light would be better than something sad. "What was her favorite dish at the *céilís*?"

"Bread pudding," he answered without hesitation. "I've never known anyone with such a love of bread pudding. She was a tiny thing, but I swear to you, she ate it by the pound."

"I am the same way with berry pie—any kind of berry, it doesn't matter," Cecily confessed. "I haven't so much as an ounce of restraint."

"Come this summer when my berries are ripe, I will bake—no, I will have someone who actually knows how to—bake you a pie with my berries. They are the best in the entire territory."

"I have heard something along those lines," she said. It seemed best not to remind him that she would be leaving in the spring. She'd rather not think on it herself.

He took a step forward. Only one, but a significant one. Then he took another. Theirs was a halting, painstaking progress, but progress just the same.

"Did she have a favorite song or tune?" Cecily thought it best to keep him talking so his mind could focus on something other than a quickly approaching headstone.

"Oddly enough," he said, "'The Parting Glass.'"

She wasn't familiar with the tune. "Why is that odd?"

"It is a song honoring the memory of those who've passed on before us."

"Is it a sad song?"

Their progress slowed noticeably. "No, actually. It's rather celebratory."

"And it was her favorite." How Cecily hoped what she was about to say was not overstepping herself, but Tavish needed permission to be honestly happy again, deeply and truly, not merely a facade that didn't quite reach the innermost bits of his heart. "If that was a favorite, then she must have prescribed to that school of thought. She preferred happy memories and celebrations of a life rather than endless mourning and regrets."

"I think—" His thick voice broke. He cleared his throat. "I think that is one of the hardest parts. If she had seen how broken I've been since she—since then, she would be sorely disappointed in me. I hate the thought of her being disappointed in me."

Cecily could hear tears in his voice. Though she hated the idea of him hurting, he needed to finally feel the grief. "From what I know of her, she would simply want you be happy again. I don't think she would begrudge you the time it took to find that happiness."

They stopped walking altogether. Had she said too much? Had he lost his nerve? A number of voices floated on the breeze. Perhaps he had too much of an audience.

"This is her," he whispered.

Her breath caught even as her pulse pounded in her head. "What would you like me to do?"

She heard him swallow. "Just don't leave me."

She slipped her arm from his and wrapped it around his middle, offering what support she could. Each breath shook from him. Here was a man trying desperately to be stalwart in the face of more than a half-decade of pain.

He broke his silence, not with spoken word, but with a broken, quiet song.

"Since it fell unto my lot,
that I should rise and you should not."

The note cracked with emotion, but he pushed on.

"I'll gently rise and softly call,
'Goodnight and joy be to you all.'"

A sniff. Then another.

"So fill to me the parting glass—"

His voice broke again. Now she understood. This was his Bridget's song. A song offered to those who have passed on. Tears formed hot in her eyes as he tried valiantly once more.

"So fill to me the parting—"

Again the lyrics stopped.

"The parting—"

She couldn't help; she didn't know the song. She simply held him as the cold wind pounded against them.

"I can't do this, Cecee," he whispered.

But from behind them, a woman's voice began to sing, strong and determined.

"So fill to me the parting glass,
and drink a health whate'er befalls."

More voices joined the first.

"Then gently rise and softly call,
'Goodnight, and joy be to you all.'"

The song continued, with voices joining from all around, but at a distance. They must have all stood at the fence of the graveyard, singing to Tavish, and to their own loved ones buried here.

Tavish had stopped singing, and he seemed to have stopped weeping as well. The strength of his neighbors was buoying him up.

"I miss her," he said quietly, emotion still heavy in his words, as the song continued around them.

"I know you do." She still missed her parents, though they'd been gone for years and years as well. "You always will. But perhaps now you can find a way to honor the life she lived and begin living yours as you were meant to do."

His arms settled more firmly around her, pulling her close. "It's going to hurt more before it hurts less, isn't it?"

"I believe so."

"But . . . I'm realizing that it's a pain I needn't face alone." He pushed out a breath and turned them both around. "Can you see them, Cecee?"

"The people singing?"

"Aye."

She leaned against him, thankful for his strength and his presence. "I'm not at all certain if the shapes I see are people or trees or simply flaws in my vision. But I can hear them. And I can feel them."

"It's all my Irish neighbors." He spoke in a tone of amazement. "Some didn't even know my Bridget."

"But they know you. And they care about you."

His arms wrapped around her. "My family's here as well."

"Of course they are."

"'Twas Ciara who took up the song when I couldn't continue." Pain, worry, and gratitude all filled his words. "She's singing yet, though she's crying something fierce."

Ciara Fulton was mourning her own loss, Cecily would wager, something her own family didn't see or wasn't aware of.

The chorus continued around them.

"Fill to me the parting glass,
and drink a health whate'er befalls.
Then gently rise, and softly call,
'Goodnight, and joy be to you all.'"

Such poignant words, tender and heartbreaking all at the same time.

A breath shook from Tavish. "This is every bit as difficult as I feared it would be. More so, truth be told."

"And you are every bit as strong in the face of it as I knew you would be."

"I'd not expected anyone to join me," Tavish said, "standing there like battlements, fortified against the coming onslaught. A man could feel safe conquering anything with such a force at his side."

His family, his neighbors, were his strength and his support. They would be the same for Finbarr.

While Cecily would miss him terribly after she left, there was some solace in knowing he would not be alone.

Chapter Thirty-one

When Tavish arrived at his parents' home that night for the weekly O'Connor Sunday supper, Ma threw her arms around him and didn't let go for what felt like hours. Da looked on, his expression both tender and amused.

"Have I contracted a fatal disease no one's told me about?" Tavish asked.

"I just love you, m' boy. You do know that, don't you?"

"Of course I do." He set his hands at her waist and pulled her a bit away from him. "Has something happened?"

He saw heartache in her expression, but he also saw hope. "You were there, Tavish. *You* were what happened."

The graveyard. He managed a fleeting smile, one that felt a bit pulled. "Thank you for standing in support of me. All of you." He eyed the rest of the room. "'Twas time and past I began making my peace with Bridget's passing. She'd not have wanted me to be unhappy for so long."

"Have you been unhappy?" Ma asked quietly. "Truly unhappy?"

"No," he reassured her. "But I've not let myself grieve, and that's left me hurting more than it needed to. Cecee was right about that."

Her pinch-browed gaze hadn't left his face. "You've been crying," she whispered.

"Here and there." He felt a little foolish admitting that, but there was no point lying. Apparently, the truth of it was clear enough. "Oddly enough, I feel better for it."

Ma put her arm around him as she walked with him farther into the room. She motioned to the corner, where Finbarr sat with Ian and Biddy's tiny one on his lap.

"I think your brother needs a cry himself," she said, keeping the comment between the two of them. "He's not grieved for his losses, either. This morning is the closest I've seen him come to it."

"I'd imagine it'll come for him in time." Tavish only hoped the lad didn't push it away for years on end. He knew all too well how doing so magnified the burden.

"Ciara's here," Ma said.

That stopped him in his tracks, and Ma with him. "She's come for Sunday supper?"

Ma nodded. "Hugged us all in turn, she did. Said nothing explaining the last months, but I think she's coming back to us."

Relief bubbled in his heart. He'd worried for her. "Do you think she'd welcome a hug from her blubbering older brother?"

"I believe she would." Ma slipped her arm away and gave him a tiny nudge toward the small lean-to that served as the family kitchen.

Ciara was inside, along with Mary, the two gabbing up a storm as they'd once done regularly.

"Thomas spoke of staying," Mary said as she mashed a bowl of boiled potatoes. "Not in sure terms or like one convinced, but I think he may at least be considering it. Seeing the strength of this town and family today touched him as none of my words managed these past months."

Tavish kept silent, not wishing to interrupt nor to miss a word. Mary and Thomas, it seemed, might not be leaving Hope Springs. There was at least the possibility.

"I hope you'll stay," Ciara said. "We'd miss you if you left."

Mary didn't look at her sister, but Tavish felt certain that all her attention was on Ciara. "We've missed you these past months. 'Tis a good thing to have you here tonight."

Ciara turned away but didn't leave. "It is good to be here." Her eyes met Tavish's. He gave her a smile he hoped was welcoming. "I'm wanting to give Tavish a hug," Ciara said, as if still speaking to Mary though her gaze was on him. "And I couldn't hug him if I wasn't here."

He hooked an eyebrow upward. "Why is it the women in this family are all wishing to hug me tonight? Makes me wonder if you've all gone mad."

Mary looked up from her mashing. Her eyes pulled wide. "Tavish."

She crossed the room and reached him just as Ciara did. They embraced him, one on either side. He wrapped an arm around each of his sisters. "If I didn't know better, I'd think you're rather fond of me."

Mary stepped away first, rolling her eyes at him. "We love you, you difficult man."

Tavish looked down at Ciara still holding on to him. "Is that true, Baby Sister?"

"Thank you for singing today." Her whisper wavered with emotion.

He gave Mary a quick look. She nodded, understanding without explanation that he meant to slip out with Ciara for a bit of privacy.

He guided her to a near corner far enough from the rest of the family for some degree of quiet. "It's I who ought to thank you," he said, keeping a supportive arm around her. "I faltered. I couldn't push through those words. 'Twas you who took them up in m' place, who helped me over that barricade."

"I thought back on our time in New York, to those late nights you spoke of a few weeks ago, when we walked home from the factory together." Ciara hadn't spoken of New York in ages. She'd been so young when they'd left, only a few years older than Emma Archer was now. "You sang to me then, whenever I needed comfort and reassurance."

She had needed more than mere comfort and reassurance, though he hadn't realized it at the time. Only in a few discussions since coming west had she told him of the misery inflicted on her by some of the other factory girls or the leering and suggestive comments she'd endured from young men on the streets during the last few months they'd lived there. He hoped he had managed to offer her some support.

"I wanted to give you some of that today," Ciara went on, "a little hope, a little strength. You needed it." She took a deep breath. "*I* needed it."

"And I've needed you, Ciara. You've been far away these last months."

She adjusted her position so her arm threaded through his rather than wrapped around him. "I've had grief of my own to walk through, but I'm coming out the other side. The singing today helped a bit. 'Twas a good start."

"It helped me as well." How he wanted to ask what burden she was carrying so he could ease some of it. He knew instinctively that voicing the question would push her away again. She was choosing to address her troubles without his direct assistance, and he would respect that. "Perhaps we could get together now and then and sing a spell. 'Twould be a welcome release for us both, I'd wager."

She nodded and smiled. "I would like that."

"And if we are very fortunate, Mary and Thomas'll be around long enough to join the party."

“I hope so.” She turned her head in the direction of the fireplace. “And Finbarr?”

“We’ll find his song as well.” Tavish made the declaration as much to himself as to her. “We’ll find it.”

Keefe, Ciara’s husband, approached in the next moment. “Might I steal this sweet lass away from you?”

“If you promise you’ll keep bringing her back.”

Keefe slipped his arm around his wife, even as he reached out and dropped a hand on Tavish’s shoulder. “You’ve my word on that.”

Tavish watched the couple return to the other O’Connors. His family was healing, slowly but surely. He didn’t know the most personal aspects of everyone’s struggles, but he knew enough to have worried and fought on their behalf. Seeing his family tiptoeing closer to whole once more lifted a weight from his heart.

Biddy approached. She hugged him fiercely. The women in the family really were determined to see to it he was embraced all the evening long. Tavish simply shook his head and chose to appreciate the shows of support and love.

“Cecee told me today’s undertaking would do my soul a lot of good,” Tavish said, hugging her in return, “but I didn’t realize it’d earn me so much attention tonight.”

“It did us all good,” Biddy said. “Every last one of us.”

Chapter Thirty-two

Cecily's day was not going according to plan. Finbarr was working at the Archers', and Granny was spending the day with Mrs. O'Connor, so Cecily had the day to herself. Rather than transcribe more of *The Light Princess*, as she'd planned, Cecily paced in front of the fireplace, frustrated by how quickly her sight was deteriorating.

The afternoon had not entirely passed when a knock sounded. She opened the door but could see nothing but a slightly darker form against the dim background of the shadowed porch. Her vision was too poor to know how many people might be standing there, let alone identify anyone.

"Good afternoon to you, Cecily."

She knew the voice. "Katie."

"I've come with Biddy O'Connor and her littlest one, as well as my Emma."

Biddy had come to call? Biddy, who avoided her as one would a carrier of an infectious disease? Who left the room every single time Cecily entered it? To say her arrival was unexpected didn't come close to the whole of it. She only hoped her shock had not been obvious.

Cecily motioned them inside. She listened to their footsteps and the sounds of their rustling dresses, attempting to place them in the room. They had all come inside. Beyond that, she could not say. Her thoughts were too distracted.

"Is something the matter?" she asked.

"Actually, yes," Biddy said. She was not too far away and likely standing. "Something is the matter with me, with how I have been."

Cecily didn't fully understand, but she knew the sound of someone desperately pushing through an uncomfortable conversation.

"I don't know if anyone has told you what that moment at the graveyard yesterday meant to all of us." Of all the topics Biddy might have chosen to pursue, Cecily would not have guessed at this one. "The fever that took Bridget Claire claimed many lives. Not a single family was spared at least one loss." Not a single person moved. Biddy took an audible breath. "Ian and I lost a child."

Was there a soul amongst the O'Connors who was not deeply grieving?

"Though Tavish has struggled more than most to make his peace with that dark time," Biddy continued, "we've all carried the pain of it these years. Singing as we did yesterday helped heal some of that. We were singing for Tavish and Bridget, yes, but for so many others as well. For ourselves. For the hopes and dreams and loved ones we've buried over the years."

"I know you couldn't see it," Katie jumped in, "but Finbarr was standing along the fence with all of us."

"Truly?" Cecily tried not to let her hopes soar too high. "He stood with you?"

"The family can speak of nothing else," Biddy said. "Tavish visiting the graveyard at long last, and singing his pain and his grief—he always used to be a singer, you know, but he stopped after Bridget's passing. But seeing him singing again. And Ciara joining the undertaking. Then Finbarr witnessing and partaking of that small bit of healing. 'Twas all a miracle unfolding right there before our eyes. A full miracle."

"Did Finbarr sing?" How she hoped he had.

"No," Biddy said, "but he was there. He was there."

Amazement filled every inch of Cecily's heart. "Oh, thank the heavens. They need this healing so desperately. I've worried over them."

"You've worked miracles for this family," Biddy said. "'Tis time I acknowledged that."

This was a change, indeed.

"I cannot promise I'll never again think of you unfairly," Biddy said, "but I mean to try."

Cecily offered her hand. "That is good enough for me."

Biddy shook it firmly and enthusiastically.

"Miss Attwater?" That was Emma. "What are all these things on the desk?"

The current banes of my existence.

"Those are instruments for writing words that can be read by fingers instead of eyes. I had planned to spend today continuing to work on transcribing this book into words for the blind, but my efforts are proving futile."

"Why is that?" Katie asked.

Cecily hadn't much discussed this aspect of her life's work since coming to Hope Springs. She struggled to admit when she was incapable of doing something she'd put her mind to. But today, she was overwhelmed and frustrated. Perhaps talking about it would help. How often had she told her students that?

"My sight has diminished further," she said. "I can no longer read printed words even with my face all but touching the lantern."

"What will you do?" Katie asked.

"I don't know." Cecily crossed back to the desk. "I had hoped to finish many more books before I was rendered entirely blind." She ran her fingers over the leather cover of *The Light Princess*. "I was going to create an entire library."

"On your own?" Katie asked, clearly shocked at the idea. "By hand?"

"It is tedious and slow work, but I love it." She pushed the book a little away.

"Reverend Ford says I am a very good reader," Emma said. "He asks me to help teach the younger children. I'm teaching Katie." The sweet child had a teacher's heart, something Cecily understood well.

"I could read the words to you," Emma continued. "If I read them, you could write them in dots, couldn't you?"

"Well, yes, but . . . This takes hours and hours, over many, many weeks. Years, if the book is long."

"Or *forever*, if you never work on it again," Emma declared.

Cecily couldn't argue with the truth of that.

"Her father says our Emma is a force to be reckoned with," Katie said. "I tend to believe him."

"I, for one, applaud a bit of fierceness in a woman, however young," Cecily said. "This is a difficult world *with* strength of character, and an impossible one without it."

"That is the truth, and no denying it," Biddy said.

"I also advocate for humility enough to accept help when it is needed and offered." Cecily sometimes struggled to admit when she was out of her depth. She did try, though. Here was an opportunity to do so again. "If you have a few moments to spare, Emma, I would appreciate you lending me your vision and your literacy."

"You speak like my grandmother," Emma said. "She's not from England, like you are, but she uses fancy words like you do."

Cecily had noticed Joseph Archer's tendency to speak more formally as well. He likely hailed from America's east coast and from a family of some means. Sorting the complicated puzzle of all their lives was endlessly intriguing, yet she needed to focus on the matter at hand.

"Katie?" Somehow Cecily had lost track of where everyone was standing.

"Over here."

"Are you pressed for time, or may Emma help me for a little while?"

"She is welcome to help you. I came hoping to do a bit of baking for Granny," Katie said. "I won't be done for a couple of hours."

"Well, then. Let's begin. We'll need to move my tools from the desk to the table, where we'll have more room."

They managed the task quickly then settled in. Cecily found the ribbon marking the page she was on. She opened the book with a small thud against the tabletop and slid it closer to Emma. Cecily ran her fingertips over the last couple of lines on her parchment and read the words aloud.

"'So he went the next morning to the house of the princess, and, making a very humble apology, begged her to undo the spell.' That's where I left off."

After a moment, Emma piped up. "I found it."

"Read me one sentence at a time," Cecily instructed. "I'll tell you when I'm ready for more. This process is very slow."

"I am very patient," Emma assured her.

She was as good as her word. They worked for an entire hour without Emma giving any indication of being anything but perfectly pleased with her task. Cecily would need time to adjust to the necessity of this new method. So much of what she'd done for her students was meant to give them back their lives, but as her vision continued to fail, she felt as though she continually lost bits of her own.

Just as sweet Emma's voice was beginning to show signs of fatigue, the door opened—Tavish. She knew his walk straight off. A moment more, and she recognized Finbarr's footsteps as well. He'd come for his Braille lesson, no doubt.

"Finbarr is here." Emma spoke no louder than a whisper.

"I thought I recognized his footsteps."

The book closed softly. "I would like to go home now."

"Because Finbarr is here?" Cecily asked gently.

Emma didn't answer. Tension and distrust filled her silence.

Cecily wasn't sure how that friendship would be mended, or if it would be. The two would have to work it out between themselves.

"Why, Miss Emma," Tavish greeted. "What a delight. I've a butterscotch for you, your favorite."

"You remembered."

"Of course I did." His footsteps brought him to where they sat. He set something, the butterscotch, no doubt, on the table.

"I hope you've brought some for the whole class, young man," Cecily said.

"A class, is this?"

She nodded regally. "I believe this gathering could be described as having a great deal of class, in fact."

He chuckled. "That bit of wordplay deserves a butterscotch."

She held her palm up. He set a candy in her hand, then folded her fingers around it. The gesture, though seemingly nothing of significance, felt surprisingly intimate. How she hoped the heat she felt steeling over her face wasn't obvious to everyone.

"She's nearly as good at turning a phrase as you are, Tavish O'Connor," Katie said.

"Nearly as good?" Biddy countered. "I'd say she's even better."

"Either way, they're quite two peas in a pod."

That caused more of a blush. The subject would have to be turned before she was rendered red as a rose. "Do you need a bite to eat before we get to work, Finbarr?" she asked. "If so, Tavish, apparently, carries about a large supply of butterscotch."

"I'm not hungry just now," Finbarr said. He'd come closer than she'd realized and likely stood just on the other side of Emma. The girl hadn't fled at his approach. That seemed like a good sign. "Here is this, Miss Emma." He set something on the table.

"My wooden horse." Her tone was full of amazement. "However did you find it? We looked and looked."

"You like to play with it in the back corner of the barn," he said. "I thought perhaps it had fallen behind something."

"And you stumbled upon it?"

"Not—not exactly."

"You searched for it?" She didn't sound as though she fully believed him. "You did that . . . for me?"

"I wished for you to have your horse back." Finbarr left the explanation at that. His heavy but careful footfall came around the table. The chair legs scraped. "I've managed to write and can read my name in dots." He was now talking to Cecily. "I'm slow, but I'm getting better."

"The 'dots' are known as Braille," she reminded him. "Referring to the system by its true name makes it more real. This needs to be real to you. A real method, a real way of writing and reading. If you treat Braille as a second-class method, using it will always feel like something of a failure."

"But I'm so slow."

"Give it time," she told him. "If you can summon the patience and wherewithal to search out a small, wooden horse in an enormous, dark barn, you can certainly give yourself time to master Braille. The two are not so different, you know. You didn't give up on the horse because it was important to Emma. You won't give up on Braille because it is important to you."

"I feel stupid," he muttered.

She quickly pressed a sentence into a fresh sheet of parchment. "Do you think you can read this?"

"Probably not."

She pushed the paper over to him. "Try, Finbarr."

Emma still hadn't left the table, and no one else had joined them, though she could hear Tavish, Biddy, and Katie in low conversation behind her.

In the next moment, Finbarr burst out laughing. Deep, belly-shaking laughter. The rest of the room went silent.

"The question is, Finbarr," Cecily said, "do you agree?"

He only laughed more.

"What did you write?" Emma asked.

Cecily remained as solemn as she could. "A secret . . . about Tavish."

"About *me*?" Tavish moved closer. "Cecee, what mischief is this?"

She stood and held her hands up in a show of innocence. "Braille lessons, Tav."

"Tav?" He was there beside her, his tantalizing scent filling the air, and his nearness warming her.

"Why should you be the only one handing out nicknames?"

He ran his hand down her arm. She loved that rare gesture from him. "Could you not think of something better than 'Tav'?"

"What do you think, Finbarr? Am I capable of thinking of something better than 'Tav'?"

That started the laughing again.

"What did you write, Cecee?"

She wiggled her brows saucily.

"You don't mean to tell me?" He pulled her a touch closer.

"Not even if you torture me."

"I'd not be so sure if I were you, miss. I'm a dab hand at torture."

She had missed this light, teasing banter. So much of their interactions of late had been heavy and mournful. Did he need this return to playfulness as much as she did? "Finbarr would stand with me. We are co-conspirators in this."

"We could defeat him with our eyes closed," Finbarr declared.

She almost could not hold back her grin, though she tried valiantly. "Especially since Tavish is so very old."

"The two of you joining forces against me is entirely unfair." Tavish's words were filled with his deep, rumbling laughter, belying his words.

"I can't deny it, brother." Paper rustling followed Finbarr's words. "I have it in writing."

"That's what you put in your secret note?"

She leaned her forehead against his shoulder and just let herself laugh. Feeling his arms around her and the joy of his teasing, she could breathe again. Her burdens lifted and lightened. She didn't feel alone. He was a miracle in her life.

"What's that look for, Katie?" Tavish asked, still as jovial and amused. "Is this a conspiracy you're part of as well?"

"Oh, Tavish. 'Tis a grand thing to hear you laugh again."

"Come now, Katie. I laugh all the time." He pulled Cecily fully into his arms once more and pressed a kiss to the top of her head. "Lately."

Lately. Cecily had been happier and more buoyant lately as well. She leaned into his embrace and let herself imagine what it would be like if she never had to let go.

Chapter Thirty-three

You won't give up on this because it is important to you.

Cecily's words wouldn't leave Tavish's mind. She was helping Finbarr hold on to things that mattered to him, but who would help her claim the things she longed for? She'd spoken of wanting to see the ocean, the Rocky Mountains. She wanted to go home.

Every time he held her, he sensed in her another wish, another hope, she'd left unspoken. She wanted to be happy, to be loved, to not be alone. He recognized the need because he longed for the same thing.

He didn't know how to give it to her. His own attempts at happiness and love and companionship never ended well. The people he cared about had left him, over and over again. He could, however, help her with the rest: the oceans and the mountains.

On the next sunny day, Tavish borrowed the buggy from Ian and set off to find Cecily, a plan in mind that he hoped would bring her a bit of joy. The fates were smiling on him; he happened upon her just as she and Katie stepped out of the mercantile, where he'd decided to begin his search.

She used her cane as she walked. He was glad it was helpful, but more than that, he was infinitely pleased to know that something he'd done for her mattered. 'Twas as if he'd given her a bit of himself to carry about, to offer support and strength.

"A good afternoon to you, ladies," he said, hopping down from the buggy. "Are you done with your business here?"

"We are," Cecily said.

"Well, then, allow me to offer the both of you a ride back home." He tossed her his most winning smile before remembering she likely couldn't see it. Though the day was bright, and they were out of doors, he didn't think her sight was that acute.

"You've only just arrived," Katie objected. "We've no wish to keep you from your own errand."

"I came with no other goal but to fetch a couple of sweet colleens back to their homes."

Katie leveled him a dry look. "You've known me going on two years, Tavish O'Connor. When are you going to get it into your head that, though I am a lot of things, 'sweet' is not one of them?" The old argument between them had begun in earnest on her side and in jest on his, but had long since become a welcome reason to laugh.

"My apologies," he said in a tone of exaggerated regret. "I should have said one sweet colleen and one rather difficult one."

"Why can't *I* be 'rather difficult'?" Cecily asked, a dramatic air of offense heavy in her demeanor and words.

"The two of you together are trouble," he said with a laugh. "Hop in the buggy before I change m' mind."

Katie managed the thing on her own, something she'd always preferred while they were courting, something that used to bother him, especially as she'd allowed Joseph the privilege of assisting her. Looking back, that ought to have served as a clue as to where her deepest affections had been, but now he found he didn't particularly care one way or the other any longer if Katie didn't want his assistance.

He set his attention, instead, on Cecily. "This is a new vehicle for you," he warned. "Let me know how I can best help you climb up safely."

She considered. "How high does it sit? Would it be a simple matter of stepping up, or would I need to use the wheel hub?"

He eyed the buggy, never having given much thought to the mechanics of getting in. "'Tisn't so high as a proper wagon. You'll find a step on the side bridging the gap between the ground and the floor of the buggy."

She nodded. "If you'll lend me a hand and talk me through where to put my foot, and perhaps put a hand on my back for stability, I think I can manage it."

"And if you think wrong? Ought I to have the preacher prepare a eulogy?"

She grinned. "Only if the preacher promises to say nice things about me. They needn't be true, only very, very flattering."

"What do you say we focus on safely navigating the treacherous ascent, and not bother Reverend Ford with concocting such a pack of lies?"

She nodded solemnly. "A very wise course of action."

In the end, she needed only a bit of assistance to find the step, and the lightest, steadying touch on her back to get up and settle on the front bench. Katie sat in back, and Tavish took his place beside Cecily.

Applying his heaviest accent, he said, "Tavish's hackney at your service, ladies. We'll be on our way presently."

He saw Katie safely to her door, and soon the buggy was rolling over the wooden bridge.

"The river is running," Cecily said in surprise. "Do you hear it?"

"Honestly, I don't," he admitted. "But now that you said so, looks like a bit in the middle has thawed."

"Does the river usually thaw in January?" she asked.

"Sometimes," he said, "when the winter has turned unseasonably warm as this one has, though it usually freezes over again and won't entirely thaw until April or so."

They talked about winter and freezes and more about the weather. Even the most mundane of topics was interesting when the two of them were discussing it.

He guided the buggy off the road to the path leading past his house.

"Why are we going to your home?" she asked.

"How did you—? Do you know how far it is from the bridge to my—"

"I can see your house right there." She pointed directly at it.

That seemed an encouraging thing. "Then your vision isn't entirely gone yet."

"The day is bright. We're outdoors. A house is large, which helps. I can't see many details, but I can see the outline well enough to know it's yours."

"That bodes very well for the rest of our afternoon, *a chara*," he said. "You see, I am kidnapping you and taking you on an adventure. And if you can see my house, you'll likely be able to see what it is I'm taking you to see."

"What are you taking me to see?" she said, with not so much as a moment's uncertainty over spending the day with him or the unplanned excursion. Perhaps she enjoyed his company as much as he enjoyed hers.

"It is a surprise, love." The *love* slipped out naturally. Cecily didn't seem at all struck by it. That could either be good or bad.

They continued up the path that bordered his fields, past the rows and rows of dormant berry bushes and vines. On and on. Farther and farther back until they reached their destination.

"Stay put for just a moment," he instructed. "I'll come around and help you down. 'Tis a bit icy."

She didn't argue or object. He hurried to her side of the buggy and reached up for her hand, talking her through the descent and seeing her safely on her feet once more.

"Will I need my cane?" she asked.

"I'll happily walk you about," he said. "But if you'd like your cane, you're welcome to it." He knew using her cane represented freedom to her, and he'd no desire to take that away.

"I suppose you're trustworthy." She set the cane on the buggy seat.

"I'll fetch it for you if you change your mind."

Her smile was sweet and light. "Thank you."

He pulled a blanket from the basket in the back of the buggy and set it around her shoulders.

"Thank you, again."

He snatched two more blankets and tucked them under one arm, then held out his other arm for her to take hold of. "Just this way."

As they walked together, he kept a slow pace so she could be certain of her footing. They hadn't far to go.

Having reached the area he wanted, he pulled his arm away and flicked open one of the blankets, laying it across a bench he'd made from a log many years earlier. This was a spot he'd frequented, and he'd quickly discovered the importance of having a place to sit that wasn't muddy.

He guided Cecily and saw her situated on the bench, then sat beside her. He set the third blanket across their laps. The winter was warmer than usual, but the air was still quite frigid.

"I am entirely turned around," she said. "I haven't the slightest idea where we are."

"This is the far end of my property," he said, "and quite possibly my favorite place in all the world, excepting Ireland."

She set her head against the side of his shoulder. "The pull of home is a strong one, isn't it?"

'Twas a gift from above to have another person understand him the way she did. To be able to turn to her with thoughts and worries without any need to defend those feelings, nor even to explain them.

"You told me many weeks ago that you'd dreamed of seeing the Rocky Mountains before your sight was gone entirely. Our mountains, those just off in the distance, are a branch of the Rockies. They aren't the majestic ones you were likely hoping for, but they are the Rockies." He glanced at her face, hoping to gauge her reaction. He'd grown more adept at determining her thoughts without seeing her eyes. In that moment, she looked thoughtful.

"I wasn't certain you'd be able to see them from this distance, but 'tisn't safe yet to travel much closer. Even when we take sleighs out to gather firewood, we don't go that direction."

"I can see their outline—not sharply, but I can see them." She didn't lift her head from his shoulder.

Did she need comfort, or was she simply weary? He couldn't say with any degree of certainty.

"It is lovely the way the view is framed by the trees," she said. She could see that much, then. He'd hoped she would.

"This pond in front of us is mine. A larger one is farther, outside of town. The ranchers water their cattle there. But this one is mine."

"We had a lake at my home in England." Emotion touched her words. "This is almost like being there again."

He'd struggled to think of a means of giving her back a glimpse of her homeland. Had he accidentally managed it?

"I hoped the lake would serve as an almost-acceptable substitute for the Pacific Ocean, which I realize is giving it a great deal too much credit. But I cannot get you to the ocean, sweetheart, and I cannot get you back to England. This is all I have to offer."

She pulled her blanket more tightly around her shoulders. "I've spent so much time over the last years looking after myself, by myself. I'd almost forgotten what it's like to have someone care about me. But this . . . This is wonderful, Tavish."

Relief and joy and the welcome whisper of peace he always felt with her settled over him once more. “Do you like it, then?”

“It is beautiful.”

He slipped his arm around her and pulled her close, both of their gazes resting on the horizon ahead. “It truly is. I knew the moment I saw the view that I wanted this farm. ’Tis a fine thing to have m’ own pond, as well.”

“Do you come here often?”

“I do, but only ever by myself. I’ve only ever shown it to one other person.”

“Bridget,” she guessed.

“She loved it as well, though she hardly held still long enough to truly see it.” He found he could laugh lightly at the memory. “She overflowed with energy, never able to entirely stop moving.”

“You must find me unbearably sedate,” she said. “I tend to be quite still.”

“I have gained an appreciation for stillness,” he said.

Her shoulders rose and fell with a deep breath. “I don’t think anyone could help but be peaceful in this place. I can imagine the sound of the pond in the warmer months. It must be very soothing.”

“When the thaw’s complete and it’s safe to do so, I’ll take you nearer the mountains,” he offered. “Then you can see them more clearly.”

She didn’t immediately answer, which wasn’t like her.

“Cecee?”

“My eyes have been hurting again,” she said quietly.

He knew what that meant. She was losing more of her vision. He hadn’t the first idea what to say to ease her heartache.

“What if this time, I lose what little sight I have left?”

“Oh, darling.”

She pulled off her spectacles and dabbed at her eyes with the corner of her blanket. “I’ve known this was coming for years, but I’m not at all ready.”

She had helped him face so many of his burdens. Yet he couldn't take this pain from her. He couldn't do a thing to make it better. He simply held her closer, struggling for words in the midst of frustrating helplessness.

"I keep telling myself that while some of the things I wanted to do won't happen, the things I want most—helping others who have lost their sight, making their lives better—I can still do. I can look after myself. I can work at the school where I was educated. Though I will need to find someone to dictate the books for me to transcribe, I can still work on my Braille library. I can still do all of those things. So there's no reason for me to be upset."

Her emotion grew thicker with each word. "It isn't as if I wasn't forewarned. It isn't as if my entire world is crumbling unexpectedly. I—I shouldn't be crying over this. I should be stronger."

"It isn't weakness to cry or to struggle," Tavish said. She herself had told him so. "And leaning on someone when you're burdened doesn't mean you're not strong."

She trembled with her next difficult, shaking breath. "I feel like I'm falling apart, Tavish."

He rested his head against hers and rubbed her arm with his hand. "You're facing a loss. I think, *a mhuirnín*, you need to let yourself grieve."

"I'm not certain I can." She held tight to her spectacles. "I've leaned so long on the hope that somehow this would not be the end result. Grieving would make it real."

He'd finally faced that same daunting part of acceptance, but thanks to her, he hadn't done so alone. He would not abandon her to her own mourning now.

"You needn't face this alone," he told her. "This place is magical. We can visit here as long and as often as you need. I'll sit here with you and hold you while you grieve, just as you've done for me."

"You're offering to carry this burden with me for a time?"

Oh, Cecily. I am offering so much more than that. If only . . . If only.

Chapter Thirty-four

Cecily knocked hard on Tavish's front door. The hour was yet early. Surely he'd awoken by now. But the knock went unanswered. A second one received no response either.

"Where are you?" she called. She forced herself to think. When she'd come daily for Finbarr's lessons, he'd been in the barn before breakfast.

The barn. Of course.

Cecily set one hand on the side of the house and held her cane out with the other. She carefully made her way to the back of the house. The dim morning light made the distant structure almost impossible to make out, but she could see just enough to know which direction to go. Even so, if not for her cane, the short journey would have resulted in a number of stumbles and stubbed toes. Tavish's gift meant more than he likely realized.

When she reached the barn, she pushed open the door and stepped inside. It was too dark for her to make out anything.

"Tavish?" she called out. "Tavish?"

"Cecee?" His confused voice echoed from some distance away. "What in the name of the saints has you here so early?"

"Granny is ill."

He was at her side in but an instant. "What's wrong with her?"

"She's feverish, and she's been moaning. I can't see if her coloring is bad or much of anything else. I need your help."

"Of course. Finbarr, can you finish up in here?"

"I can."

Tavish pulled her hand into the crook of his arm and guided her outside. "How feverish?"

"Quite warm to the touch but not the least bit clammy." Had she been sweating, Cecily might not have been so worried. A breaking fever was reason for relief.

"And the moans. Are they of pain, or discomfort or . . . ?"

"Discomfort, I would guess. I can't say for certain." How she wished she could. "It's her cough that has me most concerned. It's worse than before. Tavish, I'm worried."

They moved at a swift clip. She held her cane high enough in her hand to clear the ground. With Tavish guiding her, she didn't worry about losing her footing. She was anxious to return to Granny. The dear woman had offered her kindness when the rest of the Irish had treated her with suspicion and disdain. She and Granny had begun on something of an awkward footing, but in the end, they'd found a friendship, one Cecily deeply cherished.

Tavish didn't say much as they made their short journey. His mind was no doubt too heavy for conversation. They went through the door, across the house, and into Granny's room. The path didn't deviate in the least.

"Now what's this I hear about you being under the weather, Granny?" Tavish had somehow summoned a chipper tone. "Were you wanting a bit of attention, is that it?"

Granny's response consisted of a chest-rattling cough, not one brought on by a laugh or an attempt at speech, but by the simple act of breathing.

"Sit with her," Cecily whispered. "You are always a comfort to her."

He didn't need to be told twice. He slipped his arm free of hers, and his distinctive footfalls took him to Granny's bedside.

"You feel terrible warm, Granny," he said. "I think we'd best lay a cool cloth across your forehead, see if we can't bring your fever down a bit."

"That might help." Though feeble, her response was encouraging; it was complete, coherent, and spoken aloud.

"And perhaps a bit of broth to keep your strength up." Tavish's tenderness with his adoptive grandmother couldn't help but touch the heart of all who witnessed it.

"I . . . will try," Granny said.

"Tend to her fever," Cecily told Tavish. "I'll make some broth."

She left them there as she set her mind on her task. Granny had seemed frailer of late, even before this alarming turn for the worse. Cecily hadn't been sure if the change was simply the result of winter taking its toll on an aged body or if Granny was truly growing weaker.

Tavish cannot endure another loss. He is only now beginning to face Bridget's passing.

She wouldn't allow herself to think in such terms. Granny might simply be tired and a bit under the weather. And the cough might be nothing more than . . .

Cecily could find no satisfactory answer.

She had a pot of water and vegetables simmering when Tavish joined her in the kitchen. "How is she?" she asked.

His slow, lung-emptying breath told its own story. "I'd best fetch Ma."

"Granny is that ill?" She'd so hoped that wasn't the case.

"It isn't so much that this illness is severe, I don't think. She's simply so frail. I don't know if she has the strength to fight even the most minor of sicknesses."

Pain stabbed deep at those truthful, difficult words. "Oh, Tavish."

"Don't you start crying, or I will. And I'm not ready for that yet."

She brushed away a hair tickling her nose and blinked back the threat of tears.

"Although," Tavish said, "I could use a hug if you've one to spare."

She had no need to think. She stepped forward and wrapped her arms around him. He held her fast in return. She felt every breath he took, the strength of his embrace, the firm, stalwartness of this man who'd remained standing through so much tragedy and struggle, who'd shown her that she could admit to her limitations and not be weaker for them.

Did anyone around him see those things? Did they notice anything but the jesting and lighthearted side he showed the world? Did they understand the depth of his strength? She doubted it.

"How are your eyes?" he asked, still holding her.

"Excruciating," she said. "I've not yet taken my powders today."

"Darling, you must look after yourself. You needn't suffer."

She leaned in to him ever more. "The powders make me sleepy. And Granny needs me awake."

"Ma will look after Granny and me."

"And I'll look after myself." Cecily had been doing precisely that for half her life; she could continue doing the same.

"No, *a mhuirnín*. We will look after you."

"You don't call me *a chara* any longer, but I don't know what this new word means."

"You tell me what smell it is that gives me away, seeing as I've my doubts it's berries and berries alone you're smelling, and I will tell you what *a mhuirnín* means."

"I can't," she said.

"And why not?" He still hadn't released her. Perhaps he knew she needed his reassurance. Perhaps she was offering him a bit of it herself.

"Because I don't know how to describe it. You simply smell like you."

"And is it an unpleasant scent?" He sounded genuinely worried.

She couldn't help but laugh, and heavens, it felt good. "Yes, Tavish, you stink. That's what I've been trying to tell you all along, that you are in sore need of a bath."

"And that's why you're hugging me all the time, is it? To get a bit closer to my stench."

"Mmm. Delicious."

"You're a gem, you know." He pressed a kiss to her forehead. "I'll be back in two shakes of a rabbit's tail." He stepped away, across the room.

"You never translated that term for me," she called after him.

"Ask Granny. She knows."

"That wasn't what we agreed on," she reminded him.

His footsteps stopped at the doorway. "I'm a terrible person, Cecee. I mean to make you wait."

She shook her head at his teasing tone. What a joy it was to have a reprieve from the very real pain of life. "Fetch your mother," she said. "But be prepared to make good on your promise."

"I'll be quaking with worry all the way there and back."

The door scraped as it opened. A gush of bitterly cold air rushed inside, before a snap of the door signaled Tavish's departure. He would be back; she didn't doubt that. But her heart missed him already. That, she knew, was a dangerous thing.

She tried to keep thoughts of him out of her mind as she strained a bowl of hot broth. Carefully, she brought it to Granny's room and set it on the bureau, not trusting herself to find the bedside table without some instructions.

"Are you awake?" Cecily whispered.

"I am," came the feeble response. Granny did not sound well at all.

Cecily felt her way to the chair Tavish had occupied. "How are you?"

"Ill. More than that—I am dying."

"Granny, you—"

"Don't you be saying I'm not," Granny warned. "I know I am."

Cecily felt it and was nearly certain Tavish did, as well. "Please, don't speak so bluntly of this to Tavish when he returns. He's not holding up well of late."

"You've seen a side of him few—few ever get more than a glimpse of." Granny ran short of breath. Her sentences emerged in bits. "He feels deeply. Be it love. Or heartache"—a shaking breath—"or joy or pain. He feels it to his very bones."

"I know. I think that's why he turns so often to humor and laughter in the face of tragedy. He must relieve the ache somehow, or it will drown him."

After a rattling breath, Granny made a firm declaration. "You love him, don't you?"

Cecily had never given voice to the feelings that had been growing over the weeks. She'd hardly allowed herself to examine them. But there was no denying truth, not to this woman who saw so clearly what Cecily thought she'd kept hidden. "I do love him. How could I not?"

"I think he may love you as well, dear," Granny said. "'Tis difficult to—to be certain. He guards himself closely."

"And his family's wishes weigh heavily on him," Cecily acknowledged. "He knows they would never accept anything but friendship between us. They've become more civil—even a little friendly—but I'm still an Englishwoman and that is—" How could she explain?

"Like a cat falling in love with a dog." Granny stopped for a tight breath. "Even if they got along"—another breath—"the cat's family could never be at ease."

A rather cruel comparison, but also the truth.

"I cannot do that to him or to his family. And he'd never really be happy if he made them unhappy."

Granny began coughing once more. Cecily helped her sit up a bit, though the effort only barely eased the horrible rattling. After a time, the attack died down, and Granny could lie back again.

"I wish I could say you're wrong," Granny said. "But you *would* be a wedge in the O'Connor family—not one put there purposely—but real all the same. Centuries of animosity cannot be erased in a moment."

"It will be for the best when I leave in the spring." She was telling herself as much as Granny.

"Another student?"

"No. I'll be returning to the school in Missouri. I haven't enough sight left to continue traveling."

"You don't sound happy—at the prospect."

She wasn't. "It is not what I would have chosen for myself," Cecily admitted. She pressed her palms against her burning eyes to relieve some of the pain. The pressure didn't help much this time. "But it will be fine. I will make the best of my circumstances."

"What would you have chosen for yourself?" Granny's question emerged weaker than her previous words. She was growing more tired, and that worried Cecily a great deal. What if Tavish didn't return quickly? What if his mother didn't know how to ease Granny's misery?

"I would have chosen to keep my sight long enough to see the things I've wished to see." Everyone had impossible dreams, didn't they? "Barring that, I would choose to belong somewhere, and for my life to have mattered."

"And you want to have a choice." Granny seemed determined to continue their discussion despite her obvious exhaustion. "You don't like having your hand forced."

"I have always been stubbornly independent."

Another coughing fit stole Granny's breath. Cecily comforted her the best she knew how, but she could do so little.

"My husband thought independent women were the best sort." Each breath sounded more labored than the last. "He said 'twas his favorite thing about me, though I've my doubts. My hardheadedness certainly made his life more difficult."

"But he loved you," Cecily said. "No matter the difficulties, life with someone you love is better than a life without them, isn't it?"

"Yes." Granny kept her eyes closed for a drawn-out moment. "I've been without him six years now."

Cecily could think of no helpful or comforting words. Everything felt trite, insignificant.

"But we won't be apart, he and I. Not much longer."

Oh, how she hoped Granny didn't speak this way when Tavish returned. Cecily wasn't at all certain he was equal to hearing it.

Chapter Thirty-five

Word of Granny Claire's illness spread quickly through Hope Springs. The next two days were filled with townspeople checking on her. Though no one said as much to him directly, Tavish knew they came to say their goodbyes.

He greeted them, asked after their families, and generally managed lighthearted quips and smiles. Seeing their burdens lifted even the smallest bit by his words helped him forget about his own burden, if briefly. But the pain never went away completely. It gnawed at him, tearing at his heart. He was losing Granny, and he could do nothing to stop it.

As the second afternoon marched on, the number of visitors trailed off. Most everyone had paid their respects, and Granny no longer had the strength for visits. Tavish didn't either. Keeping his spirits up was exhausting. He could feel every gap in his armor, and he had no desire to fall to pieces.

As Da slipped from the house near about dinner time, giving Tavish a quick, silent nod on his way out, Ma remained in Granny's room. In the parlor, Tavish forced himself to breathe. He rested his arm against the fireplace mantel and set his gaze on the flickering flames.

He heard Cecily approach. Ever since she'd told him that people's footsteps were different from one another, he'd been listening to hers. He could generally pick them out: slow but confident, small strides without being timid.

"How are you, Tavish?"

"Warm, thanks to this fire. Must've been built by someone very skilled." He'd started the fire himself, of course.

"I don't know about that," Cecily drawled. "I've seen better."

"Have you now?" He looked over at her. "An expert on fires, are you?"

She shrugged lightly. "It's a hobby."

"You English have odd ways of passing the time."

Far from scolding him for jesting during a difficult moment, she seemed to appreciate the diversion. She stepped closer and took his hand. He clung to it, needing to feel that connection.

"Now," she said, "how are you *really*?"

He couldn't answer. Instead, he pushed out a breath, one heavy with regret and worry and pain. She set her other hand around their entwined ones, cupping his between both of hers.

"I'm not ready to let her go," Tavish admitted.

"I don't know if anyone is truly ready for that." She held tightly to him. "At least no one who is left behind."

That brought a fresh surge of regret. He'd had to face a difficult truth these past two days. "I suspect she's held on the past years out of worry for me. She felt responsible for the pain I couldn't escape. I'm afraid she's enduring this pain longer than she needs to because—" He took a difficult breath. "Because she doesn't want to hurt me."

"She loves you," Cecily said. "And she wants what's best for you. I am entirely certain you feel the same way about her."

"She is the dearest woman in all the world. I couldn't care more for her if she were my real grandmother. In my heart, she is." He could hardly breathe for the pain in his chest.

"Tavish." Cecily's voice had dropped to little more than a whisper. She stepped closer and set her free hand on his other arm. "You must let her go so she can be at peace, so she can rest her weary bones. She needs to know she's free to go."

He tilted his head upward, his gaze on the rough-hewn planks that made up the roof of Granny's house. He didn't think he was strong enough, but there was no denying the truth of Cecily's words.

"At the graveyard, you said you wouldn't leave me," he reminded her. "Does that promise still stand?"

"Of course it does."

He raised her hand to his lips and kissed her fingers. Once. Twice. The third time, he found some relief in the tenderness of her touch. She'd let him laugh when he'd needed to. She'd given direction when he'd felt lost. How could he have helped but be drawn to her?

"What would I do without you, Cecily Attwater?"

"If I had a penny for every time someone had said that to me, I'd be a wealthy woman." She had an innate sense for knowing when he needed a bit of levity.

Tavish breathed now—truly breathed—a near miracle, considering how difficult he'd found that basic act the last two days. "You make me feel rather ashamed for having called you 'Your Majesty.'"

"For all I know, the new term you've fashioned is every bit as bad. You still haven't told me what it means, you know."

Keeping her hand in his, he led her to the bench alongside the fireplace. "Haven't I?"

"You know you haven't," she answered.

He took a seat and gently nudged her to do the same. "It means 'my darling.'"

"Ah." Her look of understanding was too exaggerated to be anything but teasing. "It is sarcastic, then."

He laughed. 'Twas a quiet laugh and a brief one, but a laugh all the same. "You are a great deal of trouble, you know that?"

"I do."

He leaned in close and whispered, "I find I rather like trouble."

A clearing throat captured his attention. He turned in the direction of the corridor. Ma stood a single step from its edge. "Son, Granny is asking for you."

Tavish's heart dropped. He took a fortifying breath and stood, keeping Cecily's hand in his.

"She didn't ask for Miss Attwater," Ma said, though there was no real malice in the declaration.

"Perhaps not," Tavish said. "But I need her with me."

Ma didn't argue. She simply nodded and stepped aside.

The fifteen feet or so separating him from Granny's door felt like hundreds. With each step, the short walk stretched out before him. *She needs to know she's free to go.* But did he have the strength to endure losing her?

The instant he stepped inside, he knew Granny hadn't much time left. A grayish hue had taken hold of her pallor. Though her mouth still pulled in a tight line of pain, something of a softening had come to her face, as if she was no longer as aware of her suffering.

Tavish crossed to the chair at her bedside and lowered himself into it. Cecily walked beside him, her fingers laced through his. "Well, Granny. It's come to this, has it?"

"It always comes to 'this,' lad. 'Tis the way of life." Her voice had never been so quiet and fragile.

He released Cecily's hand, trusting she'd be true to her word by staying with him. He took Granny's chilled hand in his. Her skin was paper thin, spotted with years and pulled by joints distorted with age. Yet they still carried a gentle strength that he'd depended on many times. This was his turn to be her strength.

Granny took a shallow breath. "You've been good to me over the years," she said. "I don't know that I've ever told you how much you mean to me, lad."

"We've been good to each other." He couldn't keep the pain from his voice any longer—wasn't sure there was any point in trying.

"I've seen a change in you lately," Granny went on. "You're happier, and that has lifted a burden from my heart." Her breaths grew more labored with each passing moment, and an earnestness entered her feeble features. "You were meant to be joyful, Tavish O'Connor. Remember that. Live your life with joy."

"I am beginning to."

"I know it. And when I see her, I mean to tell Bridget that you are going to be happy again. That you've learned to remember her with happiness instead of sorrow."

With his free hand, he brushed at one of the tears trailing down his cheek. "I hope you will also tell her that she is missed."

"I suspect she knows, lad."

Ma sniffled quietly behind him. Cecily yet stood directly at his side, strong and supportive, though her stalwartness spoke of strength rather than indifference. Tavish looked up at her. She pressed her lips so tightly together they'd begun to lose their color. Each swallow travelled the length of her throat slowly, as if fighting its way past a physical barrier of grief. Yet, there she stood, unmoving, unbroken, unyielding. She would not leave him. He wished he could meet her eye and offer a silent *thank you*.

"I mean to see your brothers who've gone on," Granny said. "And my children. And my husband. They had all best be there to greet me, or I'll be very cross."

At her lighter tone, he allowed himself a moment's release. "Heaven itself would quake at the thought of earning your wrath, Granny."

"Hold my hand, Tavish," she said weakly. "It won't be long."

Ma stepped up beside him, opposite Cecily. "Your father's gone for the preacher," she whispered.

He nodded silently and waited.

The moments pulled longer. Granny didn't speak. Her eyes fluttered, sometimes remaining open, other times drifting closed. Each breath seemed slower than the last.

Reverend Ford arrived after a time. "Mrs. Claire," he said, in his gentle way. "I am grateful you've sent for me. I am certain you would prefer a priest, but I will do all I can for you."

The nearest Catholic church was thousands of miles away. There would be no official rites. Yet the reverend's presence, Tavish felt certain, would still bring Granny a measure of comfort.

Da slipped inside, taking his place beside Ma.

"You'd best . . . begin . . . Reverend." Granny was nearly spent.

Tavish kept her hand in his, as she'd asked him to, while Reverend Ford read from the Bible a few verses of comfort and spoke to Granny of the rest promised to the faithful. Ma cried quietly, Da's arm wrapped around her.

Granny's hand shook with the effort to keep a tight hold of Tavish's. Her eyes struggled to focus on his face.

She needs to know she is free to go, Tavish thought again.

He leaned in close to Granny's ear and whispered, "'Tis time you were on your way, my dear. You've a great many people eager to see you again."

A small smile tugged at her lips as the tension slipped away. A final breath shuddered through her. A final movement. A final sound. Then all was still. So very still.

And though his tears fell like rain in the spring, he found a degree of solace looking on her beloved face.

She was at peace.

Chapter Thirty-six

Cecily had never known the Irish's equal for finding happiness and joy amidst sorrow. She felt the strength inherent in that ability as she sat in Mr. and Mrs. O'Connor's house only a few days after Granny's funeral.

The family was celebrating Finbarr's birthday. The aroma of cakes and pies, as well as potatoes and soups, filled the air. Laughter bounced off the walls. She knew they were still mourning their loss, but they allowed themselves joy as well. They faced their difficulties as they had since Granny's passing: together. The family had turned to one another in love and support.

Cecily thanked the heavens that Tavish had his family, and that they all had each other. But the long, quiet hours alone in Granny's now-empty house had been difficult, a stark reminder that she didn't truly belong with these people. They weren't as unwelcoming as they'd once been, but in the days since the funeral, it had never been clearer that she was not, nor ever would be, one of them.

Finbarr had issued her the invitation to his birthday gathering. Though she'd been hesitant to accept, she was glad she'd come. Hearing Tavish's voice striking a happy tone, laughing with his loved ones, helped her worry less about how he was enduring this most recent loss. He'd come by to see Cecily twice since losing Granny, but the visits had been short, and he'd been understandably distant, wading as he was through grief.

"I've a present for our man, here," Tavish called out, bringing the din in the room down once more. "Though 'tis something of a gift to my own self, as well."

Something metal clanked on the floor.

"What is it?" Finbarr asked after a moment.

"Bring the lantern closer," Mrs. O'Connor instructed someone.

"I still can't say what it is." Finbarr sounded as confused as intrigued. "Oddest thing I ever saw."

"It's a milking pail," Tavish said. "Seamus and I concocted one with a wide base. It won't tip over easily should some milker, whom I'll not name to protect his reputation, keep knocking into it in the dim barn."

Finbarr laughed, something he did more of late. He still kept himself at an emotional distance from others, but he joined conversations, he laughed with his family, he no longer kept to the dim corners of the house, alone. "This'll save you a great deal of spilled milk."

"I'm looking forward to it," Tavish said.

"I have a gift for you as well," Joseph Archer said. "I won't make you guess at what it is, though—a pair of heavy work gloves. I fully intend to have you help me repair fences as spring approaches. You'll need a good pair of gloves."

"Do you think I'm ready?" He clearly hoped the answer was yes.

"I know you are. And as Tavish said, I am looking forward to it."

Jeremiah Johnson and his family had come as well. Finbarr's efforts to save their daughter from the fire that had nearly taken his own life had bonded them to him. "We have something for you," Mr. Johnson said.

A few footsteps, then silence.

"A cane?" Finbarr said after a moment.

"Miss Attwater said that having one was important for you," Mr. Johnson said. "We couldn't send for one, so I whittled this."

Finbarr had a cane. Cecily didn't bother hiding her happiness, but let her smile fully bloom. He'd rely less heavily on the assistance of others now. He could be more independent. More free.

"The family has a gift for you, too."

As Cecily couldn't see anything indoors any longer, she could only assume Mr. O'Connor had given his son something.

"A stack of paper," Finbarr said. Then, after a moment, his voice softened. "They're notes. In Braille. When did—How did you know how to—"

"We've been learning Braille," Mrs. O'Connor said. "We're not terribly good at it yet, but each of us wanted to tell you how much we love you, and we wanted to do it in a way that was just for you."

"Just for him?" Ian called out in tones of teasing mockery. "I learned so I can pass m' sweetheart notes under the table. Finbarr had nothing to do with it."

Laughter filled the room once more. The O'Connors truly were a happy group of people. Cecily loved that about them. She envied it a little, as well. Smiles and laughter weren't as joyous when one was alone.

"I believe we need a bit of music," one of the O'Connors' sons-in-law declared. His suggestion was immediately taken up. The O'Connors were also a very musical family.

Over the many sounds echoing madly around her, Cecily heard approaching steps. She couldn't be certain of the person's identity other than knowing it wasn't the person she most wanted to sit with her: Tavish. Perhaps he would before the evening was over.

"Cecily, may I have a moment?" Joseph.

"Of course."

Chair legs scraped as well as the sound of stiff fabric bending as he sat. "This is an awkward topic for a birthday party, but the spring thaw is fast approaching, so you have decisions to make. Granny Claire appointed me the task of—She asked me to make certain all was in order for her house and land to be left to you."

Cecily could not possibly have anticipated that declaration. Granny had shown her great kindness. Cecily had loved her and had felt deeply cared about in return. But this was too much, too unexpected. "You must be mistaken."

"I assure you, I am not. She was quite clear. She wanted you to have a home to call your own. To be able to stay in Hope Springs if you wished. I was instructed specifically not to force your hand or try to convince you one way or the other, only to inform you of the option and then honor your decision."

She could do nothing but sit in mute shock. Granny had given her a choice, a new path to consider. Granny had given her the possibility of a home to call her own.

"You needn't decide immediately," Joseph continued. "There is no urgency. Whenever you are ready to make a decision, no matter what you choose, simply let me know."

She nodded. "I will. Thank you for telling me."

"Thank you for all you've done for Finbarr," Joseph said. "To me, he is like a younger brother, a son, and a friend all mixed in one. Seeing him lost for so long broke my heart. But now he is slowly but surely coming back to us."

"That is always my hope for my students," she said. "I know what it is to be lost."

Joseph's chair creaked as he shifted position. "I should warn you, a very determined-looking Irishman is headed directly for you," he said. "If I don't miss my mark, I believe he means to ask you to dance."

Her heart flipped over in her chest. She hadn't danced with Tavish since that long-ago evening during the snowstorm, but she'd thought of it often since.

"Cecee, come dance with me." What the invitation lacked in elegance, it more than made up for in enthusiasm. "'Tis a reel they're beginning. You dance a reel, do you not?"

"I never have," she confessed.

"No matter." His hand took hers. "Simply hold on, and I'll spin you through it."

What could she do but laugh and cling to him? Around and around he spun her, the music bright and cheerful and so very Irish. By the way voices swung past her, Cecily could tell that others were dancing, too, moving and twirling as much as she was.

"Please don't let go," she begged even as she grinned ever more broadly. "I have absolutely no idea which way I'm facing, and I'm going to be dizzy."

His cheek brushed against hers, and he spoke softly into her ear. "I've no intention of letting go."

She forced herself not to believe his words meant anything deeper than a reference to the dance, though she wanted to believe it possible. Her admission to Granny had been entirely true. Cecily loved this man. She suspected he might love her in return, but too much was still uncertain and unsettled for her to allow for any thoughts beyond this moment.

The fast clip of music slowed, and the rhythm changed to the familiar 1–2–3 of a waltz. Tavish's arm snaked around her middle. "Here's what I was hoping for," he said. "Even my difficult family can't object to me holding you close when we're dancing to an air."

"Perhaps we can convince them to play six or seven of them." She set her hand at his neck.

"I'll see what I can do."

They settled into the movements of this dance with even greater ease than the reel.

"I am glad Finbarr convinced you to come tonight," Tavish said. "I've not seen you as much these past days as I'd've liked."

"Has your family been looking after you?" She didn't doubt they had, but she wanted to be certain he wasn't being left to face his grief unsupported.

"They have been very good to me. I grieved Bridget too long alone. I'll not do that this time. Not ever again."

She sighed with real relief and laid her head against him. "You need them. And they need you."

"It's something I've come to understand more over the past year and half than in all the years before that." His hand splayed across her back, holding her to him. "We'd all be lost without each other."

That was the undeniable truth about this family. Their strength came from one another. The loss of that connection would be devastating to them all. It was why Finbarr's situation had been so dire when she first arrived. He hadn't been the only one crippled by his injuries and losses. They had all been falling apart under the strain and suffering.

If she were to stay in Hope Springs, if she and Tavish were to grow ever closer, fall more in love, would she be welcomed into that circle of love and protection? Or would Tavish, however subtly, be pushed out of it? The O'Connors were no longer unkind to her, but an Irishman making a life with an Englishwoman was unfathomable in ways most people outside the tiny British Isles couldn't comprehend. She'd never quite be part of this family. She had seen these past days how this family turned to each other for strength, but they had not extended that same comfort to her. Her grief was kept separate from theirs, just as her life would always be.

Tavish would, at some point, be forced to choose between her and his family. No matter who he gave his loyalty to, he would be hurt by having to make the choice.

Granny had said that she wanted Tavish to be happy. How could Cecily wish for anything less?

"Cecee?" Tavish snapped her wandering thoughts back to the moment. "The music's stopped, dear. If you stand here hanging off me like this with no music as an excuse, we'll scandalize the entire room."

He was teasing, of course, but she felt a subtle reality behind the words. How many times had she resolved not to pursue these feelings, knowing that doing so could only end in disaster? He wove a spell, one she needed to slip free of.

No sooner had he guided her to the side of the room than Finbarr spoke. "Cecily, may I ask a question?"

Too much weighed on her mind for responding beyond a quiet, "Yes."

"How did my family learn Braille?"

"With great determination."

Tavish jumped in, offering his own answer. "Cecily has been spending her evenings and many of her free days giving lessons and creating instruction sheets for us. She's been neglecting her book project to make it happen. And it hasn't been only our family, you know. The Archers have been studying it as well."

"But why?" Finbarr asked. "Why would all of you learn something you have so little use for?"

He still did not truly comprehend the depth of love around him. He needed to.

Cecily pushed aside her own grief and sorrow and spoke with a tender firmness. "They didn't learn as a convenience to themselves. Learning Braille is important to them because it is important to you. This family . . ." How did she put her thoughts into words? "I have spent time with a great many families throughout my travels, but yours is special. The O'Connors have a strength here that runs deep, but it runs in both directions. You are in as much of a position to help and strengthen them as you ever were. You need them, yes, but they need you just as much. That is a gift, and a reason to keep going. I hope you understand that. I hope you appreciate that."

"I am beginning to," Finbarr said.

A weight lifted from her heart. Finbarr would recover. Tavish would heal. This family would again be whole.

And she . . . she wouldn't do anything to undermine that.

Chapter Thirty-seven

Tavish stood at the cemetery fence after services on a mild Sunday afternoon, watching Cecily lay flowers on Granny's grave. He'd not seen hide nor hair of her in nearly two weeks. No one had.

She seldom ventured outside Granny's house. Finbarr managed most of his lessons on his own and spent a great deal of time working either at Joseph's house or helping Tavish around his. On several occasions, Tavish had gone to look in on her, but the house was always dark, and she never answered his knocks. No denying it: she was avoiding him. But why?

Everything had seemed wonderful between them until the night of Finbarr's birthday. What had gone wrong since?

Katie stepped next to him. "'Tis a solemn place, this. Are you enduring Granny's passing?"

He nodded. "Well enough. How are you feeling? You were a bit poorly at the party a fortnight ago."

Katie set her hand low on her abdomen. "This little pea seems determined to make certain I am well aware of who is to be the ruler between the two of us."

"Then I'd wager the wee one is a boy. No lad avoids making trouble for the women in his life."

Katie's gaze drifted to Cecily, then she motioned toward her with a quick lift of her chin. "She must miss Granny a great deal. I do, too. No one who lived in that house could help but love that dear woman."

"Perhaps it is grief, then," Tavish said to himself.

"Beg your pardon?"

He resumed his normal tone. "I've been trying to sort out why it is she's avoiding everyone, myself included. We've none of us truly seen her since Finbarr's birthday."

"'Tis nearly spring," Katie said by way of explanation. "It must always be a difficult thing to be saying goodbye to places and to people she's come to care for. What a shame she turned down Granny's bequest."

Tavish looked over at Katie. "What bequest?"

"Granny's home," Katie said.

That made little sense. "I'm still unsure what you're speaking of."

Katie's brow arched upward in surprise. "You don't know, then."

"Obviously not."

"Granny gave Joseph instructions that he was to offer Cecily her home to have as her own," Katie said. "Granny worried that Cecily was returning to Missouri only because she'd no other choice. She felt strongly that of all the things a woman ought to have in life, a choice of what to do with that life ought to be one of them."

This was all new information to him. "But Cecee said no? She turned it down?"

"The day after Finbarr's birthday, she told Joseph that she had decided to go back to Missouri. She'll travel with the Johnsons to the depot in three weeks' time."

Tavish didn't know what to say. Indeed, he couldn't so much as form a coherent thought. Cecily could live in Hope Springs. She could stay, have a home of her own. Live nearby.

Instead, she was leaving. She had the choice, and she was choosing to go.

"I was certain you knew," Katie said. "I assumed Granny made the offer in large part because of you."

"I'd nothing to do with it," he insisted.

"Not directly," Katie said. "You must realize not a soul in this town is unaware of how you feel about Cecily."

"And now they're all aware of how she feels—or *doesn't* feel—about me."

Katie shook her head firmly. "I don't believe that's the situation at all."

"Then what is it?" He could think of no other reason she'd so easily choose to abandon him.

"Why don't you ask her yourself, you stubborn man? She's nearly here."

Sure enough, Cecily was making her way along the fence toward the gate where he stood, her cane tapping the fence posts as she passed them. She was yet a few yards away.

"Joseph and I were planning to drive her home," Katie said, "but we'll happily cede that task if you're looking for a few minutes of her time."

"I'd be grateful," he answered.

Katie simply smiled and stepped away.

Tavish turned his attention fully to Cecily, who'd nearly reached him.

She took a noseful of air. "Tavish?"

"Oh, come now. I can't possibly smell that badly."

The light expression she assumed didn't bring a smile to her lips nor smooth the lines of worry in her forehead. "I was only teasing. I recognized the sound of your voice."

"You were listening, then?" That might simplify the unavoidable conversation lying ahead of them.

"I couldn't make out what you were saying, but I recognized the timbre."

"I've been granted the privilege of seeing you home," Tavish said, "if you've no objections."

She hesitated. Apparently she did object, at least a little. "I hadn't intended to inconvenience you."

"I suspect what you intended to do was avoid me."

"Tavish." Her tone was scolding.

He stepped through the open gate in the cemetery fence and slipped his hand around hers. "Will you let me see you home, dear? I've no doubt you could manage it on your own if you wish. I simply want a bit of your company, and I hope you'd enjoy a bit of mine."

"I always enjoy your company," she said quietly.

He slipped her hand through his arm in the way he'd found helped her the most when navigating about. They walked from the graveyard and turned toward the river.

"You're leaving for Missouri." He figured there was no point stating it as a question, as everything was settled.

"You have known since I arrived in October that I would be leaving."

"I thought so only because you had no other option." He kept his focus on the road ahead, afraid that if he looked over, he'd be defeated by the determination in her voice. "I know about Granny's house." Her posture stiffened, but her expression remained neutral. "What I don't understand is why you turned it down. You could stay here, Cecee. You could have a home."

"And what would I do? I have no means of supporting myself here. Beyond that, I would be abandoning all of the people I could help."

He thought frantically, needing to convince her that making her home here was not merely possible but right. "You could still transcribe. That is important to you."

"Yes, but so is eating. Transcription does not provide an income. A person must have something to live on."

"I wouldn't let you go hungry, Cecily." Surely she knew that.

"In which case, I would be destined to be both a thorn in your family's side and the recipient of your unending charity." She spoke more tightly. "Forgive me if that does not sound appealing."

The prim and prickly Cecily had made an unexpected reappearance after all these months.

"I was not speaking of charity," Tavish said. "There is far more between us than that. I—We could—"

"No." She cut him off.

"No?" Did she understand what he'd been speaking of? "You don't—you don't want to stay?"

She held her chin at a proud angle, something he'd not seen from her since her early days in town. "I don't want to stay."

He'd no intention of letting her lie to them both, not when both of their happiness was on the line. "I don't believe you."

"Tavish, I have given it thought. I have weighed my options." Her tone left absolutely no room for discussion. She pulled her arm free of his. "I am choosing to go."

A fist to the gut would likely not have hurt more. After thought and deliberation, she was choosing to go. *Choosing* to.

"You promised, Cecily. Everyone I've ever cared about has left me, but you—" The words stuck as his heart lodged in his throat. "You promised you wouldn't. You promised."

"I am sorry." Her words were quiet but unrelenting.

No. Cecily could not simply walk away. He couldn't bear to lose her. "Do you love me?" He only hoped she would give an honest answer.

"That's not what this is about." She pushed ahead of him and took her first step onto the bridge. Her cane searched the area in front of her.

"That is absolutely what this is about." He caught up to her, keeping pace at her side. "Love doesn't abandon; it doesn't give up. Even when everything else falls apart, love remains."

"Love makes the difficult choice," she said, continuing her forward trek. "Love chooses not to inflict more pain or extend pain. Love puts the other person first, refusing to take away essential pieces of his life." With each word, her emotion rose. "Love is not selfish. Love does the right thing . . . no matter how much it hurts."

"Cecily." He set a hand on her arm and stopped her at the midpoint of the bridge. "Please, Cecily."

She turned back enough for him to see the pain in her expression—not physical suffering, but pain of the heart, an ache he knew all too well.

"Please," he repeated, stepping around to fully face her once more. He brushed his hand along her cheek, cupping his hand behind her head. "Please, Cecee."

"Oh, Tavish." She set her open palms against his chest and leaned in to him.

He pulled her ever closer with one arm and tipped her face to him with his other hand. "I do love you, you know that, don't you?"

"I know."

He'd leaned close enough that her whispered response puffed against his lips. "And you've said you love me," he pled.

"I do." Again, he felt the words as clearly as he heard them. "I've loved you for weeks and weeks."

"Then"—his lips brushed hers as he spoke—"don't leave me."

Her hand slid up his chest, her fingers settling against the base of his neck, teasing the gap in his collar. He held her to him, so close that the cold in the air gave way to her warmth. He closed the tiny gap, pressing his lips fervently, hopefully to hers. She returned the intimate gesture with the same earnestness.

He broke the contact between them only long enough to whisper her name. She did not pull away, nor give any indication she wished to. He kissed her again, and she him. As tightly as he held her, she held him just as close, just as fervently.

"I love you," he said after a time, not releasing her. "I need you to know that."

"And I love you. I truly do." Yet she pulled away.

"Cecee?"

"I do love you," she repeated, "so I won't hurt you. Sometimes love means walking away."

Shock rendered him unable to respond or move as she stepped farther from him. The cold air wrapped itself around him, stealing the lingering remnants of the warmth she'd lent him.

"Your family has allowed me to be a neighbor, a teacher. They've stopped seeing me as their enemy, and I am grateful for that. But there is one thing I can never be to them, and that is family." She took a steadying breath, and her posture rallied. "There would always be a barrier, a gap in your family circle, Tavish. And though I am blind, I can see quite clearly what that would do to them—and to you. The strain would gnaw at you. Caught between your wife and your family. My place in your life could never happily intersect with theirs. You would be forever divided between us, and you'd never truly be happy or whole. I cannot be the cause of that kind of pain."

"But, Cecily, you would be my family." He reached out and took her hands. "We would be family. That would be enough."

She shook her head. "For a time, perhaps. But the O'Connors have a bond that was forged in the fires of suffering. That bond cannot be easily broken, nor should it be." She slipped her hands free once more. "How long before your love for me turned to resentment—in small measure, perhaps, but real all the same? I won't do that to either of us. You will stay here with your family, and I will return to Missouri."

"Alone," he added.

For a moment, she looked as though she meant to say something more. But in the end, she walked away without another word.

She was leaving him because she thought that would make him happy. She thought it would save him heartache. Nothing, he suspected, could be more painful than losing her. How in heaven's name could he possibly convince her to stay when she believed so entirely that leaving was best for him?

It seemed he needed to have a rather pointed discussion . . . with his family.

Tavish tossed open the door of his parents' home. "I'm in love with an Englishwoman," he announced.

Da clutched at his heart, eyes pulled wide. "The shock, lad. I'm near to dying of it."

Ciara, whom Tavish hadn't spied at the table upon first entering, rolled her eyes. "You're not telling us anything we don't already know, brother."

He hadn't expected to find her there. "Has something happened?" She'd all but avoided the family for months, though she'd come around more and more ever since the singing at the churchyard. "Are you unwell?"

She rose from the table. "That is the Tavish we know and love: always jumping to our rescue, even when there is nothing to rescue us from." Ciara gave him a quick hug before turning back to look at Ma and Da. "Thanks for the gab. I'll see you for Sunday supper, though I expect a full accounting of Tavish's reason for bursting in here to declare something so obvious."

Her teasing was welcome. 'Twas a sign she was returning to herself once more.

"Ciara seems to be doing better," he said once she'd left.

"I believe she is." Ma sighed with clear relief. "Though she's not said as much, I suspect she and Keefe lost a baby. A few things here and there point to it. That is a difficult grief to bear, made worse by how unseen it often is."

Poor Ciara.

"But it needn't have been unseen." Tavish said. "This family would rally around her, offer comfort, grieve with them."

"Perhaps," Da said, "she's coming to a place where she is ready for us to be part of her pain. Seeing you face your own has helped her. It's helped us all."

That brought them back to the original reason he'd come. "I was able to face my grief only because of Cecily, you know. She's offered me hope. She offered it to us all."

Da nodded. "That she has."

Such easy agreement. Tavish had fully expected to plead and argue and struggle to convince them to see her as the remarkable person she was. "Why do you continue being so cold to her?"

Ma took up her sewing and motioned him to take the seat beside hers. "Have we been cold of late? We've been uncomfortable; I'll admit that. There's still a bit of unease between us. But overcoming such long-held ideas takes time, son."

"We don't have time." He looked at them each in turn. "Cecily intends to leave for Missouri in three weeks, when Johnson and his oldest make their first trip to the depot. She's leaving, not because she must, but because she's convinced that staying will turn my family against me. She's doing this for my sake, because she sees no other option."

Da, to his credit, looked more than a little worried. "I thought she was leaving because of a job she has waiting there."

"She does want to continue helping the blind, but she can do that with her books. She loves that part. And she could do that here. I am convinced she would stay if she felt there was any hope that this family would eventually accept her as one of our own. It's that impossibility compelling her to go."

"Would you follow her to Missouri?" Ma asked.

"In a heartbeat, if it would fix the problem, but it wouldn't. She'd always worry that I regretted leaving all of you, and that worry would hang over us forever. She could never truly be happy so long as she wondered if I regretted my choice." He squared his shoulders. "Her happiness is more important than my own. But following her wouldn't make her happy. Convincing her to stay if she's not wanted wouldn't make her happy either." He sat on the bench facing his parents. "I believe in this family. Help me show her that we can move beyond the prejudices we inherited, that we can see people for who they are and not simply as a product of the place they came from."

Ma reached over and took his hand. Da leaned forward and met his gaze.

"Tell us what we can do," Da said.

Tavish released his pent-up breath. "I have a plan."

Chapter Thirty-eight

Cecily stood on Granny's front porch. The air felt warmer than it had in months. She could smell the soil again, something that didn't happen during the freeze of winter. Spring was fast approaching. She'd stepped out not to sniff about for dirt, but to test the state of her vision. Much of the past week had been spent inside with no lanterns burning—there'd been little point in lighting any—and taking her powders on a regular schedule in the hope of enduring this latest awakening of her much-despised disease.

The pain had eased. This latest deterioration would be complete. She was ready to discover how bad things had become.

The sun warmed her face, so it was bright out. Leaves rustled in the breeze. A bird sang somewhere nearby. She could piece together all of these bits of her surroundings. But what she could not do was see them.

She tried to breathe, but the pain in her heart made it difficult. The doctors had predicted twenty years, perhaps thirty. She'd had seventeen. Fate, in all its cruelty, had plunged her into blackness early. The darkness seeped into her, wrapping its fingers around her aching heart. Every bit of light was gone, and she would never have it back.

A lifetime of knowing this moment would come had not truly prepared her for the reality of it. Everything was gone.

Everything.

The sound of approaching wheels forced her to push aside the crushing disappointment. She didn't care to wear personal struggles on her sleeve for everyone to see. She'd be gone soon, and while the town would remember her as nothing but an outsider, she hoped they would remember her as a stalwart outsider. Fiercely independent. Determined. Strong.

"A fine day, is it not?" called out an achingly familiar voice. It was almost as if the silent pleas of her heart had been sent to heaven itself, who had mercifully delivered precisely the person she needed.

She wanted to answer Tavish's greeting with a cheerful one of her own. But no words came. Indeed, only tears made any sort of an appearance, but she forced them back.

The wagon stopped. His boots landed on the ground with a thud; he always hopped off whichever vehicle he was driving. Though he'd once described his late fiancée as a bundle of energy, the description was apt for him as well. More subdued than he'd described Bridget, perhaps, but just as full of life. Cecily loved that about him. She loved so many things about this man.

His footsteps drew closer, then came up the steps. Heavens, she couldn't see enough to make out so much as his shadow crossing her face, though she felt the loss of sunlight.

It really is gone, then. She took a shaky breath, hoping against hope that she could keep a tight hold on her emotions.

"What's the matter, *a mhuirnín*?" His concern nearly undid her.

"I've had a difficult morning," she managed.

Quick as anything, his arms were around her. So she set hers around his waist, leaning into his desperately needed embrace. For the first time since stepping onto the heartbreakingly dark porch, she could breathe. But how could she allow herself to depend on him for comfort again? She needed to learn to bear her heartaches alone as she used to.

"Are you up for a little excursion?" he asked. "Or would you feel better spending your day like this, no doubt marveling that you're embracing a fine specimen of a man?"

"And a humble one, too." Only a moment earlier, she'd been trying not to sob. Tavish, with his heaven-sent humor and compassion, had lightened her heart as only he could. How was she to go on without him? She feared her grief would consume her without him in her life.

His arms loosened a bit, and he leaned back. "Will you go for a ride with me?"

"I would like that." More than *like* it, she *needed* it. Needed him and the strength he offered.

As they drove from Granny's house, Cecily forced herself to simply breathe. She'd long known that losing her sight was inevitable. Nothing could have prevented it. She knew that the final descent into darkness ought not to be seen as a defeat, but it felt like one anyway. Heaven help her, it felt so horribly that way.

Tavish turned the buggy—she could tell by the length of the bench that this was not his wagon—off the road only a short pace from where they'd entered it. They were going to his house, then. But when they didn't stop, she knew where he was taking her. Their spot at the lake. The lake she wouldn't be able to see ever again.

"You're quiet this afternoon," Tavish said as he pulled the wagon to a stop.

"I suppose I'm feeling a bit contemplative."

His hands settled on her waist, and he helped her to the ground. "Let me tell you my secret for when I'm thinking so much that I find m'self in the doldrums." He threaded her arm through his and guided her forward. "My secret is this: I quit thinking so much."

She offered a theatrical, "Ah. If only I'd known this secret years ago, I could have saved myself a great deal of . . . thinking."

"The bench is just here," he said. "I'm certain you used your magical abilities to discern where it is I've brought you."

Soon they were settled cozily. He took her hand in his, and she clung to it, needing his strength.

"I can't say there's a time of year when I don't care for this view," he said. "But the changing of seasons is something special. Just now there're still bits where winter is hanging on fiercely, but other spots where spring is clearly making herself known. The contrast is beautiful in and of itself."

She swallowed the rise of thick emotion in her throat. A quick cough didn't dispel the weight that had settled on her lungs.

"Cecee?"

"I can't see it." The confession did not emerge whole. She heard the words echo inside her, a bullet ricocheting off every tender corner of her heart. "That is why I was on the porch, to test my vision, to see how much I had left."

"And?"

"Nothing. I can't see shadows or even the sun shining directly on my face." She pushed out a breath, trying to maintain her increasingly perilous hold on her composure. "It's all gone."

He shifted, and his arm wrapped around her shoulders, pulling her against him. He kissed the top of her head. Cecily braced herself for words of pity, or the insistence that she didn't need to be sad. Or that she'd known this would happen, so that ought to make the loss easier to accept. She'd heard such things from countless doctors, from many of her own teachers when she'd lamented each further deterioration.

Tavish said none of those things. "The mountains are still covered in snow," he said instead. "I've always been convinced that Winter, herself, resides there. The snow retreats very slowly on the mountains, sometimes never leaving the peaks all summer long. But down here in the valley, Spring is waging a mighty war against her coldhearted sister, banishing her to her mountain home. There is no clear winner yet. Spring has claimed only the smallest of victories. The trees near us have shaken the snow from their branches, replacing it with a sprinkling of the tiniest dots of green buds. The ground has pulled the snow down in many places, and the rich soil is making a reappearance, preparing for the arrival of lush, green grass that is Spring's way of claiming her territory."

On and on he described the scene, in words so poetic even scholars would have been hard-pressed to believe they'd been improvised. His musical, Irish manner of speaking turned his beautiful descriptions into a soothing lullaby. Cecily's heart ceased its seizing and settled, cocooned for the moment, back into its normal rhythm. She forced away all thoughts of darkness and simply let his words wash over her.

"In the midst of this battle"—Tavish had described nearly every imaginable detail but was, apparently, not done yet—"is a rough-hewn bench, obviously crafted by someone with more determination than ability. And on that bench sits a man of such handsomeness as defies all description."

Her lips twitched upward.

"Women have been known to faint dead away at the smallest glance of his heart-capturing smile. Which makes one wonder: is the breathtakingly beautiful woman sitting in his muscular embrace still conscious, or has she, too, fallen victim to the overwhelming nature of his good looks?"

"The narrator of your story needs to be told that the woman's eyes don't function. That would answer his question."

His hand rubbed her arm in a slow caress. "The narrator would be happy to offer a full description of her eyes, but he, alas, has never seen them."

"I don't want to hear a description of my eyes." She began to pull away, but his gentle, reassuring embrace kept her there. The fight drained from her. "The last time I saw them, they were hideous. They will be even more so now."

He turned a little, likely looking nearly directly at her now. "The green spectacles are meant only to hide your eyes? They don't protect them from the light or anything like that?"

"I grew tired of being stared at," she said. "It was far easier to simply hide this part of me from the world."

"But I am not *the world*," he said. "Do you not trust me?"

"Of course I trust you." There was no question about that.

"You saw the pain, and grief, and guilt I hid from even my own family," he said. "Do you trust me enough to let me see what you hide from everyone?"

Could she? Of all people, Tavish would not think less of her because of her deformity. He might very well be horrified, and his stomach might turn at the sight, but he wouldn't make her feel hideous because of it.

She sat up straighter. His arms fell away. Her hands shook a little as she reached up and removed her spectacles, slowly lowering them to her lap. Her eyes were yet closed; habit wouldn't allow her to do otherwise. Not yet. Heavens, she was trembling.

His fingers lightly brushed her jaw line. "Take your time, love."

"I don't know if I can do it."

He continued his caress. "I'll not pressure you. I only want you to know that you're safe to share anything at all with me."

She felt a lot of things whenever she was with him, including safe. He was her refuge. So yes, she could share this vulnerability with him. After a moment's fluttering, she opened her eyes entirely and held perfectly still, waiting for his reaction.

He didn't gasp. That seemed like a good sign. His fingers brushed along her face, softly and slowly. She didn't know whether to lean in to his touch or pull away from it. Her spectacles had been a shield, the size of which she was just realizing. Without them, she felt exposed, defenseless.

"My eyes are likely entirely milky now."

"They are." A simple statement. No pity or disgust touched the words. He would be honest with her.

"Is there any other color left at all, or is it only white?"

"Only white." His hand slipped behind her neck, inching her closer to him.

"At least you didn't run away screaming," she said.

"Oh, Cecee," he whispered. "I have no intention of running away."

His hand slid down her back, resting at her waist. The air grew quickly warmer, and the welcoming scent of him enveloped her. She felt his breath against her lips in the instant before she felt their touch.

His kiss was gentle. Tender. Earnest. He held her as though she were the most precious of treasures. She wrapped her arms around his neck, holding tight to him, and returned his kiss with fervor. Her heart skipped and jumped and pounded, yet somehow, she still felt utterly and completely at peace.

His forehead pressed to hers, he said, "I am so glad you didn't turn out to be a man."

How was it he could make her laugh no matter the jumbled state of her mind? A person couldn't help but live her life happy and joyful with this man a part of it.

But that didn't bear thinking on. Their lives were taking different paths.

"As much as I'd love to sit here kissing you all afternoon," Tavish said, "I do need to get you back home. The family has plans this afternoon."

She nodded. "I won't keep you."

"Won't keep *us*. You're a part of their plans as well."

Bless his optimistic heart. "I doubt that."

"You shouldn't." He helped her to her feet.

"Forcing them to invite me to a gathering isn't going to change—"

"Your first lesson in your soon-to-be family is this: the O'Connors cannot be forced to do anything. They are far too headstrong."

His words pulled her up short. "My 'soon-to-be family'?"

"You don't think I go about kissing lasses I'm not desperately in love with, do you?" He clicked his tongue in disapproval.

"Love isn't always enough," she reminded him.

He helped her into the buggy once more then climbed up himself. "I think you've underestimated the power of love, my dear. More of it is playing a role in this than you know."

The buggy began moving again. She hadn't the heart to continue reminding him of the inevitable. He didn't want to admit how hopeless their situation truly was; she rather hated the reality of it. She slipped her spectacles on once more and folded her hands on her lap. A quiet ride back seemed best.

But when they reached the front of Granny's home, suddenly "quiet" was out of the question. "I hear voices. A lot of voices."

"I'd wager all of Wyoming hears their voices," Tavish laughed. "They're making quite a ruckus in there."

"Who is?"

His footsteps brought him around, and he lifted her down. They were getting quite adept at that. So long as she was in Hope Springs, she would never worry about navigating the short distance from a wagon or buggy to the ground.

"We've something of a surprise for you." As he always did, Tavish took her arm and walked her to the front porch.

The air inside the house was warm, though whether someone had built a fire, or it was simply the result of so many people occupying the relatively small space, she couldn't say. Neither could she distinguish how many people were inside or who they were.

The chatter died down. Suddenly nervous and uncertain, Cecily slipped her hand into Tavish's.

"They'll not eat you, *a mhuirnín*," he said. "Ma made certain they were all well fed, just in case."

"We hope you won't think we've overstepped ourselves." That was Mr. O'Connor. "We've come to make a proposition and a plea."

Cecily stepped closer to Tavish, her nervousness momentarily overriding her curiosity.

"We're wanting to help you with your books," Mr. O'Connor said. "We've been practicing, so we're faster, though you'd likely laugh yourself into a fit to see what we consider 'faster.' On the table there are a new half dozen Braille slates and styluses, extras that'd be kept here. We're making more. You'd have a small army helping with your work."

"I don't understand," she said quietly.

"We believe in what you do," Mr. O'Connor said. "Our Finbarr's a changed person because of you. We all are, changed for the better, and we want to help you work that change for others. It's important that we do."

"But . . . why?"

Why would they help someone who had only recently moved up from the rank of adversary?

Mrs. O'Connor answered. "To summarize what someone once told my youngest boy, 'It is important to us because it's important to you.'"

The emotion Cecily had been fighting all afternoon bubbled anew. She held ever tighter to Tavish's hand, needing his anchor in these uncharted waters.

"We want you to stay," Mr. O'Connor said. "Not because we've been coerced or are pitying you or any such thing. We want you here as a part of our lives."

She shook her head. "But I'm English. That won't ever change."

"We can't promise to not ever be uncomfortable or, I'm sorry to say it, rather stubborn in the assumptions we've been taught to make," Mr. O'Connor said. "But you've given us back two of our sons."

Tavish slipped his hand from hers and put his arm around her.

"We O'Connors are not the brightest in the bunch," Mr. O'Connor continued, "but we do learn from our mistakes. We tried to separate Tavish from you early on, and nearly lost him because of it. He'd hidden behind his pain and grief for so long, and only you were able to bring him back once more. We've a lifetime of wrong-headed lessons to relearn, but heaven help us, we mean to try."

She hardly dared hope, but she wanted so desperately to believe them. Leaning toward Tavish, she whispered, "Are they in earnest?"

"Utterly."

She turned to face him more fully. Her mind spun with all she was hearing, all she was struggling to understand. "What about the rest of the Irish in town? They are none too pleased with my origins."

Tavish rubbed her back reassuringly. "They'll be slower to come around, I'd imagine. But you'll have us, and this family rallies around its own."

"I am not one of your own," she reminded him.

"Did I not tell you just today that you soon will be?" he said. "You need to start believing me, you stubborn woman."

"You've not told her the best part yet," Ian's voice called out. "Don't underestimate the power of a good bit of bribery. Go on, then." Bribery? This conversation grew stranger and stranger.

"Matthew Scott, an Irishman here in town, worked in a printing office for a time before coming to Hope Springs," Tavish said. "He is very familiar with printing presses and such. Seamus Kelly happens to be something of a dab hand at inventing new-fangled bits of equipment. The two of them have agreed to help the lot of us, with your expert guidance, in designing a press to print entire pages at a time in Braille."

"A Braille press?" Her heart leapt at the very thought. Though books in France were printed in Braille, only one press in the United States did. This was the gap she was attempting to fill for her students and for the pupils at the Missouri School. She could do so much faster with a press.

"It may take a great deal of time and a great deal of trial," Tavish said. "But in the meantime, you have an entire family wanting to help you reach your goals and live your dream of creating your lending library."

"I don't—I don't know what to say."

"Whatever you mean to say," Mr. O'Connor jumped in, "sit on it a moment. We're all going to slip out onto the porch and let the two of you have a moment alone."

As a cacophony of footsteps made their way to the door, Cecily's mind spun. Could she trust this offer? She didn't doubt the O'Connors' desire to help with the books, or that it was a gesture of friendliness and support made from love for their son. But would that be enough to see her accepted as part of the family? Was being accepted too much to hope for? Was their support and apparent determination to not reject her outright enough to ensure that she wouldn't be pulling Tavish away from the family he'd dedicated his life to supporting and protecting?

"I've come to know your expressions fairly well, Cecee, and I can tell that you are at war with yourself." He hadn't waited a single moment after the door closed. "I know the questions you're asking; I've asked them myself. And I will tell you this: I cannot guarantee that my family will be the warm and loving one you deserve, but I do know that they don't mean to turn you out. I cannot promise that everything will be fairy tale perfect, but I swear to you that there is a very real chance it could be."

"I don't want you to be unhappy." That fate was, in fact, one of her greatest worries.

"And, my dear, darling Cecily, I don't want you to be either."

She took a steadying breath. "So what do we do? How do we know what comes next?"

"We take one step at a time." His hands slid down her arms and threaded his fingers through hers. "Rather than leaving in another week or so, give us the summer. See if m' family can be as good as their word, see if you can make a home for yourself here. If everything falls apart, and we find that the O'Connors cannot overcome the burden of history, we will decide what to do then. If, however, we find more and more reason to hope, if we discover that all of these fears and hesitations are unfounded, then I hope you will stay through the fall. Through the next winter. Through the coming of another spring. You could simply stay. Stay here. With me."

For once she could not hear the objections of her mind. Her heart shouted that he was right, that she shouldn't leave, that she couldn't.

"Please, Cecee," Tavish whispered. "Stay with me."

"Through the summer," she said.

"For now," he added on a whisper. "For now."

Chapter Thirty-nine

August

Tavish was finally home after spending several weeks driving all over the territory and a bit beyond, making his annual deliveries of preserves, cordials, and bushels of late-summer berries. He'd gained quite a reputation thereabouts for having a fine crop and products worth the asking price. No one else grew so much variety this far from civilization. He made a decent living off his crop, something not all farmers could say.

He'd not wanted to leave with Cecily's future yet undecided, but he'd taken out an extra note on his land the previous autumn, one that needed paying off. Further, he'd skipped deliveries the summer before to take Finbarr to the doctor in St. Louis. He couldn't have afforded to lose another year's sales, or he might very well lose his land.

He only prayed that the progress he'd seen in the relationship between Cecily and his family had continued during his absence. He meant to look in on his parents and ask a good many questions, but they were not his first stop. Not remotely.

Tavish knocked at the door to Cecily's home, not bothering to hide the gift he'd brought for her. She would not be able to see it either way, so the element of surprise was rather guaranteed. His heart pounded in anticipation as he waited. He'd not seen her in weeks. Heavens, he'd missed her.

If the fates chose to smile upon him, he'd take her with him on next year's deliveries. He couldn't imagine a better way to undertake the trek.

The door opened. Tavish's grin bloomed on the instant. The interior of the house was dim, but he had no difficulty seeing Cecily in the doorway. She wore the blue dress he'd always liked so much. Her distinctive green spectacles sat the tiniest bit askew on her nose. Her golden hair hung in a loose bun. But what truly drew his attention was her brows turned downward in confused concentration. Apparently his scent was not so distinctive today; she didn't appear to realize who'd come to call.

"You've baffled me," she said after a moment. "I'll need some idea who you are."

"I've not been gone so long as all that," he said. "Surely you still remember me."

Her hand flew to her heart. "Tavish." The way she whispered his name, with such a mixture of earnest longing and relief, warmed him through. "You've returned at last."

"That I have."

She held her arms out to him, an invitation he didn't need explained. He leaned her present against the wall of the house, then took her into his embrace. She wrapped her arms about his neck and clung to him, fiercely and firmly.

"You were gone entirely too long, Tavish O'Connor," she said.

"Couldn't be helped, dear. I'm needing to make a living."

She smiled. How he loved that smile.

"I've missed you is all," she said.

"Has my family been good to you?"

She nodded. "They've been good as gold. The rest of the Irish in town are following their examples. Seamus Kelly hasn't sung a single tune about the horrible English at any of the *céilis*. And though a few of the stories shared around the fire have touched upon our difficult history, none have been directed at me. I've received compliments on the food I've brought, invitations to dance—"

"From whom?" he asked firmly.

She ignored the question. "And I never want for company when I wish for it. We haven't yet worked out a usable design for the Braille press, but we're getting closer. Finbarr is advancing in his studies. And I've not been kissed in six weeks. That last bit needs addressing."

"It most certainly does."

He kissed her long, and he kissed her well. The ferventness with which she returned the affections gave him a great deal of hope. A woman intending to leave a man behind wasn't likely to kiss him so enthusiastically.

Feeling lighter and more hopeful than he had in ages, Tavish rested his forehead against hers, his arms still wrapped lovingly about her. "I've a present for you."

"I should hope so. After so many weeks away, you had best be making up sweet to me."

He made a sound of feigned frustration. "What did I do to deserve so many headstrong women in m' life?"

"You are too much like your Grandfather Claire, I would guess. He, I was once told, had a weakness for determinedly independent women."

"The very best kind, they are," he said. "They'll let a fellow hold 'em for minutes on end right on the porch for all the world to see."

He felt her laugh. "No one passing by would discover anything they don't already know."

"Have we been so obvious?"

She only smiled.

"Set yourself down on the swing, *a mhuirnín*. I'll sit beside you while you sort out what it is I've brought for you."

A moment later, they were quite snuggly, situated on the swing he'd installed at the beginning of summer for just such a purpose. She leaned against him, comfortable as can be. How far they'd come in under a year. She'd been nothing but prickles back then, and he'd been anything but welcoming.

"Though I dearly love a guessing game," he said, "I'm far too excited about my offering to make you sort it." He hopped up and fetched his gift, leaning against the house where he'd left it mere moments earlier. He retook his seat and set the gift in her hands.

She needed but the briefest of moments to identify it. "A cane."

"Not just any cane," he said. "I whittled it for you, but not like the rough job I did on your other one. This here's a bit of art, if I say it myself."

Her fingers ran slowly over the surface, studying it. "So many patterns and details. This must have taken a great deal of work."

He pressed a kiss to her temple. "I had a lot of time on m' hands while I was traveling the territory, delivering my jams and jellies and such."

"You must think rather highly of me to spend your free time on this."

"'Think highly'?" He snorted a bit at that very staid turn of phrase. "Is that all you think this is?"

She set the tips of her right hand fingers softly against his cheek. "No. That is not all I think this is. I would not, however, object to hearing you say as much."

He slipped his hand around hers, kissing her lowermost knuckles before setting their entwined hands against his heart.

"I spent a good many years hiding behind a light word and an easy jest, protecting a heart that seemed as though it'd never stop breaking. You found me there, Cecee. You found me, and you guided me back into the light. 'This' is far more than mere fondness, more than friendship, more than affection." He clutched her hand ever more fervently. "I love you, Cecily Attwater. I love you with every bit of my soul, with the bits that are broken and the bits that have mended."

"*Are* they mended?" Her voice emerged hardly louder than a whisper. "You were so deeply shattered when we met. I feared nothing would make you whole again."

He raised her hand to his lips once more. "You helped me find the strength to finally heal, and you've taught me how to love again. I only hope that, in time, you can be convinced to stay, to keep walking this path with me."

"I do have a reliable cane now," she said. "That strengthens the argument considerably."

How long he had wanted someone to smile with, to laugh with. "My reason for whittling it."

"Then I suppose I would be wise to remain, wouldn't I?"

He sat in perfect stillness, studying her expression, her posture. Had she just agreed to stay in town after the summer was out? He had to know for sure, yet he was almost afraid to ask.

"You are either grinning unrepentantly or giving me a look of terrified confusion," she said.

"Terrified confusion."

She set her cane against the side of the swing then laid her now-free hand against his chest. Though she could not see him, she turned her face up to his. "I told you once that I longed to return home."

"I remember."

"I have come to realize these past few months that I misunderstood that longing. I wanted not to go back home, but to *find* home. And I have, Tavish. Here. With you."

He took a tight breath. "You have?"

"I don't need until the end of the summer to decide. This is home. You are my home, and I want to stay."

He let out the breath he'd been holding.

She laughed. "Unrepentant grin now, I'm guessing."

"Entirely unrepentant."

"Rumor has it your smile is irresistible."

He pulled her to him once more. "I think we had best test that theory."

Once more he kissed her, relief and joy and celebration filling the moment, for she was not the only one of them who had, at last, found home.

Chapter Forty

Tavish took another bite of bread pudding. "We should've started inviting the English to our *céilís* ages ago."

Ma nodded. "Who knew they could cook?"

He shot her a grin. "'Tis a very good thing she puts up with our teasing, else I'd have no one to dance with tonight."

"Speaking of which . . ." Ma motioned toward the musicians. "Cecily looks anxious to be up and twirling again."

Tavish gave his mother a swift kiss on the cheek. "Thank you again for being kind to her this summer, for working at learning to love her."

She patted his cheek. "I've not seen you this happy in . . . I'd wager to say ever. For that, she'll have a place in my heart 'til the day I die. Now"—she nudged him away—"go make up sweet to her. She's missed you."

He'd not told anyone of his visit to Cecily's home earlier that day, preferring to keep that tender moment and the decision she'd made. That moment was theirs and theirs alone. The town would know soon enough.

He set aside his empty plate and crossed to where his Cecee sat.

He took the seat beside hers, and, with an ease that spoke of familiarity, dropped his arm around her. "Would you care to dance, my love?"

"I've another task for you first, if you've no objections." She had, over the summer, begun using phrases that leaned more toward the Irish. Did she realize it? Or was it simply a sign of her becoming more comfortable among them?

"I'd do anything at all for you."

She leaned in to him. The position was one they struck every time she sat in the circle of his arms.

"What's the task, dear?"

"This. I wanted you to hold me."

He chuckled. "It'll be a sore trial to me, but I'll do m' best to endure."

"The two of you ought to finally get married and take all of this nauseating nonsense behind closed doors." Finbarr, who sat on Cecily's other side, grumbled, though there was nothing but good-natured jesting behind his words.

"If your brother keeps talking that way, Tavish, I'll begin thinking you're fond of me."

"I'm far more than merely fond of you, you troublesome woman." In fact, he had every intention of marrying her.

Emma approached, her quiet steps no doubt going unheard by either of Tavish's companions over the loud music and voices. "Miss Attwater?"

Cecily didn't seem startled. "Good evening, Emma."

"Katie asked me to ask you if you would give Mrs. Smith your recipe for bread pudding. Papa has come early every week to make certain he gets a piece, and Katie is afraid he'll simply die of disappointment once the summer is over and there are no more *céilís*."

Cecily nodded solemnly. "We cannot allow your father to waste away. I will make certain your housekeeper receives it."

"You could write it out in Braille if you'd like," Emma said hesitantly. "I'm getting much better at reading it. I've been studying the key you gave me, and I've been practicing."

"That key didn't include numbers," Cecily said. "They're tricky. They're also very important in a recipe."

Emma's expression fell. "I hadn't thought of that," she said quietly.

"I know the numbers," Finbarr jumped in. "I could teach them to you, if you'd like."

Emma eyed him with uncertainty. Their once close friendship had not been repaired yet—life had taught Emma to be wary, and grief still pricked sharply at Finbarr.

"I can learn them on my own," Emma said.

"I know you can, but I would like to help." Finbarr, bless his heart, sounded nervous.

Emma pressed her lips together a moment, her earnest gaze never leaving Finbarr. At last, she spoke again. "I will think about it."

Finbarr accepted her answer with a silent nod.

Emma kept to the spot, not moving. Her brow pulled deep in thought. What was she debating now? For clearly something was spinning about in her mind.

"You—" She stopped short, then tried again. "You could sit with us during the storytelling, if you'd like."

Finbarr barely held back a look of eagerness. He kept his tone neutral. "I would like that, Miss Emma."

She gave a quick nod. "I'll find you when the time comes. Or Papa will. Probably Papa."

"I'll be here."

Finbarr had made great progress. He'd begun attending the *céilís* again, which amounted to something of a miracle. He still didn't dance but generally picked a chair and stayed there for the duration. Tavish hoped that would change. In time, perhaps he'd take up his penny whistle and rejoin the musicians. He prayed the lad would find a way to regain Emma's trust. Losing her treasured sisterly affection had dealt him a terrible blow.

A tune began that Tavish recognized, one disparaging of the English. "Not that one, Seamus," he called out.

Seamus's rumbling laughter responded. "Only checking to see if you're paying us any heed."

"I am, and don't you doubt it. Play us an air so I can dance with this colleen."

They obeyed. Thomas Dempsey trilled the opening notes of "Miss McCleod's Reel."

He leaned in and whispered to Cecily. "Dance with me, dear?"

She didn't hesitate. He led her in their usual way to the area set aside for dancing. Tavish took her in his arms and slowly spun her around the open area. She fit so perfectly in his arms and in his life. With her, he could smile through his difficulties without the expression being a mask. He was supported in his griefs, strengthened in his trials, joined in his joy. And she was staying. When so many others had left him behind, she was staying.

He pressed a quick kiss to her lips, earning him a whispered, "Behave."

"Not a chance of it," he replied. "I've too much to celebrate tonight."

"You're not hoping I've changed my mind, then?" She didn't sound worried at all that he had.

"On the contrary, Cecee."

When the time came for the storytelling, Joseph fetched Finbarr and guided him to where the Archer family sat. Joseph—not Emma. The tear in the fabric of their friendship didn't seem likely to mend soon or easily.

Cecily sat beside Tavish. He slipped his hand in hers as Seamus stood before the gathering.

"We've a treat for you tonight," Seamus announced. "'Tisn't myself who'll be opening up our tales for the night, but a new storyteller who, I'm told, has quite a tale to share. What say you? Shall we hear a new story?"

The crowd answered with hollered agreement, even a few cheers.

"I'll warn you, though," Seamus added, "her accent is terribly thick and difficult to understand. She hails from an odd, strange, foreign place and uses words with far too many parts."

Tavish eyed Cecily sidelong, a suspicion forming in his mind.

"I think we ought to give her a chance," Seamus continued. "Let her try her hand." Over the chuckles of the crowd, Seamus confirmed what Tavish had begun to piece together. "Up you go then, Miss Attwater. Tell us a tale."

Cecily was being called on to spin a yarn.

"You don't have to," Tavish assured her.

"Nonsense," she said. "I arranged this."

She rose and stepped forward, the cane he'd made held firmly in her grasp. The two of them had sat at the very front, so she hadn't far to go. Seamus stepped aside and sat with his own family.

Cecily cleared her throat. Heavens, but she was anxious. He hadn't the slightest idea why she'd chosen to do this. If only he could reach out and hold her hand, reassure her and support her.

"My tale will likely not be so diverting as those Seamus improves upon every week."

Laughter followed. Seamus was known for tales that grew bigger with each telling.

"I think it is a good story, though," Cecily continued. "However, I don't know how it ends. I am hopeful all of you can help me sort out that part."

She certainly had their attention.

"Many years ago, a little girl lived near a stream in a part of the world so green it was as beautiful as Ireland."

"We'll take leave to disagree with you there, lass," Seamus called out good-naturedly, earning a great deal of laughter.

Cecily smiled in acknowledgement. "Very nearly," she amended. "And this little girl had a great many dreams for her life. But they slipped away, one by one, even as the world around her did as well.

"The darkness tiptoed closer, stealing away the things most dear to her. She traveled the land, searching. She knew that somewhere in the vastness of the quickly dimming world, a spark of light was waiting, and in that spark were the wishes she'd never stopped hoping would still come true.

"After years and years, in a tiny town, far away from her childhood home, she found what she'd been searching for. She found . . . him."

Tavish didn't think he'd breathed for long, drawn-out minutes.

"She found someone who learned to love her despite her struggles, who saw the person she kept hidden out of fear and worry. He saw the dreams she hadn't dared let free again." Cecily clutched her hands together, a tension in her posture that spoke of hope and uncertainty all at once. "But she feared she couldn't stay."

Though his heart halted for a moment, it resumed its natural rhythm in the next. Despite the ending she'd chosen for that sentence, she'd already told him she meant to stay, and he trusted her.

"She wanted—she *wants* to stay." A quick breath. A tightening of her already white knuckles. "This man, this incredible, dear, beloved man wants her to stay, wishes for her to, but she needs to know if the tiny town will let her. She must be certain that her presence among them will not cause pain to the person she loves most in the world." The entire gathering must have heard her thick, nervous swallow. "That's the ending I haven't sorted through yet. Is there room for her—for *me*—among you?"

Not a soul said a word. Tavish couldn't say if they appeared more shocked or hopeful or touched, because he wasn't looking at anyone but her.

He rose from his seat and took the few steps to where she stood. He wrapped one arm around her and faced the crowd.

"How's the tale to end?" He met his ma's eye, then Da's. Ian's. Biddy's. Each family member's in turn. "Have you room enough?"

Ma stood and moved toward them. She, who only a year earlier had recoiled at the idea of a golden-haired Englishwoman, pulled Cecily into a motherly embrace. "There is room and plenty."

An instant later, Da had joined the embrace, followed by the remainder of Tavish's family. Even Finbarr found his way to them, having grown adept at navigating with his cane. They stood in a bundle of family.

All around them, the town cheered. Seamus loudly declared that Cecily wasn't a bad sort, for an Englishwoman. Anne Scott offered a welcome in Irish, something Tavish would need to teach Cecily to recognize. Katie pushed her way through the gathering to join the O'Connors' embrace.

"You're one of us now," Tavish told Cecily. "You'll never be rid of us."

"Perfect," she said.

Some hours later, as the *céilí* wound to a close, he stood beside the dwindling fire, Cecily still in his arms. Life had been difficult, heart breaking, at times even miserable. But that moment, all was right in the world.

"*A mhuirnín*," he sighed, content.

She slid her hands up his chest. "I do like when you call me that."

He leaned in and whispered against her lips. "*A mhuirnín.*'"

He kissed her with every ounce of feeling he had for her, no longer afraid to love fully and vulnerably. He had found in her a safe haven and a place of hope and healing.

He kissed her again with all the tenderness and adoration he felt, with every ounce of happiness she'd brought him, and with the hope he now had for the future.

"I love you," he whispered in her ear.

"I love you, my dearest, most wonderful, Tavish. I'll love you forever."

He held her close as the stars peeked through the thin layer of clouds and the breeze whipped through the trees. The voices of family and friends filled the night. His family was whole. The woman he loved was in his arms, in his life.

"Forever," he repeated. "Forever and ever."

Acknowledgments

With sincerest gratitude to:

Annette Lyon, whose careful and expert hand was invaluable in making this story far better than I could ever have made it on my own.

Heather Moore, who saw value in this story when others did not and helped make it a possibility. Thank you for your confidence, encouragement, and expertise.

Pam Victorio, who picks me up and dusts me off when the path I'm walking trips me up and knocks me down.

Karen Adair, who nudges me forward when I want nothing more than to throw in the towel.

My family, who endures cold dinners and a dirty house when I'm under deadline, and sudden bouts of deep cleaning and experimental recipes when I'm supposed to be writing.

About the Author

Photograph © Annalisa Rosenvall

SARAH M. EDEN is the USA Today bestselling author of multiple historical romances, including Foreword Review's 2013 "IndieFab Book of the Year" gold medal winner for Best Romance, *Longing for Home*, and two-time Whitney Award Winner *Longing for Home: Hope Springs*. Combining her obsession with history and affinity for tender love stories, Sarah loves crafting witty characters and heartfelt romances. She has thrice served as the Master of Ceremonies for the Storymakers Writers Conference and acted as the Writer in Residence at the Northwest Writers Retreat. Sarah is represented by Pam Victorio at D4EO Literary Agency.

Visit Sarah at www.sarahmeden.com

Made in United States
North Haven, CT
27 January 2023